Praise for Jennifer Weiner

'Witty, compelling and utterly unforgettable' *Heat*

'This incredibly funny book is so engrossing it should come with the warning: "Do not read on trains" – as you will miss your stop' *Now*

'Immensely readable . . . Weiner's gift lies in her ability to create characters who both amuse us and make us care' *The Washington Post*

'Weiner balances romantic formula with fresh humour, deft characterizations and literary sensibility' *Guardian*

'Weiner has been compared to both Helen Fielding and Candace Bushnell but I'd put her in a category of her own' *Sunday Express*

'Hilarious and heartwarming' *Cosmopolitan*

'Positively delightful . . . Cannie was appealing as a lovelorn career girl, but she's even more likeable as a sanguine matron with a mini-van and a Crock Pot . . . Enjoy the charisma of Cannie's earthy and mature female voice' *Entertainment Weekly*

'A fresh, funny feast of a novel' Anna Maxted

Jennifer Weiner

SIMON &
SCHUSTER

London · New York · Sydney · Toronto

A CBS COMPANY

First published in Great Britain by Pocket Books, 2001
An imprint of Simon & Schuster UK Ltd
A CBS COMPANY

This paperback edition first published by Simon & Schuster UK Ltd, 2011

1 3 5 7 9 10 8 6 4 2

Simon & Schuster UK Ltd
1st Floor
222 Gray's Inn Road
London
WC1X 8HB

www.simonandschuster.co.uk

Simon & Schuster Australia
Sydney

A CIP catalogue record for this book is available from the British Library

ISBN 978-1-84983-747-7

Printed and bound by CPI Group (UK) Ltd, Croydon, CR0 4YY

Home is so sad. It stays as it was left,
Shaped to the comfort of the last to go
As if to win them back. Instead, bereft
Of anyone to please, it withers so,
Having no heart to put aside the theft
And turn again to what it started as,
A joyous shot at how things ought to be,
Long fallen wide. You can see how it was:
Look at the pictures and the cutlery.
The music in the piano stool. That vase.
                                        —Philip Larkin

Love is nothing, nothing, nothing like they say.
                                        —Liz Phair

PART ONE

Good in Bed

ONE

"Have you seen it?" asked Samantha.

I leaned close to my computer so my editor wouldn't hear me on a personal call.

"Seen what?"

"Oh, nothing. Never mind. We'll talk when you get home."

"Seen what?" I asked again.

"Nothing," Samantha repeated.

"Samantha, you have never once called me in the middle of the day about nothing. Now come on. Spill."

Samantha sighed. "Okay, but remember: Don't shoot the messenger."

Now I was getting worried.

"*Moxie.* The new issue. Cannie, you have to go get one right now."

"Why? What's up? Am I one of the Fashion Faux Pas?"

"Just go to the lobby and get it. I'll hold."

This was important. Samantha was, in addition to being my best friend, also an associate at Lewis, Dommel, and Fenick. Samantha put people on hold, or had her assistant tell them she was in a meeting. Samantha herself did not hold. "It's a sign of weakness," she'd told me. I felt a small twinge of anxiety work its way down my spine.

I took the elevator to the lobby of the *Philadelphia Examiner*, waved at the security guard, and walked to the small newsstand, where I found *Moxie* on the rack next to its sister publications, *Cosmo* and *Glamour* and *Mademoiselle*. It was hard to miss, what with the supermodel in sequins beneath headlines blaring "Come Again: Multiple Orgasm Made Easy!" and "Ass-Tastic! Four Butt Blasters to Get your Rear in Gear!" After a quick minute of deliberation, I grabbed a small bag of chocolate M&M's, paid the gum-chomping cashier, and went back upstairs.

Samantha was still holding. "Page 132," she said.

I sat, eased a few M&M's into my mouth, and flipped to page 132, which turned out to be "Good in Bed," *Moxie*'s regular male-written feature designed to help the average reader understand what her boyfriend was up to . . . or wasn't up to, as the case might be. At first my eyes wouldn't make sense of the letters. Finally, they unscrambled. "Loving a Larger Woman," said the headline, "By Bruce Guberman." Bruce Guberman had been my boyfriend for just over three years, until we'd decided to take a break three months ago. And the Larger Woman, I could only assume, was me.

You know how in scary books a character will say, "I felt my heart stop?" Well, I did. Really. Then I felt it start to pound again, in my wrists, my throat, my fingertips. The hair at the back of my neck stood up. My hands felt icy. I could hear the blood roaring in my ears, as I read the first line of the article: "I'll never forget the day I found out my girlfriend weighed more than I did."

Samantha's voice sounded like it was coming from far, far away. "Cannie? Cannie, are you there?"

"I'll kill him!" I choked.

"Take deep breaths," Samantha counseled. "In through the nose, out through the mouth."

Betsy, my editor, cast a puzzled look across the partition that separated our desks. *"Are you all right?"* she mouthed. I squeezed my eyes shut. My headset had somehow landed on the carpet. "Breathe!" I could hear Samantha say, her voice a tinny echo from the floor. I was wheezing, gasping. I could feel chocolate and bits of candy shell on my teeth. I could see the quote they'd lifted, in bold-faced pink letters that screamed out from the center of the page. "Loving a larger woman," Bruce had written, "is an act of courage in our world."

"I can't believe this! I can't believe he did this! I'll kill him!"

By now Betsy had circled around to my desk and was trying to peer over my shoulder at the magazine in my lap, and Gabby, my evil coworker, was looking our way, her beady brown eyes squinting for signs of trouble, thick fingers poised over her keyboard so that she could instantly e-mail the bad news to her pals. I slammed the magazine closed. I took a successful deep breath, and waved Betsy back to her seat.

Samantha was waiting. "You didn't know?"

"Didn't know what? That he thought dating me was an act of courage?" I attempted a sardonic snort. "He should try *being* me."

"So you didn't know he got a job at *Moxie.*"

I flipped to the front, where Contributors were listed in thumbnail profiles beneath arty black-and-white head shots. And there was Bruce, with his shoulder-length hair blowing in what was assuredly artificial wind. He looked, I thought uncharitably, like Yanni. "'Good in Bed' columnist Bruce Guberman joins the staff of *Moxie* this month. A freelance writer from New Jersey, Guberman is currently at work on his first novel."

"His first *novel?*" I said. Well, shrieked, maybe. Heads turned. Over the partition, Betsy was looking worried again, and Gabby had started typing. "That lying sack of shit!"

"I didn't know he was writing a novel," said Samantha, no doubt desperate to change the subject.

"He can barely write a thank-you note," I said, flipping back to page 132.

"I never thought of myself as a chubby chaser," I read. "But when I met C., I fell for her wit, her laugh, her sparkling eyes. Her body, I decided, was something I could learn to live with."

"I'll KILL HIM!"

"So kill him already and shut up about it," muttered Gabby, shoving her inch-thick glasses up her nose.

Betsy was on her feet again, and my hands were shaking, and suddenly somehow there were M&M's all over the floor, crunching beneath the rollers of my chair.

"I gotta go," I told Samantha, and hung up.

"I'm fine," I said to Betsy. She gave me a worried look, then retreated.

It took me three tries to get Bruce's number right, and when his voice mail calmly informed me that he wasn't available to take my call, I lost my nerve, hung up, and called Samantha back.

"Good in bed, my ass," I said. "I ought to call his editor. It's false advertising. I mean, did they check his references? Nobody called me."

"That's the anger talking," said Samantha. Ever since she started dating her yoga instructor, she's become very philosophical.

"Chubby chaser?" I said. I could feel tears prickling behind my eyelids. "How could he do this to me?"

"Did you read the whole thing?"

"Just the first little bit."

"Maybe you better not read any more."

"It gets worse?"

Samantha sighed. "Do you really want to know?"

"No. Yes. No." I waited. Samantha waited. "Yes. Tell me."

Samantha sighed again. "He calls you. . . . Lewinsky-esque."

"With regards to my body or my blow jobs?" I tried to laugh, but it came out as a strangled sob.

"And he goes on and on about your . . . let me find it. Your 'amplitude.' "

"Oh, God."

"He said you were succulent," Samantha said helpfully. "And zaftig. That's not a bad word, is it?"

"God, the whole time we went out, he never said anything . . ."

"You dumped him. He's mad at you," said Samantha.

"I didn't dump him!" I cried. "We were just taking a break! And he agreed that it was a good idea!"

"Well, what else could he do?" asked Samantha. "You say, 'I think we need some time apart,' and he either agrees with you and walks away clinging to whatever shreds of dignity he's got left, or begs you not to leave him, and looks pathetic. He chose the dignity cling."

I ran my hands through my chin-length brown hair and tried to gauge the devastation. Who else had seen this? Who else knew that C. was me? Had he shown all his friends? Had my sister seen it? Had, God forbid, my mother?

"I gotta go," I told Samantha again. I set down my headset and got to my feet, surveying the *Philadelphia Examiner* newsroom—dozens of mostly middle-aged, mostly white people, tapping away at their computers, or clustered around the television sets watching CNN.

"Does anybody know anything about getting a gun in this state?" I inquired of the room at large.

"We're working on a series," said Larry the city editor—a small, bearded, perplexed-looking man who took everything absolutely seriously. "But I think the laws are pretty lenient."

"There's a two-week waiting period," piped up one of the sports reporters.

"That's only if you're under twenty-five," added an assistant features editor.

"You're thinking of rental cars," said the sports guy scornfully.

"We'll get back to you, Cannie," said Larry. "Are you in a rush?"

"Kind of." I sat down, then stood back up again. "Pennsylvania has the death penalty, right?"

"We're working on a series," Larry said without smiling.

"Oh, never mind," I said, and sat back down and called Samantha again.

"You know what? I'm not going to kill him. Death's too good for him."

"Whatever you want," Samantha said loyally.

"Come with me tonight? We'll ambush him in his parking lot."

"And do what?"

"I'll figure that out between now and then," I said.

I had met Bruce Guberman at a party, in what felt like a scene from somebody else's life. I'd never met a guy at a social gathering who'd been so taken with me that he actually asked me for a date on the spot. My typical m.o. is to wear down their resistence with my wit, my charm, and usually a home-cooked dinner starring kosher chicken with garlic and rosemary. Bruce did not require a chicken. Bruce was easy.

I was stationed in the corner of the living room, where I had a good view of the room, plus easy access to the hot artichoke dip. I was doing my best imitation of my mother's life partner, Tanya, trying to eat an Alaskan king crab leg with her arm in a sling. So the first time I saw Bruce, I had one of my arms jammed against my chest, sling-style, and my mouth wide open, and my neck twisted at a particularly grotesque angle as I tried to suck the imaginary meat out of the imaginary claw. I was just getting to the part where I accidentally jammed the crab leg up my right nostril, and I think there might have been hot artichoke dip on my cheek, when Bruce walked up. He was tall, and tanned, with a goatee and a dirty-blond ponytail, and soft brown eyes.

"Um, excuse me," he said, "are you okay?"

I raised my eyebrows at him. "Fine."

"You just looked kind of . . ." His voice—a nice voice, if a little high—trailed off.

"Weird?"

"I saw somebody having a stroke once," he told me. "It started off like that."

By now my friend Brianna had collected herself. Wiping her eyes, she grabbed his hand. "Bruce, this is Cannie," she said. "Cannie was just doing an imitation."

"Oh," said Bruce, and stood there, obviously feeling foolish.

"Not to worry," I said. "It's a good thing you stopped me. I was being unkind."

"Oh," said Bruce again.

I kept talking. "See, I'm trying to be nicer. It's my New Year's resolution."

"It's February," he pointed out.

"I'm a slow starter."

"Well," he said, "at least you're trying." He smiled at me, and walked away.

I spent the rest of the party getting the scoop. He'd come with a guy Brianna knew from graduate school. The good news: He was a graduate student, which meant reasonably smart, and Jewish, just like me. He was twenty-seven. I was twenty-five. It fit. "He's funny, too," said Brianna, before delivering the bad news: Bruce had been working on his dissertation for three years, possibly longer, and he lived in central New Jersey, more than an hour away from us, picking up freelance writing work and teaching the occasional bunch of freshmen, subsisting on stipends, a small scholarship, and, mostly, his parents' money.

"Geographically undesirable," Brianna pronounced.

"Nice hands," I countered. "Nice teeth."

"He's a vegetarian," she said.

I winced. "For how long?"

"Since college."

"Hmph. Well, maybe I can work with it."

"He's . . ." Brianna trailed off.

"On parole?" I joked. "Addicted to painkillers?"

"Kind of immature," she finally said.

"He's a guy," I said, shrugging. "Aren't they all?"

She laughed. "And he's a good guy," she said. "Talk to him. You'll see."

That whole night, I watched him, and I felt him watching me. But he didn't say anything until after the party broke up, and I was walking home, feeling more than a little disappointed. It had been a while since I'd even seen someone who'd caught my fancy, and tall, nice hands, nice-white-teeth grad student Bruce appeared, at least from the outside, to be a possibility.

But when I heard footsteps behind me, I wasn't thinking about him. I was thinking what every woman who lives in a city thinks when she hears quick footsteps coming up behind her and it's after midnight and she's between streetlights. I took a quick glance at my surroundings while fumbling for the Mace attached to my keychain. There was a streetlight on the corner, a car parked underneath. I figured I'd Mace whoever it was into temporary immobility, smash one of the car windows, hoping the alarm would go off, scream bloody murder, and run.

"Cannie?"

I whirled around. And there he was, smiling at me shyly. "Hey," he said, laughing a little bit at my obvious fear. He walked me home. I gave him my number. He called me the next night, and we talked for three hours, about everything: college, parents, his dissertation, the future of newspapers. "I want to see you," he told me at one in the morning, when I was thinking that if we kept talking I was going to be a wreck at work the next day. "So we'll meet," I said.

"No," said Bruce. "Now."

And two hours later, after a wrong turn coming off the Ben Franklin Bridge, he was at my door again: bigger than I'd remembered, somehow, in a plaid shirt and sweatpants, carrying a rolled-up sleeping bag that smelled like summer camp in one hand, smiling shyly. And that was that.

And now, more than three years after our first kiss, three months after our let's-take-a-break talk, and four hours after I'd found out that he'd told the entire magazine-reading world that I was a Larger Woman, Bruce squinted at me across the parking lot in front of his apartment where he'd agreed to meet me. He was blinking double-time, the way he did when he was nervous. His arms were full of things. There was the blue plastic dog-food dish I'd kept in his apartment for my dog, Nifkin. There, in a red wooden frame, was the picture of us on top of a bluff at Block Island. There was a silver hoop earring that had been sitting on his night table for months. There were three socks, a half-empty bottle of Chanel. Tampons. A toothbrush. Three years' worth of odds and ends, kicked under the bed, worked down into a crack in the couch. Evidently, Bruce saw our rendezvous as a chance to kill two birds with one stone—endure my wrath over the "Good in Bed" column and give me back my stuff. And it felt like being punched in the chest, looking at my girlie items all jumbled up in a cardboard Chivas box he'd probably picked up at the liquor store on his way home from work—the physical evidence that we were really, truly over.

"Cannie," he said coolly, still squinching his eyes open and shut in a way I found particularly revolting.

"Bruce," I said, trying to keep my voice from shaking. "How's that novel coming? Will I be starring in that, too?"

He raised his eyebrow, but said nothing. "Remind me," I said. "At what point in our relationship did I agree to let you share intimate details of our time together with a few million readers?"

Bruce shrugged. "We don't have a relationship anymore."

"We were taking a break," I said.

Bruce gave me a small, condescending smile. "Come on, Cannie. We both know what that meant."

"I meant what I said," I said, glaring at him. "Which makes one of us, it seems."

"Whatever," said Bruce, attempting to shove the stuff into my arms. "I don't know why you're so upset. I didn't say anything bad." He straightened his shoulders. "I actually thought the column was pretty nice."

For one of the few times in my adult life, I was literally speechless. "Are you high?" I asked. With Bruce, that was more than a rhetorical question.

"You called me fat in a magazine. You turned me into a joke. You don't think you did anything wrong?"

"Face it, Cannie," he said. "You are fat." He bent his head. "But that doesn't mean I didn't love you."

The box of tampons bounced off his forehead and spilled into the parking lot.

"Oh, that's nice," said Bruce.

"You absolute bastard." I licked my lips, breathing hard. My hands were shaking. My aim was off. The picture glanced off his shoulder, then shattered on the ground. "I can't believe I ever thought seriously for even one second about marrying you."

Bruce shrugged, bending down, scooping feminine protection and shards of wood and glass into his hands and dumping them back into the box. Our picture he left lying there.

"This is the meanest thing anyone's ever done to me," I said, through my tear-clogged throat. "I want you to know that." But even as the words were leaving my mouth, I knew it wasn't true. In the grand, historical scheme of things, my father leaving us was doubtlessly worse. Which is one of the many things that sucked about my father—he forever robbed me of the possibility of telling another man, *This is the worst thing that's ever happened to me,* and meaning it.

Bruce shrugged again. "I don't have to worry about how you feel anymore. You made that clear." He straightened up. I hoped he'd be angry—passionate, even—but all I got was this maddening, patronizing calm. "You were the one who wanted this, remember?"

"I wanted a break. I wanted time to think about things. I should have just dumped you," I said. "You're . . ." And I stood, speechless again, thinking of the worst thing I could say to him, the word that would make him feel even a fraction as horrible and furious and ashamed as I did. "You're small," I finally said, imbuing that word with every hateful nuance I could muster, so that he'd know I meant small in spirit, and everywhere else, too.

He didn't say anything. He didn't even look at me. He just turned around and walked away.

Samantha had kept the car running. "Are you okay?" she asked as I slid into the passenger's seat clutching the box to my chest. I nodded silently. Samantha probably thought I was ridiculous. But this wasn't a situation I expected her to sympathize with. At five foot ten, with inky black hair, pale skin, and high, sculpted cheekbones, Samantha looks like a young Anjelica Huston. And she's thin. Effortlessly, endlessly thin. Given a choice of any food in the world, she'd probably pick a perfect fresh peach and Rya crispbreads. If she wasn't my best friend, I'd hate her, and even though she is my best friend, it's sometimes hard not to be envious of someone who can take food or leave it, whereas I mostly take it, and then take hers, too, when she doesn't want any more. The only problem her face and figure had ever caused her was too much male attention. I could never make her feel what it was like to live in a body like mine.

She glanced at me quickly. "So, um, I'm guessing that things with you two are over?"

"Good guess," I said dully. My mouth tasted ashy, my skin,

reflected in the passenger's side window, looked pale and waxen. I stared into the cardboard box, at my earrings, my books, the tube of MAC lipstick that I thought I'd lost forever.

"You okay?" asked Samantha gently.

"I'm fine."

"Do you want to get a drink? Some dinner, maybe? Want to go see a movie?"

I held the box tighter and closed my eyes so I wouldn't have to see where we were, so I wouldn't have to follow the car's progress back down the roads that used to lead me to him. "I think I just want to go home."

My answering machine was blinking triple-time when I got back to my apartment. I ignored it. I shucked off my work clothes, pulled on my overalls and a T-shirt, and padded, barefoot, into the kitchen. From the freezer I retrieved a canister of frozen Minute Maid lemonade. From the top shelf of the pantry I pulled down a pint of tequila. I dumped both in a mixing bowl, grabbed a spoon, took a deep breath, a big slurp, settled myself on my blue denim couch, and forced myself to start reading.

Loving a Larger Woman

by Bruce Guberman

I'll never forget the day I found out my girlfriend weighed more than I did.

She was out on a bike ride, and I was home watching football, leafing through the magazines on her coffee table, when I found her Weight Watchers folder—a palm-sized folio with notations for what she'd eaten, and when, and what she planned to eat next, and whether she'd been drinking her eight glasses of water a day. There was her name. Her identification number. And her weight, which I am too much of a gentleman to reveal here. Suffice it to say that the number shocked me.

I knew that C. was a big girl. Certainly bigger than any of

the women I'd seen on TV, bouncing in bathing suits or drifting, reedlike, through sitcoms and medical dramas. Definitely
bigger than any of the women I'd ever dated before.

What, I thought scornfully. Both of them?

I never thought of myself as a chubby chaser. But when I
met C., I fell for her wit, her laugh, her sparkling eyes. Her
body, I decided, was something I could learn to live with.

Her shoulders were as broad as mine, her hands were almost
as big, and from her breasts to her belly, from her hips down
the slope of her thighs, she was all sweet curves and warm welcome. Holding her felt like a safe haven. It felt like coming
home.

But being out with her didn't feel nearly as comfortable.
Maybe it was the way I'd absorbed society's expectations, its
dictates of what men are supposed to want and how women
are supposed to appear. More likely, it was the way she had. C.
was a dedicated foot soldier in the body wars. At five foot ten
inches, with a linebacker's build and a weight that would have
put her right at home on a pro football team's roster, C.
couldn't make herself invisible.

But I know that if it were possible, if all the slouching and
slumping and shapeless black jumpers could have erased her
from the physical world, she would have gone in an instant.
She took no pleasure from the very things I loved, from her
size, her amplitude, her luscious, zaftig heft.

As many times as I told her she was beautiful, I know that
she never believed me. As many times as I said it didn't matter,
I knew that to her it did. I was just one voice, and the world's
voice was louder. I could feel her shame like a palpable thing,
walking beside us on the street, crouched down between us in
a movie theater, coiled up and waiting for someone to say what
to her was the dirtiest word in the world: *fat*.

And I knew it wasn't paranoia. You hear, over and over, how

fat is the last acceptable prejudice, that fat people are the only safe targets in our politically correct world. Date a queen-sized woman and you'll find out how true it is. You'll see the way people look at her, and look at you for being with her. You'll try to buy her lingerie for Valentine's Day and realize the sizes stop before she starts. Every time you go out to eat you'll watch her agonize, balancing what she wants against what she'll let herself have, what she'll let herself have against what she'll be seen eating in public.

And what she'll let herself say.

I remember when the Monica Lewinsky story broke and C., a newspaper reporter, wrote a passionate defense of the White House intern who'd been betrayed by Linda Tripp in Washington, and betrayed even worse by her friends in Beverly Hills, who were busily selling their high-school memories of Monica to *Inside Edition* and *People* magazine. After her article was printed, C. got lots of hate mail, including one letter from a guy who began: "I can tell by what you wrote that you are overweight and that nobody loves you." And it was that letter—that word—that bothered her more than anything else anyone said. It seemed that if it were true—the "overweight" part—then the "nobody loves you" part would have to be true as well. As if being Lewinsky-esque was worse than being a betrayer, or even someone who was dumb. As if being fat were somehow a crime.

Loving a larger woman is an act of courage in this world, and maybe it's even an act of futility. Because, in loving C., I knew I was loving someone who didn't believe that she herself was worthy of anyone's love.

And now that it's over, I don't know where to direct my anger and my sorrow. At a world that made her feel the way she did about her body—no, herself—and whether she was desirable. At C., for not being strong enough to overcome what the world told her. Or at myself, for not loving C. enough to make her believe in herself.

I wept straight through Celebrity Weddings, slumped on the floor in front of the couch, tears rolling off my chin and soaking my shirt as one tissue-thin supermodel after another said "I do." I cried for Bruce, who had understood me far more than I'd given him credit for and maybe had loved me more than I'd deserved. He could have been everything I'd wanted, everything I'd hoped for. He could have been my husband. And I'd chucked it.

And I'd lost him forever. Him and his family—one of the things I'd loved best about Bruce. His parents were what June and Ward would have been if they were Jewish and living in New Jersey in the nineties. His father, who had perpetually whiskered cheeks and eyes as kind as Bruce's, was a dermatologist. His family was his delight. I don't know how else to say it, or how much it astonished me. Given my experience with my own dad, watching Bernard Guberman was like looking at an alien from Mars. *He actually likes his child!* I would marvel. *He really wants to be with him! He remembers things about Bruce's life!* That Bernard Guberman seemed to like me, too, might have had less to do with his feelings about me as a person and more to do with my being a), Jewish, and hence a marriage prospect; b), gainfully employed, and thus not an overt gold digger; and c), a source of happiness for his son. But I didn't care why he was so nice to me. I just basked in his kindness whenever I could.

Bruce's mother, Audrey, had been the tiniest bit intimdating, with manicured fingernails painted whatever shade I'd be reading about in *Vogue* the next month, and perfectly styled hair, and a house full of glass and wall-to-wall white carpeting and seven bathrooms, each kept immaculately clean. The Ever-Tasteful Audrey, I called her to my friends. But once you got past the manicure, Audrey was nice, too. She'd been trained as a teacher, but by the time I met Audrey her working-for-a-living days were long past and she was a full-time wife, mother, and volunteer—the perenniel PTA mom, Cub Scout leader, and Hadassah president, the one who could always be counted on to organize the synagogue's annual food drive or the Sisterhood's winter ball.

The downside of parents like that, I used to think, was that it killed your ambition. With my divorced parents and my college debts I was always scrambling for the next rung on the ladder, the next job, the next freelance assignment; for more money, more recognition, for fame, insofar as you could be famous when your job was telling other people's stories. When I started at a small newspaper in the middle of nowhere, covering car crashes and sewage board meetings, I was desperate to get to a bigger one, and when I finally got to a bigger one, I wasn't there two weeks before I was already plotting how to move on.

Bruce had been content to drift through graduate school, picking up a teaching assignment here, a freelance writing gig there, making approximately half of what I did, letting his parents pick up the tab for his car insurance (and his car, for that matter), and "help" with his rent and subsidize his lifestyle with $100 handouts every time he saw them, plus jaw-droppingly generous checks on birthdays, Chanukah, and sometimes just because. "Slow down," he'd tell me, when I'd slip out of bed early to work on a short story, or go into work on a Saturday to send out query letters to magazine editors in New York. "You need to enjoy life more, Cannie."

I thought sometimes that he liked to imagine himself as one of the lead characters in an early Springsteen song—some furious, passionate nineteen-year-old romantic, raging against the world at large and his father in particular, looking for one girl to save him. The trouble was, Bruce's parents had given him nothing to rebel against—no numbing factory job, no stern, judgmental patriarch, certainly no poverty. And a Springsteen song lasted only three minutes, including chorus and theme and thundering guitar-charged climax, and never took into account the dirty dishes, the unwashed laundry and unmade bed, the thousand tiny acts of consideration and goodwill that actually maintaining a relationship called for. My Bruce preferred to drift through life, lingering over the Sunday paper, smoking high-quality dope, dreaming of bigger papers and better assignments without doing much to get them. Once, early in our relationship, he'd sent his clips to the *Examiner,* and gotten a curt "try us in five years" postcard in response. He'd shoved the letter in a shoebox, and we'd never discussed it again.

But he was happy. "Head's all empty, I don't care," he'd sing to me, quoting the Grateful Dead, and I'd force a smile, thinking that my head was never empty and that if it ever was, you could be darn sure I'd care.

And what had all my hustle gotten me, I mused, now slurping the boozy slush straight from the bowl. What did it matter. He didn't love me anymore.

I woke up after midnight, drooling on the couch. There was a pounding in my head. Then I realized it was someone pounding at the door.

"Cannie?"

I sat up, taking a moment to locate my hands and my feet.

"Cannie, open this door right now. I'm worried about you."

My mother. Please God no.

"Cannie!"

I curled tight onto the couch, remembering that she'd called me in the morning, a million years ago, to tell me she'd be in town that night for Gay Bingo, and that she and Tanya would stop by when it was over. I got to my feet, flicking off the halogen lamp as quietly as I could, which wasn't very quietly, considering that I managed to knock the lamp over in the process. Nifkin howled and scrambled onto the armchair, glaring at me reproachfully. My mother started pounding again.

"Cannie!"

"Go 'way," I called weakly. "I'm . . . naked."

"Oh, you are not! You're wearing your overalls, and you're drinking tequila, and you're watching *The Sound of Music*."

All of which was true. What can I say? I like musicals. I especially like *The Sound of Music*—particularly the scene where Maria gathers the motherless Von Trapp brood onto her bed during the thunderstorm and sings "My Favorite Things." It looked so cozy, so safe—the way my own family had been, for a minute, once upon a time, a long time ago.

I heard a muttered consultation outside my door—my mother's voice, then another, in a lower register, like Marlboro smoke filtered through gravel. Tanya. She of the sling and the crab leg.

"Cannie, open up!"

I struggled back into a sitting position and heaved myself into the bathroom, where I flicked on the light and stared at myself, reviewing the situation, and my appearance. Tear-streaked face, check. Hair, light brown with streaks of copper, cut in a basic bob and shoved behind my ears, also present. No makeup. Hint—well, actuality—of a double chin. Full cheeks, round, sloping shoulders, double D-cup breasts, fat fingers, thick hips, big ass, thighs solidly muscled beneath a quivering blanket of lard. My eyes looked especially small, like they were trying to hide in the flesh of my face, and there was something avid and hungry and desperate about them. Eyes exactly the color of the ocean in the Menemsha harbor in Martha's Vineyard, a beautiful grapey green. My best feature, I thought ruefully. Pretty green eyes and a wry, cockeyed smile. "Such a pretty face," my grandmother would say, cupping my chin in her hand, then shaking her head, not even bothering to say the rest.

So here I am. Twenty-eight years old, with thirty looming on the horizon. Drunk. Fat. Alone. Unloved. And, worst of all, a cliché, Ally McBeal and Bridget Jones put together, which was probably about how much I weighed, and there were two determined lesbians banging on my door. My best option, I decided, was hiding in the closet and feigning death.

"I've got a key," my mother threatened.

I wrested the tequila bowl away from Nifkin. "Hang on," I yelled. I picked up the lamp and opened the door a crack. My mother and Tanya stared at me, wearing identical L.L. Bean hooded sweatshirts and expressions of concern.

"Look," I said. "I'm fine. I'm just sleepy, so I'm going to sleep. We can talk about this tomorrow."

"Look, we saw the *Moxie* article," said my mother. "Lucy brought it over."

Thank you, Lucy, I thought. "I'm fine," I said again. "Fine, fine, fine, fine."

My mother, clutching her bingo dauber, looked skeptical. Tanya, as usual, just looked like she wanted a cigarette, and a drink, and for

...nd my siblings never to have been born, so that she could have / mother all to herself and they could relocate to a commune in Northampton.

"You'll call me tomorrow?" my mother asked.

"I'll call," I said, and closed the door.

My bed looked like an oasis in the desert, like a sandbar in the stormy sea. I lurched toward it, flung myself down, on my back, my arms and legs splayed out, like a size-sixteen starfish stapled to the comforter. I loved my bed—the pretty light blue down comforter, the soft pink sheets, the pile of pillows, each in a bright slipcover—one purple, one orange, one pale yellow, and one cream. I loved the Laura Ashley dust ruffle and the red wool blanket that I'd had since I was a girl. Bed, I thought, was about the only thing I had going for me right now, as Nifkin bounded up and joined me, and I stared at the ceiling, which was spinning in a most alarming way.

I wished I'd never told Bruce I wanted a break. I wished I'd never met him. I wished that I'd kept running that night, just kept running and never looked back.

I wished I wasn't a reporter. I wished that my job was baking muffins in a muffin shop, where all I'd have to do was crack eggs and measure flour and make change, and nobody could abuse me, and where they'd even expect me to be fat. Every flab roll and cellulite crinkle would serve as testimony to the excellence of my baked goods.

I wished I could trade places with the guy who wore the "FRESH SUSHI" sandwich board and walked up and down Pine Street at lunch hour, handing out sushi coupons for World of Wasabi. I wished I could be anonymous and invisible. Maybe dead.

I pictured myself lying in the bathtub, taping a note to the mirror, taking a razor blade to my wrists. Then I pictured Nifkin, whining and looking puzzled, scraping his nails against the rim of the bathtub and wondering why I wasn't getting up. And I pictured my mother having to go through my things and finding the somewhat battered copy of *Best of Penthouse Letters* in my top dresser drawer, plus the pink fur-lined handcuffs Bruce had given me for Valentine's Day. Finally, I pictured the paramedics trying to maneuver my dead, wet body down three flights of stairs. "We've got a big one here," I imagined one of them saying.

Okay. So suicide was out, I thought, rolling myself into the comforter and arranging the orange pillows under my head. The muffin shop/sandwich board scenario, while tempting, was probably not going to happen. I couldn't see how to spin it in the alumni magazine. Princeton graduates who stepped off the fast track tended to own the muffin shops, which they would then turn into a chain of successful muffin shops, which would then go public and make millions. And the muffin shops would only be a diversion for a few years, something to do while raising their kids, who would invariably appear in the alumni magazine clad in eensy-beansy black-and-orange outfits with "Class of 2012!" written on their precocious little chests.

What I wanted, I thought, pressing my pillow hard against my face, was to be a girl again. To be on my bed in the house I'd grown up in, tucked underneath the brown and red paisley comforter, reading even though it was past my bedtime, hearing the door open and my father walk inside, feel him standing over me silently, feeling the weight of his pride and his love like it was a tangible thing, like warm water. I wanted him to put his hand on my head the way he had then, to hear the smile in his voice when he'd say, "Still reading, Cannie?" To be little, and loved. And thin. I wanted that.

I rolled over, groped for my nightstand, grabbed a pen and paper. *Lose weight,* I wrote, then stopped and thought. *Find new boyfriend,* I added. *Sell screenplay. Buy large house with garden and fenced yard. Find mother more acceptable girlfriend.* Somewhere between writing *Get and maintain stylish haircut* and thinking *Make Bruce sorry,* I finally fell asleep.

Good in bed. Ha! He had a lot of nerve, putting his name on a column about sexual expertise, given how few people he'd even been with, and how little he'd known before he'd met me.

I had slept with four people—three long-term boyfriends and one ill-considered freshman year fling—when Bruce and I hooked up, and

I'd fooled around extensively with another half-dozen. I might've been a big girl, but I'd been reading *Cosmopolitan* since I was thirteen, and I knew my way around the various pieces of equipment. At least I'd never had any complaints.

So I was experienced. And Bruce . . . wasn't. He'd had a few harsh turn-downs in high school, when he'd had really bad skin, and before he'd discovered that pot and a ponytail could reliably attract a certain kind of girl.

When he'd shown up that first night, with his sleeping bag and his plaid shirt, he wasn't a virgin, but he'd never been in a real relationship, and he'd certainly never been in love. So he was looking for his lady fair, and I, while not averse to stumbling into Mr. Right, was mostly looking for . . . well, call it affection, attention. Actually, call it sex.

We started off on the couch, sitting side by side. I reached for his hand. It was ice-cold and clammy. And when I casually slung an arm over his shoulder, then eased my thigh against his, I could feel him shaking. Which touched me. I wanted to be gentle with him, I wanted to be kind. I took both of his hands in mine and tugged him off the couch. "Let's lie down," I said.

We walked to my bedroom hand in hand, and he lay on my futon, flat on his back, his eyes wide open and gleaming in the dark, looking a bit like a man in a dentist's chair. I propped myself up on my elbow and let the loose ends of my hair trail gently across his cheek. When I kissed the side of his neck he gasped as if I'd burned him, and when I eased one hand inside his shirt and gently tugged at the hair on his chest, he sighed, "Ah, Cannie," in the tenderest voice I'd ever heard.

But his kisses were horrible, slobbery things, all bludgeoning tongue and lips that felt as if they were somehow collapsing when they met mine, so that I was left with a choice between teeth and mustache. His hands were stiff and clumsy. "Lie still," I whispered.

"I'm sorry," he whispered back unhappily. "I'm all wrong, aren't I?"

"Shh," I breathed, my lips against his neck once more, the tender skin right where his beard ended. I slid one hand down his chest, lightly feathered it over his crotch. Nothing doing. I pressed my breasts into his side, kissed his forehead, his eyelids, the tip of his nose, and tried again. Still nothing. Well, this was curious. I decided to show him a trick, to teach him how to make me happy whether he could get hard or not. He moved me enormously, this six-foot-tall guy with a ponytail and a look on his face like I might electrocute him instead of . . . this. I wrapped both of my legs around one of his, took his hand, and slid it into my panties. His eyes met mine and he smiled when he felt how wet I was. I put his fingers where I needed them, with my hand over his, pressing his fingers against myself, showing him what to do, and I moved against him, letting him feel me sweat and breathe hard and moan when I came. And then I pressed my face into his neck again, and moved my lips up to his ear. "Thank you," I whispered. I tasted salt. Sweat? Tears, maybe? But it was dark, and I didn't look.

We fell asleep in that position: me, wearing just a T-shirt and panties, wrapped around him; him, with only his shirt unbuttoned, only halfway, still in underwear, sweatpants, socks. And when the light crept through my windows, when we opened our eyes and looked at each other, it felt like we had known each other much longer than just one night. As if we could never have been strangers. "Good morning," I whispered.

"You're beautiful," he said.

I decided that I could get used to hearing that in the mornings. Bruce decided that he was in love. We were together for the next three years, and we learned things with each other. Eventually, he told me the whole story, about his limited experience, about always being either drunk or stoned and always very shy, about how he'd been turned down a few times his first year in college and just decided to be patient. "I knew I'd meet the right girl someday," he said, smiling at me, cradling me close. We figured it out—the things he liked, the things I liked, the things we both liked. Some of it was straightforward. Some of it would have been raunchy enough to raise eyebrows even in *Moxie,* where they ran regular features on new "sizzling sexy secrets!"

But the thing that galled me, that chewed at my heart as I tossed and turned, feeling clammy and cotton-mouthed from the previous night's tequila binge, was the column's title. "Good in Bed." It was a lie. It wasn't that he'd been some kind of sexual savant, a boy wonder under the sheets . . . it was that we had loved each other, once. We'd been good in bed together.

TWO

I woke up on Saturday morning to the sound of the telephone. Three rings, then silence. A ten-second pause, then three more rings, followed by more silence. My mother was not a fan of answering machines, so if she either knew or believed that I was home, she'd just keep calling until I picked up. Resistance was futile.

"This is so obnoxious," I said, in lieu of "hello."

"This would be your mom," said my mother.

"I'm shocked. Could you call me back later? Please? It's very early. I'm very tired."

"Oh, quit whining," she said briskly. "You're just hung over. Pick me up in an hour. We'll go to the cooking demonstration at Reading Terminal."

"No," I said. "Absolutely not." Knowing, even as I said it, that I could protest and complain and come up with seventeen different excuses, and, come noon, I'd still be in the Reading Terminal, cringing as my mother offered a high-volume play-by-play critique of the hapless chef's menu selection and cooking skills.

"Drink some water. Take some aspirin," she said. "I'll see you in an hour."

"Ma, please . . ."

"I'm assuming you read Bruce's article," she said. My mother is not big on elaborate transitions.

"Yeah," I said, knowing, without having to ask, that she had, too. My sister Lucy, a charter subscriber to *Moxie* and eager reader of any and all things related to femininity, still had her copy delivered to our house. After last night's door-pounding debacle, I could only assume that she'd pointed it out to my mother . . . or that Bruce had. The very thought of that conversation—"I'm just calling to let you know that I had an article published this month and I think Cannie's pretty upset by it"—made me want to hide under the bed. If I could even fit. I didn't want to walk around in a world where *Moxie* was on the news-stands, in mailboxes. I felt scalded by shame, like I was wearing a gigantic crimson C., like everyone who saw me would know that I was the girl from "Good in Bed," and that I was fat and that I'd dumped some guy who'd tried to understand and love me.

"Well, I know you're upset. . . ."

"I'm not upset," I snapped. "I'm fine."

"Oh," she said. This, obviously, was not the response she was expecting. "I thought it was kind of crummy of him."

"He's a crummy guy," I said.

"He wasn't a crummy guy. That's why it was so surprising."

I slumped against my pillows. My head hurt. "Are we going to debate his crumminess now?"

"Maybe later," said my mother. "I'll see you soon."

There are two kinds of houses in the neighborhood where I grew up—the ones where the parents stayed married, and the ones where they didn't.

Given only a cursory glance, both kinds of houses look the same—big, rambling, four- and five-bedroom colonials set well back from the sidewalk-less streets, each on an acre of land. Most are painted conservative colors, with contrasting shutters and trim—a slate-gray house with blue shutters, for example, or a pale beige house with a red door. Most have long driveways, done in gravel, and many have in-ground pools out back.

But look closer—or, better yet, stay a while—and you'll start to see the difference.

The divorce houses are the ones where the Chem-Lawn truck doesn't stop anymore, the ones the plowing guy drives past on the mornings after winter storms. Watch, and you'll see either a procession of sullen-faced teenagers, or sometimes even the lady of the house, emerge to do the raking, mowing, shoveling, trimming, themselves. They're the houses where Mom's Camry or Accord or minivan doesn't get replaced every year, but just keeps getting older and older, and where the second car, if there is one, is more likely some fourth-hand piece of automotive detritus purchased from the *Examiner*'s classified ads than the time-honored stripped-down but brand-new Honda Civic or, if the kid's really lucky, Dad's cast-off midlife crisis sports car.

There's no fancy landscaping, no big pool parties in the summer, no construction crews making a racket at seven A.M. adding on that new home office or master bedroom suite. The paint job lasts for four or five years instead of two or three, and is more than a little bit flaky by the time it gets redone.

But mostly, you could tell on Saturday mornings, when what my friends and I dubbed the Daddy Parade began. At about ten or eleven o'clock every other Saturday, the driveways up and down our street, and the neighboring streets, would fill with the cars of the men who used to live in these big four- and five-bedroom houses. One by one, they'd exit their cars, trudge up the walkways, ring the bells of the homes where they used to sleep, and collect their kids for the weekends. The days, my friends would tell me, would be full of every kind of extravagance—shopping excursions, trips to the mall, the zoo, the circus, lunch out, dinner out, a movie before and after. Anything to keep the time passing, to fill the dead minutes between children and parents who suddenly had very little to say to each other once they'd got done either mouthing pleasantries (in the cordial no-fault cases) or spitting vitriol (in the contested cases, where the parents paraded each other's shortcomings and infidelities in front of a judge—and, by extension, in front of a gossipy public, and, eventually, their children as well).

My friends all knew the drill. My brother and sister and I did it a few times in the early days of my parents' split, before my father announced that he wanted to be less like a father, more like an uncle, and that our weekend visits didn't fit in with his vision. Saturday nights would be spent on a pullout bed in his condo across town—a small, dusty space full of too much expensive stereo equipment and top-of-the-line TVs, and either too many pictures of the children, or, eventually, none at all. At my dad's place Lucy and I would huddle on the thin mattress of the pullout couch, feeling the metal frame poke us all night long, while Josh would sleep beside us in a sleeping bag on the floor. Meals would be taken in restaurants exclusively. Few of the newly single dads had the skills to cook, or the desire to learn. Most of them, it turned out, were just waiting for a replacement wife or girl-friend to come along, to stock the refrigerators and have dinner wait-ing every night.

And on Sunday morning, in time for church or Hebrew school, the parade would begin again, only in reverse: the cars pulling up and disgorging the kids, who'd hustle up the driveway trying not to run or look too relieved, and the fathers trying not to drive away too fast, try-ing to remember that this was supposed to be a pleasure, not a duty. For two years, three years, four years they'd come. Then they'd van-ish—remarried, mostly, or moved away.

It wasn't that bad, really—not third-world bad, not Appalachia bad. There was no physical pain, no real hunger. Even with the drop in the standard of living, the suburbs of Philadelphia were still a damn sight better than the way most people in the world—or the country—lived. Even if our cars were older and our vacations less lavish and our in-ground swimming pools less than pristine, we still had cars, and vacations, pools in the backyards, and roofs over our heads.

And the mothers and children learned how to lean on each other. Divorce taught us how to deal with stuff, whether it was reduced cir-cumstances, or what to say when the Girl Scout leader asked what you'd like to bring to the Father/Daughter banquet. ("A father," was the preferred answer.) My girlfriends and I learned to be flippant and tough, a posse of junior cynics, all before we hit sixteen.

I always wondered, though, what the fathers felt as they drove up the street they used to drive down every night, and whether they really saw their former houses, whether they noticed how things got frayed and flaky around the edges now that they were gone. I wondered it again as I pulled up to the house I'd grown up in. It was, I noticed, looking even more Joad-like than usual. Neither my mother nor the dread life partner, Tanya, was much into yard work, and so the lawn was littered with drifts of dead brown leaves. The gravel on the driveway was as thin as an old man's hair combed across an age-spotted scalp, and as I parked I could make out the faint glitter of old metal from behind the little toolshed. We used to park our bikes in there. Tanya had "cleaned" it by dragging all the old bikes, from tricycles to discarded ten-speeds, out behind the shed, and leaving them there to rust. "Think of it as found art," my mother had urged us when Josh complained that the bike pile made us look like trailer trash. I wonder if my father ever drove by, if he knew about my mother and her new situation, if he thought about us at all, or whether he was content to have his three children out there in the world, all grown up, and strangers.

My mother was waiting in the driveway. Like me, she's tall, and heavy (a Larger Woman, I heard Bruce's voice taunt in my head). But whereas I am an hourglass (an extremely full hourglass), my mother is shaped like an apple—a round midsection on toned and muscular legs. A former high-school standout in tennis, basketball, and field hockey, and the current star of the Switch Hitters (her inevitable lesbian softball team), Ann Goldblum Shapiro has retained both the carriage and the sensibilities of a onetime jock, a woman who believes there's no problem that can't be solved, and no situation that can't be improved, by a good brisk walk or a few laps in the pool.

She wears her hair short and lets it stay gray and dresses in comfortable clothes in shades of gray and beige and pale pink. Her eyes are the same green as mine, but wider and less anxious, and she smiles a lot. She's the kind of person who's constantly being approached by strangers—for directions, for advice, for honest assessments of whether bathing suits made the would-be wearer's butt look big in the communal dressing room at Loehmann's.

Today, she was dressed for our outing in wide-legged pale pink sweatpants, a blue turtleneck sweater, one of her fourteen pairs of activity-specific sneakers, and a windbreaker accented with a small triangular, rainbow-colored pin. She wore no makeup—she never wore it—and her hair was in its usual air-dried spikes. She looked happy as she climbed into the car. For her, the free cooking demonstrations at Philadelphia's premiere downtown food market *cum* meeting place were better than standup comedy. They weren't intended to be participatory, but nobody bothered to tell her that.

"Subtle," I said, pointing at her pin.

"You like?" she asked, oblivious. "Tanya and I picked them up in New Hope last weekend."

"Did you get me one?" I asked.

"No," she said, refusing to take the bait. "We got you this." She handed me a small rectangle wrapped in purple tissue paper. I unwrapped it at a red light, to find a magnet depicting a cartoon girl with squiggly curled hair and glasses. "I'm not gay, but my mother is," it read. Perfect.

I fiddled with the radio and kept quiet during the half hour drive back to town. My mother sat quietly beside me, obviously waiting for me to bring up Bruce's latest opus. On the way into the Terminal, in between the vegetable vendor and the fresh fish counter, I finally did.

"Good in bed," I snorted. "Hah!"

My mother gave me a sideways glance. "So I take it he wasn't?"

"I don't want to be having this conversation with you," I grumbled, as we worked our way past the bakeries and the Thai and Mexican food stalls and found seats in front of the demonstration kitchen. The chef—a semiregular I remembered from the Southern Favorites lesson three weeks before—blanched as my mother sat down.

She shrugged at me, and stared at the blackboard. This week it was American Classics with Five Easy Ingredients. The chef launched into his spiel. One of his assistants—a gangly, pimply kid from The Restaurant School—started hacking away at a head of cabbage. "He's going to cut his finger off," my mother predicted.

"Shh!" I said, as the front-row regulars—mostly senior citizens who took these sessions way too seriously—scowled at us.

"Well, he is," said my mother. "He's holding the knife all wrong. Now, getting back to Bruce . . ."

"I don't want to talk about it," I said. The chef melted a gigantic glob of butter in a pan. Then he added bacon. My mother gasped as if she'd witnessed a beheading, and raised her hand.

"Is there a heart-healthy modification for this recipe?" she inquired. The chef sighed and started talking about olive oil. My mother returned her attention to me. "Forget Bruce," she said. "You can do better."

"Mother!"

"Shh!" hissed the front-row foodies. My mother shook her head. "I can't believe this."

"What?"

"Would you look at the size of that pan? That pan's not big enough." Sure enough, the chef-in-training was cramming way too much imperfectly chopped cabbage into a shallow frying pan. My mother raised her hand. I yanked it down.

"Just let it go."

"How's he going to learn anything if nobody tells him when he's making a mistake?" she complained, squinting at the stage. "That's right," agreed the woman sitting next to her.

"And if he's going to dredge the chicken in that flour," my mother continued, "I really think he needs to season it first."

"You ever try cayenne pepper?" asked an elderly man in the row ahead. "Not too much, you understand, but just a pinch gives it a really nice flavor."

"Thyme's nice, too," said my mother.

"Okay, Julia Child." I closed my eyes, slumping lower in my folding chair as the chef moved on to candied sweet potatoes and apple fritters, and my mother continued to quiz him about substitutions, modifications, techniques that she'd learned in her years as a homemaker, while offering running commentary to the bemusement of the people sitting near her and the fury of the entire front row.

Later, over cappuccinos and hot buttered pretzels from the Amish pretzel stand, she gave me the speech I was sure she'd been preparing since last night. "I know your feelings are hurt right now," she began. "But there are a lot of guys out there."

"Yeah, right," I muttered, keeping my eyes on my cup.

"Women, too," my mother continued helpfully.

"Ma, how many times do I have to tell you? I'm not a lesbian! I'm not interested."

She shook her head in mock sadness. "I had such high hopes for you," she fake-sighed, and pointed toward one of the fish stalls, where pike and carp were stacked on top of each other, open-mouthed and googly-eyed, their scales gleaming silver under the lights. "This is an object lesson," she said.

"This is a fish stall," I corrected.

"This is telling you that there are plenty of fish in the sea," she said. She walked over and tapped one fingernail on the glass case. I followed her reluctantly. "You see that?" she said. "Think of each one of those fish as a single guy."

I stared at the fish. The fish, stacked six high on the crushed ice, seemed to gape back. "They have better manners," I observed. "Some of them are probably better conversationalists, too."

"You want fish?" asked a short Asian woman in a floor-length rubber apron. She had a filleting knife in one hand. I thought, briefly, about asking to borrow it, and what it would feel like to gut Bruce. "Good fish," she urged.

"No thanks," I said. My mother led me back to the table.

"You shouldn't be so upset," she said. "That article will be lining birdcages by next month. . . ."

"What an uplifting thought to share with a journalist," I said.

"Don't be sarcastic," she said.

"I don't have any other way to be." I sighed.

We sat down again. My mother picked up her coffee cup. "Is it because he got a job at a magazine?" she ventured.

I took a deep breath. "Maybe," I acknowledged. And it was true, seeing Bruce's star rise while mine just stayed in place would have hurt even if his first story hadn't been about me.

"You're doing fine," said my mother. "Your day will come."

"What if it doesn't?" I demanded. "What if I never get another job, or another boyfriend. . . ."

My mother waved her hand dismissively, as if this was too silly to even consider.

"But what if I don't?" I asked raggedly. "He's got this column, he's writing a novel. . . ."

"He says he's writing a novel," said my mother. "Doesn't mean it's true."

"I'm never going to meet anyone else," I said flatly.

My mother sighed. "You know, I think some of this is my fault," she finally said.

That got my attention.

"When your father used to say things . . ."

This was definitely a turn I didn't want the conversation to take. "Mom . . ."

"No, no, Cannie, let me finish." She took a deep breath. "He was awful," she said. "Mean and awful, and I let him get away with way too much, and I let it go on for too long."

"Water under the bridge," I said.

"I'm sorry," said my mother. I had heard her say this before, of course, but it hurt every time, because every time it made me remember just what she was apologizing for, and how bad it had been. "I'm sorry because I know it's what's made you this way."

I stood up, grabbing her cup and mine, our used napkins, the remains of the pretzels, and headed off to find a garbage can. She followed behind me. "Made me how?" I asked.

She thought about it. "Well, you're not great with criticism."

"Tell me about it."

"You don't seem very comfortable with how you look."

"Show me a woman who is," I shot back. "It's just that not all of us get to enjoy having our insecurities exploited for millions of *Moxie* readers."

"And I wish . . ." She looked ruefully toward the tables at the center of the market, where families were gathered, having sandwiches or coffee, passing sections of the *Examiner* back and forth. "I wish you believed in yourself more. Like with . . . romantic stuff."

Yet another conversation I didn't want to be having with my late-in-life-lesbian mother.

"You'll find the right guy," she said.

"I've been underwhelmed by the choices so far."

"You stayed with Bruce too long. . . ."

"Ma, please!"

"He was a nice guy. But I knew you didn't love him that way."

"I thought you were out of the heterosexual advice-giving arena."

"I'm making a special guest appearance on an as-needed basis," she said cheerfully. Outside, by the car, she gave me a rough hug—a big step for her, I knew. My mother is a great cook, a sympathetic listener, and a good judge of character, but she's never been big on touchy-feely stuff. "I love you," she said, which was also out of character for her. But I wasn't going to object. I needed all the love I could get.

THREE

On Monday morning I sat in a waiting room full of women too big to cross their legs, all of us wedged into inadequate armchairs on the seventh floor of the University of Philadelphia Weight and Eating Disorders Center, thinking that if I ran the place I'd make sure to have couches.

"A few surveys," the smiling, skinny secretary behind the desk had said, handing me a half-inch thick slab of forms, a clipboard, and a pen. "There's breakfast," she added chirpily, pointing at a stack of desiccated bagels, a tub of fat-free cream cheese, and a pitcher of orange juice with a thick film of pulp floating on the top. Like anyone would eat in here, I thought, bypassing the bagels and sitting down with my forms beneath a poster that read "Taking it off . . . one day at a time!" and depicted a model in a leotard romping through a field full of flowers, which was not something I planned on doing, no matter how skinny I got.

Name. That was easy. Height. No problem. Current weight. Ack. Lowest weight maintained as an adult. Did fourteen count as an adult? Reason for wanting to lose weight. I thought for a minute, than scribbled, *Was humiliated in national publication.* I thought for a minute, than added, *Would like to feel better about myself.*

Next page. Diet history. Highest weights, lowest weights, programs I'd enrolled in, how much I'd lost, how long I'd kept it off. "Please use reverse side if more space is needed," read the form. I needed. In fact, judging from a quick glance around the room, everybody needed. One woman even had to ask for extra paper.

Page three. Parents' weights. Grandparents' weights. Siblings' weights. I took guesses for all of them. These weren't things that were discussed around the table at family gatherings. Did I binge and purge, fast, abuse laxatives, exercise compulsively? If I did, I thought, would I look like this?

Please list your five favorite restaurants. Well, this would be easy. I could just walk down my street and pass five fabulous places to eat—everything from spring rolls to tiramisu before I'd gone three blocks. Philadelphia still lived in the shadow of New York City and often had the character of a sulky second sister who'd never made the honor roll or the homecoming court. But our restaurant renaissance was for real, and I lived in the neighborhood that boasted the first crêperie, the first soba noodle shop, and the first drag show dinner theater (so-so female impersonators, divine calamari). We also had the obligatory two coffee shops per block, which had hooked me on three-dollar lattes and chocolate-chip scones. Not, I knew, the breakfast of champions, but what was a girl to do, except try to compensate by avoiding the cheesesteak shops on every corner? Plus which, Andy, the one real friend I'd made at the paper, was the food critic, whom I often accompanied on review meals, eating foie gras and rabbit rillettes and veal and venison and pan-seared sea bass at the finest restaurants in town while Andy murmured into the microphone wire running through his collar.

Five favorite foods. Now this was getting tricky. Desserts, in my opinion, were an entirely separate category from main dishes, and breakfast was another thing altogether, and the five best things I could cook bore no relation to the five best things I could buy. Mashed potatoes and roast chicken were my go-to comfort foods, but could I really compare them to the chocolate tarts and crème brûlée from the Parisian bakery on Lombard Street? Or the grilled stuffed grape leaves at Viet Nam, the fried chicken at Delilah's, and the brownies from Le

Bus? I scribbled, crossed out, remembered the chocolate bread pudding at the Silk City Diner, heated and with fresh whipped cream, and had to start again.

Seven pages of physical history. Did I have a heart murmur, high blood pressure, glaucoma? Was I pregnant? No, no, and a thousand times no. Six pages of emotional history. Did I eat when I was upset? Yes. Did I eat when I was happy? Yes. Would I be tearing through those bagels and that funky-looking cream cheese at this very moment, were it not for the present company? You betcha.

On to the psychology pages. Was I frequently depressed? I circled *sometimes*. Did I have thoughts of suicide? I winced, then circled *rarely*. Insomnia? No. Feelings of worthlessness? Yes, even though I knew I wasn't worthless. Did I ever fantasize about cutting off fleshy or flabby areas of my body? What, doesn't everyone? Please add any additional thoughts. I wrote, *I am happy with every aspect of my life except my appearance.* Then I added, *And my love life.*

I laughed a little bit. The woman stuffed into the seat next to mine gave me a tentative smile. She was wearing one of those outfits I always thought of as fat-lady chic: leggings and a tunic top in a soft, periwinkle blue, with silk-screened daisies across her chest. A beautiful outfit, and not cheap, either, but play clothes. It's as if the fashion designers decided that once a woman hit a certain weight, she'd have no need for business suits, for skirts and blazers, for anything except glorified sweatsuits, and they tried to apologize for dressing us like overaged Teletubbies by silk-screening daisies on the tops.

"I'm laughing to keep from crying," I explained.

"Gotcha," she said. "I'm Lily."

"I'm Candace. Cannie."

"Not Candy?"

"I think my parents decided not to give the kids on the playground any extra ammunition," I said. She smiled. She had glossy black hair twisted back with lacquered chopstick-y things, and diamond studs the size of cocktail peanuts in her ears.

"Do you think this will work?" I asked. She shrugged her thick shoulders.

"I was on phen-fen," she said. "I lost eighty pounds." She reached into her purse. I knew what was coming. Regular women carry pictures of their babies, their husbands, their summer houses. Fat ladies carry pictures of themselves at their skinniest. Lily showed me the full-figure view, in a black suit, and then the side profile, in a miniskirt and sweater. Sure enough, she looked terrific. "Phen-fen," she said, and sighed gigantically. Her bosom looked like something governed by tides and gravity, not mere human will. "I was doing so great," she said. Her eyes took on a faraway look. "I was never hungry. It was like flying."

"Speed'll do that to you," I observed.

Lily wasn't listening. "I cried the day they took it off the market. I tried and tried, but I gained everything back in, like, ten minutes." She narrowed her eyes. "I would kill to get more phen-fen."

"But . . . ," I said hesitantly. "Wasn't it supposed to cause heart problems?"

Lily snorted. "Given a choice between being this big and being dead, I swear I'd have to think about it. It's ridiculous! I could walk down two blocks and buy crack cocaine on the corner, but I can't get phen-fen for love or money."

"Oh." I couldn't think of anything else to say.

"You never tried phen-fen?"

"No. Just Weight Watchers."

That brought a chorus of complaints and rolled eyes from the women sitting around me.

"*Weight* Watchers!"

"That's a crock."

"Expensive crock."

"Standing in line so some skinny thing can weigh you. . . ."

"And those scales were never right," said Lily, to a chorus of enthusiastic *uh-huhs!* The size six behind the desk was looking worried. Fat lady insurrection! I grinned, imagining us surging down the hall, a righteous, stretch-pant-wearing army, tipping over the scales, toppling the blood-pressure machine, tearing the height-weight charts off the walls and making all the skinny clinicians eat them, while we feasted on bagels and fat-free cream cheese.

"Candace Shapiro?"

A tall doctor with an extremely deep voice was calling my name. Lily squeezed my hand.

"Good luck," she whispered. "And if he's got any samples of phen-fen in there, grab 'em!"

The doctor was fortyish, thin (of course), and going gray at the temples, with a warm handshake and big brown eyes. He was also extremely tall. Even in my thick-soled Doc Martens I barely came up to his shoulders, which meant he had to be at least six and a half feet. His name sounded like Dr. Krushelevsky, only with more syllables. "You can call me Dr. K," he said, in his absurdly deep, absurdly slow voice. I kept waiting for him to drop what I took for a misguided Barry White impression and talk normally, but he didn't, so I guessed that basso profundo was the way he did talk. I sat, holding my purse against my chest, while he flipped through my forms, squinting at a few answers, laughing out loud at others. I looked around, trying to relax. His office was nice. Leather couches, a comfortably cluttered desk, a real-looking Oriental rug covered with piles of books, papers, magazines, and a television/VCR in one corner, a small refrigerator with a coffee machine perched on top in another. I wondered if he'd ever slept there . . . if maybe the couch unfolded into a bed. It looked like the kind of place you'd want to stay in.

"Humiliated in national publication?" he read out loud. "What happened?"

"Ugh," I said. "You don't want to know."

"No, really. I do. I think that's the most unusual answer anyone's ever given."

"Well, my boyfriend . . ." I winced. "Ex-boyfriend. Excuse me. He's writing this column for *Moxie*. . . ."

"Good in Bed?" asked the doctor.

"Why, yes, I like to think so."

The doctor blushed. "No . . . I mean . . ."

"Yeah, that's the column Bruce writes. Don't tell me you read it," I said, thinking, if some fortysomething diet doctor had seen it, I could pretty much assume that everyone else in my life had, too.

"I actually clipped it out," he told me. "I thought our patients might enjoy it."

"What? Why?"

"Well, it was actually a fairly sensitive appreciation of . . . of . . ."

"A fat lady?"

The doctor smiled. "He never called you that."

"Just everything but."

"So you're in here because of the article?"

"Partly."

The doctor looked at me.

"Okay, mostly. It's just, I don't . . . I never thought of myself . . . that way. As a larger woman. I mean, I know I am . . . larger . . . and I know I should lose weight. I mean, it's not like I'm blind, or oblivious to the culture, and how Americans expect women to look . . ."

"So you're here because of America's expectations?"

"I want to be thin." He looked at me, waiting. "Well, thinner, anyhow."

He flipped through my forms. "Your parents are overweight," he said.

"Well . . . kind of. My mom's a little heavy. My father, I haven't seen in years. He had kind of a belly when he left, but . . ." I paused. The truth was, I didn't know where my father was living, and it was always awkward when it came up. "I have no idea what he looks like now."

The doctor looked up. "You don't see him?"

"No."

He scribbled a note. "How about your siblings?"

"Both skinny." I sighed. "I'm the only one who got hit with the fat stick."

The doctor laughed. "Hit with the fat stick. I've never heard it put quite that way."

"Yeah, well, I got a million more of 'em."

He flipped some more. "You're a reporter?"

I nodded. He flipped back. "Candace Shapiro . . . I've seen your byline."

"Really?" This was a surprise. Most civilians skipped right over the bylines.

"You write about television sometimes." I nodded. "You're very funny. Do you like your job?"

"I love my job," I said, and meant it. When I wasn't obsessing over the high-pressure, in-the-public-eye nature of being a reporter, or scrapping for good assignments with territorial coworkers, and entertaining dreams of the muffin shop, I managed to have a good time. "It's really fun. Interesting, challenging . . . all those things."

He wrote something down in the folder. "And do you feel like your weight affects your job performance . . . how much money you make, how far you've advanced?"

I thought for a minute. "Not really. I mean, sometimes, some of the people I interview . . . you know, they're thin, I'm not, I get a little jealous, maybe, or wonder if they think I'm lazy or whatever, and then I have to be careful when I write the articles, not to let the way I'm feeling affect what I say about them. But I'm good at my job. People respect me. Some of them even fear me. And it's a union paper, so financially I'm okay."

He laughed, and kept flipping, slowing at the psychology page.

"You were in therapy last year?"

"For about eight weeks," I said.

"May I ask what for?"

I thought for a minute. There is no easy way to say to someone you'd just met that your mother had announced, at fifty-six, that she was gay. Especially not to someone who sounded like a thin, white James Earl Jones, and would probably be so tickled he'd repeat it out loud. Possibly even more than once.

"Family things," I finally said.

He just looked at me.

"My mother was . . . in a new relationship, that was moving very quickly, and it kind of freaked me out."

"And did the therapy help?"

I thought of the woman my HMO assigned me to, a mousy woman with Little Orphan Annie curls who wore her glasses chained around her neck and seemed a little bit afraid of me. Maybe hearing about the newly lesbian mother and my absent father within the first five minutes of taking my history was more than she'd planned on. She always had this vaguely cringing look, as if she feared that at any moment I would charge across her desk, knock her box of Kleenex to the floor, and try to throttle her.

"I guess so. The therapist's main point was that I can't change things other people in my family do, but I can change how I react to them."

He scratched something in my folder. I tried to do a subtle lean so I could make some of it out, but he had the page tilted at a difficult angle. "Was that good advice?"

I shuddered inwardly, remembering how Tanya moved in six weeks after she and my mother had started dating, and her first act of residence was to move all of the furniture out of what had been my bedroom and replace it with her rainbow-striped sun catchers and self-help books, plus her two-ton loom. By way of saying thanks, she wove Nifkin a small striped sweater. Nifkin wore it once, then ate it.

"I guess so. I mean, the situation's not perfect, but I'm sort of getting used to it."

"Well, good," he said, and flipped my folder closed. "Here's the thing, Candace."

"Cannie," I said. "They only call me Candace when I'm in trouble."

"Cannie, then," he said. "We're running a year-long study of a drug called sibutramin, which works somewhat the way phen-fen did. Did you ever take phen-fen?"

"No," I said, "but there's a lady in the lobby who misses it sorely."

He smiled again. He had, I noticed, a dimple in his left cheek. "I consider myself warned," he said. "Now, sibutramin's a lot milder than phen-fen, but it does the same thing, which is basically to fool your brain into thinking that you're full longer. The good news is, it doesn't have the same health risks and potential complications that have been associated with phen-fen. We're looking for women who are at least thirty percent above their ideal weight . . ."

". . . and you're delighted to inform me that I qualify," I said sourly.

He smiled. "Now, the studies that have been done already show patients losing between five and ten percent of their body weight in a year's time."

I did some quick calculations. Losing ten percent of my body weight was still not going to put me anywhere near the weight I wanted to be.

"Does that disappoint you?"

Was he kidding? It was so frustrating! We had the technology to replace hearts, to put septuagenarians on the moon, to give old geezers erections, and the best modern science could do for me was a lousy ten percent?

"I guess it's better than nothing," I said.

"Ten percent is a lot better than nothing," he said seriously. "Studies show that even losing as little as eight pounds can have a dramatic effect on blood pressure and cholesterol."

"I'm twenty-eight years old. My blood pressure and cholesterol are fine. I'm not worried about my health." I heard my voice rising. "I want to be thin. I need to be thin."

"Candace . . . Cannie . . ."

I took a deep breath and rested my forehead in my hands. "I'm sorry."

He put his hand on my arm. It felt nice. It was probably something they'd taught him to do in medical school: If patient becomes hysterical at prospect of relatively minute weight loss, place one hand gently on forearm. . . . I moved my arm away.

"Look," he said. "Realistically, given your heredity, and your frame, it may be that you were just never meant to be a thin person. And that's not the worst thing in the world."

I didn't lift my head. "Oh, no?"

"You're not sick. You're not in any pain. . . ."

I bit my lip. He had no idea. I remember when I was fourteen or so, on summer vacation somewhere by the beach, walking down a sidewalk with my sister, my slender sister, Lucy. We were wearing baseball caps and shorts and bathing suits and flip-flops. We were eating ice-cream cones. I could close my eyes and see the way my tanned legs looked against my white shorts, the sensation of the ice cream melting on my tongue. A kindly-looking white-haired lady had approached us with a smile. I thought she'd say something like how we reminded her of her granddaughters, or made her miss her own sister and the fun they'd had together. Instead, she nodded at my sister, walked up to me, and pointed at the ice cream cone. "You don't need that, dearie," she'd said. "You should be on a diet." I remembered things like that. A lifetime's accretion of unkindnesses, all of those little lingering hurts that I carried around like stones sewn into my pockets. The price you paid for being a Larger Woman. *You don't need that.* Not in pain, he'd said. What a joke.

The doctor cleared his throat. "Let's talk about motivation for a minute."

"Oh, I'm very motivated." I lifted my head, managed a small, crooked smile. "Can't you tell?"

He smiled back. "We're also looking for people who have the right kind of motivation." He shut my folder and crossed his hands over his nonexistent belly. "You probably know this already, but people who have the best long-term success with weight management decide to lose weight for themselves. Not for their spouses, or their parents, or because their high-school reunion's coming up, or they're embarrassed over something that somebody wrote."

We stared at each other silently.

"I'd like to see," he said, "if you can come up with some reasons to lose weight, other than the fact that you're angry and upset right now."

"I'm not angry," I said angrily.

He didn't smile. "Can you think of other reasons?"

"I'm miserable," I blurted. "I'm lonely. Nobody's going to date me looking like this. I'm going to die alone, and my dog's going to eat my face, and no one will find us until the smell seeps out under the door."

"I find that highly unlikely," he said with a smile.

"You don't know my dog," I said. "So am I in? Do I get drugs? Can I have some now?"

He smiled at me. "We'll be in touch." I stood up. He pulled a stethoscope around his neck and patted the examining table. "They'll draw some blood on your way out. I just need to listen to your heart for a minute. Hop up here for me, please."

I sat up straight on the crinkly white paper on top of the table and closed my eyes as his hands moved against my back. The first time a man had touched me with any regard or kindness since Bruce. The thought made my eyes fill. Don't do it, I thought fiercely, don't cry now.

"Breathe in," Dr. K. said calmly. If he had any idea what was going on, he didn't let on. "Nice deep breath . . . and hold it . . . and let it out."

"Is it still there?" I asked, staring at his head, bent over, as he wedged the stethoscope beneath my left breast. And then, before I could stop myself, "Does it sound broken?"

He straightened up, smiling. "Still there. Not broken. In fact, it sounds like you have a strong and healthy heart." He offered his hand. "I think you're going to be fine," he said. "We'll be in touch."

Out in the lobby, Lily the daisy-shirt woman was still wedged into her chair, half of a plain bagel balanced on one knee. "So?" she asked.

"They're going to let me know," I said. There was a piece of paper in her hand. I was unsurprised to see that it was a Xeroxed copy of "Loving a Larger Woman" by Bruce Guberman. "You seen this?" she asked me.

I nodded.

"This is great," she said. "This guy really gets it." She shifted as much as her seat would allow and looked me right in the eye. "Can you imagine the idiot who'd let someone like this get away?"

FOUR

I think every person who is single should have a dog. I think the government should step in and intervene: If you're not married or coupled up, whether you've been dumped or divorced or widowed or whatever, they should require you to proceed immediately to the pound nearest you and select an animal companion.

Dogs give your days a rhythm and a purpose. You can't sleep ridiculously late, or stay out all day and all night, when there's a dog depending on you.

Every morning, no matter what I'd drunk, what I'd done, or whether or not my heart had been broken, Nifkin woke me up by gently applying his nose to my eyelids. He is a remarkably understanding little dog, willing to sit patiently on the couch with his paws crossed gracefully in front of him while I sang along to *My Fair Lady* or clipped recipes from *Family Circle*, which I subscribed to even though, as I liked to joke, I had neither family nor circle.

Nifkin is a small and neatly made rat terrier, white with black spots and brown markings on his long, spindly legs. He weighs precisely ten pounds and looks like an anorexic and extremely high-strung Jack Russell, with a Doberman pinscher's ears, pointing permanently upright, tacked onto his head. He's a secondhand dog. I inherited him from three sportswriters I knew at my first paper. They were renting a house, and they decided that a house required a dog. So they got Nifkin from the pound believing that he was actually a Doberman pinscher puppy. Of course, he was no such thing . . . just a full-grown rat terrier with oversized ears. Truthfully, he looks like pieces of a few different dogs that someone put together as a joke. And he's got a permanent, Elvis-like sneer on his face—the result, the story goes, from when his mother bit him when he was a puppy. But I refrain from remarking on his shortcomings when he's within earshot. He's also very sensitive about his looks. Just like his mother.

The sportswriters spent six months alternately showering him with attention, letting him lap beer out of his water bowl, or leaving him penned up in their kitchen, completely ignored, all the while waiting for him to grow into his Doberman pinscher-hood. Then one of them got a job at the *Fort Lauderdale Sun-Sentinel,* and the other two decided to split up and move to their own apartments. Neither one wanted to take along anxious little Nifkin, who did not in any way resemble a Doberman pinscher.

Employees could run free classified ads in the paper, and their ad, "One dog, small, spotted, free to a good home" ran for two weeks with no takers. Desperate, with their bags packed and security deposits already paid on their new places, the sportswriters double-teamed me in the company cafeteria. "It's you or the pound again," they said.

"Is he housebroken?"

They exchanged an uneasy look. "Kind of," said one. "For the most part," said the other.

"Does he chew things?"

Another uneasy look. "He likes rawhide," said one. The other one kept his mouth shut, from which I inferred that Nifkin probably also enjoyed shoes, belts, wallets, and anything else that came his way.

"And has he learned to walk on a leash, or is he still pulling all the time? And do you think he'd answer to something other than Nifkin?"

The guys looked at each other. "Look, Cannie," one of them finally said, "you know what happens to dogs in the pound . . . unless they can convince somebody else that he's a Doberman pinscher. And that's unlikely."

I took him in. And, of course, Nifkin spent the first months of our time together pooping furtively in a corner of the living room, chewing a hole in my couch, and acting like a spastic rabbit whenever his leash was attached to his collar. When I moved to Philadelphia I decided that things would be different. I put Nifkin on a rigorous schedule: a walk at 7:30 A.M., another one at 4 P.M., for which I paid the kid next door $20 a week, then a brief constitutional before I went to sleep. We did six months of obedience boot camp, after which point he'd pretty much stopped chewing, was thoroughly housebroken, and was generally content to walk politely beside me, unless a squirrel or a skateboarder distracted him. For his progress, he was allowed on the furniture. He sat beside me on the couch while I watched TV, and slept curled up on a pillow next to my head every night.

"You love that dog more than me," Bruce would complain, and it was true that Nifkin was spoiled rotten, with all manner of fluffy toys, rawhide bones, small fleece sweaters, and gourmet treats, and, I am embarrassed to say, a small dog-size sofa, upholstered in the same denim as my couch, where he sleeps when I'm at work. (It was also true that Bruce had no use for Nifkin, and couldn't be bothered to walk him. I'd come home from the gym, or a bike ride, or a long day at work, to find Bruce sprawled on my couch—frequently with his bong nearby—and Nifkin perched, quivering, on one of the pillows, looking as if he were going to explode. "Has he been out?" I'd ask, and Bruce would shrug shamefacedly. After this happened a dozen times or so I just quit asking). Nifkin's picture is my screen saver at work, and I subscribe to the online newsletter *Ratter Chatter,* although I've managed to refrain from sending in his picture—so far.

In bed together, Bruce and I used to make up stories about Nifkin's history. I was of the opinion that Nifkin had been born into a well-to-do British family, but that his father had disowned him after catching him in a compromising position in the hayloft with one of the stable boys, and banished him to America.

"Maybe he worked as a window dresser," Bruce had mused, cupping one hand over my head.

"Hand hat," I cooed, and snuggled into him. "I'll bet he hung out at Studio 54."

"He probably knew Truman."

"And he'd wear custom-made suits, and carry a cane."

Nifkin looked at both of us as if we were nuts, then strolled off to the living room. I tilted my head up for a kiss, and Bruce and I were off to the races again.

But as much as I'd rescued Nifkin from the sportswriters, the classified ads, and the pound, he had rescued me, too. He kept me from being lonely, he gave me a reason to get up every morning, and he loved me. Or maybe he just loved the fact that I had opposable thumbs and could work a can opener. Whatever. When he laid his little muzzle next to my head at night and sighed and closed his eyes, it was enough.

The morning after my appointment at the weight management clinic I hitched Nifkin to his extend-o-leash, tucked a plastic Wal-Mart bag into my right pocket, four small dog biscuits and a tennis ball into my left. Nikfin was jumping about crazily, caroming from my couch to his couch, down the hall to the bedroom and back again at warp speed, pausing only to dart a lick toward my nose. Every morning, to him, is a celebration. Yay! he seems to say. It's morning! I love morning! Morning! Let's go for a walk! I finally got him out the door, but he kept prancing at my side as I fished my sunglasses out of my pocket and put them on. We proceeded down the street, Nifkin practically dancing, me dragging behind.

The park was almost empty. Just a pair of golden retrievers sniffing at the bushes, and a haughty cocker spaniel in the corner. I unleashed my dog, who promptly and without provocation made a beeline for the cocker spaniel, barking frantically.

"Nifkin!" I hollered, knowing that as soon as he got within a foot or two of the other dog he'd stop, give a deep, disdainful sniff, perhaps bark a few more times, and then leave the other dog alone. I knew that, Nifkin knew that, and it was more than likely that the cocker spaniel knew it, too (it's been my experience that other dogs mostly ignore the Nif when he goes into his attack mode, probably because he's very small and not all that menacing, even when he's trying). But the dog's owner looked alarmed as he saw a spotted, sneering rat terrier missile streaking toward his pet.

"Nifkin!" I called again, and my dog for once listened to me, stopping dead in his tracks. I hurried over, trying to look dignified, and scooped Nifkin into my arms, holding him by his scruff, looking into his eyes and saying, "No," and "Bad," the way I'd learned in Remedial Obedience. Nifkin whined and looked disgruntled at having his fun interrupted. The cocker spaniel wagged his tail hesitantly.

The cocker spaniel guy was looking amused.

"Nifkin?" he asked. I could see he was getting ready to pop the question. I wondered if he'd have the nerve. I made myself a bet that he would.

"Do you know what a nifkin is?" he asked. Score 1, Cannie. A nifkin, according to my brother's fraternity friends, is the area between a guy's balls and his ass. The sportswriters had named him.

I put on my best puzzled look. "Huh? It's his name. Does it mean something?"

The guy blushed. "Uh, yeah. It's, um . . . it's kind of a slang term."

"For what?" I asked, trying to look innocent. The guy shuffled his feet. I looked at him expectantly. So did Nifkin.

"Um," said the guy, and stopped. I decided to have mercy.

"Yes, I know what a nifkin is," I said. "He's a secondhand dog." I gave him the abbreviated version of the sportswriter story. "And by the time I figured out what a nifkin was, it was too late. I tried calling him Nifty . . . and Napkin . . . and Ripken . . . and, like, everything else I could think of. But he won't respond to anything but Nifkin."

"That is rough," said the guy, laughing. "I'm Steve," he said.

"I'm Cannie. What's your dog's name?"

"Sunny," he said. Nifkin and Sunny sniffed each other tentatively as Steve and I shook hands.

"I just moved here, from New York," he said. "I'm an engineer. . . ."

"Family in town?"

"Nope. The single guy." He had nice legs. Tanned, slightly furry.

And those dumb Velcro-strapped sandals that everyone was wearing that summer. Khaki shorts, a gray T-shirt. Cute.

"Would you like to have a beer maybe sometime?" he asked.

Cute, and evidently not averse to the sweaty, queen-size woman.

"Sure. That'd be great."

He smiled at me from under his baseball cap. I gave him my number, trying not to get my hopes up, but feeling pleased with myself nonetheless.

Back home, I gave Nifkin a cup of Small Bites kibble, ate my Special K, then gargled, flossed, and took deep, calming breaths, preparing for my interview with Jane Sloan, lady director extraordinaire who I'd be profiling for next Sunday's paper. In deference to her fame, and because we'd be lunching at the *très chic* Four Seasons, I took extra care with my clothes, struggling into both a panty girdle and control-top pantyhose. Once my midsection was secured, I pulled on my ice-blue skirt, ice-blue jacket with funky star-shaped buttons, the requisite chunky black loafers, uniform shoe of twentysomething would-be hipsters. I prayed for strength and composure, and for Bruce's fingers to be broken in some bizarre industrial accident guaranteeing that he'd never write again. Then I called a cab, grabbed my notebook, and headed to the Four Seasons for lunch.

I cover Hollywood for the *Philadelphia Examiner*. This is not as easy as you'd think, because Hollywood is in California, and I, alas, am not.

Still, I persist. I write about trends, about gossip, the mating habits of stars and starlets. I do reviews, and even the occasional interview with the handful of celebrities who deign to stop by the East Coast on their promotional juggernauts.

I wandered into journalism after graduating from college with an English degree and no real plans. I wanted to write. Newspapers were one of the few places I could locate that would pay me to do it. So, the September after graduation, I was hired at a very small newspaper in central Pennsylvania. The average age of a reporter was twenty-two. Our combined years of professional experience were less than two years, and boy, did it show.

At the *Central Valley Times,* I covered five school districts, plus assorted fires, car crashes, and whatever features I could find time to churn out. For this I was paid the princely sum of $300 a week— enough to live on, just barely, if nothing went wrong. And of course, something was always going wrong.

Then there were the wedding announcements. The *CVT* was one of the last newspapers in the country that still ran, free of charge, lengthy descriptions of weddings—and, woe to me, of wedding dresses. Princess seams, alençon lace, French embroidery, illusion veils, beaded headpieces, gathered bustles . . . all of these were terms I found myself typing so often that I put them on a save-get key. Just one key-stroke, and out would pop complete phrases: *freshwater pearl embroidery,* or *ivory taffeta pouf.*

One day I was wearily typing the wedding announcements and musing on the injustice of it all when I came across a word I couldn't read. Many of our brides filled their forms in by hand. This particular bride had written in looping cursive, in purple ink, a word that looked like CFORM.

I carried the form over to Raji, another cub reporter. "What's this say?"

He squinted at the purple. "C-FORM," he read slowly. "Like MDOS, or something."

"For a dress, though?"

Raji shrugged. He'd grown up in New York City, then attended Columbia Journalism School. The ways of Central Pennsylvanians were strange to him. I headed back to my desk; Raji went back to his dread chore, typing in a week's worth of school lunch menus. "Tater Tot," I heard him sigh. "Always, the Tater Tot."

Which left me with C-FORM. Under "contact for questions" the bride had scribbled her home phone number. I picked up the phone, and dialed.

"Hello?" answered a cheerful-sounding woman.

"Hello," I said, "this is Candace Shapiro calling from the *Valley Times.* I'm trying to reach Sandra Garry. . . ."

"This is Sandy," chirped the woman.

"Hi, Sandy. Listen, I do the wedding announcements here, and I'm reading your form and there's a word . . . C-FORM?"

"Seafoam," she answered promptly. In the background I could hear a kid screaming, "Ma!" and what sounded like a soap opera on TV. "That's the color of my dress."

"Oh," I said, "well, that's what I needed to know, so thanks. . . ."

"Except, well, maybe . . . I mean, do you think people will know what seafoam is? Like, what do you think of when you think of seafoam?"

"Green?" I ventured. I really wanted to get off the phone. I had three baskets of laundry reposing in the trunk of my car. I wanted to get out of the office, go to the gym, wash my clothes, buy some milk. "Like a pale green, I guess."

Sandy sighed. "See, that's not it," she said. "It's really more blue, I think. The girl at the Bridal Barn said the color's called seafoam, but that's really more of a green-sounding thing, I think."

"We could say blue," I said. Another sigh from Sandy. "Light blue?" I essayed.

"See, but it's not really blue," she said. "You say blue, and people think, you know, blue like the sky, or navy blue, and it's not, like, dark or anything . . ."

"Pale blue?" I offered, running through my bridal announcement-gleaned gamut of synonyms. "Ice blue? Robin's egg blue?"

"I just don't think any of those are quite right," Sandy said primly.

"Hmm," I said. "Well, if you want to think about it and call me back . . ."

Which was when Sandy started to cry. I could hear her sobbing on the other end of the phone as the soap opera droned in the background and the child, who I imagined, had sticky cheeks and possibly a stubbed toe, continued to whine, "Ma!"

"I want it to be right," she said between her sobs. "You know, I waited so long for this day . . . I want everything to be perfect . . . and I can't even say what color my dress is. . . ."

"Oh, now," I said, feeling ridiculously ineffectual. "Oh, listen, it's not that bad. . . ."

"Maybe you could come here," she said, still crying. "You're a reporter, right? Maybe you could look at the dress and say what's right."

I thought of my laundry, my plans for the night.

"Please?" asked Sandy, in a tiny, pleading voice.

I sighed. The laundry could wait, I supposed. And now I was curious. Who was this woman, and how did someone who couldn't spell seafoam find love?

I asked her for directions, mentally cursed myself for being such a softie, and told her I'd be there in an hour.

To be perfectly honest, I was expecting a trailer park. Central Pennsylvania has plenty of those. But Sandy lived in an actual house, a small white Cape Cod with black shutters and the proverbial picket fence out front. The backyard boasted a plastic orange SuperSoaker, an abandoned Big Wheel, a new-looking swingset. There was a shiny black truck parked in the driveway, and Sandy stood at the door—thirtyish, tired-looking around her eyes, but with a tremulous species of hope there, too. Her hair was pale blond, fine as spun sugar, and she had the tiny snub nose and wide cornflower-blue eyes of a painted figurine.

I got out of the car with my notebook in my hand. Sandy smiled through the screen door. I could see two small hands clutching her thigh, a child's face peeping around her leg, then vanishing behind it.

The house was cheaply furnished, but neat and clean, with stacks of magazines on the pine-veneer coffee table: *Guns & Ammo*, *Road & Track*, *Sport & Field*. The ampersand collection, I thought to myself. Powder-blue wall-to-wall carpet lined the living room floor; fresh white linoleum—the kind you roll down in a single sheet, with patterns stamped on it to make it look like separate tiles—covered the kitchen. "Do you want a soda? I was just about to have one myself," she said shyly.

I didn't want soda. I wanted to see the dress, come up with an adjective, hit the road, and be good & gone by the time *Melrose Place* was on. But she seemed desperate, and I was thirsty, so I sat down at her kitchen table under the stitched sampler that read "Bless This Home," with my notebook at my side.

Sandy took a gulp of her drink, burped gently against the back of her hand, closed her eyes, and shook her head. "Excuse me, please."

"Are you nervous about the wedding?" I asked.

"Nervous," she repeated, and laughed a little. "Honey, I'm terrified!"

"Is it . . ." I wanted to tread carefully here, "have you done the whole wedding thing before?"

Sandy shook her head. "Not like this. My first time I eloped. That was when I found out I was pregnant with Trevor. Justice of the peace over in Bald Eagle," she said. "I wore my prom dress to that one."

"Oh," said I.

"Second time," she continued, "there never was a wedding at all. That was Dylan's daddy, who I guess you could call my common-law husband. We were together seven years."

"Dylan, that's me!" piped up a little voice from underneath the table. A small, sleek blond head peeked out. "My daddy's in the army."

"That's right, honey," said Sandy, absently tousling Dylan's hair with one hand. She raised her eyebrows significantly toward me, shook her head, and whispered, "J-a-i-l."

"Oh," I said again.

"For stealing cars," she whispered. "Not anything, you know, too bad. I actually met Bryan, my fiancé, when I went visiting Dylan's dad," she said.

"So Bryan's . . ." I was just starting to learn how the long pause could sometimes be a reporter's best friend.

"Going to be paroled tomorrow," Sandy said. "He was in for fraud."

Which, I guessed from the pride in her voice, was a step up even from grand theft auto.

"So you met him in prison?"

"We were actually corresponding for some time before then," Sandy said. "He put an ad in the classified section . . . here, I saved it!"

She hopped up, causing our soda glasses to rattle, and came up with a laminated piece of paper no bigger than a postage stamp. "Christian gentleman, tall, athletic build, Leo, seeks sensitive pen-pal for letters and maybe more," it read.

"He got twelve responses," Sandy said, beaming. "He said he liked my letter the best."

"What did you tell him?"

"I was real honest," she said. "I explained my situation. How I was a single mother. How I wanted a role model for my boys."

"And you think . . ."

"He'll be a good daddy," she said. She sat down again, staring into her glass like it contained the mysteries of the ages instead of flat generic cola. "I believe in love," she said, her voice strong and clear.

"Did your parents . . ." I began. She waved one hand in the air, as if to shoo away the very idea.

"My father left when I was four, I think," she said. "Then it was just my mom and one boyfriend after another. Daddy Rick, Daddy Sam, Daddy Aaron. I swore it wasn't gonna go that way for me. And it's not," she said. "I think . . . I know . . . that this time I got it right."

"Mom?" Dylan was back, his lips dyed Kool-Aid red, holding his brother's hand. Where Dylan was small and fine-boned and blond, this boy—Trevor, I guessed—was darker and sturdier, with a thoughtful look on his face.

Sandy stood up and shot me a tentative smile. "You wait right here," she said. "Boys, you come with me. Let's show the reporter lady momma's pretty dress!"

After all of that—the prison, the husbands, the Christian classified ad—I was prepared for something dreadful, some off-the-rack horror show of a dress. The Bridal Barn specialized in those.

But Sandy's dress was beautiful. Tightly fitted on top, a fairytale princess boned bodice spangled with snowflake-sized crystals that caught the light, a deeply scooped neckline that showed off the creamy skin of her chest, swelling into a wave of tulle that swished around her feet. Her cheeks were flushed, her blue eyes sparkled. She looked like Cinderella's fairy godmother, like Glinda the good witch. Trevor held her hand solemnly as she made her way into the kitchen, humming "Here Comes the Bride." Dylan had appropriated her veil and popped it on his own head.

Sandy stood under the kitchen light and twirled. The edge of her skirt whispered along the floor. Dylan laughed and clapped his hands, and Trevor stared up at his mother, how her bare arms and shoulders rose out of the dress, how her hair fell against her skin. She twirled and twirled and her sons stared at her as if they were under a spell, until finally she stopped. "What do you think?" she asked. Her cheeks were flushed, and she was breathing hard. I could see each breath make her bosom swell against the tight-fitted scalloped edges of the bodice. She turned once more, and I could see tiny cloth rosebuds stitched all down the back, tight as a baby's pursed lips. "Is it blue? Green?"

I looked at her for a long moment, her pink cheeks and milky skin, and her sons' delighted eyes.

"I'm actually not sure," I said. "But I'll figure something out."

I missed the deadline, of course. The city editor was long gone by the time I made it back to the newsroom, after Sandy had shown me her pictures of Bryan, and told me all about their honeymoon plans, after I'd watched her read her sons *Where the Wild Things Are,* and kiss their foreheads and their cheeks, and add a finger's worth of bourbon to her soda, and half as much to mine. "He's a good man," she'd said dreamily. Her lit cigarette moved through the room like a firefly.

I had three inches to fill, and I had to write to fit, write only enough to fill the allotted space beneath the blurry picture of Sandy's smiling face. I sat at my computer, my head spinning a little, and keyed up my fill-in-the-blank marriage form, the one with spaces: bride's name, groom's name, attendants' names, description of dress. Then I pressed the "escape" key, cleared the screen, took a deep breath, and wrote:

Tomorrow Sandra Louise Garry will marry Bryan Perreault in Our Lady of Mercy Church on Old College Road. She will walk down the aisle with antique rhinestone combs in her hair and will promise to love and to honor and cherish Bryan, whose letters she keeps folded beneath her pillow, each one read so many times it's worn thin as a butterfly's wing.

"I believe in love," she says, even though a cynic might say there's every indication that she shouldn't. Her first husband left her, her second is in jail—the same jail where she met Bryan, whose parole begins two days before the wedding. In his letters, he calls her his little dove, his perfect angel. In her kitchen, the last of the three cigarettes she allows herself each night burning between her fingers, she says he is a prince.

Her sons, Dylan and Trevor, will attend the bride. Her dress is a color called seafoam, a color perfectly balanced between the palest blue and the palest green. It isn't white, a color for a virgin, a teenager with her head full of sugar-spun romances, or ivory, which is white tinged with resignation. Her dress is the color of dreams.

Well. A little florid, a little overwritten and overwrought. A dress the color of dreams? The whole thing had "Recent Graduate of College Creative Writing Workshop" stamped on every syllable. The next morning I came to work and there was a copy of the page splayed over my keyboard, the offending passage circled in red copy-editor's grease-paint pencil. "SEE ME," said the two-word message scrawled in the margin, in the unmistakable hand of Chris, the executive editor, an easily distractible Southerner who'd been lured to Pennsylvania with the promise of moving on to a bigger, better paper in the chain (that, plus unparalleled trout fishing). I knocked timidly at his office door. He beckoned me inside. A second copy of my story was opened on his desk.

"This," he said, pointing with one spindly finger. "What was this, exactly?"

I shrugged. "It was just . . . well, I met this woman. I was typing her announcement and there was a word I couldn't read, so I called her, then I met her, and then . . ." My voice trailed off. "I guess I thought it sounded like a story."

He looked up at me. "You were right," he said. "Want to do it again?"

And a star was born . . . well, sort of. Every other week I'd find a bride and write a short column about her—who she was, her dress, the church and the music and the party afterward. But most of all, I wrote about *how*: how my brides decided to get married, to stand up in front of a minister or rabbi or justice of the peace and promise forever.

I saw young brides and old brides, blind and deaf brides, teenage brides pledging themselves to their first loves and cynical twentysomethings taking vows with the men they called their baby's fathers. I attended first, second, third, fourth, and a single fifth wedding. I saw eight-hundred-guest extravangazas (an Orthodox wedding, where the men and women danced in separate ballrooms and there were a total of eight rabbis in attendance, all wearing Tina Turner–style glitter wigs by the end of the night). I saw a couple get married in adjoining hospital beds after a car accident that had left her a quadriplegic. I saw a bride left at the altar, watched her face crumple when the best man, his face pale and grave, made his way down the aisle and whispered, first into her mother's ear, and then into hers.

It was ironic, I knew, even then. While my peers were writing hip, sarcastic first-person columns for nascent online magazines about being single in the nation's big cities, I was toiling at a little local newspaper—a dinosaur, quivering on the tar pit of extinction in the evolutionary scale of the media—investigating marriage, of all things. How quaint! How charming!

But I couldn't have written about myself the way my classmates did, even if I'd wanted to. The truth was, I didn't have the brio to chronicle my own sex life. Nor did I have the kind of body I'd be comfortable exposing, even in print. And sex didn't interest me the way marriage did. I wanted to understand how to be part of a couple, how to get brave enough to take someone's hand and leap across the chasm. I would take each bride's story, each halting narrative of how they met and where they went and when they knew, and turn them over and over in my mind, looking for the loose thread, the invisible seam, the crack I could pry open so I could turn the story inside out and figure out the truth.

If you read that little paper in the early 1990s, you could probably see me at the edges of a hundred different wedding pictures, in the blue linen dress that I wore—plain, so as not to call attention to myself, but dressy, in deference to the solemnity of the occasion. See me in the aisle seats, my notebook tucked into my pocket, staring at a hundred different brides—old, young, black, white, thin, not thin—looking for answers. How do you know when a guy is the right guy? How can you be sure enough to promise someone forever and mean it? How can you believe in love?

After two-and-a-half years of the wedding beat, my clips happened to cross the right editor's desk at the precise moment that my hometown's big daily paper, the *Philadelphia Examiner,* had, as an institution, decided that attracting Generation X readers was of utmost importance, and that a young reporter would, by her very existence, draw those readers in. So they invited me to move back to the city of my birth and be their eyes and ears on twentysomething Philadelphia.

Two weeks later, the *Examiner* decided as an institution that attracting Generation X readers mattered not a whit, and went back to desperately trying to shore up circulation among soccer moms in the suburbs. But the damage had been done. I'd been hired. Life was good. Well, mostly.

From the start, the single biggest drawback to my job was Gabby Gardiner. Gabby is a massive, ancient woman, with a cap of bluish-tinged white curls and smeary, thick glasses. If I'm big, she's super-size. You'd think we would enjoy some solidarity because of our shared oppression, our common struggle to survive in a world that deems any woman above a size twelve grotesque and laughable. You would think wrong.

Gabby is the entertainment columnist for the *Philadelphia Examiner* and has filled that post, as she's fond of reminding me and anyone else within earshot, "for longer than you've been alive." This is both her strength and her weakness. She's got a network of contacts that spans both coasts and two decades. Unfortunately, those decades were the 1960s and 1970s. She stopped paying attention somewhere between Reagan's election and the advent of cable, so there's a whole universe of stuff, from MTV on down, that simply doesn't register on her radar the way, say, Elizabeth Taylor does.

Gabby's age could be anywhere from sixty on up. She has no children, no husband, no discernible hint of sexuality or hint of any life at all outside of the office. Her lifeblood is Hollywood gossip, and her attitude toward her subjects is rarely anything less than reverential. She talks about the stars she covers, mostly thirdhand, in reprinted bits of regurgitated gossip from the New York City tabloids and *Variety,* as if they are her intimates, her friends. Which would be pathetic if Gabby Gardiner were the least little bit likable. And she's not.

She is, however, lucky. Lucky that most of the *Examiner's* readers are over forty and not interested in learning anything new, so her "Gabbing with Gabby" column remains one of the most popular parts of our section—another fact that she frequently remarks upon, at top volume (allegedly she shouts because she's deaf, but I'm convinced that she does it because it's more annoying than simply talking).

For my first few years at the *Examiner* we left each other alone. Unfortunately, things escalated last summer, when Gabby took a two-month leave to address some nasty-sounding medical problem ("polyps" was the only word I caught, before Gabby and her friends shot me laser-beam hate looks, and I scurried out of the mailroom without even having retrieved my copy of *Teen People*). In her absence, I got to write her daily column. She lost the war, but won the battle: They kept calling the damn thing "Gabbing with Gabby," appending a short note in an embarrassingly small font about how Gabby was "on assignment" and that *"Examiner* staff writer Candace Shapiro is filling in."

"Good luck, kid," Gabby had said grandly, waddling over to my desk for her farewell, beaming as if she hadn't spent the past two weeks lobbying for the editors to run wire copy instead of giving me a chance while she was off, presumably being de-polyped. "Now, I told all my best sources to call you."

Terrific, I thought. Hot gossip about Walter Cronkite. Can't wait.

That should have been the end of it, but it wasn't. Every morning, Monday through Friday, I could look forward to my daily call from Gabby.

"Ben Affleck?" she'd rasp. "What's a Ben Affleck?"

Or, *"Comedy Central?* Nobody watches it."

Or, pointedly, "Saw something on Elizabeth on *ET* last night. Why didn't we have it?"

I tried to ignore her—to be pleasant on the phone and every once in a while, when she got particularly crabby, to toss in a line about "Gabby Gardiner will return at the end of September" at the end of the column.

But then one morning she called and I wasn't there to pick up my phone, so Gabby got my voice mail, which was basically me saying, "Hello, you've reached Candace Shapiro, entertainment columnist at the *Philadelphia Examiner.*" I didn't realize my misstep until the paper's executive editor stopped by my desk.

"Have you been telling people you're the entertainment columnist?" he asked.

"No," I said. "I'm not. I'm just filling in."

"I got a very irate call from Gabby last night. Late last night," he emphasized, with the expression of a man who did not appreciate having his sleep interrupted. "She thinks you're giving people the impression that she's gone for good and you've taken over."

Now I was confused. "I don't know what she's talking about."

He sighed again. "Your voice mail," he said. "I don't know what it says, and, frankly, I don't want to know what it says. Just fix it so Gabby isn't waking up my wife and kids anymore."

I went home and wept to Samantha ("She's completely insecure," she observed, and passed me a pint of half-melted sorbet as I moped on her couch). I raged on the phone to Bruce ("Just change the damn thing, Cannie!"). So I took his advice, altering my voice mail to say, "You've reached Candace Shapiro, temporary, transient, impermanent, just-filling-in, in-no-way-here-for-good entertainment columnist." Gabby called the next morning. "Love the message, kid," she said.

But the damage was done. When Gabby returned from her break

she took to calling me "Eve"—as in *All About*—when she spoke to me at all. I just tried to ignore her, and focus on my extracurricular activities: short stories, scraps of a novel, and *Star Struck,* the screenplay I'd been laboring over for months. *Star Struck* was a romantic comedy about a big-city reporter who falls for one of the stars she interviews. They meet cute (after she falls off a bar stool ogling him at the hotel bar), get off on the wrong foot (after he assumes she's just another plus-size groupie), fall for each other, and, after the appropriate Act Three complications, end up in each other's arms as the credits roll.

The star was based on Adrian Stadt, a cute comedian on *Saturday Night!* whose sense of humor seemed in sync with my own—even when he was doing his memorable three-month stint as the Projectile Vomiting Pilot. He was the guy I'd watched all through college and beyond and thought, if he were here, or if I were there, we'd probably get along. The reporter, of course, was me, only I named her Josie, made her a redhead, and gave her stable, straight, still-married parents.

The screenplay was what I'd pinned my dreams on. It was my answer to all of my good grades, to every teacher who'd ever told me I was talented, to every professor who'd ever said I had potential. Best of all, it was a hundred-page response to a world (and to my own secret fears) that told me that plus-size women couldn't have adventures, or fall in love. And today I was going to do something gutsy. Today, over lunch at the Four Seasons, I was interviewing actor Nicholas Kaye, star of the forthcoming *Belch Brothers,* a teen-pleasing comedy featuring twin brothers whose gas gives them magical powers. More importantly, I was also interviewing Jane Sloan, who'd executive-produced the movie (with one hand holding her nose, I figured). Jane Sloan was a hero of mine, who, before her slide toward the crassly commercial, had written and directed some of the sharpest, funniest films Hollywood had ever seen. Better yet, they were films with sharp, funny women in them. For weeks I'd been distracting myself from the missing-Bruce blues by constructing an elaborate daydream of how we'd meet and she'd immediately recognize me as a kindred spirit and potential collaborator, slipping me her business card and insisting that I contact her the moment I turned my attention from journalism to screenwriting. I even smiled a little, imagining the look of delight on her face when I modestly confessed that I had indeed penned a screenplay, and that I'd send it to her if she liked.

She was a writer, I was a writer. She was funny, I figured, and I'm funny, too. True, Jane Sloan was also rich and famous, successful beyond my wildest dreams, and about the size of one of my thighs, but sisterhood, I reminded myself, is powerful.

Almost an hour after I arrived, forty-five minutes after we were scheduled to meet, Jane Sloan seated herself across from me and laid a large mirror and a larger bottle of Evian next to her plate. "Hello," she said, her throaty voice emerging through her clenched teeth, and proceeded to give her face a few healthy squirts. I squinted at her, waiting for the punch line, waiting for her to crack up and say she was kidding. She didn't. Nicholas Kaye sat down beside her and shot me an apologetic grin. Jane Sloan finally put the mirror and bottle down.

"I'm sorry we're late," said Nicholas Kaye, who looked much like he did on TV—cute as a button.

Jane Sloan shoved the butter dish aggressively across the table. She picked up her napkin, which had been folded into the shape of a swan, opened it with one dismissive flick of her wrist, and carefully wiped her face with it. Only after she'd set the napkin, now stained ecru and crimson and mascara-black, onto the table, did she deign to speak.

"This city," she pronounced, "is wreaking havoc on my pores."

"I'm sorry," I said, feeling stupid as soon as the apology had left my mouth. What was I sorry for? I wasn't doing anything to her pores.

Jane waved one pale hand languorously, as if my apology for Philadelphia was of no more consequence then a mold spore, then picked up her silver butter knife and started poking at the flower-shaped butter pat in the dish she'd just banished to my side of the table. "What do you need to know?" she asked, without looking up.

"Umm," I said, fumbling for my pen and my notebook. I had a whole list of questions ready, questions about everything from how she'd cast the movie to who her influences were, and what she liked on TV, but all I could think of was, "Where'd you get the idea?"

Without lifting her eyes from the butter, she said, "Saw it on TV."

"That late-night sketch comedy show on HBO?" Nicholas Kaye said helpfully.

"I called the director. Said I thought it should be a movie. He agreed."

Great. So that was how movies got made. Strange little butter-averse pint-size Elvira with squirt bottle makes phone call, and voilà, instant film!

"So . . . you wrote the script?"

Another wave of that ghostlike hand. "I just oversaw."

"We hired a few guys from *Saturday Night!*," said Nicholas Kaye.

Double great. Not only did I not work for *Saturday Night!*, I wasn't even a guy. I quietly abandoned my plan of telling her that I'd written a screenplay. They'd probably laugh me all the way to Pittsburgh.

The waiter approached. Both Jane and Nicholas scowled at their menus in silence. The waiter shot me a desperate look.

"I'll have the osso bucco," I said.

"Excellent choice," he said, beaming.

"I'll have . . ." said Nicholas. Long, long pause. The waiter waited, pen poised. Jane poked at the butter. I felt a drop of sweat descend from the nape of my neck, down my back, and into my underwear. "This salad," he finally said, pointing. The waiter leaned in for a look. "Very good, sir," he said, relieved.

"And for the lady?"

"Lettuce," Jane Sloan mumbled.

"A salad?" the waiter ventured.

"Lettuce," she repeated. "Red leaf, if you have it. Washed. With vinegar on the side. And I don't want the leaves cut in any way," she continued. "I want them torn. By hand."

The waiter scribbled and fled. Jane Sloan slowly lifted her eyes. I fumbled my notebook open again.

"Umm . . ."

Lettuce, I was thinking. Jane Sloan is eating lettuce for lunch, and I'm going to sit here and suck down veal in front of her. And, worse yet, I couldn't think of a thing to ask.

"Tell me your favorite scene in the movie," I finally managed. A horrible question, a freshman-at-the-school-paper question, but better than nothing, I thought.

She smiled, finally—faintly, fleetingly, but still, it was undeniably a smile. Then she shook her head.

"Can't," she said. "Too personal."

Oh, God, help me. Rescue me. Send a tornado shrieking through the Four Seasons, uprooting businessmen, sending fine china flying. I'm dying here. "So what's up next?"

Jane just shrugged and looked mysterious. I felt the waistband of my control-top pantyhose give up the fight and slide down my midsection, coming to rest at the top of my thighs.

"We're working on something new together," Nicholas Kaye volunteered. "I'm going to write . . .with a couple of my friends from college . . . and Jane's going to show it to the studios. Would you like to hear about that?"

He launched into an enthusiastic description of what sounded like the world's dumbest movie—something about a guy who inherits his father's whoopie cushion factory, and how his father's partner doublecrosses him, and how he and the spunky cleaning lady triumph in the end. I took notes without hearing, my right hand moving mechanically over the page as my left hand ferried food to my mouth. Meanwhile, Jane was dividing her lettuce into two piles—one of mostly leaf pieces, the other of mostly stem pieces. Once this division was complete, she proceeded to dip the top third of the tines of her fork into the vinegar pot, then carefully spear a single piece of lettuce from the mostly leaf side and place it precisely in her mouth. After exactly six bites— during which time Nicholas polished off his salad and two pieces of bread and I downed half my osso bucco, which was, all things considered, delicious—she patted her lips dry with her napkin, picked up her butter knife, and started poking the butter again.

I reached over and pulled the butter dish away, thinking that I couldn't stand to see this, and, also, that I had to try something, because the interview was going down the crapper. "Cut it out," I said sternly. "That butter hasn't done anything to you."

There was a pause. A pregnant pause. An icy, yawning crevasse of a pause. Jane Sloan stared at me with her dead black eyes.

"Dairy," she said, as if it were a curse.

"Third largest industry in Pennsylvania," I countered, without any idea of whether it was true. It sounded about right, though. Whenever I went for a bike ride that took me more than a few miles out of the city, I saw cows.

"Jane's allergic," Nicholas said quickly. He smiled at his director, and took her hand, and then it hit me: They're a couple. Even though he is twenty-seven and she is . . . well, God, at least fifteen years older than that. Even though he is recognizably human and she . . . isn't. "What else?"

"Tell me . . . ," I stammered, my mind stuck on blank at the sight of their interlaced fingers. "Tell me something about the movie that not everybody knows."

"Part of it was shot where they shot *Showgirls,*" offered Nicholas.

"That's in the press packet," Jane said suddenly. I knew that, but I'd decided to be polite, take the quote, and get the hell out of Dodge before I found out what a woman who ate six lettuce leaves for lunch did when they asked if she wanted dessert.

"I'll tell you something," she said. "The girl in the flower shop? She's my daughter."

"Really?"

"Her first role," Jane said, sounding almost proud, almost shy. Almost real. "I've been discouraging her . . . she's already obsessing over the way she looks. . . ."

Wonder where she gets that, I thought, but said nothing.

"I haven't told anyone else that," Jane said. The corners of her lips twitched. "But I like you."

Heaven help the reporters you don't like, I thought, and was trying to construct a reasonable response when she suddenly stood up, taking Nicholas along with her. "Good luck," she murmured, and they swept out the door. Just as the dessert cart arrived.

"Something for mademoiselle?" said the waiter sympathetically.

Can you blame me if I said yes?

* * *

"So?" asked Samantha, on the phone that afternoon.

"She ate lettuce for lunch," I moaned.

"A salad?"

"Lettuce. Plain lettuce. With vinegar on the side. I almost died."

"Just lettuce?"

"Lettuce," I repeated. "Red leaf lettuce. She specified a variety. And she kept squirting her face with Evian."

"Cannie, you're making this up."

"I'm not! I swear! My Hollywood idol, and she's this lettuce-eating freak, this, this miniature Elvira with tattooed eyeliner. . . ."

Samantha listened dispassionately. "You're crying."

"I am not," I lied. "I'm just disappointed. I thought . . . you know . . . I had this idea that we'd hit it off. And I'd send her the screenplay, but I'm never going to get to give anyone the screenplay, because I didn't go to college with a single cast member of *Saturday Night!,* and those are the guys who get their scripts read." I glanced down at myself. More bad news. "Also I got osso bucco on my jacket."

Samantha sighed. "I think you need an agent."

"I can't get an agent! Believe me, I've tried! They won't even look at your stuff unless you've had something produced, and you can't get producers to look at something unless it comes from an agent." I wiped my eyes viciously. "This week sucks."

"Mail call!" said Gabby gleefully. She dropped a stack of papers on my desk and waddled off. I said good-bye to Sam, and turned to my correspondence. Press release. Press release. Fax, fax, fax. Envelope with my name carefully lettered in the handwriting I had long since learned to identify as Old Person, Angry. I ripped the envelope open.

"Dear Miss Shapiro," read the shaky letters. "Your article on Celine Dion's special was the filthiest, nastiest smear piece of garbage I have seen in my fifty-seven years as a loyal *Examiner* reader. Bad enough that you mocked Celine's music as "bombastic, overblown ballads," but then you had to go and make fun of her looks! I'll bet you're no Cindy Crawford yourself. Sincerely, Mr. E. P. Deiffinger."

"Hey, Cannie."

Jesus Christ. Gabby was forever sneaking up behind me. For being massive, and old, and deaf, she could be quiet as a cat when it suited her. I turned around and there she was, squinting over my shoulder at the letter in my lap.

"Did you get something wrong?" she asked, her voice full of sympathy as thick, and fake, as Cheez Whiz. "Do we need to run a correction?"

"No, Gabby," I said, trying not to scream. "Just a little opposing viewpoint."

I tossed the letter in the trash can and shoved my chair back so fast I almost ran over Gabby's toes.

"Jeez!" she hissed and retreated.

"Dear Mr. Deiffinger," I composed in my head. "I may not be a supermodel, but at least I've got enough working brain cells to know what sucks when I hear it."

"Dear Mr. Deiffinger," I thought, walking the mile and a half from work to the Weight and Eating Disorders office where my first Fat Class was meeting. "Sorry you took offense at my description of Celine Dion's work, but I actually thought I was being charitable."

I stomped into the conference room, seated myself at the table, and looked around. There was Lily, from the waiting room, and an older black woman, about my size, with a bulging briefcase beside her, poking away at one of those hand-held e-mail readers. There was a blond teenager, her long hair swept off her face in a hairband, her body hidden beneath a bulky oversized sweatshirt and gigantic droopy jeans. And there was a woman of perhaps sixty who had to weigh at least four hundred pounds. She followed me into the room, walking with the aid of a cane, and surveyed the seats carefully, measuring her bulk against their parameters, before easing herself down.

"Hey, Cannie," said Lily.

"Hey," I grumbled. The words *Portion Control* were written on a white wipable message board, and there was a poster of the food pyramid on one wall. This shit again, I thought, wondering if I could place out of the class. I'd been to Weight Watchers, after all. I knew all about portion control.

The skinny nurse I remembered from the waiting room walked through the door, her hands full of bowls, measuring cups, a small plastic replica of a four-ounce pork chop.

"Good evening, everyone," she said, and wrote her name—Sarah Pritchard, R.N.—on the board. We went around the table, introducing ourselves. The blond girl was Bonnie, the black woman was Anita, and the very large woman was Esther from West Oak Lane.

"I'm having a flashback of college," whispered Lily, as Nurse Sarah distributed booklets full of calorie counts, and packets of printouts on behavior modification.

"I'm having a flashback of Weight Watchers," I whispered back.

"Did you try that?" asked Bonnie the blond girl, edging closer to us.

"Last year," I said.

"Was that the One Two Three Success program?"

"Fat and Fiber," I whispered back.

"Isn't that a cereal?" asked Esther, who had a surprisingly lovely voice—very low, and warm, and free of the dread Philadelphia accent that causes natives to swallow their consonants like they're made of warm taffy.

"That's Fruit and Fiber," the blond girl said.

"Fat and Fiber was where you had to count the grams of fat and the grams of fiber in every food, and you were supposed to eat a certain number of grams of fiber, and not go over a certain number of grams of fat," I explained.

"Did it work?" asked Anita, setting down her Palm Pilot.

"Nah," I said. "But that was probably my fault. I kept mixing up which number I was supposed to stay below and which one I was supposed to go above . . . and then I found, like, these really high-fiber brownies that were made with iron filings or something. . . ."

Lily cracked up.

"They had a zillion calories apiece but I figured it didn't matter because they were very low in fat and very high in fiber. . . ."

"A common mistake," said Nurse Sarah cheerfully. "Fat and fiber are both important, but so is the total number of calories you take in.

It's very simple, really," she said, turning back to the board and scribbling the kind of equation that had confounded me in eleventh grade. "Calories taken in versus calories expended. If you take in more calories than you burn, you'll gain weight."

"Really?" I asked, my eyes wide.

The nurse looked at me suspiciously.

"Are you serious? It's that simple?"

"Um," she began. I suspected that she was probably used to fat ladies sitting meekly in the chairs, like overfed sheep, smiling and nodding and being grateful for the wisdom she was imparting, staring at her with abashed, admiring eyes, all because she'd had the good fortune of being born thin. The thought infuriated me.

"So if I eat fewer calories than I burn . . ." I slapped my forehead. "My God! I finally get it! I understand! I'm cured!" I stood up and pumped my hands in the air as Lily snickered. "Healed! Saved! Thank you, Jesus, and the Weight and Eating Disorders Center, for taking the blinders from my eyes!"

"Okay," said the nurse. "You've made your point."

"Damn," I said, resuming my seat. "I was going to ask if I could be excused."

The nurse sighed. "Look," she said. "The truth of it is, there're a lot of complicating factors . . . and science doesn't even understand all of them. We know about metabolic rates, and how some people's bodies just seem to want to hang on to excess weight more than other people's do. We know this isn't easy. I would never tell you that it was."

She stared at us, breathing rapidly. We stared right back.

"I'm sorry," I finally said into the silence. "I was being fresh. It's just that . . . well, I don't want to speak for anybody else, but I've had this explained to me before."

"Uh-huh," said Anita.

"Me, too," said Bonnie.

"Fat people aren't stupid," I continued. "But every single weight-loss program I've ever been to treats us like we are—as if as soon as they explain that broiled chicken is better than fried, and frozen yogurt's better than ice cream, and that if you take a hot bath instead of eating pizza, we're going to all turn into Courteney Cox."

"That's right," said Lily.

The nurse looked frustrated. "I'd certainly never mean to suggest that any of you are stupid," she said. "Diet is part of it," she added. "Exercise is part of it, too, although probably not as big a part as we used to believe."

I frowned. That was just my luck. With all of the biking and walking I did, plus regular workouts at the gym with Samantha, exercise was the one part of a healthy lifestyle that I had down pat.

"Now today," she continued, "we're going to be talking about portion size. Did you know that most restaurants serve portions that are well over the recommended USDA guidelines of what most women require over an entire day?"

I groaned softly to myself as the nurse arrayed the plates and cups and little plastic pork chop on the table. "The correct portion of protein," she said, speaking in the slow, loud, careful voice commonly employed by kindergarten teachers, "is four ounces. Now, can anyone tell me about how much that is?"

"Size of your palm," muttered Anita. "Jenny Craig," she said to the nurse's surprised look.

Nurse Sarah took a deep breath. "Very good!" she said, making a visible effort to sound happy and upbeat. "Now, how about a portion of fat?"

"Tip of your thumb," I muttered. Her eyes widened. "Look," I said, "I think we all know this stuff. . . am I right?"

I looked around the table. Everyone nodded. "The only thing we're here for, the only thing that this program has to offer us, is the drugs. Now, are we going to get them today, or do we have to sit here and act like you're telling us things we don't already know?"

The nurse's face went from frustrated (and slightly dismissive) to angry (and more than slightly scared). "There's a procedure to this," she said. "We explained it. Four weeks of behavior-modification classes . . ."

Lily started thumping her fist on the table. "Drugs . . . drugs . . . drugs . . ." she chanted.

"We can't just hand out prescription medication. . . ."

"Drugs . . . drugs . . . drugs . . ." Now Bonnie the blond girl and Esther were chanting along as well. The nurse opened her mouth, then closed it again. "I'll get the doctor," she said, and bolted. The five of us stared at each other for a moment. Then we all burst out laughing.

"She was scared!" Lily hooted.

"Probably thought we'd crush her," I muttered.

"Sit on her!" gasped Bonnie.

"I hate skinny people," I said.

Anita looked very serious. "Don't say that," she said. "You shouldn't hate anyone."

"Agh," I sighed. Just then, Dr. K. stuck his head through the door, with the chastened-looking nurse right behind him, practically clinging to the hem of his white coat.

"I understand there's a problem," he rumbled.

"Drugs!" said Lily.

The doctor had the look of a man who wanted very badly to laugh and was trying very hard not to.

"Is there a movement spokeswoman?" he asked.

Everyone looked at me. I got to my feet, smoothed my shirt, and cleared my throat. "I think that it's the feeling of the group that we've all been through different lectures and courses and support groups concerning behavior modification." I looked around the table. Everyone seemed to be nodding in agreement. "It's our feeling that we've tried to change our behavior, and eat less, and exercise more, and all of those things that they tell you to do, and what we'd really like . . . what we're really here for, what we've all paid for, is something new. Namely, drugs," I concluded, and sat back in my seat.

"Well, I know how you feel," he said.

"I doubt that very much," I shot back.

"Well, maybe you can tell me," he said mildly. "Look," he said. "It's not like I know the secrets to lifelong weight loss and I'm here to tell them to you. Think of this as a journey . . . think of it as something we're in on together."

"Except that our journey led us to the wonderful world of plus-size shopping and lonely nights," I grumbled.

The doctor smiled at me—a very disarming grin. "Let's forget about fat or thin for a minute," he said. "If you guys already know the calorie counts of everything, and what a serving of pasta's supposed to look like, then I'm sure you all know that most diets don't work. Not over the long term, anyhow."

Now he had our attention. It was true, we'd all figured this out (from bitter personal experiences, in most cases), but to hear an authority figure, a doctor, a doctor who was running a weight-loss program say it . . . well, that was practically heresy. I half expected security guards to come rushing through the door and drag him off to be re-brainwashed.

"I think," he continued, "that we'll all have much better luck—and we'll be happier—if we think instead about small lifestyle changes—little things that we can do every day that won't prove unsustainable over the long term. If we think about getting healthier, and feeling happier with ourselves, instead of looking like Courteney . . ."

He looked at me, eyebrows raised.

"Cox," I supplied. "Actually, Cox-Arquette. She got married."

"Right. Her. Forget her. Let's concentrate on the attainable, instead. And I promise that nobody here will treat you like you're stupid, no matter what your size is."

I found I was touched in spite of myself. The guy was actually making sense. Better yet, he wasn't talking down to us. It was . . . well, revolutionary, really.

The nurse gave us one last disgruntled glance and scurried away. The doctor closed the door and took a seat. "I'd like to do an exercise with you," he said. He looked around the table. "How many of you ever eat when you're not hungry?"

Dead silence. I closed my eyes. Emotional eating. I'd been through this lecture, too.

"How many of you eat breakfast, and then maybe you come to the office and there's a box of doughnuts and they look good and you'll have one just because they're there?"

More silence. "Dunkin' Donuts or Krispy Kremes?" I finally asked.

The doctor pursed his full lips. "I hadn't thought about it."

"Well, it makes a difference," I said.

"Dunkin' Donuts," he said.

"Chocolate? Jelly? Glazed that somebody from Accounting ripped in half, so there's only half a doughnut left?"

"Krispy Kremes are better," said Bonnie.

"Especially the warm ones," said Esther.

I licked my lips.

"The last time I had doughnuts," said Esther, "someone brought them to work, just like we're talking about, and I picked out one that looked like a Boston cream . . . you know, it had the chocolate on top?"

We nodded. We all probably knew how to recognize a Boston cream doughnut on sight.

"Then I bit into it," Esther continued, "and it was . . ." Her lips curled. "Lemon."

"Ick," said Bonnie. "I hate lemon!"

"Okay," said the doctor, laughing. "My point is, they could be the best doughnuts in the world. They could be the Platonic ideal of doughnut-ness. But if you've already had breakfast, and you aren't really hungry, ideally, you should be able to walk right by."

We thought about this for a minute. "As if," Lily finally said.

"Maybe you could try telling yourself that when you are really hungry, if what you're really hungry for is a doughnut, then you can go get one."

We thought again. "Nope," said Lily. "I'm still eating the free doughnuts."

"And how do you know what you're really hungry for?" asked Bonnie. "Like, me . . . I'm always hungry for the stuff I know I shouldn't be eating. But, like, give me a bag of baby carrots and I'm all, like, whatever."

"Did you ever try boiling them and mashing them with ginger and orange rind?" asked Lily. Bonnie wrinkled her nose.

"I don't like carrots," said Anita, "but I do like butternut squash."

"That's not a vegetable, though. It's a starch," I said.

Anita looked confused. "How can it not be a vegetable?"

"It's a starchy vegetable. Like a potato. I learned that in Weight Watchers."

"On Fat and Fiber?" asked Lily.

"Okay then!" said the doctor. I could tell from his eyes that the unruly chatter of five veterans of Weight Watchers, Jenny Craig, Pritikin, Atkins, et al., was starting to get to him. It couldn't be fun.

"Let's try something," he said. He walked to the door and flicked off the lights. The room dimmed. Bonnie giggled. "I want you all to close your eyes," he said, "and try to figure out how you feel right now, right this minute. Are you hungry? Tired? Are you sad, or happy, or anxious? Try to really concentrate, and then, try to really separate the physical sensations from what's happening emotionally."

We all closed our eyes.

"Anita?" asked the doctor.

"I'm tired," she said immediately.

"Bonnie?"

"Oh, maybe tired. Maybe a little hungry, too," she said.

"And emotionally?" he prodded.

Bonnie sighed. "I'm sick of my school," she finally muttered. "The kids say rotten things to me." I snuck a peek at her. Her eyes were still tightly screwed shut, and her hands were clenched into fists on top of her oversized jeans. High school, evidently, had not gotten any kinder or gentler since my own attendance ten years prior. I wished I could put my hand on her shoulder. Tell her that things would get better . . . except, given recent events in my own life, I wasn't sure it was the truth.

"Lily?"

"Starving," Lily said promptly.

"And emotionally?"

"Umm . . . okay," she said.

"Just okay?" asked the doctor.

"There's a new episode of *ER* on tonight," she said. "I can't be anything less than okay."

"Esther?"

"I'm ashamed," said Esther, and burst into tears. I opened my eyes. The doctor pulled a small packet of Kleenex out of his pocket and handed it over.

"Why ashamed?" he asked gently.

Esther smiled weakly. "'Cause before we started I was looking at the plastic pork chop, and I was thinking that it didn't look half bad."

That broke the tension. We all started laughing, even the doctor. Esther sniffled, wiping her eyes.

"Don't worry," Lily said. "I was thinking the exact same thing about the pat of butter on the food pyramid."

The doctor cleared his throat. "And Candace?" he asked.

"Cannie," I said.

"How are you?"

I closed my eyes, but only for a second and what I saw was Bruce's face, Bruce's brown eyes close to mine. Bruce saying that he loved me. Then I opened them and looked right at him. "Fine," I said, even though it wasn't true. "I'm fine."

"So how'd it go?" asked Samantha. We were panting on side-by-side StairMasters that night at the gym.

"So far, not bad," I said. "No drugs yet. The doctor who's leading the class seems okay."

We climbed in silence for a few minutes, the belts grinding and squeaking beneath our feet as a Funky Fitness class blared away beside us. Our gym seemed determined to attract new members by offering every flavor-of-the-week fitness class, so we had Pilates, gospel aerobics, interval spinning, and something called the Fireman's Full-Body Workout, complete with hoses, ladders, and a one-hundred-pound mannequin to be hauled up and down the stairs. Meanwhile, the roof leaked, the air conditioners were iffy, and the Jacuzzi always seemed to be under repair.

"And how was the rest of your day, dear?" asked Sam, wiping her face with her sleeve. I told her about Mr. Deiffenger's angry defense of Celine Dion.

"I hate readers," I gasped, as my StairMaster kicked into a higher gear. "Why do they have to get so personal?"

"I guess he probably figures that you were messing with Celine, so you deserve it."

"Yeah, but she's public property. I'm just me."

"But not to him, you're not. Your name's in the paper. That makes you public property, just like Celine."

"Only bigger."

"And with better taste. And not," said Samantha sternly, "with any plans to marry your seventy-year-old manager who's known you since you were twelve."

"Oh, now who's being critical?" I asked.

"Damn Canadians," said Samantha. She'd spent a few years work-ing in Montreal, had endured a disastrous love affair with a man there, and never had anything nice to say about our neighbors to the North, including Peter Jennings, whom she steadfastly refused to watch, arguing that he'd taken a job that should have rightfully gone to an American—"someone who knows how to say the word *about*."

After forty miserable minutes, we adjourned to the steam room, wrapped ourselves in towels, and assumed prone positions on the benches.

"How's the Yoga King?" I inquired. Sam gave a satisfied-looking smile and raised her arms above her head, reaching toward the ceiling.

"I'm feeling very flexible," she said smugly. I threw my towel at her head.

"Don't torture me," I said. "I'm probably never going to have sex again."

"Oh, cut it out, Cannie," said Samantha. "And you know this won't last. Mine never do." Which was true. Sam's love life, of late, had been uniquely cursed. She'd meet a guy and go out with him once, and everything would be wonderful. They'd meet again, and things would be clicking along. And then, on the third date, there'd be some horrible awkward moment, some unbelievable revelation, something that would basically make it impossible for Sam to see the guy again. Her last guy, a Jewish doctor with a fabulous résumé and enviable physique, had looked like a contender until Date #3, when he'd taken Sam home for dinner and she'd been disturbed to find a picture of his sister prominently displayed in the entryway hall.

"What's wrong with that?" I'd asked.

"She was topless," Samantha'd replied. Exit Dr. Right, enter the Yoga King.

"Look at it this way," said Samantha. "It was a lousy day, but now it's over."

"I just wish I could talk to him."

Samantha brushed her hair back over her shoulders, propped her head on an elbow, and stared down at me from her perch on one of the upper tiers of wooden benches. "To Mr. Deiffledorf?"

"Deiffinger. No, not him." I ladled more water on the hot rocks so the steam billowed around us. "To Bruce."

Samantha squinted at me through the haze. "Bruce? I don't get it."

"What if . . . ," I said slowly. "What if I made a mistake?"

She sighed. "Cannie, I listened to you for months talk about how things weren't right, how things weren't getting better, how you knew that taking a break would be the right thing to do in the long run. And even though you were upset right after it happened, I never heard you say that you'd made the wrong decision."

"What if I think something different now?"

"Well, what changed your mind?"

I thought about my answer. The article was part of it. Bruce and I had never talked about my whole weight thing. Maybe if we had . . . if he had some sense of how I felt, if I had some inkling of how much he understood . . . maybe things could have been different.

But more than that, I missed talking to him, telling him how my day went, blowing off steam about Gabby's latest salvos, reading him potential leads for my stories, scenes from my screenplays.

"I just miss him," I said lamely.

"Even after what he wrote about you?" asked Sam.

"Maybe it wasn't so bad," I muttered. "I mean, he didn't say that he didn't find me . . . you know . . . desirable."

"Of course he found you desirable," Sam said. "You didn't find *him* desirable. You found him lazy, and immature, and a slob, and you told me not three months ago lying on this very bench that if he left one more used piece of Kleenex in your bed you were going to kill him and leave his body on a New Jersey Transit bus."

I winced. I couldn't remember the line exactly, but it sure sounded like something I'd say.

"And if you called him," Samantha continued, "what would you say?"

"Hi, how are you, planning on humiliating me in print again anytime soon?" I'd actually had a monthlong reprieve. Bruce's October "Good in Bed" had been called "Love and the Glove." Someone— Gabby, I was practically sure—had left a copy on my desk at work the day before, and I'd read it as fast as I could, with my heart in my throat, until I'd determined that there wasn't a word about C. Not this month, at least.

Real men wear condoms, was his first line. Which was a hoot, considering that during our three years together Bruce had been almost completely spared the indignities of latex. We'd both tested clean, and I went on the pill after a handful of dismaying times when his erection would wilt the instant I produced the Trojans. That minor detail was, of course, notably absent from the story, along with the fact that I'd wound up putting the thing on him—an act that left me feeling like an overprotective mother tying her little boy's shoes. *Donning the glove is more than a mere duty,* he'd lectured *Moxie*'s readers. *It's a sign of devotion, of maturity, a sign of respect for all womankind—and a sign of his love for you.*

Now, the memory of the way he'd really been regarding condoms seemed too tender to even consider. And the thought of Bruce and I in bed together made me cringe, because of the thought that came dashing in on its heels: *We'll never be like that again.*

"Don't call him," said Sam. "I know it feels awful right now, but you'll get through it. You'll survive."

"Thank you, Gloria Gaynor," I grumbled, and went to take a shower.

When I got home, my answering machine was blinking. I hit "play" and heard Steve. "Remember me? The guy in the park? Listen, I was just wondering if you'd like to get that beer this week or maybe dinner. Give me a call."

I smiled as I walked Nifkin, grinned when I cooked myself a chicken breast and a sweet potato and spinach for dinner, beamed all through my twenty-minute consultation with Sam on the question of Steve, Cute Guy from the Park. At nine o'clock precisely I dialed his number. He sounded glad to hear from me. He sounded . . . great, in fact. Funny. Considerate. Interested in what I did. We quickly covered the basics of each other's lives: ages, colleges, oh-did-you-know-Janie-from-my-high-school, a little bit about parents and family (I left out the whole lesbian mother thing, in order to have something to talk about in the event of a second date), and a little bit about why-we're-single-right-now (I gave the two-sentence synopsis of the Bruce denouement. He told me he'd had a girlfriend back in Atlanta, but she'd gone to nursing school and he'd moved here). I told him about covering the Pillsbury bake-off. He told me that he'd taken up kayaking. We decided to meet for dinner on Saturday night at the Latest Dish and maybe catch a movie after that.

"So maybe this will be okay," I told Nifkin, who didn't seem to care much, one way or the other. He turned three times and settled himself on a pillow. I put on my nightgown, trying to avoid glimpses of my body in the bathroom mirror, and went to sleep feeling cautiously optimistic that there was at least a chance that I wouldn't die alone.

Samantha and I had long since identified Azafran as our designated first date restaurant. It had all the advantages: It was right around the corner from her house and my apartment. The food was good, it wasn't too expensive, it was BYOB, which gave us the chance to a) impress the guy by bringing a good bottle of wine, and b) eliminate the possibility of the guy getting blotto, because there'd be nothing more than the single bottle. And, best of all, Azafran had floor-to-ceiling windows, and waitresses who worked out at our gym, who knew us, and who would obligingly seat us at the window tables—our backs to the street, with the guy facing forward—so that whichever one of us didn't have the date could stroll by with Nifkin and scope out the prospect.

I was congratulating myself, because Steve looked eminently scopable. Short-sleeved polo shirt, neat khakis that looked as though he might actually have ironed them, and a pleasant whiff of cologne. A nice change from Bruce, who was given to stained T-shirts and droopy shorts and who could, absent frequent reminders on my part, be somewhat haphazard in his deodorant use.

I smiled at Steve. He smiled back. Our fingers brushed over the calamari. The wine was delicious, perfectly chilled, and it was a perfect night, with a clear, starry sky and just a hint of fall in the wind.

"So what did you do today?" he asked me.

"Went for a bike ride, up to Chestnut Hill," I said. "Thought about you . . ."

Something flickered across his face then. Something bad.

"Look," he said quietly. "I ought to tell you something. When I asked if you wanted to have a beer with me . . . well, I told you I was new to the neighborhood . . . I mean, I was really just looking for . . . you know. For friends. For people to hang out with."

The calamari turned into a lead ball in my stomach. "Oh."

"And I guess I didn't make that clear enough . . . that, I mean that this isn't a date or anything . . . oh, God," he said. "Don't look at me like that."

Don't cry, I told myself. Don't cry don't cry don't cry. How had I misread this so badly? I was pathetic. A walking joke. I wanted Bruce back. Hell, I wanted my mother. Don't cry don't cry don't cry.

"Your eyes," he said softly. "Your eyes are killing me."

"I'm sorry," I said dumbly. Apologizing as always. This cannot get any worse, I thought. Steve stared over my head, out the window.

"Hey," he said, "isn't that your dog?"

I turned, and, sure enough, there was Samantha, and Nifkin, both peering through the window. Sam looked impressed. As I stared, she flashed me a quick thumbs-up.

"Will you excuse me?" I murmured. I stood up, forcing my feet to move. In the ladies' room I splashed cold water on my face, concentrating on not breathing, feeling the tears I couldn't cry mass behind my forehead and instantly transform themselves into a headache. I considered the night ahead: dinner, then we were supposed to go see the latest world-ending disaster flick at the multiplex. But I couldn't. I couldn't spend the whole night sitting next to a guy who'd just declared himself an un-date. And maybe that made me too sensitive, or ridiculous, but the truth was, I couldn't do it.

I went to the kitchen and found our waitress.

"Almost ready," she said, then looked at my face. "Oh, God . . . what? He's gay. He's an escaped convict. He used to date your mother."

"Along those lines," I said.

"Want me to tell him you're sick?"

"Yeah," I said, then thought again. "No. Tell you what . . . pack up the food, and don't tell him anything. Let's see how long he sits there."

She rolled her eyes. "That bad?"

"There's another way out of here, right?"

She pointed to the fire exit, which was propped open by a chair containing a busboy on a break. "Go for it," she said, and a minute later, clutching two to-go containers and what remained of my pride, I slunk past the busboy and out into the night. My head was pounding. Fool, I thought fiercely. Idiot. Stupid, stupid idiot to think that somebody who looks like that would be interested in someone who looks like you.

I got upstairs, dumped the food, took off my dress, pulled on my ratty overalls, thinking furiously that I probably looked like Andrea Dworkin. I stomped down the stairs, out the door, and started walking, first down to the river, then north, toward Society Hill and Old City, and finally, west toward Rittenhouse Square.

Part of me—the reasonable part—was thinking that this was not a big thing, just a minor bump on life's bicycle path, and that he was the idiot, not me. *The single guy,* he'd said. Was I wrong to think that he was asking me out on a bona fide date? And so what if this wasn't a date after all? I'd had dates before. I'd even had boyfriends. It was completely reasonable to think that I'd have them both again, and this guy wasn't worth another second of my time.

But another part—the shrill, hysterical, hypercritical, and, unfortunately, much louder part—was saying something else entirely.

That I was dumb. That I was fat. That I was so fat that nobody would ever love me again and so dense that I couldn't see it. That I'd been a fool, or, worse, been made a fool of. That Steve, the Teva-wearing engineer, was probably sitting at an empty table, eating calamari and laughing to himself about big, dumb Cannie.

And who was I going to tell? Who could comfort me?

Not my mother. I couldn't really talk to her about my love life after I'd made it so clear that I didn't approve of hers. And plus, with Bruce's column, she'd learned enough about my after-dark activities for the time being.

I could tell Samantha, certainly, but she'd think I was crazy. "Why are you assuming this is about the way you look?" she'd demand, and I'd mutter that it could probably have been about something else, or just a plain old misunderstanding, all the while feeling the truth in my bones, the Gospel according to my father: I was fat and I was ugly and nobody would ever love me. And it would be embarrassing. I wanted my friends to think of me as someone who was smart and funny and capable. I didn't want them to feel sorry for me.

What I wanted to do was call Bruce. I wouldn't tell him about this latest humiliation—I didn't want his pity, either, or for him to think I'd come crawling back, or was planning to, simply because some fuzzy-legged jerk had rejected me—but I wanted to hear his voice. No matter what he'd said in *Moxie,* no matter how he'd shamed me. After three years, he knew me better than probably anyone else in the world, except Samantha, and at that moment, standing on the sidewalk on 17th and Walnut, I wanted to talk to him so badly that I got weak in the knees.

I hurried home and heaved myself up the stairs two at a time. Sweaty, hands shaking, I sprawled on the bed and reached for the phone, punching in his number as fast as I could. He picked up instantly.

"Hey, Bruce," I began.

"Cannie?" His voice sounded strange. "I was just going to call you."

"Really?" I felt a small spark of hopefulness flare in my chest.

"I just wanted to let you know," he began, and his voice dissolved into harsh, ragged sobs. "My father died this morning."

I don't remember what I said then. I remember that he told me the details: He'd had a stroke and he'd died in the hospital. It had been very fast.

I was crying, Bruce was crying. I couldn't remember when I'd felt so horrible about something. It was so unfair. Bruce's father was a wonderful man. He had loved his family. He had even, I thought, maybe loved me, too.

But even as I was feeling horrible, I felt the spark growing. *He'll get it now,* a voice in my head whispered. Once you've had a loss like that, doesn't it change the way you see the world? And wouldn't it change the way he saw me, my own fractured family, my own lost father? Plus, he'd need me. He'd needed me once before, to rescue him from loneliness, from sexual ignorance and shame . . . and surely he would need me again to help him get through this.

I imagined us at the funeral, and how I'd hold his hand, how I'd help him, hold him up, be there for him to lean on, the way I wished I could have leaned on him. I imagined him looking at me with new respect and understanding, new consideration, with the eyes of a man, not a boy.

"Let me help. How can I help?" I said. "Do you want me to come over?"

His reply was dismayingly instant. "No," he said. "I'm going home, and there's a ton of people there now. It would be weird. Could you come to the funeral tomorrow?"

"Of course," I said. "Of course. I love you," I said, the words out of my mouth almost before I'd finished thinking them.

"What does that mean?" he asked me, still crying.

To my credit, I recovered fast. "That I want to be there for you . . . and help you any way I can."

"Just come tomorrow," he said dully. "That's all you can do right now."

But something perverse in me persisted.

"I love you," I said again, and left the words hanging there. Bruce sighed, knowing what I wanted, and unwilling, or unable, to give it to me.

"I have to go," he said. "I'm sorry, Cannie."

PART TWO

Reconsider Me

FIVE

Thinking back, there was probably some way I could have felt worse at Bernard Guberman's funeral. Like if I'd killed him myself.

The service started at two o'clock. I got there early, but the parking lot was already full, with cars backed down the driveway, spilling onto the highway. I finally parked across the street, dashed across four lanes of traffic and straight into a cluster of Bruce's friends. They were standing in the vestibule, in what were surely their interview suits, hands in their pockets, talking quietly and looking at their feet. It was a brilliantly sunny fall afternoon—a day to look at leaves, to buy apple cider and build the first fire of the year. Not a day for this.

"Hey, Cannie," George said softly.

"How's he doing?" I asked.

George shrugged. "He's inside," he said.

Bruce was sitting in a little vestibule, holding a bottle of Evian water and a handkerchief in his right hand. He was wearing the same blue suit he'd worn on Yom Kippur, when we'd sat side by side in temple. It was still too tight, the tie still too short, and he was wearing canvas sneakers that he'd decorated with drawings of stars and swirls during some particularly boring lecture. The second I saw him it was as if our recent history fell away—my decision to ask for a break, his decision to describe my body in print. It was as if nothing was left but our connection—and his pain. His mother stood above him with one hand on his shoulder. There were people everywhere. Everyone was crying.

I went over to Bruce, knelt down, and hugged him.

"Thank you for coming," he said, coolly. Formally. I kissed his cheek, scratchy with what looked like three days' growth of beard. He didn't appear to notice. The hug his mother gave me was warmer, her words a marked contrast to his. "Cannie," she whispered. "I'm glad you're here."

I knew it was going to be bad. I knew I'd feel terrible, being there, even after our parking-lot breakup, even though, of course, there was no earthly way I could have known that this would happen.

But it wasn't just bad. It was agony. Agony when the rabbi, whom I'd seen at Bruce's house at dinner a few times, talked about how Bernard Leonard Guberman had lived for his wife and his son. About how he'd take Audrey to toy stores, even though they didn't have grandchildren. "Just to be ready," he'd say. Which was when I lost it, knowing that I was the one who was supposed to produce those grandchildren, and how much the kids would have loved him, and how lucky I would have been to have that kind of love in my life.

And I sat there on the hard wooden bench in that funeral parlor, eight rows back from Bruce, who was supposed to have been my husband, thinking how all I wanted was to be beside him, and how I'd never felt farther away.

"He really loved you," Bruce's Aunt Barbara whispered to me as we stood washing our hands outside the house. There were cars double-parked in the cul-de-sac, cars circling the block, so many cars that they'd had to station a policeman outside the cemetery for the burial service. Bruce's father had been active in the temple, and had had a thriving practice as a dermatologist. Judging from the throngs, it looked like every Jew or teenager with a skin condition had shown up to pay their respects.

"He was a wonderful man," I said.

She looked at me curiously. "Was?"

Which was when I realized that she was talking about Bruce, who was still alive.

Barbara wrapped her maroon fingernails around my forearm and dragged me into the immaculate, Downy-scented laundry room.

"I know you and Bruce broke up," she said. "Was it because he didn't propose?"

"No," I said. "I guess . . . I just felt more and more that maybe we weren't a good fit."

It was as if she hadn't heard.

"Audrey always told me that Bernie said how happy he'd be to have you in the family," she said. "He always said, 'If Cannie wants a ring, she'll have a ring in a minute.'"

Oh, God. I felt tears starting to build behind my eyes. Again. I'd wept during the service, when Bruce stood on the bimah and talked about how his father taught him to catch a ball and drive, and I'd cried at the cemetery when Audrey sobbed over the open grave and said, over and over, "It isn't fair, isn't fair."

Aunt Barbara handed me a handkerchief.

"Bruce needs you," she whispered, and I nodded, knowing that I couldn't trust my voice. "Go," she said, pushing me into the kitchen. I wiped my eyes and went.

Bruce was sitting on the porch with his friends around him in a forbidding-looking circle. When I approached, he squinted at me, observing me like a specimen on a slide.

"Hey," I said softly. "Is there anything I can do for you?"

He shook his head and looked away. There was someone in every chair on the porch, and nobody looked like they were moving. As gracefully as I could, I squatted down on the step behind them, just outside of the circle, and sat there, holding my knees. I was cold, and hungry, but I hadn't brought a jacket, and there wasn't anywhere to balance a plate. I listened to them talk about nothing—about sports, and concerts, and their jobs, such as they were. I watched as Bruce's mother's friends' daughters, a trio of interchangeable twentysome-things, made their way onto the porch with paper plates full of petit fours, and gave Bruce their condolences, and their smooth cheeks to kiss. It felt like swallowing sand, watching him go out of his way to smile at them and show how he'd remembered all their names, when he could barely spare me a glance. Sure, I knew when—if—we decided to break up, he'd most likely find somebody else. I just never thought I'd have to suffer through a preview. I sat on my hands feeling wretched.

When Bruce finally stood up, I got up to follow him, but my leg had fallen asleep, and I stumbled and went sprawling, wincing as a splinter dug its way into my palm.

Bruce helped me up. Reluctantly, I thought.

"Do you want to take a walk?" I asked him. He shrugged. We walked. Down the driveway, down the street, where more cars were massing.

"I'm so sorry," I told him. Bruce said nothing. I reached for his hand, my fingertips brushing the back of his palm. He didn't reach back. "Look," I said, feeling desperate, "I know things have been . . . I know that we . . ." My voice trailed off. Bruce looked at me coldly.

"You aren't my girlfriend anymore," he said. "You were the one who wanted a break, remember? And I'm small," he practically spat.

"I want to be your friend," I said.

"I've got friends."

"I noticed," I told him. "Mannerly bunch."

He shrugged.

"Look," I told him. "Could we . . . could we just . . ." I put my fist against my lips. Words were failing me. All I had left were sobs. I swallowed hard. Get through this, I told myself. "Whatever happened between us, however you're feeling about me, I want you to know that your father was a wonderful man. I loved him. He was the best father I ever saw, and I'm sorry he's gone, and I just feel so terrible about all of this . . ." Bruce just stared at me. "And if you want to call me . . ." I finally managed.

"Thanks," he finally said. He turned to walk toward the house, and after a moment I turned to follow him, like a chastened dog, walking numbly behind him with my head hanging down.

I should have just left, but I didn't. I stayed on through the evening prayers, when men with tallits over their shoulders crowded

Audrey's living room, bumping their knees on the hard wooden mourning benches, pressing their shoulders against the covered mirrors. I stayed when Bruce and his friends gathered in the white-and-chrome kitchen to pick over deli trays and make small talk. I hung on the edge of the group, so full of sadness I thought I would burst, right there on Audrey's Spanish-tiled floor. Bruce never looked at me. Not even once.

The sun set. The house slowly emptied. Bruce collected his friends and took us up to his bedroom, where he sat down on his bed. Eric and Neil and Neil's hugely pregnant wife took the couch. George took the chair at Bruce's desk. I folded myself up on the floor, outside of the circle, thinking with some small and primitive part of my brain that he'd have to talk to me again, he'd have to let me comfort him, if our years together were to have meant anything.

Bruce unfastened his ponytail, shook out his hair, and tied it back again. "I've been a child my whole life," he announced. Nobody seemed to know quite how to respond to that, so they did what I supposed they normally did, up in Bruce's room. Eric filled the bong, and George fished a lighter out of his suit jacket pocket, and Neil shoved a towel under the door. Unbelievable, I thought, biting back a burst of hysterical laughter. They cope with death the exact same way they cope with a Saturday night when there's nothing good on cable.

Eric passed the bong to Neil without even asking me if I wanted it. I didn't, and he probably knew it. The only thing pot ever did for me was make me want to sleep and eat even more than I already did. Not exactly the kind of drug I needed. Still, it would have been nice if he'd offered.

"Your father was really cool," George mumbled, and everyone else mumbled his assent, except for Neil's pregnant wife, who made a big production of heaving herself to her feet and walking out the door. Or maybe it's always a production to get up and go when you're that pregnant. Who knows? Neil gazed at his sneakers. Eric and George said again how sorry they were. Then everybody started talking about the playoffs.

Always a child, I thought, looking at Bruce through the haze. For a minute, I caught his eye, and we looked right at each other. He tilted the bong toward me: Want some? I shook my head no, and took a deep breath into the silence.

"Remember when the swimming pool was finished?" I asked.

Bruce gave me a small but encouraging nod.

"Your father was so happy," I said. I looked at his friends. "You guys should have seen it. Dr. Guberman couldn't swim . . ."

". . . he never learned how," Bruce added.

"But he insisted—absolutely insisted—that this house have a swimming pool. 'My kids aren't going to sweat for another summer!'"

Bruce laughed a little bit.

"So the day the pool was finished, he threw this gigantic party." Now George was nodding. He'd been there. "He had it catered. He ordered, like, a dozen watermelon baskets . . ."

". . . and a keg," said Bruce, laughing.

"And he walked around all afternoon in this monogrammed bathrobe that he'd bought just for the occasion, smoking this gigantic cigar, and looking like a king," I concluded. "There must have been a hundred people here . . ." My voice trailed off. I was remembering Bruce's father in the hot tub, a steaming cigar clenched between his teeth, a Dixie cup full of beer sweating on the ledge beside him, and the full moon hanging like a circle of gold in the sky.

And finally I felt that I was on more stable ground. I couldn't smoke pot, and he wouldn't let me kiss him, but I could tell stories all night long. "He looked so happy," I said to Bruce, "because you were happy."

Bruce started to cry quietly, and when I got up and crossed the room and sat beside him, he didn't say anything. Not even when I reached for him. When I put my arm around his shoulders he leaned into me, holding me and crying. I closed my eyes so I only heard his friends getting up and filing out the door.

"Ah, Cannie," he said.

"Shh," I said, and rocked him, moving him back and forth with my whole body, easing him back onto the bed, beneath a shelf lined with his Little League trophies and perfect attendance plaques from

Hebrew school. His friends were gone. We were finally alone. "Sshh now, shh now." I kissed his wet cheek. He didn't resist. His lips were cool underneath mine. He wasn't kissing me back, but he wasn't pushing me away, either. It was a start.

"What do you want?" he whispered to me.

"I would do whatever you wanted," I said. "Even . . . if you wanted that . . . I'd do it for you. I love you . . ." I said.

"Don't say anything," he whispered, sliding his hands up under my shirt.

"Oh, Bruce," I breathed, unwilling to believe that this was happening, that he wanted me, too.

"Shh," he said, shushing me the way I'd quieted him moments before. His hands were fumbling with the many clasps of my bra.

"Lock the door," I whispered.

"I don't want to let you go," he said.

"You don't have to," I told him, tucking my face into his neck, breathing in the smell of him, sweet smoke and shaving cream and shampoo, glorying in the feel of his arms around me, thinking that this was what I wanted, was what I'd always wanted—the love of a man who was wonderful and sweet and who, best of all, understood me. "You don't have to ever again."

I tried to make it good for him, to touch him in his favorite places, to move the way that I remembered he liked. It felt wonderful to me, to be with him again, and I thought, holding his shoulders as he thrust himself into me and moaned, that we could start over; that we *were* starting over. The *Moxie* article I was willing to write off as water under the bridge, provided he'd swear a solemn oath to never again mention my body in print. And the rest of it, his father's death, we'd get through as a couple. Together. "I love you so much," I whispered, kissing the side of his face, holding him close, trying to quiet the small voice inside of me that noticed, even in the throes of passion, that he wasn't saying anything back.

Afterward, with my head on his shoulder and my fingertips tracing circles on his chest, I thought that nothing had ever felt so right. I thought that maybe I'd been a child, a girl, but now I was ready to step up to the plate, to do the right thing, to be a woman, and to stand beside him, holding him up, starting tonight.

Bruce, evidently, had other thoughts. "You should get going," he said, removing himself from my arms and walking into the bathroom without looking back at the bed.

This was unexpected. "I can stay," I called.

Bruce came out of the bathroom with a towel wrapped around his waist. "I've got to go to temple with my mom in the morning, and I think it would, um, complicate things if . . ." His voice trailed off.

"Okay," I said, remembering my vow, to be an adult,·to think of what he needed instead of what I wanted, even though what I wanted was more along the lines of a long, slow, sweet snuggle, followed by both of us drifting gently off to sleep—not this hasty retreat. "No problem," I said, and pulled my clothes back on. No sooner had I straightened my panties then Bruce was grabbing my elbow and walking me toward the door, hustling me past the kitchen and the living room, where, presumably, his mother was waiting and his friends had regrouped.

"Give me a call," I said, hearing my voice trembling, "whenever you want."

He looked away. "I'm going to be kind of busy," he said.

I took a deep breath, willing the panic to subside. "Okay," I said. "Just know that I'm there for you."

He nodded gravely. "I appreciate that, Cannie," he said, as if I'd just offered him financial planning advice instead of my heart on a platter. I went to kiss him. He offered me his cheek. Fine, I thought, getting into the car, gripping the steering wheel tightly so he wouldn't see my hands shake. I can be patient. I can be mature. I can wait for him. He loved me so much, I thought, speeding home through the dark. He'll love me again.

SIX

When I took Psychology 101, the professor taught us about random reinforcement. Put three groups of rats in three separate cages, each equipped with a bar. The first group of rats got a pellet every time they pressed the bar. The second group never got pellets, no matter how often they pressed. And the third group got pellets just once in a while.

The first group, the professor said, eventually gets bored with the guaranteed reward and the rats who never get treats give up, too. But the random rats will press on that bar forever, hoping each time they press that this time the magic will happen, that this time they'll get lucky. It was at that moment in class that I realized that I had become my father's rat.

He'd loved me once. I remembered it. I had a handful of mental pictures, postcards that had gotten soft around the edges from being handled so often. Scene one: Cannie, age three, snug in her father's lap, her head against his chest, feeling his voice rumble through her as he read *Where the Wild Things Are.* Scene two: Cannie, age six, holding hands with her daddy as he led her through the doors of the elementary school on a warm summer Saturday to take her first grade readiness test. "Don't be shy," he tells her, kissing both her cheeks. "You'll do great."

I remember being ten years old spending whole days with my father, running errands, meeting his secretary, and Mrs. Yee at the dry cleaners who did his shirts, the salesman at the clothing store who looked at my father with respect as he paid for his suits. We'd pick up brie at the fancy cheese shop that smelled wonderfully of freshly roasted coffee beans, and jazz records at Old Vinyl. Everyone knew my father's name. "Dr. Shapiro," they'd greet him, smiling at him, at us, lined up in a row, from oldest to youngest, with me at the head of the line. He'd put one big warm hand on my head, stroking my ponytail. "This is Cannie, my oldest," he'd say. And all of them, from the clerks at the cheese store to the security guards in his building, seemed to know not just who he was, but who I was, too. "Your father says you're very smart," they'd say, and I'd stand there, smiling, trying to look smart.

But days like that became rare as I got older. The truth was, my father mostly ignored me. He ignored all of us—Lucy, and Josh, and even my mother. He came home late, he left home early, he spent his weekends in the office or on long drives "to clear my head." Whatever affection we got, whatever notice he paid us, was parceled out in small doses, administered infrequently. But oh, when he loved me, when he put his hand on my head, when I leaned my own head against him . . . there was no feeling in the world that could beat it. I felt important. I felt cherished. And I would do whatever it took, press the bar until my hands bled, to get that feeling again.

He left us for the first time when I turned twelve. I came home from school and there he was, unexpectedly, in the bedroom, piling undershirts and sock balls into a suitcase. "Dad?" I asked him, startled to see him in the daytime. "Are you . . . are we . . ." I wanted to ask if we were going somewhere—a trip, maybe? His eyes were heavy and hooded. "Ask your mother," he said. "She'll explain."

And my mother did explain it—that both she and my father loved us very much, but they couldn't work things out between the two of them. I was still numb from the shock of that when I found out the truth of what was going on from Hallie Cinti, one of the popular girls. Hallie was on my soccer team, but in a completely different league socially. On the field she frequently looked as though she'd prefer that I not pass to her, as if my foot on the ball could transmit my own personal taint and send nerd-germs creeping through her cleats. Three years later she'd be infamous for administering restorative blow-jobs to three of the five starters on the boys' basketball team during halftime of the state play-offs, and we'd all be calling her Hallie Cunti, but I didn't know that yet.

"Heard about your father," she said, plunking herself down at my table, which was in a corner of the lunchroom where Hallie Cinti and her ilk rarely ventured. The chess club kids and my friends from Junior Debaters stared, open-mouthed, as Hallie and her friend Jenna Lind slung their purses over the backs of two plastic chairs and stared at me.

"Heard what?" I asked warily. I didn't trust Hallie, who'd ignored me through six years of school, or Jenna, whose hair was always perfectly feathered.

Hallie, as it turned out, couldn't wait to tell me. "I heard my Mom talking about it last night. He moved in with some dental technician on Copper Hill Road."

I toyed with my peanut butter sandwich, buying time. Was this true? How could Hallie's mother know? And why was she talking about it? My mind was fluttering with questions, plus the half-remembered faces of all the women who'd ever scraped my teeth.

Jenna leaned in to deliver the coup de grace. "We heard," she said, "that she's only twenty-seven."

Well. So that would explain the gossip. Hallie and Jenna stared at me, and my debate-team friends stared at them staring. I felt like I'd been suddenly thrust onstage, and I didn't know my lines, or even what I was supposed to be performing.

"So is it true?" Hallie asked impatiently.

"It's no big deal," said Jenna, evidently hoping to get me to spill via sympathy. "My parents are divorced."

Divorced, I thought, tasting the word. Was this really what was happening? Would my Dad do this to us?

I lifted my eyes to the popular girls. "Go away," I told them. I heard one of my debate friends gasp. Nobody talked to Jenna and Hallie that way. "Leave me alone. Go away!"

Jenna rolled her eyes. Hallie shoved her seat back. "You're a big fat loser," she opined, before scurrying back to the popular kids' tables, where everyone's shirts had little alligators, and all the girls ever had for lunch was Diet Coke.

I walked home slowly and found my mother in the kitchen, with about ten half-unpacked bags of groceries arrayed on the counters and dining room table. "Is Dad living with someone else?" I blurted. She shoved three packages of chicken breasts into the freezer and sighed, her hands on her hips.

"I didn't want you to find out like this," she murmured.

"Hallie Cinti told me," I said.

My mother sighed again.

"But she doesn't know anything," I said, hoping my mother would agree.

Instead she sat at the kitchen table and motioned for me to join her. "Mrs. Cinti works at the same hospital as your Dad," she said.

So it was true.

"You can tell me things. I'm not a little kid." But at that moment, I wished that I was a little kid—the kind whose parents still read to her in bed and held her hands when she crossed the streets.

My mother sighed. "I think this might be for your father to tell you."

But that conversation never happened, and two nights later, my father had moved back. Josh and Lucy and I stood in the backyard and watched him pull the suitcase out of the trunk of his little red sports car. Lucy was crying, and Josh was trying not to. My father never even looked at us as he crossed the gravel driveway, the heels of his boots crunching with each step.

"Cannie?" Lucy sniffled. "If he's back now, that's good, isn't it? He won't leave anymore, right?"

I stared at the door, watching it slowly close behind him. "I don't know," I said. I needed answers. My father was unapproachable, my mother was no help. "Don't worry," she scolded me. Her own face was etched with lines of sleeplessness. "Everything's going to be fine, honey." This from my mother, who never called me honey. As much as I dreaded it, I would have to go right to the source.

I found Hallie Cinti in the girls' room the next Monday afternoon. She was standing at the mirror, squinted as she reapplied Bonnie Belle lip gloss. I cleared my throat. She ignored me. I tapped her on her shoulder and she turned to face me, her lips pursed in distaste.

"What?" she spat.

I cleared my throat as she glared at me. "Um . . . that thing . . . about my father," I began.

Hallie rolled her eyes and pulled a pink plastic comb out of her purse.

"He moved back," I said.

"How swell for you," said Hallie, now combing her bangs.

"I thought maybe you might have heard why. From your mom."

"Why should I tell you anything?" she sneered.

I'd spent the whole weekend planning for this contingency. What could I, plump and unpopular Cannie Shapiro, offer sleek, beautiful Hallie? I pulled two items out of my backpack. The first was a five-page paper on light and dark imagery in *Romeo and Juliet*. The other was a fifth of vodka that I'd swiped from my parents' liquor cabinet that morning. Hallie and her crew might not have been as academically advanced as I was, but they made up for it in other fields of endeavor.

Hallie snatched the bottle out of my hands, checked to see that the seal was unbroken, then reached for the paper. I yanked it back.

"First, tell me."

She gave a little shrug, slipped the bottle into her purse, and turned back toward the mirror. "I heard my mother talking on the phone. She said that his dental friend told him that she wanted children," she said. "And I guess your father doesn't want any more. And looking at you," she continued, "I can understand why." She turned to me, smirking, extending her hand for the paper.

I threw it at her. "Just copy it over in your own handwriting. I put in some spelling mistakes, so they'll know it's you, not me."

Hallie took the paper and I went back to class. *No more children.* Well, the way he treated us, that made sense.

He stayed with us for almost six years after that, but he wasn't the same. The little moments of kindness and love, the nights he'd read to us in bed, the Saturday afternoon ice-cream cones and the Sunday afternoon drives, were gone. It was as if my father had fallen asleep, alone, on a bus or a train, and woken up twenty years later, surrounded by strangers: my mother, my sister, my brother, and me, all wanting things—help with the dishes, a ride to band practice, $10 for the movies, his approval, his attention, his love. He looked out at us, mild brown eyes swimming with confusion, then hardening with anger. Who are these people? he seemed to be wondering. How long will I have to travel beside them? And why do they think I owe them anything?

He went from being loving, in an absent-minded, occasional way, to being mean. Was it because I knew his secret—that he didn't want more children, that he'd probably never wanted us? Was it that he missed the other woman, that she was his one true love, forever denied to him? I thought that was some of it. But there were other things, too.

My father was—is, I suppose—a plastic surgeon. He started off in the Army, working with burn victims, wounded soldiers, men who'd come back from the war with their skin pink and puckery from chemicals, or lumpy and disfigured from shrapnel.

But he discovered his true genius after we moved to Pennsylvania. There, the bulk of his practice involved not soldiers but society ladies, women whose only wounds were invisible and who were willing to drop thousands of dollars on a discreet, skilled surgeon who'd make their bellies tight, their eyelids less droopy, who'd eliminate saddle-bags and double chins with a few deft strokes of the scalpel.

He was successful. By the time he left us for the first time Larry Shapiro was known as the man to see in the greater Philadelphia area for tummy tucks, chin lifts, nose jobs, boob jobs. We had the requisite big house, the curved driveway, the in-ground swimming pool with hot tub in the back. My father drove a Porsche (although, thankfully, my mother was able to talk him out of the NOSEDOC vanity plates). My mom drove an Audi. We had a maid clean twice a week; my parents threw catered dinner parties every other month, and we went on vacations to Colorado (for skiing) and Florida (for sun).

And then he left, and came back, and our lives fell apart, like a well-loved book that you'd read and read again, until one night you picked it up to read yourself to sleep and the binding collapsed, sending dozens of pages spiraling toward the floor. He didn't want this life. That much was clear. He was miserable tethered to this suburb, to the never-ending schedule of soccer games and spelling bees and Hebrew schools, tied down by mortgage payments and car payments, habit and obligation. And he took his misery out on all of us—and, for some reason, on me especially.

Suddenly, it was as if he couldn't bear to look at me. And nothing I could do was right, or even close.

"Look at this!" he'd thunder, of my B+ in algebra. He was sitting at the dining room table, a familiar glass of scotch at his elbow. I was skulking in the doorway, trying to hide myself in the shadows. "What is your excuse for this?"

"I don't like math," I'd tell him. In truth, I was just as ashamed of the grade as he was angry about it. I'd never gotten anything less than an A in my life. But no matter how hard I tried, or how much extra help I got, algebra confounded me.

"Do you think I liked medical school?" he snarled. "Do you have any idea how much potential you have? Do you have any inkling what a waste it is to squander your gifts?"

"I don't care what my gifts are. I don't like math."

"Fine," he'd say with a shrug, flinging the report card across the table like it had suddenly acquired an offensive smell. "Be a secretary. See if I care."

He was like that with all of us—snarly, surly, dismissive, and rude. He'd come home from work, drop his briefcase in the hall, pour himself the first in a series of scotch on the rocks, and storm by us, upstairs into the bedroom, locking the door behind him. He'd either stay up there, or retreat to the living room, with the lights turned low, listening to Mahler's symphonies. Even at thirteen, even without the benefit of a basic music appreciation class, I knew that nonstop Mahler, backed by the rattle of ice cubes in his glass, could portend nothing good.

And when he did bother to speak to us, it was only to complain: how tired he was, how little appreciated; how hard he worked to provide things for us, "you little snobs," he'd slur, "with your skis and your swimming pool."

"I hate to ski," said Josh, who did. One run and he'd head back to the lodge to drink hot chocolate and fret, and if we forced him back out he'd convince the Ski Patrol that he was suffering from imminent frostbite, and we'd have to collect him at the first aid cabin, stripped down to his long underwear and basting under the heat lamps.

"I'd rather swim with the other kids at the Rec Center," said Lucy, which was true. She had more friends than the rest of us put together. The phone was always ringing. Another sore spot with my father. "That goddamn phone!" he'd yell when it rang during dinner. But we weren't allowed to take it off the hook. It could be his office, after all.

"If you hate us so much, why did you even have kids?" I'd scream at him, taunting him with what I knew was the truth. He never had an answer—just more insults, more anger, more scalding, punishing rage. Josh, just six, was "a baby." Lucy, who was twelve, he either ignored or berated. "Stupid," he'd say, shaking his head at her grades, "Clumsy," when she'd drop a glass. And, at thirteen, I became "the dog."

It's true, thirteen was not the year when I was looking my best. In addition to the breasts and hips I'd sprouted, seemingly overnight, I had acquired a mouthful of complicated-looking metal and rubber bands to correct my overbite. I had a *de rigeur* Dorothy Hamill haircut, which wasn't doing my full face any favors. I bought clothes in two sizes—baggy and baggier—and spent the whole year in a perpetual stoop, trying to hide my chest. I looked like the Hunchback of Notre Dame, only with zits and braces. I felt like a walking affront, like a collection of the things my father spent his days waging war against. He was all about beauty—its creation, its maintenance, its perfection. Having a wife who'd fallen short of the mark and hadn't stayed thin was one thing, I supposed . . . but a daughter who'd failed so flagrantly was, evidently, unforgivable. And I had failed. There was nothing beautiful about me at thirteen, nothing at all, and I could feel that fact confirmed in the hard, hateful way he looked at me, and in all the things he said.

"Cannie's very bright," I heard him tell one of his golf buddies. "She'll be able to take care of herself. Not a beauty," he said, "but smart."

I stood there, hardly believing what I'd heard, and when I finally believed it, I crumpled inside, like a tin can under a car's wheels. I wasn't stupid, and I wasn't blind, and I knew that there were many ways in which I differed from Farrah Fawcett, from girls in movies and on posters in boys' bedrooms. But I'd remembered his hand on my head, his beard tickling my cheek as he kissed me. I was his daughter, his little girl. He was supposed to love me. Now he thought I was ugly. *Not a beauty* . . . but what father doesn't think his little girl is beautiful? Except I wasn't little. And, I guessed, I wasn't his girl anymore.

When I look at pictures of myself from that time—and, understandably, there are only about four—there's this horrible desperate look in my eyes. *Please like me,* I'm pleading, even as I'm trying to hide myself behind a row of cousins at a bar mitzvah, beneath the hot tub bubbles during a pool party, with my lips drawn in a pained smile, stretched tight over my braces, ducking my head into my neck, hunching my shoulders, slouching to make myself shorter, smaller. Trying to disappear.

Years later, in college, when a friend was recounting some bit of suburban childhood horror, I tried to explain how it was with my father. "He was a monster," I blurted. I was an English major, versed in Chaucer and Shakespeare, Joyce and Proust by then. I still hadn't found a better word than that.

My friend's face got very serious. "Did he molest you?" she asked. I almost laughed. Given how much of my father's conversation with me revolved around how ugly, how fat, how hideous I was, molestation was the last thing I would have expected.

"Did he abuse you?" she asked.

"He drank too much," I said. "He left us." But he never hit me. He never hit any of us. It would have been easier if he had. Then there would have been a name we could give it, a box to put it in, a label for the box. There would have been laws, authorities, shelters, TV talk shows where reporters gravely discussed what we were enduring, a built-in recognition of what we'd experienced, to help us through.

But he never raised a finger. And, at thirteen, at fourteen, I had no words for what he was doing to us. I didn't even know how to start that conversation. What would I have said? "He's mean?" Mean meant being grounded, meant no television after dinner, not the kind of daily verbal assault my father would routinely deliver over the dinner table, a scathing recitation of all the ways I'd failed to live up to my potential, the walking tour of the places that I had failed.

And who would have believed me? My father was always charm personified to my friends. He remembered their names, and their boyfriend's names, he would inquire courteously about summer plans and college visits. They wouldn't have believed me, and if they had they would have wanted me to explain. And I had no explanation, no answers. When you're on a battleground, you don't have the luxury of time to dwell on the various historical factors and sociopolitical influences that caused the war. You just keep your head down and try to survive it, to shove the pages back in the book, close the covers and pretend that nothing's broken, nothing's wrong.

The summer before my senior year of high school, my mother took Josh and Lucy to Martha's Vineyard for the weekend. A friend had a rental house, she was itching to get out of Avondale. I had my first summer job, as a lifeguard at a local country club. I told my Mom that I'd stay home, watch the dogs, hold down the fort. I figured it would be fine: I could have the house to myself, entertain my twenty-three-year-old boyfriend away from her watchful eye, come and go as I pleased.

For the first three days it was fine. Then I came home in the predawn hours of the fourth morning, and it was as if I were twelve again. There was my father in the bedroom, the suitcase on the bed, the stacks of white T-shirts and the piles of black socks—maybe the same ones, I thought wildly, that he'd taken the last time.

I stared at them, and then at him. My father looked at me for a long moment. Then he sighed.

"I'll call," he said, "when I have my new number."

I shrugged. "Whatever," I said.

"Don't talk to me like that!" he said. He hated when we were flip. He demanded respect, even—especially—when he didn't deserve it.

"What's her name?" I asked. He narrowed his eyes.

"Why do you want to know?"

I looked at him and couldn't think of an answer. Did I imagine that it made any difference? Could a name even matter?

"Tell your mother," he began. I shook my head.

"Oh, no," I said. "Don't make me do your dirty work. If you've got something to say, tell her yourself."

He shrugged, like it didn't matter. He added a few more shirts, a fistful of ties.

"I'm glad you're leaving. Do you know that?" I said. My voice was too loud in the early-morning quiet of the house. "We'll be better off without you," I said.

He looked at me. Then he nodded. "Yes," he said, "I think maybe you will."

He went back to his packing. I went back to my bedroom. I lay on the bed—the bed where my father had read to me, a million years ago—and closed my eyes. I'd been waiting for this, after all. I'd known it was coming. I thought it would feel the way it does when a scab over an old wound finally falls off—a momentary pang, a little bit of pain, a sense of absence. Then nothing. Just nothing at all. That was what I was supposed to feel, that was all I wanted to feel, I thought fiercely, tossing and turning on my bed, trying to find comfort. It didn't matter, I told myself, over and over again. I just couldn't figure out why I was crying.

I went to Princeton because he told me to, in one of his last acts of hands-on parenting. I'd wanted to go to Smith. I liked the campus, liked the crew coach, liked the idea of an all-girls' school, where the focus would be on learning, where I could be free to be who I was: your basic late-eighties model nerd with her nose in a book.

"Forget it," my father pronounced over the table. He'd been gone for six months by then: relocated to a new suburb, living in a brand-new, shiny condo with a brand-new shiny girlfriend. He'd agreed to meet us for dinner, then cancelled and rescheduled twice. "I'm not sending you to some dyke school."

"Larry," said my mother, her voice quiet and hopeless. All of her good humor and cheer had been leeched from her by then. It would be years—and Tayna—before she laughed and smiled easily.

My father ignored her, glaring at me suspiciously, a forkful of steak raised halfway to his mouth. "You aren't a dyke, are you?"

"No, Dad," I said, "I actually prefer threesomes."

He chewed. Swallowed. Patted his lips with his napkin. "That's two more people than I'd have thought would be interested in seeing you naked," he said.

As much as I'd liked Smith, I hadn't liked Princeton. The campus looked like the staging ground for a very successful eugenics experiment: everyone was blond, preppy, and perfect, except for the dark-haired girls who were sleek, exotic, and perfect. During the weekend I'd spent there I hadn't seen a single fat person, or anyone with bad skin. Just acres of shiny hair, straight white teeth, and perfect bodies in perfect clothes arrayed beneath the perfect willow trees that grew beneath perfectly Gothic stone halls.

I said I'd be miserable. My father said he didn't care. I dug my heels in. He told me it was Princeton or nothing. And by the time I'd been packed off to Campbell Hall and stayed long enough to start classes and have my graduation-present mountain bike stolen from the library bicycle rack, the divorce was final, and he was gone for good, sticking us with a tuition bill of which he'd paid just enough to make it impractical for me to start over anywhere else. So I quit the crew team—no big loss to me, or the team, I suspect, since I'd gained the requisite Freshman Fifteen, plus the fifteen pounds my roommate should have gained but didn't, thanks to her diligent bulimia—and got a job with the Department of Food Services, affectionately known as Doofus to its employees.

If college is supposed to be the best years of your life, then it's safe to say that I spent the best years of my life in a hairnet, dishing out reconstituted scrambled eggs and limp bacon, loading dirty dishes on the conveyor belt, mopping the floors, looking at my classmates out of the corner of my eyes and thinking that they were all so much more beautiful, graceful, comfortable in their own skins than I could ever be. They all had better haircuts. And all of them were thin. True, many of them were thin because they were sticking their fingers down their throats after every meal, but at times that seemed like a small price to pay for having basically everything a woman could want—brains, beauty, and a way to eat ice cream and cherry Danishes and still stay skinny.

"Good Hair" was the first article I wrote for the campus alternative newspaper. I was a freshman, and the editor-in-chief, a junior named Gretel whose own hair was kept in a paramilitary blond brush cut, asked me to write more. By sophomore year I was a columnist. By junior year I was a senior writer, spending every hour I wasn't slinging hash or pushing a mop in the *Nassau Weekly*'s cramped, dusty offices in Aaron Burr Hall, and I'd decided that this was what I wanted to do with my life.

Writing let me escape. It let me escape Princeton, where everyone was chic and stylish and, in the case of the guy down the hall, the future ruler of some minor Middle Eastern principality. It let me escape the insistent tug of my family, and its ongoing misery. Writing was like slipping into the ocean, a place where I could move easily, where I could be graceful, and playful, and invisible and visible all at once—a byline, not a body. Sitting in front of the computer, with the screen blank and the cursor blinking, was the best escape I knew.

And there was plenty to escape from. In the four years I was at Princeton, my father remarried and had two more children. Daniel and Rebecca. He had the nerve to send me pictures, and birth announcements. Did he think I'd be happy, seeing their squinched-up baby faces and tiny baby footprints? It felt like being kicked. It wasn't that he didn't want children, I realized sadly. It was that he hadn't wanted us.

My mother went back to work, and her weekly telephone calls were full of complaints about how schools, and kids, had changed since she got her teaching certificate. The subtext was clear: This wasn't the life she signed up for. This wasn't where she expected to be, at fifty, making ends meet on alimony and what the local school board paid permanent substitutes.

Meanwhile, Lucy had flunked out of her first year at school in Boston, and was living at home, attending community college haphazardly, and majoring in unsuitable men. Josh was spending three hours a day in the gym, lifting weights so frequently that his upper body looked inflated, and had pretty much stopped talking except for a series of tonal grunts and the occasional "Whatever."

"Just get your education," my mother would say wearily, after the latest recitation of how my father's checks were late again, of how her car had broken down, of how my sister hadn't come home for two nights in a row. "Just finish up. We'll be fine."

Then—finally—it was the June of my graduation.

Except for a handful of strained lunches during the summer and Christmas breaks, I hadn't seen my father. He sent birthday cards (usually on time), and tuition checks (almost always late) and usually for about half of what they were supposed to be. I felt like I'd become just one more unremarkable item on his to-do list. I hadn't expected him to come to my graduation. I never thought he'd care. But he called me a week in advance of the much-longed-for date, saying that he was looking forward to it. Him, and his new wife, whom I'd never met.

"I'm not sure . . . I don't think . . . ," I stammered.

"Cannie," he said. "I'm your father. And Christine's never seen Princeton!"

"So tell Christine you'll send her a postcard," my mother said sourly. I had dreaded telling my mother that he'd be there, but I couldn't figure out how to tell him no. He'd said the magic words, the pellet words. *I'm your father.* After everything—his distance, his desertion, the new wife and new kids—I was, it seems, still starving for his love.

My father, with new wife and kids in tow, arrived during the English Department's reception. I'd won some small award for creative writing, but they came too late to hear my name called. Christine was a petite little thing, with an aerobicized hard body and a blond perm. The children were adorable. My floral Laura Ashley dress had looked just fine in the dorm. Now it looked like a slipcover, I thought dismally. And I looked like a sofa.

"Cannie," said my father, looking me up and down. "I see college cuisine's agreed with you."

I clutched my stupid plaque tightly against me. "Thanks so much," I said. My father rolled his eyes at his new wife as if to say, *Can you believe how touchy she is?*

"I was just teasing you," he said, as his new adorable children stared at me, as if I were an animal in a zoo for the oversized.

"I, um, got you tickets for the ceremony." I didn't mention that I'd had to beg, borrow, and finally pay $100 I couldn't spare to score the tickets. Each senior was issued a total of four. The administration at Princeton hadn't yet made accomodations for those of us struggling with reconstructed families that included stepmothers, stepfathers, new half-siblings, and the like.

My father shook his head. "Won't be necessary. We're leaving in the morning."

"Leaving?" I repeated. "But you'll miss graduation!"

"We've got tickets to Sesame Place," chirped his little wife, Christine.

"Sesame Place!" repeated the little girl for emphasis.

"So Princeton was sort of on our way."

"That's . . . um . . . well." And suddenly I was blinking back tears. I bit my lip as hard as I could, and squeezed the plaque against me so tightly that I had an eight-by-twelve bruise on my midsection for the next week and a half. "Thanks for stopping by."

My father nodded, and moved as if he was going to hug me, but wound up merely grasping my shoulders and giving me the kind of shake that coaches routinely administer to underperforming athletes—a "buck up, camper" kind of shake. "Congratulations," he said. "I'm very proud of you." But when he kissed me his lips never even touched my skin, and I knew the whole time that his eyes were on the door.

Somehow I made it through the ceremony, the dismantling of my dorm room, the long ride home. I hung my diploma on my bedroom wall and tried to figure out what I'd do next. Graduate school was out of the question. Even after all those breakfasts I'd worked, all those drooly pieces of bacon and curdled scrambled eggs, I was still $20,000 or so in debt. I couldn't see borrowing more money. So I lined up job interviews with the handful of small papers who were willing to even consider a college graduate with no real-world experience, in the middle of a recession, and spent the summer driving up and down the Northeast in the thirdhand van I'd bought with some of my food-service dollars. When I loaded up the car to head out for my job interviews, I made myself a promise—I wasn't going to be my father's rat anymore. I was going to walk away from the pellet bar. He could bring me nothing but unhappiness, and I didn't need more unhappiness in my life.

I heard from my brother that our father had moved out West, but I didn't ask for specifics, and nobody offered them. Ten years after the divorce he no longer had to pay child support or alimony. The checks stopped coming. So did the birthday cards, or any acknowledgment that we even existed. Lucy's graduation came and went, and when Josh sent a card announcing his, it came back returned to sender. Our father had moved on, it seemed, without telling us where.

"We could find him on the Internet or something," I offered. Josh glared at me.

"Why?"

And I couldn't think of an answer. If we found him, would he come? Would he care? Probably not. We agreed, the three of us, to let it be. If our father wanted to stay gone, we would let him.

And we struggled into our twenties without him. Josh overcame his fear of the slopes and spent a year and a half drifting from one ski-resort town to another, and Lucy ran off briefly to Arizona with a guy she claimed was a former professional hockey player. As evidence, she'd had him remove his bridge in the middle of dinner and show that he was missing all his teeth.

And that was that, pretty much.

I know that what had happened with my father—his insults, his criticism, the way he made me feel that I was defective and deformed—had hurt me. I'd encountered enough of those self-help articles in women's magazines to know that you don't go through that kind of cruelty unscathed. With every man I met I'd watch myself carefully. Did I really like that editor, I'd wonder, or am I just searching for Daddy? Do I love this guy, I'd ask myself, or do I just think he'd never leave me, the way my father did?

And where had all the care I'd taken gotten me, I wondered? I was alone. A man who'd liked me enough to want me in his family was dead, and I couldn't even say how sorry I was properly. And now that it was possible—now that it was likely, even—that Bruce had finally gotten to the point in his life where he could understand me, where he could sympathize with what I'd been through because of what he'd gone through—he wouldn't even talk to me. It felt like the cruelest joke, like a rug being yanked out from under me—in other words, like the way my father made me feel, all over again.

SEVEN

The scales at the University of Philadelphia's Weight and Eating Disorders Center looked like meat carts. The platforms were about four times the size of normal scales, with railings all around them. It was hard not to feel like livestock when you climbed aboard, as I had every other week since September.

"That's very unusual," said Dr. K, gazing down at the red digital printout on the scale. "You lost eight pounds."

"I can't eat," I said numbly.

"You mean you're eating less," he said.

"No, I mean every time I put something in my mouth I puke."

He looked at me sharply, then back at the scale. The numbers were the same. "Let's step into my office," he suggested.

And there we were again: me in the chair, him at his desk, my ever-thickening folder spread in front of him. He was tanner than when I'd seen him last, and possibly even thinner, floating in his white laboratory coat. It had been six weeks since I'd last seen Bruce, and things were not proceeding as I'd hoped.

"Most patients gain weight before we start them on the sibutramine," he said. "They have a kind of last hurrah. So, as I said, this is unusual."

"Something happened," I said.

114

He looked at me sharply. "Another article?"

"Bruce's father died," I said. "Bruce, my boyfriend . . . ex-boyfriend. His dad died last month."

He looked down at his hands, at his folder, then, finally, up at me. "I'm sorry to hear that."

"And he called me . . . and told me . . . and asked me to go to the funeral . . . but he wouldn't let me stay. Wouldn't let me stay with him. He was so awful . . . and it was so sad . . . and the rabbi said how he used to go to toy stores, and I feel so terrible . . ."

I blinked hard against the tears. Wordlessly, Dr. K. handed me a box of Kleenex. He took off his glasses and pressed two fingers against the bridge of his nose.

"I'm a bad person," I blubbered. He looked at me kindly.

"Why? Because you broke up with him? That's silly. How could you know this was going to happen?"

"No," I said. "I know I couldn't. But now, it's like . . . all I want is to be there for him, and love him, and he won't let me, and I feel so . . . alone. . . ."

He sighed. "It's hard when things end. Even if nobody dies, even if you part on the best possible terms, and there's nobody else involved. Even if you're the one who lets go first. It's never easy. It always hurts."

"I just feel like I made this huge mistake. Like I didn't think things through. I thought I knew . . . how it would feel to be apart from him. But I didn't. I couldn't. I never imagined anything like this. And all I do is miss him. . . ." I swallowed hard, choking on another sob. I couldn't explain it—that I'd been waiting my whole life for a guy who would get me, who would understand my pain. I thought I'd known what pain was, but I knew now I'd never hurt this way.

He focused his eyes on a spot on the wall over my head as I wept. Then he opened a drawer, pulled a pad out of his desk, and started writing.

"Am I out of the study?" I asked.

"No," he said. "Of course, you're going to have to start eating again soon. But I think it might be a good idea for you to have someone to talk to."

"Oh, no," I said. "Not therapy."

He gave me a crooked smile. "Am I sensing a little antipathy here?"

"No, I don't have anything against it, but I just know it won't help," I told him. "I'm looking at the situation realistically. I made a huge mistake. I wasn't sure that I loved him enough, and now I know that I do, and his father's dead and he doesn't love me anymore." I straightened my back and wiped my face. "But I still want to do this. I really want to do this. I want to have one thing in my life I can feel good about. I want to feel like I'm doing something right."

He sat me on the examination table again, his hands gentle on my back and my arms as he tied a piece of rubber tubing around my bicep and told me to make a fist. I looked away when he slid the needle in, but he'd done it so skillfully I could barely feel it. Both of us watched the glass vial filling up with my blood. I wondered what he was thinking. "Almost done," he said quietly, before deftly removing the needle and pressing a piece of gauze over the wound.

"Do I get a lollipop?" I joked. He handed me a Band-Aid instead, and the piece of paper where he'd written two names, two phone numbers. "Take it," he said. "And, Cannie, you've got to eat, and if you find that you can't, you have to call us, and then I'd really suggest calling one of these counselors."

"I'm so huge, do you really think a few more days is going to kill me?"

"It's really not healthy," he said seriously. "It can have an adverse impact on your metabolism. My suggestion is to start off with easy stuff . . . toast, bananas, flat ginger ale."

Out in the lobby, he gave me a sheaf of papers easily three inches thick. "Keep exercising, too," he said. "It'll help you feel better."

"You sound like my mother," I said, tucking everything into my purse.

"And Cannie?" He put his hand on my forearm. "Try not to take it so hard."

"I know," I said. "I just wish things were different."

"You'll be fine," he told me firmly. "And . . ."

His voice trailed off. He looked uncomfortable.

"You know how you said you were a bad person?"

"Oh," I said, embarrassed. "Sorry. I just have this tendency to get a little melodramatic. . . ."

"No, no. That's okay. I just meant . . . I wanted to tell you . . ."

The elevator doors slid open, and the people on it looked at me. I looked at the doctor and stepped backward.

"You aren't," he told me. "I'll see you in class."

I went home and lunged for the telephone. My one message was from Samantha.

"Hi, Cannie, it's Sam . . . no, not Bruce, so get that pathetic look off your puss and call me if you feel like going for a walk. I'll buy you an iced coffee. It'll be great. Better than a boyfriend. 'Bye."

I set down the phone, and picked it up again when it started ringing. Maybe it was Bruce this time, I thought.

Instead, it was my mother.

"Where have you been?" she demanded. "I've been calling and calling."

"You didn't leave a message," I pointed out.

"I knew I'd get you eventually," she said. "How's it going?"

"Oh, you know . . . ," I said, my voice trailing off. My mother had really been making an effort since Bruce's father had died. She'd sent a card to the family and made a donation to the temple. She'd been calling me every night, and insisted that I come to her softball league's play-off series and watch the Switch Hitters take on Nine Women Out. It was all attention I could have done without, but I knew she meant well.

"Are you walking?" she asked me. "Are you riding your bike?"

"A little bit," I sighed, remembering how Bruce used to complain that spending time at my house was more like triathlon training sessions than a vacation, because my mother was always trying to organize a walk, a bike ride, two-on-two basketball at the Jewish Center, where she'd gleefully body-check my brother under the boards while I sweated on a StairMaster and Bruce read the sports section in the Seniors' Lounge.

"I'm walking," I said. "I take Nifkin out every day."

"Cannie, that's not enough! You should come home," she said. "You'll be in for Thanksgiving, right? Are you going to come Wednesday, or the day of?"

Ugh. Thanksgiving. Last year Tanya had invited another couple— both women, of course. One of them wouldn't touch meat, and referred to heterosexual people as "breeders," while her girlfriend, whose buzz cut and broad shoulders gave her a disconcerting resemblance to my senior prom date, sat beside her looking embarrassed, then vanished into the family room, where we found her, hours later, watching a football game. Tanya, whose Marlboro habit had rendered her tastebuds defunct, spent the entire meal hustling from the kitchen to the table, bearing one bowl of overcooked, overmashed, oversalted side dishes after another, plus something called Tofurkey for the vegetarian. Josh had cut out early on Thursday night, muttering something about finals, and Lucy spent the entire time on the phone with a mysterious boyfriend, who, we would later learn, was both married and twenty years her senior.

"Never again," I'd whispered to Bruce that night as I tried to find a comfortable position on the lumpy couch while Nifkin trembled behind a stereo speaker. Tanya's loom occupied the space that had formerly housed my bed, and whenever we came home I had to camp out in the living room. Plus, her two evil cats, Gertrude and Alice, took turns stalking the Nif.

"Why don't you come home for the weekend?" my mother asked.

"I'm busy," I said.

"You're obsessed," she corrected. "I'll bet you're sitting there, reading old love letters Bruce sent you and hoping I'll get off the phone in case he calls you."

Damn. How does she do that?

"I am not," I told her. "I've got call waiting."

"Waste of money," said my mother. "Look, Cannie. He's obviously angry with you. He's not going to come running back just yet. . . ."

"I'm aware of that," I said frostily.

"So what's the problem?"

"I miss him," I said.

"Why? What do you miss so much?"

I didn't say anything for a minute.

"Let me ask you something," my mother had said gently. "Have you talked to him?"

"Yeah. We talk." In truth, I'd broken down and called him twice. Both calls had lasted less than five minutes, both had ended when he told me, politely, that there were things he needed to do.

My mother persisted. "Is he calling you?"

"Not so much. Not exactly."

"And who's ending the calls? You or him?"

This was getting touchy. "I see you've returned to the heterosexual advice-giving arena."

"I'm allowed," my mother said cheerfully. "Now: Who's hanging up?"

"Depends," I lied. In truth, it was Bruce. Always Bruce. It was like Sam had said. I was pathetic, and I knew it, and I couldn't stop myself, which was even worse.

"Cannie," she said. "Why don't you give him a break? Give yourself a break, too. Come home."

"I'm busy," I demurred, but I could feel myself weakening.

"We'll bake cookies," she wheedled. "We'll go for long walks. We'll go for a bike ride. Maybe we'll go to New York for the day . . ."

"With Tanya, of course."

My mother sighed. "Cannie," she said, "I know you don't like her, but she is my partner . . . Can't you at least try to be nice?"

I thought about it. "No. Sorry."

"We can have some mother/daughter time, if you really want it."

"Maybe," I said. "It's busy here. And I've got to go to New York next weekend. Did I tell you? I'm interviewing Maxi Ryder."

"Really? Ooh, she was great in that Scottish movie."

"I'll tell her you said so."

"And listen, Cannie. Don't call him anymore. Just give him some time."

I knew she was right, of course. A), I wasn't stupid, and b), I'd been hearing it from Samantha, and from every single one of my friends and acquaintances who had an even passing familiarity with the situation, and I'd probably be hearing it from Nifkin, too, if only he could talk. But somehow I couldn't stop. I had turned into someone that I would have pitied in another life; someone who searched for signs, who analyzed patterns, who went over every word in a conversation looking for hidden meanings, secret signals, the subtext that said, *Yes, I still love you, of course I still love you.*

"I'd like to see you," I'd told him shyly, during Five Minute Phone Conversation #2. Bruce had sighed.

"I think we should wait," he said. "I don't just want to jump right back in again."

"But we'll see each other sometime?" I said, in a tiny little voice that was utterly unlike anything I'd normally use for conversation, and he'd sighed again.

"I don't know, Cannie," he said, "I just don't know."

But "I don't know" wasn't a "no," I'd reasoned, and once I had a chance to be with him, to tell him how sorry I was, to show him how much I had to give, how much I wanted to be back with him . . . well, then he'd take me back. Of course he would. Wasn't he the one who'd said "I love you" first, three years ago, as we'd held each other in my bed? And hadn't he been the one who was always bringing up marriage, always stopping on our walks to admire babies, always steering me toward jewelry shop windows when we walked on Sansom Street, and kissing my ring finger and telling me how we'd always be together?

It was inevitable, I tried to tell myself. Just a matter of time.

"Let me ask you something," I began.

Andy the food critic shoved his glasses up his nose and murmured into his sleeve. "The walls are painted pale green, with gilt on the moldings," he said softly. "It's very French."

"It's like being inside a Fabergé egg," I volunteered, looking around.

"Like being inside a Fabergé egg," Andy repeated. I heard a muted click as he turned off the tape recorder he had concealed in his pocket.

"Explain men," I said.

"Can we do the menu first?" Andy cajoled. This was our standard deal: first, the food, then, my questions about men and married life. Today we were casing the latest crêperie for a possible review.

Andy perused the menu. "I'm interested in the paté, the escargot, the greens with pear and warm Gorgonzola, and the mushroom in puff pastry to start with," he instructed. "You can get any kind of crêpe you want for a main course, except not the plain cheese."

"Ellen?" I guessed. Andy nodded. In one of life's supreme ironies, Andy's wife, Ellen, was possessed of the least adventurous palate of all time. She eschewed sauces, spices, most ethnic cuisines, and was constantly frowning over the menus, desperately scanning them for things like plain baked chicken breasts and mashed potatoes that weren't truffled, garlicked, or otherwise gussied up. Her ideal evening, she'd once told me, consisted of rented movies and frozen waffles "with the kind of syrup that has absolutely nothing maple about it." Andy adored her . . . even when she was screwing up his review meals by ordering yet another Caesar salad or plain piece of fish.

Our waiter ambled over to refill our water glasses. "Any questions?" he drawled. From his offhand manner, plus the blue paint caked under his fingernails, I had him pegged as a waiter by day, artiste by night. He seemed hugely, supremely, unassailably indifferent. *Pay attention,* I tried to tell him telepathically. It didn't seem to work.

I ordered the escargot and a crêpe with shrimp, tomatoes, and creamed spinach. Andy took the paté and the salad, and a crêpe with wild mushrooms, goat cheese, and toasted almonds. We each had a glass of white wine.

"Now," he said, as the waiter loped back to the kitchen. "How can I help you?"

"How can they . . ." I began. Andy raised his hand.

"Are we speaking in the abstract or the specific here?"

"It's Bruce," I acknowledged. Andy rolled his eyes. Andy was not a fan of Bruce . . . not since the first and last review dinner he'd come out for. Bruce was even worse than Ellen. "A picky vegetarian," Andy had messaged me at work the next day, "is basically a food critic's worst nightmare." In addition to not finding a single thing he wanted to eat, Bruce also managed to tip his menu far enough toward the candle that lit our table to actually set the menu on fire, bringing three waiters plus the sommelier running and sending Andy, a stickler for anonymity, dashing into the men's room lest he risk discovery. "It's hard to keep a low profile," he carefully pointed out the next day, "when you're being sprayed with a fire extinguisher."

"I just want to know," I said. "I mean, the thing that I don't understand . . ."

"Spit it out, Cannie," Andy urged. The waiter returned, dumped my escargot in front of Andy, Andy's paté in front of me, and hastily departed. "Excuse me," I called toward his back. "Could I have some more water? When you get a minute? Please?" The waiter's whole body seemed to sigh as he reached for the pitcher.

Once our glasses were filled, Andy and I traded plates, and I waited for him to describe, and taste, before continuing.

"Well, it's like, okay, I know that I was the one who wanted to take a break, and now I miss him, and it's like, this pain . . ."

"Is it a sharp stabbing pain, or more of a constant throbbing ache?"

"Are you making fun of me?"

Andy stared into my eyes, his own brown eyes wide and innocent behind his gold-rimmed glasses. "Well, maybe a little bit," he finally said.

"He's completely forgotten me," I grumbled, spearing a snail. "It's as if I never even mattered . . . like I never meant anything to him."

"I'm confused," said Andy. "Do you want him back, or are you just concerned about your legacy?"

"Both," I said. "I just want to know . . ." I gulped a mouthful of wine to stave off tears. "I just want to know that I meant something, somehow."

"Just because he's acting like you didn't mean anything doesn't mean that you really didn't," said Andy. "It's probably just an act."

"You think?"

"The guy adored you," Andy said. "That wasn't an act."

"But how can he not even want to talk to me now? How can it just be so completely . . ." I sliced one hand through the air to indicate a violent and absolute ending.

Andy sighed. "For some guys, it's just like that."

"For you?" I asked.

He paused, then nodded. "For me, when it was over, it was always over."

Over his shoulder, I could see our waiter approaching . . . our waiter, plus two other waiters, trailed by an anxious-looking dark-haired man with an apron tied over his suit. The manager, I presumed. Which could only mean the one thing that Andy dreaded most—namely, someone had figured out who he was.

"Monsieur!" the man in the suit began, as our waiter set down our entrées, another one poured us fresh water, and a third waiter carefully decrumbed our not-very-crumby table. "Is everything to your liking?"

"Just fine," said Andy weakly, as Waiter One set fresh silverware beside our plates, Waiter Two whisked fresh bread and butter to the center of the table, and Waiter Three hustled over with a lit candle.

"Please let us know if there's anything else we can bring you. Anything!" the manager fervently concluded.

"I will," Andy said, as the three waiters lined up and stared at us, looking anxious and vaguely resentful, before finally retreating to the corners of the restaurant where they watched our every mouthful.

I didn't even care. "I just think that I made a mistake," I said. "Did you ever break up with someone and think you made a mistake?"

Andy shook his head, wordlessly offering me a bite of his crêpe.

"What should I do?"

He munched, looking thoughtful. "I don't know if these are actual wild mushrooms. They taste kind of domestic to me."

"You're changing the subject," I grumbled. "You're . . . oh, God. I'm boring, aren't I?"

"Never," said Andy loyally.

"No, I am. I've turned into one of those horrible people that just talks about their ex-boyfriend all the time, until nobody can stand to be around them and they don't have any friends . . ."

"Cannie . . ."

". . . and they start drinking alone, and talking to their pets, which I do anyway . . . oh, God," I said, only half-faking a collapse into the bread dish. "This is a disaster."

The manager hurried over. "Madame!" he cried. "Is everything all right?"

I straightened myself up, flicking bits of bread from my sweater. "Just fine," I said. He bustled off, and I turned back to Andy.

"When did I become a madame?" I asked mournfully. "I swear, the last time I was at a French restaurant they called me Mademoiselle."

"Cheer up," said Andy, handing me the last of the paté. "You're going to find someone much better than Bruce, and he won't be a vegetarian, and you'll be happy, and I'll be happy, and everything's going to be fine."

EIGHT

I tried. Really, I did. But I found myself so preoccupied with Bruce misery that it was hard to get anything done at work. This is what I considered as I sat on an Amtrak Metroliner bound for New York and Maxi Ryder, famously ringletted and frequently dumped costar of last year's Oscar-nominated romantic drama, *Trembling,* in which she'd played a brilliant brain surgeon who eventually succumbs to Parkinson's disease.

Maxi Ryder was British, twenty-seven or twenty-nine, depending on which magazines you believed, and had been known, early in her career, as something of an ugly duckling until, through the miracle of rigorous diet, Pilates, and the Zone (plus, it was whispered, some discreet plastic surgery), she'd managed to transform herself into a size-two swan. In fact, she'd been a size two to start off with, and a beauty to boot, but had gained twenty pounds for her breakthrough role in a foreign film called *Advanced Placement,* playing a shy Scottish schoolgirl who has a torrid affair with her headmistress. By the time that film had reached the States, she'd shed the twenty pounds, dyed her hair auburn, ditched her British manager, hooked up with the hottest agency in Hollywood, founded the inevitable production company (Maxi'd Out, she'd called it), and been featured in a *Vanity Fair* spread of homes of the stars, wearing only a black feather boa, curled seductively beneath the headline "Maxi's Pad." Maxi, in other words, had arrived.

But for all her talent and her beauty, Maxi Ryder kept getting dumped, in the most public ways you could think of.

She'd done the typical starlet-in-her-twenties thing, popularized by Julia Roberts and practiced by the generation that followed, which was to fall in love with her costars. But while Julia would have them yanking her toward the altar, poor Maxi just got her heart broken, again and again and again. And it didn't happen quietly, either. The assistant director she'd fallen for on *Advanced Placement* showed up at the Golden Globes sucking face with one of the girls from *Baywatch*. Her costar on *Trembling*—the one with whom she'd played a half-dozen torrid love scenes, where the chemistry between them was so palpable it practically soaked your popcorn—had broken the news to her, and the rest of the world at the same time, during a Barbara Walters' "Ten Most Fascinating People" interview. And the nineteen-year-old rock star she'd picked up on the rebound had gotten married in Vegas two weeks after they met to a woman who was not Maxi.

"It's a wonder she's doing any press at all," Roberto, the publicist at Midnight Oil, had told me the week before. Midnight Oil was a very small, somewhat obscure New York PR firm—leagues below the big agencies that Maxi'd typically deal with. But between *Advanced Placement* and *Trembling,* she'd spent six weeks in Israel making a tiny little movie, a period piece about a kibbutz during the Seven Day War . . . and tiny little movies generally had small-time publicity agencies, which was where Roberto came in.

Seven Day Soldier would probably never even have made it to American art houses, had it not been for the Oscar nomination Maxi had gotten for *Trembling.* And Maxi would probably never have done any publicity for the movie, except she'd signed on to it before she'd made it big, which meant she'd agreed to be paid bupkes, and to publicize the film "in any way the producers deem appropriate."

So, needless to say, the producers saw a chance to at least have an enormous opening weekend based on the strength of Maxi buzz. They'd flown her in from a shoot in Australia, set her up in the penthouse of the Regency on the Upper East Side, and invited in what Roberto referred to as "a select group of reporters" to enjoy twenty-minute audiences with her. And Roberto, bless his loyal heart, had called me first.

"Are you interested?" he'd asked.

Of course I was, and Betsy was thrilled in the way that editors usually are when plummy scoops fall into their laps, even though Gabby grumbled about one-hit wonders and flashes in the pan.

I was happy. Roberto was happy. Then Maxi's personal publicist got in on the act.

There I was, moping at my desk, counting the days since Bruce and I had spoken (ten), the length in minutes of the conversation (four), and contemplating making an appointment with a numerologist to figure out if the future held anything good for us, when the phone rang.

"This is April from NGH," rapped the voice on the other end. "We understand you're interested in speaking with Maxi Ryder?"

Interested? "I'm interviewing her Saturday at ten in the morning," I told April. "Roberto from Midnight Oil set it up."

"Yes. Well. We have a few questions before we sign off."

"Who are you again?" I asked.

"April. From NGH." NGH was one of the hugest and most notorious public relations firms in Hollywood. They were the people you called if you were famous, under forty, found yourself in the midst of some kind of unsavory and/or illegal mess and wanted to keep all but the most fawning and tractable press far, far away. Robert Downey hired NGH after he passed out in someone else's bedroom in a heroin haze. Courtney Love had NGH redo her image after she'd redone her nose, her breasts, and her fashion, and they smoothed her transition from foul-mouthed grunge goddess to couture-clad sylph. At the *Examiner,* we called them Not Gonna Happen . . . as in, that interview you were hoping for, that profile you wanted to write? Not Gonna Happen. Now, evidently, Maxi Ryder had enlisted their assistance as well.

"We would like your assurance," April from NGH began, "that this interview will focus exclusively on Maxi's work."

"Her work?"

"Her roles," said April. "Her acting. Not her personal life."

"She's a celebrity," I said mildly. Or at least I thought it came out that way. "I consider that her work. Being a famous person."

April's voice could have frozen hot fudge. "Her work is acting," she said. "Any attention that she gets is only because of that work."

Normally I would have let it drop—just gritted my teeth and grinned and agreed to whatever ridiculous conditions they wanted to impose. But I hadn't slept the night before, and this April was pushing all the wrong buttons. "Oh, come on!" I said. "Every time I open *People* magazine I see her in a slit skirt and big, dark, don't-look-at-me glasses. And you're telling me she just wants to be known as an actor?"

I'd hope that April would take my remarks in the half-joking manner I'd intended them. But I wasn't sensing a thaw.

"You cannot ask her about her love life," April said sternly.

I sighed. "Fine," I said. "Terrific. Whatever. We'll talk about the movie."

"So you're agreeing to the conditions?"

"Yes. I'm agreeing. No love life. No skirts. No nothing."

"Then I'll see what I can do."

"I told you, Roberto already set up the interview!"

But I was talking to a dead line.

Two weeks later, when I finally left for the interview, it was a gray, drizzly Saturday morning in late November, the kind of day where it looks like everyone with means and money has fled the city and gone to the Bahamas, or their country cottage in the Poconos, and the streets are populated with the people they'd left behind: pockmarked delivery boys, black girls with braids, scruffy-looking dreadlocked white kids on bikes. Secretaries. Japanese tourists. A guy with a wart on his chin with two hairs sprouting from it, long, curly hairs that reached almost to his chest. He smiled and stroked them as I walked by. My lucky day.

I spent the twenty-block walk uptown trying not to think of Bruce and trying not to let my hair get too wet. The lobby of the Regency was huge, marble, blessedly quiet and mirror-lined, which let me appreciate, from three different angles, the zit that had sprouted on my forehead.

I was early, so I decided to loiter. The hotel gift shop boasted the typical assortment of overpriced bathrobes, $5 toothbrushes, and magazines in many languages, one of which happened to be the November *Moxie*. I grabbed it and flipped to Bruce's column. "Going Down," I read. "One Man's Oral Adventures." Hah! "Oral adventures" had not been Bruce's forte. He had a little problem with excessive saliva. In a moment of margarita-soaked weakness I'd once referred to him as "the human bidet." It had been that bad at the beginning. Of course, there was no way he'd mention that, I thought smugly, any more than he'd mention that I'd been the only girl he'd ever attempted that particular maneuver upon. And I flipped back to his column. *"I once overheard my girlfriend refer to me as the human bidet,"* read the pull-quote. He'd heard that? My face flamed.

"Miss? Are you planning to purchase that?" asked the woman behind the counter. So I did, with a pack of Juicy Fruit gum and a $4 bottle of water. Then I parked myself on one of the plush couches in the icy-cool lobby and began:

Going Down

When I was fifteen and a virgin, when I wore braces and the tighty whities my mother bought me, my friends and I used to laugh ourselves sick over a Sam Kinison routine.

"Women!" he'd rant, tossing his hair over his shoulder, stalking the stage like a small, rotund, beret-wearing trapped animal. "Tell us what you want! Why," he'd say, and drop to one knee, beseeching, "why is it so HARD to say YES, right THERE, that's GOOD, or NO, not THAT. TELL US WHAT YOU WANT!" he'd shriek, as the audience erupted, "WE'LL DO IT!"

We laughed without knowing precisely what made this so hysterical. What could be so hard? we wondered. Sex, insofar as we'd experienced it, did not involve much mystery. Lather, rinse, repeat. That was our repertoire. No fuss, no muss, and certainly no confusion.

When C. parted her legs and then parted herself with her fingertips . . .

Oh . . . my . . . God, I thought. It was as if he'd shoved a mirror between my legs and broadcasted the image to the whole world. I swallowed hard and kept reading.

. . . I felt a sudden and complete sympathy with every man who'd ever pumped his fist to Kinison's lament. It was like looking at a face with no features, was the best thing I could think. Hair and belly and hands above, creamy thighs to the left and the right, but in front of me, a mystery, curves and tucks and protrusions that bore, it seemed, little resemblance to the air-brushed pornography I'd seen since I was fifteen. Or maybe it was just the proximity. Or maybe it was just my nerves. Being confronted with a mystery is a scary thing.

"Tell me what you want," I whispered to her, and I remember how far away her head seemed at that moment. "Tell me what you want and I'll do it." But then I realized that by telling me what she wanted, she'd be as much as admitting that . . . well, that she knew what she wanted. That someone else had stared into this strange, unknowable heart, had learned the geography, had unfurled her secrets. And even though I knew she'd had other lovers, that seemed somehow different, more intimate. She'd let someone else see her here, like this. And I, being male and a former Sam Kinison listener to boot, resolved to bring her to paradise, to make her mewl like a sated kitty, to obliterate every trace of memory of the He Who'd Gone Before.

Strange unknowable heart, I snorted. He Who'd Gone Before. Somebody get me a shovel!

And she tried, and I tried, too. She demonstrated with her fingertips, with words, with gentle pressure and gasps and sighs. And I tried, too. But a tongue isn't like a finger. My goatee drove her crazy, in precisely the opposite of the way she wanted to be driven crazy. And when I heard her on the phone once refer to me as the Human Bidet, well, it seemed easier to rely on the things I knew I could do better.

Do any of us know what we're doing? Does any man? I ask my friends, and at first they all guffaw and swear they have to scrape their women off the ceiling. I buy them beer and keep their glasses full, and in a few hours I have my more perfect truth: We're all clueless. Every single one of us.

"She says she's coming," says Eric mournfully. "But I dunno, man . . ."

"It isn't obvious," says George. "How are we supposed to know?"

How, indeed? We're men. We need reliability, we need hard (or even liquid) evidence, we need diagrams and how-to guides, we need the mystery explicated.

And when I close my eyes I can see her, still, as she lay that first time, furled tight like the wings of a tiny bird, seashell pink, tasting like the rich ocean water, full of tiny lives, things I'll never see, let alone understand. I wish I could. I wish I had.

"Okay, Jacques Cousteau," I muttered, and struggled to my feet. When he closed his eyes he could still see me, he'd written. Well, what did that mean? And when had he written it? And if he still missed me, then why wasn't he calling? Maybe, I thought, there was hope after all. Maybe I'd call him later. Maybe we still had a chance.

I took the elevator up to the hospitality suite on the twentieth floor, where a variety of young, larva-pale publicists in variations on black stretch pants, black bodysuits, and black boots sat on couches and smoked.

"I'm Cannie Shapiro from the *Philadelphia Examiner,*" I said, to the one sitting beneath a life-size cardboard cutout of Maxi Ryder in battle fatigues, brandishing an Uzi.

Larva Girl paged languidly through some pages full of names.

"I don't see you," she said.

Great. "Is Roberto here?"

"He stepped out for a minute," she said, flip-flopping one hand toward the door.

"Did he say when he'd be back?"

She shrugged, apparently having exhausted her vocabulary.

I peered at the pages, trying to read upside-down. There was my name: Candace Shapiro. And there was a thick black line through it. "NGH" read the note in the margin.

Just then Roberto hustled in.

"Cannie," he said, "what are you doing here?"

"You tell me," I said, trying for a smile. "Last I heard I was interviewing Maxi Ryder."

"Oh, God," he said. "Nobody called you?"

"About what?"

"Maxi decided to, um, scale way back on the print interviews. She's only doing the *Times*. And *USA Today*."

"Well, nobody told me." I shrugged. "I'm here. Betsy's expecting a story."

"Cannie, I'm so sorry. . ."

Don't be sorry, you idiot, I was thinking. Do something!

". . . but there's nothing I can do."

I gave him my best smile. My most charming smile, which I hoped was underscored with my I-work-for-a-large-important-newspaper steel. "Roberto," I said, "I was planning to talk to her. We saved the space. We're counting on the story. Nobody called me . . . and I schlepped all the way up here on a Saturday, which is my day off . . ."

Roberto started wringing his hands.

". . . and I would really, really appreciate it if we could maybe just get even fifteen minutes with her."

Now Roberto was wringing his hands and biting his lip at the same time, plus shifting from foot to foot. Bad signs all.

"Listen," I said softly, leaning toward him, "I watched every single one of her movies, even the direct-to-video ones. I'm, like, the complete Maxi expert. Isn't there anything we can do?" I saw him start to waver, when the cell phone on his belt shrilled.

"April?" he said. *April,* he mouthed to me. Roberto was a sweet-heart, but not the sharpest knife in the drawer.

"Can I talk to her?" I whispered, but Roberto was already rehol-stering his phone.

"She said they weren't comfortable with your, um, compliance."

"What? Roberto, I agreed to every single one of her conditions. . . ."

My voice was rising. The larval creatures on the couch were start-ing to look vaguely alarmed. As was Roberto, who was edging out into the hallway.

"Let me talk to April," I pleaded, holding out my hand for his cell phone. Roberto shook his head. "Roberto," I said, hearing my voice breaking, imagining Gabby's gloating grin when I came back to the office empty-handed. "I can't go back without a story!"

"Look, Cannie, I am so, so sorry . . ."

He was wavering. I saw he was. And that's when a tiny woman in high-heeled calf-length black leather boots came trip-trapping down the long marble hall. There was a cell phone in one hand, a walkie-talkie in the other, and a no-nonsense look on her unlined, carefully made-up face. She could have been a very mature twenty-eight or forty-five with a great plastic surgeon. This, undoubtedly, was April.

She took me in—my zit, my anger, my black dress and sandals from last summer, far less fashionable than anything any one of the couch larvae were wearing, in one cool, dismissive glance. Then she turned to Roberto.

"Is there a problem?" she said.

"This is Candace," he said, pointing weakly at me. "From the *Examiner.*"

She stared at me. I felt—actually felt—my zit expanding beneath her gaze.

"Is there a problem?" she repeated.

"There wasn't until a few minutes ago," I said, struggling to keep my voice calm. "I had an interview scheduled for two o'clock. Roberto tells me it's been cancelled."

"That's right," she said pleasantly. "We decided to limit our print interviews to major newspapers."

"The *Examiner* has a circulation of 700,000 on Sundays, which is when we'd planned the story for," I said. "We're the fourth-largest city on the East Coast. And nobody bothered to tell me the interview was off."

"That was Roberto's responsibility," she said, raking him with her gaze.

This was clearly news to Roberto, but he wasn't going to contradict Miss Kitten with a Whip. "Sorry," he muttered to me.

"I appreciate the apologies," I said, "but as I told Roberto, we've now got a hole in our Sunday newspaper, and I've wasted my day off." Which wasn't technically true. Stories fell through all the time, as April probably knew, and we'd just pop something else in the hole. And as for wasting my day off, any time I got a free ticket to New York, I always found something to do there.

But I was furious. The nerve of these people, to treat me so rudely, and to be so patently, completely not sorry about it!

"Isn't there any way she can see me for a few minutes? Since I'm here?"

April's tone was becoming decidedly less pleasant. "She's running late as it is, and she's flying right back to location this afternoon. To Australia," she emphasized, as if this was a place a country mouse such as myself had most likely never heard of. "And," she continued, snapping a small notebook open, "we've already scheduled a telephone interview with your boss."

My boss? It was inconceivable that Betsy would do this, beyond inconceivable that she'd do this and not tell me.

"With Gabby Gardiner," April concluded.

I was stunned. "Gabby's not my boss!"

"I'm sorry," April said, sounding not sorry at all, "but those are the arrangements we've made."

I backed into the hospitality suite and plopped into a chair by the window. "Look," I said. "I'm here, and I'm sure you'd agree that it would be better for all of us to do an in-person interview—even a quick one—with someone who's seen all of Maxi's movies, who took the time to prepare for this—than something over the phone. I'm happy to wait."

April stood in the hall for a moment. "Do I have to call security?" she finally asked.

"I don't see why," I said. "I'll just sit here until Ms. Ryder finishes up with whoever she's in with, and if it happens that she's got a minute or two to spare before she has to go rushing back to Australia, I will conduct the interview that I was promised." I clenched my hands into fists so she wouldn't see how I was shaking, and played my final card. "Of course, if it should turn out that Ms. Ryder doesn't have a few minutes for me," I said sweetly, "then I'll be writing a thirty-inch story about what's happened to me here. And by the way, what's your last name?"

April glared at me. Roberto sidled closer to her, flicking his eyes back and forth between us, as if we were playing a very fast game of tennis. I stared right back at April.

"It's impossible," she said.

"Interesting last name," I said. "Is it one of those Ellis Island specials?"

"I'm sorry," she said, for what would be the last time, "but Ms. Ryder's not going to be speaking to you. You were sarcastic to me on the phone . . ."

"Ooh, a sarcastic reporter! Bet you've never seen one of those before!"

". . . and Ms. Ryder doesn't need your kind of attention . . ."

"Which is fine," I exploded, "but couldn't one of your lackeys or flunkies or interns have had the courtesy to call me before I came all the way up here?"

"Roberto was supposed to," she said again.

"Well, he didn't," I told her, and crossed my arms. Standoff. She stood and glared at me for a minute. I glared right back. Roberto leaned against the wall, actually shaking. The larvae stood in a row, their eyes darting back and forth.

"Call security," April finally said, and turned on her heel. She looked back over her shoulder at me. "You," she said. "Write whatever you want. We don't care."

And with that, they were gone: Roberto, shooting me a final, desperately apologetic look over his shoulder, the larvae, all in black boots, and April, and whatever chance I had of meeting Maxi Ryder. I sat there, until they'd all piled into an elevator. Only then did I let myself cry.

Generally speaking, hotel lobby bathrooms are great places to have breakdowns. People registered at the hotel are mostly using the bathrooms in their rooms. People on the streets don't always know that they can breeze right in to the lobby of even the fanciest hotel and almost always use the toilet unmolested. And the bathrooms tend to be spacious and fancy, with all the amenities from hairspray and tampons to actual towels for wiping your tears and drying your hands. Sometimes there's even a couch to collapse on.

I staggered down the hall, into the elevator, and through the gold door reading "Ladies" in elaborate script, heading for the handicapped stall and peace, quiet, and solitude, grabbing two neatly rolled towels on my way in. "Fucking Maxi Ryder!" I hissed, and slammed the door, sat down, and pressed my fists against my eyes.

"Huh?" said a familiar voice from somewhere over my head. "Why?"

I looked up. A face was peeking over the top of the stall.

"Why?" Maxi Ryder said again. She was just as adorable in person as she was on the big screen, with her saucer-wide blue eyes, her lightly freckled, creamy skin, her cascade of auburn curls, seemingly brighter and more glossy than standard-issue human hair was meant to be. She was gripping a slim cigarette in one tiny blue-veined hand, and as I watched she took a generous drag and blew it out toward the ceiling.

"Don't smoke in here," I told her. It was the first thing I could think of. "You'll set off the alarms."

"You're cursing me because I'm smoking?"

"No. I'm cursing you because you stood me up."

"What?"

Two sneaker-clad feet plunked lightly onto the marble and came to rest outside my stall. "Open up," she said, rapping at the door. "I want some explanation."

I slumped down on the toilet seat. First April, now this! Reluctantly I leaned forward and unlocked the door. Maxi stood outside the stall, arms crossed on her chest, waiting for her answers. "I'm from the *Philadelphia Examiner,*" I began. "I was supposed to interview you. Your little Gestapo-ette told me, after I came all the way up here, that the interview had been canceled and rescheduled with this woman at my office who's just . . ." I gulped. "Vomitous," I arrived at. "So it kind of ruined my day. Not to mention our Sunday section." I sighed. "But it's not your fault, I guess. So I'm sorry. I shouldn't have cursed at you."

"Bloody April," said Maxi. "She never even told me."

"I'm not surprised."

"I'm hiding," said Maxi Ryder, and gave a nervous giggle. "From April, actually."

In person her voice was soft, cultured. She was wearing bell-bottomed jeans and a scoop-necked pink T-shirt. Her hair was piled into the kind of artless updo that probably took a hairdresser half an hour to construct, ornamented with tiny, sparkling butterfly clips. Like most young female stars I'd met, she was thin to the point of unreality. I could make out the bones of her wrists and forearms, the pale blue tracery of veins along her neck.

Her pouty lips were painted scarlet. Her eyes were carefully lined and shadowed. And her cheeks were streaked with tears.

"Sorry about your interview," she said.

"It wasn't your fault," I said again. "So what brings you to these parts? Don't you have your own bathroom somewhere else?" I asked.

"Oh," she said, and drew a long, shuddering breath. "You know."

"Well, actually, not being a thin, rich, successful movie star, I probably don't."

One corner of her mouth quirked upward, then drew down again into a trembling crimson bow. "Ever had your heart broken?" she asked in a shaky voice.

"Actually, yes," I said.

She closed her eyes. Impossibly long lashes rested against her pale freckled cheeks, and tears slid out from beneath them.

"It's unbearable," she said. "I know how that sounds . . ."

"No. No. I know what you mean. I know that it feels like that."

I handed her one of the rolled-up towels I'd grabbed on the way in. She took it, then looked at me. It was, I thought, a test.

"My house is full of things he gave me," I began, and she nodded vigorously, curls bouncing.

"That's it," she said, "that's right."

"And it hurts to look at them, and it hurts to put them away."

Maxi slumped to the bathroom floor and leaned her cheek against the cool marble wall. After a moment's hesitation, I joined her, struck by the absurdity of it all, and how it would make a great opening for an article: *Maxi Ryder, one of the most acclaimed young actresses of her generation, is crying on the bathroom floor.*

"My mother always says that it's better to have loved and lost than never to have loved at all," I said.

"Do you believe that?" she asked.

I only had to think about it for a minute. "No. I don't even think she believes it. I wish I'd never loved him. I wish I'd never met him. Because I think that as good as the good times were, it isn't worth feeling like this."

We sat for a minute, side by side.

"What's your name?"

"Candace Shapiro. Cannie."

"What was his name?"

"Bruce. And you?"

"I'm Maxi Ryder."

"I know that. I meant, what was his name?"

She made a horrible face. "Oh, don't tell me you don't know! Everybody knows! *Entertainment Weekly* did a whole story. With a flow chart!"

"Well, I was very explicitly forbidden from even mentioning it." Plus, there was more than one candidate, but it didn't seem prudent to say so.

"Kevin," she whispered. Which would be Kevin Britton, her costar from *Trembling.*

"Still Kevin?"

"Still Kevin, always Kevin," she said sadly, fumbling for another cigarette. "Kevin who I can't forget, even after I've tried everything. Drink . . . drugs . . . work . . . other men . . ."

Jeez. I suddenly felt very innocent.

"What do you do?"

I knew what she was asking me. "Oh, you know. Probably the same kinds of things as you." I laid one hand across my forehead, affecting world-weary hauteur. "I started by running off to my private island with Brad Pitt, trying to forget the pain by buying up llama ranches in New England . . ."

She punched my arm. Her clenched fist felt like a puff of air. "Seriously! Maybe it'll be something I haven't thought of."

"Probably just more stuff that doesn't really work. Baths, showers, bike rides . . ."

"I can't go for bike rides," she said morosely.

"Because of the paparazzi?"

"No. I never learned how."

"Really? Bruce, my ex-boyfriend, couldn't ride a bike either . . ." My voice trailed off.

"God, don't you hate that?" she asked.

"The way even completely unrelated things remind you of the person you're trying to forget? Yes. I hate it." I looked at her. With her face framed by the bathroom wall marble, she looked ready for her close-up. Whereas I was probably a blotchy-faced, runny-nosed wreck. No justice, I thought. "What do you do?" I asked.

"Invest," Maxi said instantly. "Manage my money. And my parents' money, too." She sighed. "I used to manage Kevin's money. I wish he'd given me a little notice that he was going to dump me. I'd have sunk him so deep into Planet Hollywood that he'd be taking guest-shots on the WB just to make his rent."

I considered Maxi with newfound respect. "So you, like . . ." I racked my brains for the appropriate vocabulary. "Day-trade?"

She shook her head. "Nope. I don't have time to be geeking around on computers all day. I pick stocks, and I look for investment opportunities." She stood and stretched, her hands on her nonexistent hips. "I buy real estate."

My respect was turning into awe. "Like houses?"

"Yup. Buy them, have a crew renovate them, sell them at a profit, or live in them a while, if I'm between movies."

I felt my fingers reaching for my pen and notebook, creeping almost of their own accord. Maxi as real-estate mogul was something I hadn't read in any of the innumerable profiles I'd plowed through. It would make great copy. "Hey," I ventured. "Do you think . . . I mean, I know they said you were busy, but maybe . . . could we talk for a few minutes? So I can write my story?"

"Sure," said Maxi, shrugging, and looked around as if realizing for the first time that we were in a bathroom. "Let's get out of here. Want to?"

"Aren't you supposed to be heading to Australia? That's what April said."

Maxi looked exasperated. "I'm not leaving till tomorrow. April's a liar."

"Imagine that," I said.

"No, really . . . oh. Oh, I see. You're kidding." And she smiled at me. "I forget how people are."

"Well, generally, they're bigger than you."

She sighed, gazed at herself, and dragged deeply on her cigarette. "When I turn forty," she said, "I swear, I'm giving this all up, and I'm going to build a fortress on an island with a moat and electrified fences, and I'm going to let my hair go gray and eat custard until I have fourteen chins."

"That was not," I pointed out, "what you told *Mirabella*. You told them you wanted to appear in one quality movie a year, and raise your children in a country farmhouse."

She raised an eyebrow. "You read that?"

"I've read everything about you," I told her.

"Lies. All lies," she said, almost cheerfully. "Today, for example. I'm to go to some place called Mooma . . ."

"Moomba," I corrected.

". . . and have drinks with Matt Damon, or Ben Affleck. Or maybe both. And we're supposed to look very secretive and lovey, and somebody's going to call Page 6, and we're to be photographed, and then we're going to go to some restaurant that probably paid April off to have dinner, except of course I can't actually have dinner, because, God forbid, I ever get photographed with something actually in my mouth, or with my mouth open, or basically in any manner that could give any suggestion that I ever do anything with my mouth besides kiss men . . ."

". . . and smoke."

"Not that, either. The cancer lobby, you know. Which is how I got away from April. Told her I needed a cig."

"So you really want to pass up drinks and dinner with Ben . . . or Matt. . . ."

"Oh, it doesn't stop there. Then I'm supposed to be seen out dancing at some bar with pigs in its name . . ."

"Hogs and Heifers?"

"That's it. Dancing there till some ungodly hour, and then, and only then, am I permitted some sleep. And that's after I take off my brassiere and dance on the bar while I'm twirling it over my head."

"Wow. They really, um, arrange all that for you?"

She pulled a crumpled piece of paper out of her pocket. Sure enough: 4 P.M., Moomba; 7 P.M., Tandoor; 11–?, Hogs and Heifers. She reached into another pocket and produced a very small black lace Wonderbra. She wrapped the Wonderbra around her hand and started swinging it around her head while pumping her hips in a parody of a party girl's bump and grind. "See," she said, "they even made me practice. If it was up to me I'd sleep all day . . ."

"Me, too. And watch *Iron Chef*."

Maxi looked puzzled. "What's that?"

"Spoken like someone who's never been home alone on a Friday night. It's this TV show where there's this reclusive millionaire, and he's got these three chefs . . ."

"The Iron Chefs," Maxi guessed.

"Right. And every week they have cooking battles with some

challenger chef who comes in, and the eccentric millionaire gives them a theme ingredient that they have to cook with, and half the time it's something that starts off alive, like squid or giant eel . . ."

Maxi was smiling, and nodding, and looking like she couldn't wait to see the first episode. Or maybe she was just acting, I reminded myself. That was, after all, her job. Maybe she acted this excited and friendly and, well, nice, every time she met someone new, and then forgot they'd ever existed as soon as she moved on to the next movie.

"It's fun," I concluded. "Also free. Cheaper than renting a movie. I taped it last night, and I'm going to watch it when I get home."

"I'm never home on Fridays or Saturdays," she said sadly.

"Well, I almost always am. Believe me, you're not missing much."

Maxi Ryder grinned at me. "Cannie," she said, "know what I really want to do?"

And that was how I wound up in the Bliss day spa, naked on my belly, next to one of the most acclaimed young movie stars of my generation, talking about my failed love life while a man named Ricardo slathered Active Green Clay Mud all over my back.

Maxi and I had slipped out a back door of the hotel and caught a cab to the spa, where the receptionist very snippily informed us that they were booked all day, were booked for weeks, in fact, until Maxi slipped off her sunglasses and made about three seconds' worth of significant eye contact and the service improved by about 3,000 percent.

"This is so great," I told her, for about the fifth time. And it really was. The bed was cushioned with about half a dozen towels, and each one of them was easily as thick as my comforter. Soothing music played so softly in the background I thought it was a CD, until I'd opened my eyes long enough to see that there was an actual woman with an actual harp in the corner, half-hidden behind a lacy billow of curtains.

Maxi nodded. "Wait until they start with the showers and the salt rub." She closed her eyes. "I'm so tired," she murmured. "All I want to do is sleep."

"I can't sleep," I told her. "I mean, I start, but then I wake up . . ."

". . . and the bed's so empty."

"Well, I actually have a little dog, so the bed isn't empty."

"Oh, I'd love a dog! But I can't. Too much travel."

"You can come hang out with Nifkin any time," I said, knowing that it was highly unlikely that Maxi would be dropping by for an iced cappuccino and a frolic in the dog-crap-studded South Philadelphia dog park. Then again, I reasoned, as Ricardo gently rolled me over and started smearing my front, this was pretty unlikely, too.

"So what's next?" I asked. "Are you blowing off your entire agenda?"

"I think I am," she said. "I just want one day and one night to live like a normal person."

This hardly seemed like to the time to point out that normal people did not get to drop a thousand dollars on a single trip to a spa.

"What else do you want to do?"

Maxi considered. "I don't know. It's been so long . . . what would you do if you had a day to kill in New York?"

"Am I me in this scenario, or am I you?"

"What's the difference?"

"Well, do I have unlimited resources and recognition issues, or am I just plain old me?"

"Let's do plain old you first."

"Hmm. Well, I'd go to the ticket outlet in Times Square and try to get a half-price ticket for a Broadway show tonight. Then I'd go to the Steve Madden store in Chelsea and see what was on sale. And I'd look in all the galleries, and I'd buy six-for-a-dollar barrettes at the flea market on Columbus, and I'd have dinner at Virgil's, and go to the show."

"That sounds fantastic! Let's do it!" Maxi sat straight up, naked, covered in mud, with something thick slicking back her hair, and pulled the cucumber slices off her eyes. "Where are my shoes?" She looked down at herself. "Where are my clothes?"

"Lie down," I said with a laugh. Maxi lay down again.

"What's Steve Madden?"

"It's a great shoe store. One time I wandered in there, and it was the No Big Feet sale. All the size tens were half-price. I think it was the happiest day of my life, footwear-wise."

"That sounds so great," Maxi said dreamily. "Now, then. What's Virgil's?"

"Barbecue," I said. "They do these great ribs and fried chicken, and biscuits with maple butter . . . but you're a vegetarian, right?"

"Only on the record," said Maxi. "I love ribs."

"Do you think we can do it? I mean, won't people recognize you? And what about April?" I looked at her shyly. "And . . . I mean, not to pressure you or anything, but if we could talk about your movie for a little while . . . so I can write my story, and my editor doesn't kill me."

"But of course," said Maxi grandly. "Ask me anything at all."

"Later," I said. "I don't want to take advantage."

"Oh, go 'head!" She giggled merrily, and started writing my article: "Maxi Ryder is naked in a downtown spa, doused in aromatic extracts, musing on her lost love."

I heaved myself onto one elbow so that I could look at her.

"Do you really want to get into the lost love thing? I mean, that was the one thing that April was a demon about. She only wanted reporters to ask you about your work."

"But the thing about being an actor is that you get to take your life—your pain—and make it work for you." She took what sounded like a deep cleansing breath. "All things serve a purpose," she said. "I know that if I'm ever called upon to play a woman scorned . . . say, dumped publicly on a talk show . . . I'll be ready."

"You think that's bad? My ex-boyfriend writes the men's sex column for *Moxie*."

"Really?" she asked. "I was in *Moxie* last fall. 'Maxi on *Moxie*.' It was pretty stupid. Does your ex ever write about you?"

I sighed miserably. "I'm his favorite topic. It's not a lot of fun."

"What?" asked Maxi. "Did he talk about something personal?"

"Yeah," I said. "My weight, for starters."

Maxi sat straight up again. "'Loving a Larger Woman?' That was you?"

Damn. Had everyone in the world read that stupid thing?

"That was me."

"Wow." Maxi looked at me—not, I hope, to try to figure out how much I weighed, and whether it could genuinely have been more than Bruce. "I read it on the plane," she said apologetically. "I don't read *Moxie,* normally, but it was a really long flight, and I got bored, so I read, like, three months' worth. . . ."

"You don't have to apologize," I said. "I'm sure a lot of people read it."

She lay down again. "Were you the one who called him the human bidet?" she asked.

Even under the mud, I was blushing again. "Never to his face," I said.

"Well, it could be worse. I got dumped on a Barbara Walters special," said Maxi.

"I know," I said. "I saw."

We lay in silence as the attendants sprayed the mud off of us with a half-dozen hoses. I felt like a very pampered, very exotic pet . . . that, or a particularly expensive cut of meat. Then we were covered with coarse salt, scrubbed down, showered off again, then wrapped in warm robes and sent off for facials.

"I think you had it worse than I did," I reasoned, as we let our clay masks dry. "I mean, when Kevin talked about ending a long relationship, everyone who watched knew that he meant you. But with the article, the only people who knew that C. was me were . . ."

"Everyone who knew you," said Maxi.

"Yeah. Pretty much." I sighed. Between the seaweed and the salt and the New Age music and the warm and gentle almond-oiled hands of Charles the masseur, I felt like I was wrapped in some delicious cloud, miles above the world, away from telephones that didn't ring and resentful coworkers and snooty publicists. Away from my weight . . . so much so that I wasn't even worried what Charles & Company were thinking as they rubbed and oiled and rolled me around. There was just me and the sadness, but even that didn't feel very heavy just then. It just felt there, like my nose, like the scar over my belly button I got from picking at a chicken pox scab when I was six. Just another part of me.

Maxi grabbed my hand. "We're friends, right?" she said. And I thought, for a moment, that she probably didn't mean it—that this was a version of her quickie, six-week, movie-set friendships. But I didn't care.

I squeezed back. "Yes," I said. "We're friends."

"You know what I think?" Maxi asked me. She raised a single fingertip. Instantly, there were four more shots of tequila in front of us, each one paid for, no doubt, by a different adoring guy. She picked up a glass and looked at me. I did the same, and we gulped tequila. I set the glass down, wincing at the burn. We'd wound up at Hogs and Heifers after all. We'd had a late lunch at Virgil's, where we'd sampled ribs, barbecued chicken, banana pudding, and cheese grits. Then we'd each bought about six pairs of Steve Madden shoes, reasoning that although we might feel fat, our feet didn't. Then it was on to the Beauty Bar, where we'd bought all manner of cosmetics (I stuck mostly to sand-colored eyeshadow and concealing cream. Maxi splurged on everything with glitter). It all added up to much more than I'd planned on spending on either shoes or makeup in the next year, and possibly even the next several years, but I figured, when's the next time I'll be shopping with a movie star?

"You know what I think?" Maxi repeated.

"What's that?"

"I think that we actually have a lot in common. It's the body thing," she said.

I squinted at her. "Huh?"

"We're ruled by our bodies," she pronounced, and sipped at a beer that someone had sent over. To me, this sounded very profound. This, perhaps, was because I was profoundly drunk. "You're stuck with a body that you think men don't want . . ."

"It's a little more than a theory at this point," I said, but Maxi wasn't about to have her monologue interrupted.

"And I'm afraid that if I start eating things I like, I'll stop looking the way I look, and nobody will want me. Worse than that," she said, glaring through the cigarette haze, "nobody will pay me. So I'm stuck, too. But what we're really trapped by is perceptions. You think you need to lose weight for someone to love you. I think if I gain weight, no one will love me. What we really need," she said, pounding the bar for emphasis, "is to just stop thinking of ourselves as bodies and start thinking of ourselves as people."

I stared at her admiringly. "Thass very deep."

Maxi took a deep swallow of beer. "Heard it on Oprah."

I did another shot. "Oprah's deep. But I have to say that all things considered, I'd rather be trapped in your body than mine. At least I could wear bikinis."

"But don't you see? We're both in prison. Prisons of Flesh."

I giggled. Maxi looked offended. "What, you don't agree?"

"No," I said, snorting, "I just think that Prisons of Flesh sounds like the name of a porno movie."

"Fine," Maxi said when she'd stopped laughing. "But I have a valid point."

"Of course you do," I told her. "I know that I shouldn't feel the way I do about how I look. I want to live in a world where people are judged by who they are instead of what size they wear." I sighed. "But you know what I want even more than that?" Maxi looked at me expectantly. I hesitated, then took another tequila. "I want to forget about Bruce."

"I have a theory about that, too," Maxi announced triumphantly. "My theory," she said, "is that hate works." She clinked her glass against mine. We did the shot, and upended the glasses on the sticky bar top, beneath the gently swaying clothesline of brassieres that had once cupped the breasts of the famous.

"I can't hate him," I said sadly. Suddenly my lips felt as though they were forming words a good foot or two away from my face, like they'd decided to just detach themselves and head for greener pastures. It was a common side effect when I'd been enjoying too many libations. That, and a liquid sensation in my knees and wrists and elbows, like my joints were coming unhinged. When I got drunk I started remembering things. And right now, because there was Grateful Dead on the jukebox ("Cassidy," I thought), what I was remembering was how we'd gone to pick up Bruce's friend George to go to a Dead show, and while we were waiting we'd slipped into the study and I'd given him a very quick, extremely hot blow job underneath the stuffed deer's head mounted on the wall. Physically I was sitting at Hogs and Heifers, but in my head I was on my knees in front of him, my hands cupping his ass, his knees pressing my chest as he trembled and gasped that he loved me, thinking that I was made for this, made for nothing but this.

"Sure you can," Maxi urged, yanking me out of the basement and into the tequila-soaked present. "Tell me the worst thing about him."

"He was really sloppy."

She crinkled her nose adorably. "That's not that bad."

"Oh, you have no idea! He had all this hair, see, and it would get in the shower drain, and he'd never clean his shower, but every once in a while he'd just, like, scoop up a clump of this disgusting, awful, soap-scummy hair and, like, park it in a corner of the tub. The first time I saw it I screamed."

We did another shot. Maxi's cheeks were flushed bright, her eyes were gleaming.

"Also," I continued, "also he had disgusting toenails." I burped, as delicately as I could, against the back of my hand. "They were all yellow and thick and raggedy . . ."

"Fungus," said Maxi knowledgeably.

"And then there was his minibar," I said, warming to the task. "Every time his parents went on a plane, they'd bring him those mini-bottles of vodka and scotch. He'd keep them in a shoebox, and whenever anyone would come over for a drink, he'd say, 'Have something from the minibar.'" I paused, considering. "Actually, that was kind of cute."

"I was going to say," agreed Maxi.

"But it got annoying after a while. I mean, I'd come over, I'd have a terrible headache, I'd just want a vodka and tonic, and off he'd go to the minibar. I think he was just too cheap to shell out for an actual bottle of his own."

"Tell me," asked Maxi. "Was he really good in bed?"

I tried to prop my head in my hand, but my elbow wasn't doing its job, and I wound up almost bouncing my forehead off the bar. Maxi laughed at me. The bartender scowled. I asked for a glass of water. "You wanna know the truth?"

"No, I want you to lie to me. I'm a movie star. Everyone else does."

"The truth," I said, "the truth is that . . ."

Maxi was laughing, leaning in close. "C'mon, Cannie, let me have it."

"Well, he was very willing to try new things, which I appreciated . . ."

"Come on. No editori . . . editorial . . ." She closed her eyes, and her mouth. "No spin. I asked a simple question. Was he any good?"

"The truth. . . ." I tried again. "The truth is that he was very . . . small."

Her eyes widened. "Small, you mean . . . down there?"

"Small," I repeated. "Tiny. Microscopic. Infinitesimal!" There. If I could say that word, I couldn't be as wasted as I thought I was. "I mean, not when it was hard. When it was hard it was pretty normal-sized. But when it was soft, it was like it telescoped back into his body, and it just looked like this little . . ." I tried to say it, but I was laughing too hard.

"What? C'mon, Cannie. Stop laughing. Sit up straight. Tell me!"

"Hairy acorn," I finally managed. Maxi whooped. Tears came to her eyes, and somehow I was sideways, my head in her lap. "Hairy acorn!" she repeated.

"Shh!" I shushed her, trying to maneuver myself upright.

"Hairy acorn!"

"Maxi!"

"What? Do you think he's going to hear me?"

"He lives in New Jersey," I said very seriously.

Maxi climbed onto the bar and cupped her hands around her mouth. "Attention, bar patrons," she called. "Hairy Acorn resides in New Jersey."

"If you're not gonna show us your tits, then get off the bar!" shouted a drunk guy in a cowboy hat. Maxi very elegantly gave him the finger, then climbed down.

"It could almost be a proper name," she said. "Harry Acorn. Harry A. Corn."

"You can't tell anynone. Anyone," I slurred.

"Don't worry. I won't. And I seriously doubt that me and Mr. Corn travel in the same circles."

"He lives in New Jersey," I said again, and Maxi laughed until tequila came out of her nose.

"So basically," she said, once she'd stopped spluttering, "you're pining for a guy with a small willy who treated you badly?"

"He didn't treat me badly," I said. "He was very sweet . . . and attentive . . . and . . ."

But she wasn't listening. "Sweet and attentive are a dime a dozen. And so, I'm sorry to inform you, are small willies. You can do better."

"I have to get over him."

"So get over him! I insist!"

"What's the secret?"

"Hate!" said Maxi. "Like I said before."

But I couldn't hate him. I wanted to, but I couldn't. Against my will, I remembered something tremendously tender. How once, around Christmas, I'd told him to pretend he was Santa Claus, and I pretended I had come to the mall to have my picture taken. How I'd perched on his lap, taking care to plant my feet firmly on the floor so I wouldn't rest all my weight on him, and whispered in his ear, "Is it true that Santa comes just once a year?" How he'd laughed, and how he'd gasped when I put one hand against his chest and shoved him flat back on the bed and snuggled against him while he performed an impromptu and doubtlessly off-key rendition of "All I Want for Christmas Is You."

"Here," said Maxi, shoving a shot of tequila into my hand. "Medicine."

I gulped it down. She grabbed my chin and stared into my eyes. It looked like there were two of her—saucer-blue eyes, cascading hair, the geometrically perfect sprinkling of freckles, the chin just a shade too pointed, so that she wouldn't be perfect, but overwhelmingly endearing instead. I blinked, and she turned into one person again.

Maxi studied me carefully. "You still love him," she said. I bowed my head. "Yes," I whispered.

She let go of my chin. My head hit the bar. Maxi pulled me back upright by my barrettes. The bartender was looking concerned. "I think maybe she's had enough," he said. Maxi ignored him.

"Maybe you should call him," she said.

"I can't," I told her, suddenly acutely aware that I was very, very drunk. "I'll make a fool of myself."

"There are worse things than just looking foolish," she said.

"Like what?"

"Losing someone you love, because you're too proud to call and lay it on the line," she said. "That's worse. Now: What's his number?"

"Maxi . . ."

"Give me the number."

"This is a really bad idea."

"Why?

"Because . . ." I sighed, suddenly feeling all the tequila pressing against my skull. "Because what if he doesn't want me?"

"Then it's better that you know that, once and for all. We can go in like surgeons and cauterize the wound. And I'll teach you the restorative powers of hating his guts." She held out the phone. "Now. The number."

I took the phone. It was a tiny thing, a toy of a telephone, no longer than my thumb. I unfolded it clumsily, and squinted, poking at the digits with my pinkie.

He picked up on the first ring. "Hello?"

"Hey, Bruce. It's Cannie."

"Hi-ii," he said slowly, sounding surprised.

"I know this is kinda weird, but I'm in New York, in this bar, and you'll never guess who I'm here with . . ."

I paused for a breath. He didn't say anything.

"I have to tell you something . . ."

"Um, Cannie . . ."

"No, I just want, I just need . . . you just have to lishen. Listen," I finally managed. The words came in a rush. "Breaking up with you was a mistake. I know that now. And Bruce, I'm so sorry . . . and I miss you so much, and it's just getting worse and worse every day, and I know I don't deserve it, but if you could gimme 'nother chance I'd be so good to you . . ."

I could hear the springs creak as he shifted his weight on the bed. And someone else's voice in the background. A female voice.

I squinted at the clock on the wall, behind the dangling bras. It was one in the morning.

"But I'm innerupting," I said dumbly.

"Hey, Cannie, this actually isn't such a good time . . ."

"I thought you needed space," I said, "because of your father dying. But that's not it, is it? It's me. You don't want me."

I heard a bumping sound, then a far-off, murmured conversation. He'd probably put his hand over the receiver.

"Who is she?" I yelled.

"Look, is there a good time when I can call you back?" Bruce asked.

"Are you gonna write about her?" I cried. "Does she get to be an initial in your wonderful, fabulous column? Is she good in bed?"

"Cannie," Bruce said slowly, "let me call you back.".

"Don't. Don't worry. You don't have to," I said, and started stabbing at buttons on the telephone until I found the one that switched it off.

I handed the phone back to Maxi, who was staring at me gravely.

"That didn't sound good," she said.

I felt the room spinning. I felt like I was going to throw up. I felt like I'd never be able to smile again in my life, that, somewhere in my heart it was always going to be one o'clock in the morning, and I'd be calling the man I loved, and there'd be another woman in his bed.

"Cannie? Can you hear me? Cannie, what should I do?"

I lifted my head from the bar. I rubbed my eyes with my fist. I drew a deep shuddering breath. "Get me more tequila," I said, "and teach me how to hate."

Later—much later—in the cab back to the hotel, I leaned my head on Maxi's shoulder, mostly because I couldn't hold it up. I knew that this was it: the point where I had nothing left to lose, nothing left at all. Or maybe it was that I'd lost the most important thing already. And what did it matter? I thought. I reached into my purse, fumbling for the somewhat tequila-sticky copy of my screenplay that I'd tucked inside a million years ago, thinking that I'd revise the final scenes on the train ride home.

"Here," I slurred, shoving the screenplay into Maxi's hands.

"Oh, really, for me?" Maxi cooed, going into what sounded like her standard accepting-a-gift-from-a-stranger spiel. "Really, Cannie, you shouldn't have."

"No," I said, as a brief ray of sense poked through the alcohol fog. "No, I probably shouldn't have, but I'm gonna."

Maxi, meanwhile, was leafing drunkenly through the pages. "Whazzis?"

I hiccuped and figured, since I've come this far, why lie? "It's a screenplay that I wrote. I thought maybe you would like to read it, like maybe on the plane if you get bored again." I hiccuped some more. "I don't wanna impose . . ."

Maxi's eyelids had drooped to half-mast. She shoved the screenplay into her little black backpack, mangling the first thirty pages in the process. "Don' worry about it."

"You don't have to read it if you don't want to," I said. "And if you read it and you don't like it, you can tell me. Don't worry about hurting my feelings." I sighed. "Nobody else does."

Maxi leaned over and enfolded me in a clumsy hug. I could feel the bones of her elbows jabbing me as she gripped me tightly. "Poor Cannie," she said. "Don't you worry. I'm gonna take care of you."

I stared at her, as dubious as I was drunk. "You are?"

She nodded violently, with her ringlets bouncing around her face. "I'll take care of you," she said, "if you'll take care of me. If you'll be my friend, then we'll take care of each other."

NINE

I woke up in a hotel suite, in a very large bed, in my unfashionable black dress. Someone had taken off my sandals and set them neatly on the floor.

Sun was slanting through the windows, making bright stripes on the ivory-colored carpet and the pink down comforter that felt light as a kiss on my body. I lifted my head. Youch. Big mistake. I gingerly set my head back down on the pillows and closed my eyes again. It felt like someone had welded an iron band around my scalp and was tightening it slowly. It felt like my face was shrinking. It felt like there was something taped to my forehead.

I lifted my hands, removed a piece of paper that had, indeed, been taped to my forehead, and began to read.

Dear Cannie,

Sorry I had to leave you in such a state, but my plane left very early this morning (and April is livid with me . . . but that's okay. It was worth it!).

I feel very badly about what happened last night. I know that I pushed you into calling him, and that it was terrible news to receive. I can imagine how you're feeling now. I have been there myself (in terms of the tequila and the heartbreak both!).

Why don't you call me tomorrow, when you're back home and, I
hope, feeling better? My number's below. I do hope you'll forgive me,
and that we are still friends.

There will be a car waiting for you out front all day long, to take
you home—my treat. (Actually, April's!) Please call soon.

> *Sincerely,*
> *Maxi Ryder*

And then there were a string of telephone numbers: Australia.
Office. England. Pager. Cell phone. Fax. Alternate Fax. E-mail.

I made my way gingerly to the bathroom, where I was noisily and
thoroughly sick. Maxi had left aspirin on the sink, along with what
looked like several hundred dollars of unopened Kiehl's grooming
products, and two large bottles of Evian water, still chilled. I swallowed three aspirin, sipped carefully at the water, and caught a
glimpse of myself in the mirror. Ugh. Not good. Pale, pasty, blotchy
skin, greasy hair, black-circled eyes, and all the makeup I'd tried at
the Beauty Bar had smeared everywhere. I was weighing the pain-to-
benefit ratio of a long hot shower when there was a gentle knock at the
door.

"Room service," said the waiter, and wheeled in a cart. Hot coffee, hot tea, four kinds of juice, and dry toast. "Feel better," he said
sympathetically. "And Ms. Ryder made arrangements for late check-
out."

"How late?" I asked. My voice sounded creaky.

"Late as you like," he said. "Take your time. Enjoy."

He opened the curtains, displaying a panoramic view of the city.

"Wow," I said. The sunlight felt like it was stabbing my eyes, but
the power of that view was undeniable. I could see Central Park
spread out below me, dotted with people and trees, with their leaves
turning orange and gold. The the stretch of high-rises in the distance.
Then the river. Then New Jersey. *"He lives in New Jersey,"* I heard
myself saying.

"It's the penthouse suite," he said, and left me there.

I poured myself a cup of tea, added sugar, attempted a few bites of toast. The bathtub, I observed sadly, was big enough for two—in fact, it was probably big enough for three, if the occupants were so inclined. The rich are different, I reasoned, and ran the water as hot as I could stand it, dumped in some frothing lotion guaranteed to possess so many restorative powers that I should rise from the tub reborn, or at least much better looking, and pulled my sundress off over my head.

My second mistake of the morning. There were mirrors all over the bathroom, mirrors offering views you couldn't usually find outside of a department store. And the terrain was not looking good. I closed my eyes to blot out the vision of stretch marks and cellulite. "I have strong tanned legs," I recited to myself. We'd practiced positive self-talk the week before in Fat Class. "I have beautiful shoulders." Then I slipped into the tub.

So, I thought bitterly. So he had someone else. So what did I think would happen? He's Jewish, he's got an education, he's tall and he's straight and he's easy on the eyes, and somebody was bound to snatch him up.

I rolled over, sending a cascade of water to the bathroom floor.

But he loved me, I thought. And was always telling me so. He thought I was perfect . . . that we were perfect together. And ten minutes later he's got someone else in his bed? Doing the things he swore he only ever wanted me to do?

The voice returned, implacable. *But you were the one who wanted a break.* And, *What did you expect?*

"Philadelphia, right, miss?" The driver was Russian, and was actually wearing a chauffeur's cap. The car, as it turned out, was a limousine, with a backseat bigger than my bed, and probably bigger than my bedroom, too. I peeked inside. There was the requisite television set, a VCR, a fancy-looking stereo . . . and, of course, a bar. Different liquors glittering in cut-crystal decanters, and a row of empty glasses. My stomach rolled over lazily.

"Could you excuse me?" I asked, and hurried back into the lobby. Hotel lobby bathrooms are also great places to get sick.

The chauffeur looked amused when I made it back to the car. "You want to take the Turnpike?"

"Whatever's easiest," I said, slipping into the seat, while he held the door open and loaded my backpack, shoe boxes, and shopping bags from the Beauty Bar into the trunk. There was a telephone in the backseat, next to the stereo and the television set, and I grabbed it, suddenly, sweatily desperate to know whether Bruce had tried to get in touch with me last night. There was a single message on my machine. "Hey, Cannie, it's Bruce, returning your call. I'm going home for a few days, so maybe I'll try you later this week." No *I'm sorry*. No *It was all a bad dream*. The call had come at eleven in the morning, probably after he'd had time for a morning go-round and a Belgian waffle with Miss Squeaky Springs, who would, thanks to my training, never refer to him as the Human Bidet, and who probably did not weigh more than he did.

I closed my eyes. It hurt so much.

I set the phone back as we barreled down the New Jersey Turnpike at eighty miles an hour, right past the exit that would take me to his door. I tapped two of my fingers against the window as we sped past. Hello and good-bye.

Sunday passed in a blur of tears and vomit at Samantha's house, where Nifkin and I had decamped, the better not to hear the telephone not ringing. Samantha, I could tell, was doing her damnedest not to say she'd told me so. She lasted longer than I would have—all the way until Sunday night, when she finally ran out of questions to ask about Maxi and turned to the topic of Bruce, and the disastrous telephone call.

"You wanted to take a break for a reason," she told me. We were sitting at the Pink Rose Pastry Shop. She was nibbling a macaroon. I was forking my way through a baseball-shaped and baseball-sized éclair, the best legal antidote for human misery I'd found, figuring that it didn't matter, because I hadn't eaten anything since the afternoon before, in New York, with Maxi.

"I know," I said, "I just can't remember what it was anymore."

"And you did think things through before you did it, right?"

I nodded.

"So you had to at least consider the possibility that he'd find somebody else?"

It felt like an impossibly long time ago, but I had considered it. At one point I'd even hoped for it, hoped for him to find some cute little Deadhead girl with ankle bracelets and armpit hair who'd stay up late and get high with him while I worked hard, sold my screenplays, and made *Time* magazine's "Thirty Under Thirty" list. Once upon a time, I'd been able to contemplate that scenario without tears, nausea, and/or feelings that I wanted to die, wanted to kill him, or wanted to kill him and then die.

"There were reasons things weren't working out," Samantha said.

"Tell me again what they were."

"He didn't like to go to movies," said Samantha.

"I go to movies with you."

"He didn't like to go anywhere!"

"So it'd kill me to stay home?" I poked the éclair so hard it toppled over, oozing custard. "He was a really good guy. A good, sweet guy. And I was a fool."

"Cannie, he compared you to Monica Lewinsky in a national magazine!"

"Well, that's not the worst thing in the world. It's not like he cheated on me."

"I know what this is about," said Samantha.

"What?"

"It's about wanting what you can't have. It's the law of the universe: He loved you, you felt bored and suffocated. Now he's moved on, and you're desperate to have him back. But think about it, Cannie . . . has anything really changed?"

I wanted to tell her that I had—that I'd gotten an up-close look at what else was out there in my personal dating universe, and that its name was Steve, it wore Tevas, and it didn't even consider a night out with me to be a date.

"You'd just wind up dumping him again, and that's really not fair."

"Why do I have to be fair?" I moaned. "Why can't I just be selfish and lousy and rotten, like everybody else?"

"Because you're a good person," she said. "Unfortunate as it may seem."

"How do you know?" I challenged her.

"Okay. You're walking Nifkin and you go past your car and you notice that if you pulled it up a few feet there'd be another parking space, instead of just one of those annoying gaps that looks like a parking space but isn't. Do you move the car?"

"Well, yeah . . . wouldn't you?"

"That's not the point. That's the evidence. You're a good person."

"I don't want to be a good person. I want to drive to New Jersey and kick that bitch out of his bed . . ."

"I know," she said. "But you can't."

"Why not?" I demanded.

"Because you'll wind up in jail, and I'm not going to take care of your weird little dog forever."

"Fine." I sighed.

The waiter came by, glancing at our plates. "Finished?"

I nodded. "All done. No more," I said.

Sam told me I could stay over if I wanted to, but I decided that I couldn't hide forever, so I hitched up Nifkin and went back home. I hauled myself up the stairs, with my hands full of Saturday's mail, and there he was, right in front of my door. I saw him in stages—his scuffed-up, second-best sneakers . . . then mismatched athletic socks . . . then tanned, hairy legs came into view as I ascended. Sweatpants, an old college T-shirt, his goatee, his dirty-blond ponytail, his face. Ladies and gentlemen, fresh from his engagement with the Spring Squeaker, Bruce Guberman.

"Cannie?"

I felt so strange, as if my heart were trying to sink and rise at the same time. Or maybe it was just more nausea.

"Look," he said, "I, um, I'm sorry about last night."

"Nothing to apologize for," I said breezily, shouldering past him and unlocking the door. "What brings you here?"

He walked inside, keeping his eyes on his shoelaces and his hands in his pockets. "I'm on my way down to Baltimore, actually."

"How nice for you," I said, giving Nifkin a stern look in hopes that it would stop him from jumping up toward Bruce, his tail wagging triple-time. "I wanted to talk to you," he said.

"How nice for me," I replied.

"I was going to tell you. I wanted to tell you before you read about it," he said.

Oh, terrific. I was going to have to live it and read about it, too? "Read about it where?" I asked.

"In *Moxie,*" he said.

"Actually, *Moxie*'s not high on my reading list," I told him. "I already know how to give a good blow job. As you may remember."

He took a deep breath, and I knew what it was, knew what was coming, the way you can feel the air pressure change and know that a storm's on the way. "I wanted to tell you that I'm kind of seeing somebody."

"Oh, really? You mean you didn't have your eyes shut the whole time last night?"

He didn't laugh.

"What's her name?"

"Cannie," he said gently.

"I refuse to believe that you found another girl named Cannie. Now tell me. C'mon. Age? Rank? Serial number?" I asked jokingly, hearing my voice as if from a million miles away.

"She's thirty-one . . . she's a kindergarten teacher. She's got a dog, too."

"That's great," I said sarcastically. "I bet we have lots and lots of other things in common. Let me guess . . . I'll bet she's got breasts! And hair!"

"Cannie . . ."

And then, because it was the only thing I could think of, "Where'd she go to school?"

"Um . . . Montclair State."

Great. Older, poorer, more dependent, less intelligent. I was dying to ask if she was blond, too, just to make the run of clichés complete.

"Do you love her?" I blurted instead.

"Cannie . . ."

"Never mind. I'm sorry. I had no right to ask you that. I'm sorry." And then, before I could stop myself, I asked, "Did you tell her about me?"

He nodded. "Of course I did."

"Well, what did you say?" A horrible thought struck me. "Did you tell her about my mom?"

Bruce nodded again, looking puzzled. "Why? What's the big deal?"

I shut my eyes, assaulted by a sudden vision of Bruce and his new girl in his wide, warm bed, his arm wrapped companionably around her, telling my family secrets. "Her mother's gay, you know," he'd say, and the new girl would give a wise, professionally compassionate kindergarten-teacher nod, all the while thinking what a freak I must be.

From the bedroom, I heard choking noises. "Excuse me," I murmured, and ran into the bedroom, where Nifkin was busily regurgitating a Baggie. I cleaned up the mess and walked back to the living room. Bruce was standing in front of my couch. He hadn't sat down, hadn't so much as touched anything. I could tell just from looking at him how desperately he wanted to be back in his car with the windows rolled down and the Springsteen cranked up . . . to be away from me.

"Are you okay?"

I took a deep breath. I wish you were back with me, I thought. I wish I didn't have to hear this. I wish we'd never broken up. I wish we'd never met.

"Fine," I said. "I'm glad for you."

We were both quiet then.

"I hope we can be friends," said Bruce.

"I don't think so," I said.

"Well," he said, and paused, and I knew that he had nothing left to say to me, and that there was really only one thing he wanted to hear.

And so I said it. "Good-bye, Bruce," I said, and opened the door, and stood there, waiting, until he walked out.

Then it was Monday, and I was back at work, feeling both queasy and abidingly dumb. I was shuffling things around on my desk, half-heartedly going through my mail, which featured the usual spate of complaints from Old People, Angry, plus a collection of bitter missives from Howard Stern fans who were most displeased with the review I'd given his latest on-air venture. I was wondering whether I could simply come up with a form letter to the seventeen guys who'd accused me of being ugly, old, and jealous of Howard Stern, and signed themselves "Baba Booey," when Gabby sauntered over.

"How'd it go with Maxi Whosit?" she asked.

"Fine," I said, giving her my best bland smile.

Gabby raised her eyebrows. "'Cause I heard through the grapevine that she wasn't doing any interviews with print reporters. Just TV."

"Not to worry."

But Gabby was looking worried. Extremely worried. She'd probably scheduled Maxi as the main item for tomorrow's column—just for the sheer joy of undercutting me—and now she was going to wind up scrambling to fill the space. Scrambling was not something Gabby did well.

"So . . . you talked to her?"

"For about an hour," I said. "Great stuff. Really great. We really hit it off. I think," I said, drawing the words out to prolong the torture, "I think we might even be friends."

Gabby's mouth fell open. I could tell she was trying to figure out whether to ask if anyone had mentioned her planned chat with Maxi, or to just hope I hadn't learned about it.

"Thanks for asking, though," I said sweetly. "It's so nice of you to look out for me like this. It's almost like . . . gee! . . . like you're my boss." I pushed back my chair, got to my feet, and walked by her regally, my back straight, my head held high. Then I went into the bathroom and threw up. Again.

Back at my desk, I was groping through my drawers, searching desperately for a mint or some gum, when the phone rang.

"Features, Candace Shapiro," I said distractedly. Thumbtacks, business cards, three sizes of paperclips, and not an Altoid to be found. Story of my life, I thought.

"Candace, this is Dr. Krushelevansky from the University of Philadelphia," said a deep, familiar voice.

"Oh. Oh, hi," I said. "What's up?" I gave up on the desk drawer and started going through my purse, even though I'd already looked through there.

"There's something I need to discuss with you," he said.

That got my attention. "Yes?"

"Well, you know that last blood draw we did . . ." I remembered it well. "Something came up that I'm afraid makes you ineligible for the study."

I felt my palms go icy. "What? What is it?"

"I'd prefer to discuss this with you in person," he said.

I quickly ran through everything else that a blood test could reveal, each possibility more awful than the one before. "Do I have cancer?" I asked. "Do I have AIDS?"

"You don't have anything life-threatening," he said sternly. "And I'd prefer not playing Twenty Questions."

"Then just tell me what's wrong," I begged. "High cholesterol? Hypoglycemia? Scurvy? Gout?"

"Cannie . . ."

"Do I have rickets? Oh, God, please not rickets. I don't think I can stand being fat and bowlegged."

He started laughing. "No rickets, but I'm starting to think you might have Tourette's. How do you know all of these diseases anyhow? Do you have a physician's desk reference in front of you?"

"I'm glad you think this is amusing," I said plaintively. "I'm glad this is your idea of fun, calling up innocent reporters in the middle of the day and telling them there's something wrong with their blood."

"Your blood is fine," he said seriously. "And I'll be happy to tell you what we found, but I would prefer to do it in person."

* * *

He was sitting behind his desk when I came in, and he got to his feet to greet me. I noticed, once again, how very tall he was.

"Have a seat," he said. I dropped my purse and backpack on one chair and parked myself on another.

He fanned my folder out on his desk. "As I told you, we do a standard series of tests when we draw blood, looking for conditions that could possibly disqualify study participants. Hepatitis is one of them. AIDS, of course, is another."

I nodded, wondering if he'd ever get to the point.

"We also test for pregnancy," he said. I nodded again, thinking, *okay, already, but what's wrong with me?* And then I realized. *Pregnancy.*

"But I'm not . . ." I stammered. "I mean, I can't be."

He flipped the folder around and pointed to where something was circled in red. "I'd be happy to arrange for another test," he said, "but generally, we're very accurate."

"I . . . I don't . . ." I stood up. How had this happened? My mind was whirling. I sank back into the chair to think. I'd gone off the Pill after Bruce and I had broken up, figuring it would be a long, long time before I had the need to contracept again, and it hadn't even occurred to me that I was at risk during the shiva call. It had to have happened then.

"Oh, God," I said, jumping to my feet again. Bruce. I had to find Bruce, I had to tell Bruce, surely he'd take me back now. . .*except,* my mind whispered, *what if he didn't?* What if he told me that it was my concern, my problem, that he was with somebody else and I was on my own?

"Oh," I said, slumping once more into the seat and burying my face in my hands. It was too horrible to even think about. I hadn't even noticed that Dr. K. had left the room until the door opened and he was standing there. There were three Styrofoam cups in one of his hands, a fistful of creamers and sugar packets in the other. He set the cups down on the desk in front of me: tea, coffee, water. "I wasn't sure what you like," he said apologetically. I picked up the tea. He opened his desk drawer and produced a half-empty bear-shaped squeeze bottle of honey. "Can I get you anything else?" he asked kindly. I shook my head.

"Would you like to be alone for a bit?" he asked, and I remembered that this was the middle of a work day, that there was a world going on around me, and that he probably had other things to do, other fat ladies to see.

"You probably don't do this a lot, do you?" I asked. "Tell people that they're pregnant, I mean."

The doctor looked taken aback. "No," he finally said. "No, I guess I don't do it a lot." He frowned. "Did I do it wrong?"

I laughed weakly. "I don't know. Nobody's ever told me that I'm pregnant before, so I don't have much to compare it to."

"I'm sorry," he said tentatively. "I take it this is . . . unexpected news."

"You could say that," I said. Suddenly, I was gripped with a vivid memory of the Cannie and Maxi Tequila Tour. "Oh, my God," I said, imagining that the putative kid was probably pickled by this point. "Do you know anything about fetal alcohol syndrome?"

"Hang on," he said. I heard him moving quickly down the hall. He came back with a book in his hands. *What To Expect When You're Expecting.* "One of the nurses had it," he explained. He flipped to the index. "Page 52," he said, and handed me the book. I skimmed the salient paragraphs and learned that basically, provided I quit drinking to the point of incoherence for the duration, things would be okay. Assuming, of course, that I wanted things to be okay. And, at that moment, I had no idea what I wanted. Except, of course, not to be in this situation at all.

I put the book on his desk and gathered my purse and backpack. "I guess I should be going," I said.

"Would you like another test?" he asked.

I shook my head. "I'll do one at home, I guess, and then I'll figure out . . ." I closed my mouth. Truthfully, I didn't know what I'd figure out.

He pushed the book back toward me. "Would you like to hang onto it? In case you have other questions?"

He was being so nice to me, I thought. Why was he being so nice to me? He was probably some crazy right-to-lifer, I thought meanly, trying to trick me into staying pregnant with the beverage sampler and the free guidebooks.

"Won't the nurse want it back?" I asked.

"She's had her babies," he said lightly. "I'm sure she wouldn't mind. You're welcome to have it." He cleared his throat. "With regard to the study," he began. "If you choose to continue the pregnancy, you won't be eligible, of course."

"No thin pills?" I joked.

"They haven't been approved for use by pregnant women."

"Then I could be your guinea pig," I offered, feeling myself teetering on the edge of hysteria. "Maybe I'd have a really skinny baby. That'd be good, right?"

"Whatever you do, just let me know," he said, tucking a business card inside of the book. "I'll make sure you get a full refund if you decide not to continue."

I remembered, very clearly, somewhere in the sheaf of forms I'd filled out the first day, something stating that there would be no refunds allowed. Crazy right-to-lifer, for sure, I thought, and stood up, strapping my backpack over my shoulders.

He looked at me kindly. "Listen, if you want to talk about it . . . or if you have any other medical questions, I'd be happy to try to help."

"Thanks," I muttered. My hand was already on the doorknob.

"Take care of yourself, Cannie," he said. "And give us a call, either way."

I nodded again, turned the handle, and hustled out the door.

I made bargains with God the whole way home, the same way I'd invented letters to the Celine Dion fan, poor Mr. Deiffinger, the least of my concerns now. Dear God, if you make me not pregnant I'll volunteer at the pet shelter and the AIDS hospice and I'll never write anything nasty about anyone again. I'll be a better person. I'll do everything right, I'll go to synagogue and not just on high holy days, I won't be so mean and critical, I'll be nice to Gabby, only please, please, please, don't let this be happening to me.

I bought two tests at the drugstore on South Street, white cardboard boxes with beaming mothers-to-be on the front, and peed all over my hand doing the first one, I was shaking so hard. By then I was so convinced of the worst that I didn't need the plus sign on the EPT wand to tell me what Dr. Krushelevansky already had.

"I'm pregnant," I said to the mirror, and mimed a smile, like the woman on the box.

"Pregnant," I informed Nifkin later that night, as he bounded all over me and licked my face at Samantha's house, where I'd stashed him while I was at work. Samantha had two dogs of her own, plus a big, fenced-in yard and a pet door, so the dogs could go in and out as they pleased. Nifkin wasn't crazy about her dogs, Daisy and Mandy— I suspected that he much preferred the company of people to other pets—but he was a big fan of the premium lamb and rice kibble that Samantha served, and so, on balance, seemed happy to hang out at Sam's house.

"What did you say?" Samantha called from the kitchen.

"I'm pregnant," I called back.

"What?"

"Nothing," I yelled. Nifkin sat on my lap, looking gravely into my eyes.

"You heard me, right?" I whispered. Nifkin licked my nose and curled into my lap.

Samantha came into the living room, wiping her hands. "You were saying?"

"I said, I'm going home for Thanksgiving."

"Lesbian turkey again?" Samantha wrinkled her nose. "Didn't you tell me that I was under strict instructions to slap you if you ever mentioned spending another holiday with Tanya again?"

"I'm tired," I told her. "I'm tired and I want to go home."

She sat down beside me. "What's going on, really?"

And I wanted so badly to tell her then, to just turn to her and spill it all out, to tell her, help me, and tell me what to do. But I couldn't.

Not yet. I needed time to think, to know my own mind before the chorus started. I knew the advice she'd give me. It would be the same thing I'd tell her if she were in the same situation: young, single with a great career, knocked up by a guy who wasn't returning her phone calls. It was a no-brainer, a $500 afternoon in the doctor's office, a few days of cramps and crying, end of story.

But before I went for the obvious, I wanted some time, even just a few days. I wanted to go home, even if home had long since gone from a happy refuge to something closer to a Sapphic commune.

It wasn't hard. I called Betsy, who told me to take as much time as I needed. "You've got three weeks of vacation, five days you never took from last year, and comp time from New York," she said, in a message on my machine at home. "Have a happy Thanksgiving, and I'll see you next week."

I e-mailed Maxi. "Something has come up . . . unfortunately, not the thing I might have hoped for," I wrote. "Bruce is dating a kindergarten teacher. I am brokenhearted and going home to eat dried turkey and let my mother feel sorry for me."

"Good luck, then," she'd written back immediately, even though it had to be three in the morning there. "And never mind the teacher. She's his transition object. They never last. Call or write when you're home . . . I'll be in the States again in the spring."

I cancelled my haircut, postponed a few telephone interviews, arranged for my neighbors to pick up my papers and my mail. I didn't call Bruce. If I decided not to stay pregnant, there'd be no reason for him to know. At this stage in our non-relationship, I couldn't very well imagine him sitting beside me in a clinic tenderly holding my hand. If I did stay pregnant . . . well, I'd burn that bridge when I came to it, I thought.

I hitched my bicycle rack and mountain bike to the back of my little blue Honda, put Nifkin in his traveling case, and tossed my bag in the trunk. Ready or not, I was going home.

PART THREE

I Go Swimming

TEN

The summer between my junior and senior years at Princeton, I had an internship at the *Village Vanguard,* the oldest and most attitudinous of the alternative newsweeklies in the country.

It was a wretched three months. For one thing, it was the hottest summer in years. Manhattan was boiling. Every morning I'd start sweating the instant I exited the shower, keep sweating through the subway ride downtown, and basically continue sweating the whole day.

I worked for a horrible woman named Kiki. Six feet tall and skeletally skinny, with henna'd hair, cat-eye thrift shop eyeglasses, and a permanent scowl, Kiki's summer uniform was a miniskirt paired with thigh-high suede boots, or, alternately, the noisiest clogs in the world, topped with a tight T-shirt advertising Sammy's Rumanian Restaurant, or the Boy Scouts Gymboree, or something else so square that it was hip.

Initially, Kiki confounded me. The hipster garb made sense, and the bad attitude was par for the *Vanguard* course, but I couldn't figure out when she was getting any work done. She showed up late, left early, and took two-hour lunches in between, and seemed to spend most of her time in the office on the phone with a cadre of interchangeable-sounding friends. The mosaic nameplate on the white picket fence she'd ironically erected around her cubicle read "associate editor." And while she associated plenty, I'd never seen her edit.

She was, however, the master of delegating unpleasant chores. "I'm thinking about women and murder," she'd announce on a Tuesday afternoon, idly sipping her iced coffee while I stood before her, sweating. "Why don't you see what we've done?"

This was 1991. The back issues of the *Vanguard* weren't stored online, or even on microfilm, but in huge, dusty, falling-apart, over-sized binders that each weighed at least twenty pounds. These binders were housed along the hallway that linked the offices of columnists to the feeding pen of metal chairs and cigarette-scarred desks that served as workspace for the *Vanguard*'s lesser luminaries. I spent my days hauling the binders off the shelves, lugging them over first to my desk, then to the copying machine, all the while trying to avoid the gin breath and wandering hands of the nation's preeminent gun rights activist, whose office was right next to the shelves, and whose favorite summer hobby seemed to be accidentally on purpose brushing against the sides of my breasts when my arms were loaded down with binders.

It was miserable. After two weeks I gave up on the subway and started taking the bus. Even though it made the ride twice as long and just as hot, it kept me out of the sweltering, fetid pit that the 116th Street subway stop had become. One afternoon in early August, I was sitting on the M140, minding my own business and sweating as usual, when, just as the bus lurched past Billy's Topless, I heard a very small, perfectly calm voice that sounded as if it was coming from the precise base of my skull.

"I know where you're going," said the voice. The hair on my arms and the back of my neck stood straight up. I got goosebumps, and was suddenly freezing cold, and I was completely convinced that what I was hearing was ... not human. A voice from the spirit world, I might have said that summer, laughing it off with my friends. But really, I thought it was the voice of God.

Of course it wasn't God, just Ellyn Weiss, the small, strange, androgynous-looking *Village Vanguard* contributing writer who'd sat down behind me and decided to say, "I know where you're going" instead of "hello." But in my mind, I thought that if I ever got to hear the voice of God, it would sound exactly like that: small and still and sure.

Once you've heard the voice of God, it changes things. That day, when the preeminent gun rights activist waggled his fingertips against the side of my right breast as he made his lurching way back to his office, I accidentally on purpose dropped 1987 on his foot. "So sorry," I said, sweet as pie, when he turned the color of a dirty sheet and stumbled away, never to lay a finger on me again. And when Kiki told me, "I've been thinking about women and men, and how they're different," and asked whether I could start pulling pages, I told her a bald-faced lie. "My advisor says I won't get credit for this if all you've got me doing is photocopying," I told her. "If you can't use me, I'm sure the copy editors can." That very afternoon I slipped Kiki's skinny, angered clutches and spent the rest of the summer writing headlines, and going out for cheap drinks with my new copy-editing colleagues.

Now, seven years later, I sat cross-legged on a picnic table, my face turned up to the pale November sunshine and my bike parked beside me, waiting to hear that voice again. Waiting for God to take notice as I sat in the center of Pennwood State Park in suburban Pennsylvania five miles from the house I grew up in, for God to look down upon me and intone either, *Keep the baby,* or *Call Planned Parenthood.*

I stretched out my legs, lifted my arms over my head, breathing in through my nose, out through my mouth, the way Samantha's yoga instructor boyfriend said would rid my bloodstream of impurities and increase clear thoughts. If it had happened the way I figured—if I'd gotten pregnant the last time Bruce and I were together—then I was eight weeks along. How big was it, I wondered? The size of a fingertip, a pencil eraser, a tadpole?

I'd decided that I'd give God another ten minutes, when I heard something.

"Cannie?"

Ugh. That most definitely was not the voice of the divine. I felt the table tilt as Tanya hoisted herself on top of it, but I kept my eyes closed, hoping that maybe, for once, if I ignored her she'd go away.

"Is something wrong?"

Silly me. I was forever forgetting that Tanya was a participant in a clutch of self-help groups: one for families of alcoholics, another for sexual-abuse survivors, a third called Codependent No More!, with an exclamation point as part of its name. Leaving well enough alone wasn't even a possibility. Tanya was all about intervention.

"It might help if you talk about it," she rumbled, lighting a cigarette.

"Mm," I said. Even with my eyes shut I could feel her watching me.

"You got fired," she suddenly announced.

My eyes flew open in spite of myself. "What?"

Tanya looked inordinately pleased with herself. "I figured it out, didn't I? Hah! Your mother owes me ten bucks."

I lay on my back, waving her smoke away from me, feeling a growing annoyance. "No, I did not get fired."

"Was it Bruce? Did something else happen?"

"Tanya, I really don't feel like discussing it right now."

"Bruce, huh?" Tanya said mournfully. "Shit."

I sat up again. "Why does that bother you?"

She shrugged her shoulders. "Oh, your mother figured it was something with Bruce, so if she's right, I've got to pay her."

Great, I thought. My poor life reduced to a series of ten-dollar bets. Easy tears sprang to my eyes. It seemed these days I was crying about everything, starting with my situation and continuing relentlessly to human-interest stories that ran in the *Examiner*'s Lifestyle section and Campbell's soup commercials.

"I guess you saw that last article he wrote, huh?" said Tanya.

I'd seen it. "Love, Again," it was called, in the December issue, which had hit stands just in time to ruin my Thanksgiving. "I know I should be focusing on E. by herself," he'd written.

I know that it's wrong to compare. But there's no way to avoid it. After The First, it seems that the next woman is, necessarily, The Second. At least in the beginning, at least for a little while. And E. is in every way different from my first love: short where she was tall, fine and delicate where she was broad and solid, sweet where she was bitterly, mordantly funny.

"Rebound," my friends tell me, nodding their heads like ancient rabbis instead of twenty-nine-year-old full-time temps and graduate students. "She's your rebound girl." But what's wrong with rebound, I wonder? If there was a first and it didn't work out, then there has to be a second, a next. Eventually, you have to move on.

If first love was like exploring a new continent, I think that second love is like moving to a new neighborhood. You already know there will be streets and houses. Now you have the pleasure of learning what the houses look like inside, how the streets feel beneath your feet. You know the rules, the basic vocabulary: phone calls, Valentine's Day chocolates, how to comfort a woman when she tells you what's gone wrong in her day, in her life. Now you can fine-tune. You find her nickname, how she likes her hand held, the sweet spot just beneath the curve of her jaw . . .

And that was as far as I'd made it before running to the toilet for my second hurl of the day. Just the idea of Bruce kissing someone else on the sweet spot just beneath the curve of her jaw—even the thought of him noticing such a thing—was enough to send my already queasy stomach into revolt. He doesn't love me anymore. I had to keep reminding myself of that, and every time I thought those words, it was like hearing them for the first time, in all-capital italic letters, being boomed out by the guy who did voice-overs for movie previews: *HE DOESN'T LOVE ME ANYMORE.*

"It must be tough," mused Tanya.

"It's ridiculous," I snapped. And really, the whole situation was pretty ridiculous. After three years of resisting his pleas, his offers, his desperate importunings, and biweekly proclamations that I was the only woman he'd ever want, we were apart, I was pregnant, and he'd found somebody else, and I would, most likely, never see him again.

(*Never* was another word I'd hear in my head a lot, as in: You'll never wake up next to him again, or, You'll never talk to him on the telephone.)

"So what are you going to do?" she asked.

"That's the big question," I said, and hopped off the table and onto my bike, heading back home. Except it didn't feel like home anymore and, thanks to Tanya's invasion, I wasn't sure it ever would again.

The less you know about your parents' sex lives, the better. Sure, you figure, they had to have done it at least once, to get you, and then maybe a few more times, if you had brothers and sisters, but that was procreation; that was duty, and the thought of them using their various openings and attachments for fun, for pleasure—in short, in the manner you, their child, would like to be using yours—was nothing short of sick-making. Particularly if they were having the kind of trendy, cutting-edge love life that was all the rage in the late 1990s. You don't need to know about your parents having sex, and you especially don't need to know about them having hipper sex than you are.

Unfortunately, thanks to Tanya's self-help training, and my mother's being rendered senseless by love, I got the whole story.

It started when my brother, Josh, came home from college and was rummaging in my mother's bathroom for the toenail clippers, when he came across a small stack of Hallmark greeting cards—the kind with abstract watercolors of birds and trees on the front, and florid calligraphy'd sentiments inside. "Thinking of you," read the front of one, and inside, beneath the rhymed Hallmark couplet, someone had written, "Annie, after three months, the fire still burns strong." No signature.

"I think they're from this woman," said Josh.

"What woman?" I asked.

"The one who's living here," said Josh. "Mom says she's her swim coach."

A live-in swim coach? This was the first I'd heard of it.

"It's probably nothing," I told Josh.

"It's probably nothing," Bruce told me, when I'd talked to him that night.

And that was how I started my conversation with my mother when she called at work two days later: "This is probably nothing, but . . ."

"Yes?" asked my mother.

"Is there, um, someone else . . . living there?"

"My swim coach," she said.

"You know, the Olympics were last year," I said, playing along.

"Tanya's a friend of mine from the Jewish Community Center. She's between apartments, and she's staying in Josh's room for a few days."

This sounded slightly suspect. My mother didn't have friends who lived in apartments, let alone who slept over because they were between them. Her friends all lived in the houses their ex-husbands had left, just like she did. But I let it go until the next time I called home and an unfamiliar voice answered the telephone.

"H'lo?" the strange voice growled. It was, at first, impossible to tell whether I was talking to a woman or a man. But whoever it was sounded as if they'd just gotten out of bed, even though it was almost eight o'clock on a Friday night.

"I'm sorry," I said politely, "I think I have the wrong number."

"Is this Cannie?" demanded the voice.

"Yes. Who's this, please?"

"Tanya," she said proudly. "I'm a friend of your mother's."

"Oh," I said. "Oh. Hi."

"Your mother's told me a lot about you."

"Well, that's . . .that's good," I said. My mind was churning. Who was this person, and what was she doing answering our telephone?

"But she's not here right now," Tanya continued. "She's playing bridge. With her bridge group."

"Right."

"Do you want me to have her call you?"

"No," I said, "no, that's okay."

That was Friday. I didn't speak to my mother again until she called on Monday afternoon at work.

"Is there something you want to tell me?" I asked her, expecting her to say some variation of "No." Instead, she took a deep breath.

"Well, you know, Tanya . . . my friend? She's . . . well. We're in love and we're living together."

What can I say? Subtlety and discretion run in the family.

"I've got to go," I said, and hung up the phone.

I spent the whole rest of the afternoon staring blankly into space, which, believe me, did nothing to add to the quality of my article about the MTV Video Music Awards. At home, there were three messages on my machine: one from my mother ("Cannie, call me, we need to discuss this"); one from Lucy ("Mom said I have to call you and she didn't say why"); and one from Josh ("I TOLD you so!").

I ignored all of them, instead rounding up Samantha for an emergency dessert and strategy session. We went to the bar around the corner, where I ordered a shot of tequila and a slab of chocolate cake with raspberry sauce. Thus fortified, I told her what my mother had told me.

"Wow," murmured Samantha.

"Good God!" said Bruce, when I told him later that night. But it wasn't long before his initial shock turned into . . . well, call it shocked amusement. With a heavy helping of condescension. By the time he arrived at my door he was in full-blown good liberal mode. "You should be glad she's found someone to love," he lectured.

"I am," I said slowly. "I mean, I guess I am. It's just that . . ."

"Glad," Bruce repeated. He could get a little insufferable when it came to toeing the P.C. party line, and to mouthing the beliefs that were practically mandatory among graduate students in the northeast in the nineties. Most of the time I let him get away with it. But this time I wasn't going to let him make me feel like a bigot, or like I was less open-minded and accepting than he was. This time it was personal.

"How many gay friends do you have?" I asked, knowing what the answer was.

"None, but . . ."

"None that you know of," I said, and paused while he let that sink in.

"What does that mean?" he demanded.

"It means what I said. None that you know of."

"You think one of my friends is gay?"

"Bruce, I didn't even know my own mother was gay. How do you expect me to have any kind of insight about your friends' sexuality?"

"Oh," he said, mollified.

"But my point is that you don't really know any gay people. So how can you assume it's such a terrific thing for my mom? That I should be happy about it?"

"She's in love. How can that be a bad thing?"

"What about this other person? What if she's awful? What if . . ." I was starting to cry as the horrible images piled up in my head. "What if, I don't know, they're walking somewhere and someone sees them and, and, throws a beer bottle at their heads or something . . ."

"Oh, Cannie . . ."

"People are mean! That's my point! It's not that there's anything wrong with being gay, but people are mean . . . and judgmental . . . and rotten . . . and, and you know what my neighborhood's like! People won't let their kids trick or treat at our house. . . ." Of course, the truth was that nobody'd let their kids trick or treat at our house since 1985 when my father began his downhill slide by neglecting the yardwork and getting in touch with his inner artiste. He'd brought a scalpel home from the hospital and turned half a dozen pumpkins into unflatteringly accurate renditions of members of my mother's immediate family, including a truly hideous pumpkin Aunt Linda that he'd perched on our porch, topped with a platinum blond wig that he'd swiped from the hospital's lost and found. But the truth was also that Avondale wasn't an especially integrated community. No blacks, few Jews, and no openly gay people that I could recall.

"So who cares what people think?"

"I do," I sobbed. "I mean, it's nice to have ideals and hope that things will change, but we have to live in the world the way it is, and the world is . . . is . . ."

"Why are you crying?" Bruce asked. "Are you worried about your mother, or yourself?" Of course, by that time, I was crying too hard to answer, and there was also a mucus situation that needed immediate attention. I swiped my sleeve across my face and blew my nose noisily. When I looked up, Bruce was still talking. "Your mother's made her choice, Cannie, and if you're a good daughter, what you'll do is support it."

Well. Easy for him to say. It wasn't as if the Ever Tasteful Audrey had announced over one of her four-course kosher dinners that she'd decided to park on the other side of the street, as it were. I would bet a week's pay that the Ever Tasteful Audrey had never even seen another woman's vagina. She'd probably never even seen her own.

The thought of Bruce's mother in her whirlpool bathtub for two, discreetly dabbing at her own privates from beneath an Egyptian cotton washcloth with a high thread count, made me laugh a little.

"See?" said Bruce. "You just have to roll with it, Cannie."

I laughed even harder. Having discharged his boyfriendly duty, Bruce switched gears. His voice dropped from his concerned-guidance-counselor tenor to a more intimate tone. "Come here, girl," he murmured, sounding for all the world like Lionel Richie as he beckoned me beside him, tenderly kissing my forehead and not so tenderly tossing Nifkin off the bed. "I want you," he said, and placed my hand on his crotch to remove any doubt.

And so it went.

Bruce left at midnight. I fell into an uneasy sleep and woke up the morning after with the telephone shrilling on my pillow. I unglued one eyelid. 5:15. I picked up the phone. "Hello?"

"Cannie? It's Tanya."

Tanya?

"Your mother's friend."

Oh, God. Tanya.

"Hi," I said weakly. Nifkin stared at me as if to say, what is this about? Then he gave a dismissive sniff and resettled himself on the pillow. Meanwhile, Tanya was talking a blue streak.

". . . knew the first time I saw her that she could have feelings for me . . ."

I struggled to sit up, and groped for a reporter's notebook. This was too bizarre not to be recording for posterity. By the time our conversation ended, I'd filled nine pages, made myself late for work, and learned every detail about Tanya's life. I heard how she was molested by her piano teacher, how her mother died of breast cancer when she was young ("I coped with my pain with alcohol"), and how her father had remarried a not-nice book editor who refused to pay Tanya's tuition to Green Mountain Valley Community College ("they've got the third-best program in New England for art therapy"). I learned the name of Tanya's first love (Marjorie), how she wound up in Pennsylvania (job), and how she'd been in the process of ending a seven-year relationship with a woman named Janet. "She's very codependent," Tanya confided. "Maybe obsessive-compulsive, too." At this point I had retreated into full reporter mode and wasn't saying anything but "Uh-huh," or, "I see."

"So I moved out," she told me.

"Uh-huh," I said.

"And I devoted myself to weaving."

"I see."

Then it was on to how she'd met my mother (passionate glances in the ladies' locker room sauna—I'd almost been forced to put the phone down), where they'd gone on their first date (Thai food), and how Tanya had convinced my mother that her lesbian tendencies were more than a passing fancy.

"I kissed her," Tanya announced proudly. "And she tried to walk away, and I held her by the shoulders and I looked her in the eyes and I said, 'Ann, this is not going away.'"

"Uh-huh," I said. "I see."

Tanya then proceeded to the analysis and reflection portion of the speech.

"The way I see it," she began, "your mother's devoted her whole life to you kids." She said "you kids" in precisely the same tone I would have used for "you infestation of cockroaches."

"And she put up with that bastard . . ."

"Which bastard are we talking about here?" I inquired mildly.

"Your father," said Tanya, who was obviously not going to tone things down for the benefit of the bastard's offspring. "Like I was saying, she's devoted her life to you guys . . . and not that it's a bad thing. I know how much she wanted to be a mother, and have a family, and, of course, there weren't other options for dykes back then . . ."

Dykes? I could barely handle "lesbian." At what point did my mother get promoted to "dyke"?

". . . but what I think," Tanya continued, "is that now it's time for your mother to do more of what she wants. To have a life of her own."

"I see," I said. "Uh-huh."

"I'm really looking forward to meeting you," she said.

"I have to go now," I said, and hung up the phone. I didn't know whether to laugh or cry, so I wound up doing both at the same time.

"Beyond awful," I said to Samantha on the car phone.

"A freak like you wouldn't believe," I told Andy over lunch.

"Don't judge," Bruce warned me, before I'd even said a word.

"She's . . . um. She's into sharing. Lots of sharing."

"That's good," he said, doing his squinchy-blinky thing. "You should do more sharing, Cannie."

"Huh? Me?"

"You're very closed with your emotions. You keep everything so tight inside you."

"You know, you're right," I said. "Let's find a total stranger so I can tell how my piano teacher groped me."

"Huh?"

"She was molested," I said. "And she told me all the gory details."

Even Mr. Love Everyone seemed taken aback by this information. "Oh my."

"Yeah. And her mother had breast cancer, and her stepmother convinced her father not to pay her community college loans."

Bruce looked at me skeptically. "She told you all this?"

"What do you think, I drove home and read her diary? Of course she told me!" I paused to poach a few french fries off his plate. We were at the Tick Tock Diner, home of the enormous portion and the surliest waitresses south of New York. I never ordered fries there, but I used all my powers of persuasion to get Bruce to order them, so I could share. "She sounds seriously cracked."

"You probably made her uncomfortable."

"But I didn't say anything! She's never even met me! And she was the one who called me, so how could I make her uncomfortable?"

Bruce shrugged. "It's just the way you are, I guess."

I scowled at him. He reached for my hand. "Don't get mad. It's just that . . . you have this kind of judgmental thing going on."

"Says who?"

"Well, my friends, I guess."

"What, just because I think they should get jobs?"

"See, there you go. That's judgmental."

"Honey, they're slackers. Accept it. It's the truth."

"They're not slackers, Cannie. They do have jobs, you know."

"Oh, come on. What does Eric Silverberg do for a living?"

Eric, as we both knew, had a full-time temporary job at an Internet startup, where, as best we could both figure, he spent his days trading Springsteen bootleg tapes, meeting girls on one of the three online dating services he subscribed to, and arranging drug buys.

"George has a real job."

"George spends every weekend in a Civil War reenactment brigade. George owns his own musket."

"You're changing the subject," Bruce said. I could tell he was trying to stay angry, but he was starting to smile.

"I know," I said. "It's just that a guy who has his own musket is such an easy punchline."

I stood up, crossed the table, and sat down next to him on his side of the booth, squeezing his thigh and resting my head against his shoulder. "You know the only reason I'm judgmental is because I'm jealous," I said. "I wish I could have that kind of life. No college loans to pay, rent taken care of, nice, stable, married heterosexual parents who'd set me up with their slightly used furniture every time they redecorate and buy me a car for Chanukah . . ." My voice trailed off. Bruce was staring at me hard. I realized that, in addition to describing most of his friends, I'd just described him, too.

"I'm sorry," I said gently. "It's just that sometimes it feels like everybody's got things easier than I do, and that every time I get close to having things be kind of okay . . . something like this happens."

"Did you ever think that maybe these things happen to you because you're strong enough to take them?" Bruce asked. He reached down, grabbed my hand, and moved it up on his thigh. Way up. "You're so strong, Cannie," he whispered.

"I just," I said, "I wish . . ." And then he was kissing me. I could taste ketchup and salt on his lips. Then his tongue was in my mouth. I shut my eyes and let myself forget.

I spent the weekend at Bruce's apartment. It was one of those times where we got it just right: good sex, a nice meal out, lazy afternoons trading sections of the Sunday *Times,* and then I was on my way home before we started grating on each other. We talked about my mother a little bit, but mostly I got to just lose myself with him. And he gave me his favorite flannel shirt to wear home. It smelled like him, like us: like dope and sex, his skin and my shampoo. It was too tight across my chest—all of his things were—but the sleeves fell to my fingertips, and I felt enclosed, comforted, as if he was there hugging me tight, holding my hands.

Be brave, I thought back home in my bed. I pulled Bruce's shirt tight around me, tilted my cheek toward Nifkin so he could give me an encouraging lick, and phoned home.

Thankfully, my mother answered. "Cannie!" she said, sounding relieved. "Where have you been? I've been calling and calling . . ."

"I went to Bruce's," I told her. "We had theater tickets," I lied. Bruce didn't do well in theaters. Short attention span.

"Well," she said. "Well. Um, I want to tell you that I'm sorry for springing things on you like that. I guess I should have . . . well, I know I should have waited and maybe told you in person . . ."

"Or at least not at the office," I said.

She laughed. "Right. I'm sorry."

"It's okay."

"So . . ." I could almost hear her testing half a dozen opening remarks in her head. "Do you have any questions?" she finally asked.

I took a deep breath. "Are you happy?"

"I feel like I'm in high school!" my mother said jubilantly. "I feel . . . oh, I can't even describe it."

Please, don't try, I thought.

"Tanya's really terrific. You'll see."

"How old is she?" I asked.

"Thirty-six," said my fifty-six-year-old mother.

"A younger woman," I observed. My mother giggled. You have no idea how disturbing that was. My mother has never been the giggling type.

"She does seem to have a little problem with . . . boundaries," I ventured.

My mother's voice got very serious. "What do you mean?"

"Well, she called me Friday morning . . . I guess you weren't there. . . ."

A quick intake of breath. "What did she say?"

"It might take me less time to cover what she didn't say."

"Oh, God. Oh, Cannie."

"I mean, I'm sorry she was, you know, molested . . ."

"Oh, Cannie, she didn't!" But underneath the shocked, horrified tone, my mother sounded . . . almost proud. As if underneath the anger, she was indulging a favored child in the child's favorite prank.

"Yup," I said grimly. "I got the whole saga, from the piano teacher who tickled her ivories . . ."

". . . Cannie!"

". . . and the wicked stepmother, to the obsessive-compulsive co-dependent ex-girlfriend."

"Ack," said my mother. "Jeez."

"She might want to consider some therapy," I said.

"She goes. Believe me, she goes. She's been going for years."

"And she still hasn't figured out that you don't go blurting your whole life story to a complete stranger the first time you speak to them?"

My mother sighed. "I guess not," she said.

I waited. I waited for an apology, an explanation, something that could make sense of this. Nothing came. After a moment of awkward silence, my mother changed the subject, and I went along, hoping this was a phase, a fling, a bad dream, even. No such luck. Tanya had arrived for good.

What does a lesbian bring on a second date? goes the joke. A U-Haul. What does a gay guy bring on a second date? What second date?

An old joke, true, but there's a certain amount of truth to it. After they started dating, Tanya did in fact move out of the basement of her codependent obsessive-compulsive ex-girlfriend's condominium and into an apartment of her own.

But for all intents and purposes, she'd moved in on the second date. I realized this when I came home six weeks after what my siblings and I were referring to as Mom's Outage, and saw the writing on the wall.

Well, the poster on the wall. "Inspiration," it read, above a picture of a cresting wave, "is believing we can all pull together."

"Mom?" I called, dropping my bags on the floor. Nifkin, meanwhile, was whining and cringing by my legs in a most un-Nifkin-like manner.

"In here, honey," yelled my mother.

Honey? I wondered, and walked into the family room with Nifkin cowering behind me. This time, the new poster was of frolicking dolphins. "Teamwork," it said. And beneath the dolphin poster were my mother and a woman who could only be Tanya, in matching purple sweatsuits.

"Hey!" said Tanya.

"Hey," my mother repeated.

A large tangerine-colored cat leapt off of the windowsill, stalked insolently up to Nifkin, and stretched out a paw, claws extended. Nifkin gave a shrill yip and fled.

"Gertrude! Bad cat!" called Tanya. The cat ignored her and curled up in a patch of sunlight in the center of the room.

"Nifkin!" I called. From upstairs I heard a faint whine of protest— Nifkin-speak for *no way, no day*.

"Do we have employees that we're trying to motivate?" I asked, pointing at the teamwork dolphins.

"Huh?" said Tanya.

"What?" said my mother.

"The posters," I said. "We've got the exact same ones in the printing plant at work. Right next to the "27 Days Injury Free" sign. They're, like, motivational artwork."

Tanya shrugged. I'd been expecting a standard-issue gym teacher, with sinewy calves and ropy biceps and a no-nonsense haircut. Evidently I'd been expecting wrong. Tanya was a tiny boiled pea of a woman, barely five feet tall, with an aureole of frizzy reddish hair and skin tanned the color and consistency of old leather. No chest or hips to speak of. She looked like a little kid, right down to the scabby knees and the Band-Aid wrapped around one finger. "I just like dolphins," she said shyly.

"Uh-huh," I said. "I see."

And those were just the most obvious of the changes. There was a collection of dolphin figurines above the fireplace where the family pictures had been. Plastic magazine racks were bolted to the walls, giving our family room the look of a doctor's office—the better to display Tanya's copies of *Rehabilitation* magazine. And when I went to drop my bags in my room, the door wouldn't open.

"Mom!" I called, "there's something wrong up here!"

I heard a whispered consultation going on in the kitchen: my mother's voice calm and soothing, Tanya's bass grumble rising toward hysteria. Every once in a while I could make out words. "Therapist" and "privacy" seemed to comprise a dominant theme. Finally my mother walked up the stairs, looking troubled.

"Um, actually, I was going to talk to you about this."

"About what? The door being stuck?"

"Well, the door's locked, actually."

I just stared.

"Tanya's kind of been . . . keeping some of her things in there."

"Tanya," I pointed out, "has an apartment. Can't she keep her things there?"

My mother shrugged. "Well, it's a very small apartment. An efficiency, really. And it just kind of made sense . . . maybe you can sleep in Josh's room tonight."

At this point I was getting impatient. "Ma, it's my room. I'd like to sleep in my room. What's the big deal?"

"Well, Cannie, you don't . . . you don't live here anymore."

"Of course I don't, but that doesn't mean I don't want to sleep there when I come home."

My mother sighed. "We made some changes," she murmured.

"Yeah, I noticed. So what's the big deal?"

"We, um . . . well. We kind of got rid of your bed."

I was speechless. "You got rid of . . ."

"Tanya needed the space for her loom."

"There's a loom in there?"

Indeed there was. Tanya stomped up the stairs, unbolted the door, and stomped back downstairs, looking sullen. I entered my room and saw the loom, a computer, a battered futon, a few ugly pressboard bookshelves covered with plastic walnut veneer, containing volumes with titles like *Smart Women, Foolish Choices,* and *Courage to Heal,* and *It's Not What You're Eating, It's What's Eating You.* There was a rainbow-triangle suncatcher hanging in the window and, worst of all, an ashtray on the desk.

"She smokes?"

My mother bit her lip. "She's trying to quit."

I inhaled. Sure enough, Marlboro Lights and incense. Yuck. Why did she have to plant her self-help guides and her cigarette smells in my room? And where was my stuff?

I turned toward my mother. "You know, you really could have told me about this. I could have come down and taken my things with me."

"Oh, we didn't get rid of anything, Cannie. It's all in boxes in the basement."

I rolled my eyes. "Well, that makes me feel a lot better."

"Look," she said. "I'm sorry. I'm just trying to balance things here. . . ."

"No, no," I said. "'Balance' involves taking different things into account. This," I said, sweeping my hand to indicate the loom, the ashtray, the stuffed dolphin perched upon the futon, "is taking what one person wants into account, and completely screwing the other person. This is completely selfish. This is absolutely ridiculous. This is . . ."

"Cannie," said Tanya. She'd somehow come up the stairs without my hearing.

"Excuse us, please," I said, and slammed the door in her face. I took a perverse pleasure in listening to her work at the door handle after I'd locked it with her lock.

My mother started to sit down where my bed used to be, caught herself mid-sit and settled for Tanya's desk chair. "Cannie, look. I know this is a shock. . . ."

"Have you gone completely crazy? This is ridiculous! All it would have taken was one lousy phone call. I could have come, gotten my stuff . . ."

My mother looked miserable. "I'm sorry," she said again.

I wound up not staying the night. That visit occasioned my first—and, so far, my last—stint at therapy. The *Examiner*'s health plan paid for ten visits with Dr. Blum, the smallish, Little Orphan Annie–looking woman who scribbled frantically, while I told her the whole crazy-father-bad-divorce-lesbian-mother tale. I worried about Dr. Blum. For one thing, she always looked a little scared of me. And she always seemed a few twists behind the current plot.

"Now, back up," she'd say, when I'd segue abruptly from Tanya's latest atrocity to my sister, Lucy's, inability to keep a job. "Your sister was, um, dancing topless for a living, and your parents didn't notice?'

"This was '86," I'd say. "My father was gone. And my mother somehow managed to miss the fact that I was sleeping with my substitute history teacher and I'd gained fifty pounds during my freshman year of college, so yeah, she pretty much believed that Lucy was babysitting until four every morning."

Dr. Blum would squint down at her notes. "Okay, and the history teacher was . . . James?"

"No, no. James was the guy on the crew team. Jason was the E-Z-Lube poet. And Bill was the guy in college, and Bruce is the guy right now."

"Bruce!" she'd say triumphantly, having located his name in her notes.

"But I'm really worried that I'm, you know, leading him on or something." I sighed. "I'm not sure I really love him."

"Let's go back to your sister for a minute," she'd say, flipping faster and faster through her legal pad, while I sat there and tried not to yawn.

In addition to her inability to keep up, Dr. Blum was rendered less than trustworthy by her clothes. She dressed as if she didn't know there was such a thing as the petite section. Her sleeves routinely brushed her fingertips; her skirts sagged around her ankles. I opened up as best I could, answered her questions when she asked them, but I never really trusted her. How could I trust a woman who had even less fashion sense than I did?

At the end of our ten sessions, she didn't quite pronounce me cured, but she did leave me with two pieces of advice.

"First," she said, "you can't change anything anybody else in this world does. Not your father, not your mother, not Tanya, not Lisa . . ."

". . . Lucy," I corrected.

"Right. Well, you can't control what they do, but you can control how you respond to it . . . whether you allow it to drive you crazy, or occupy all of your thoughts, or whether you note what they're doing, consider it, and make a conscious decision as to how much you'll let it affect you."

"Okay. And what's thing two?"

"Hang on to Bruce," she said seriously. "Even if you don't think he's Mr. Right. He's there for you, and he sounds like a good support, and I think you're going to need that in the coming months."

We shook hands. She wished me good luck. I thanked her for her help and told her that Ma Jolie in Manayunk was having a big sale, and that they made things in her size. And that was the end of my big therapy experience.

I wish that I could say that, in the years since Tanya and her loom and her pain and her posters moved in, that things have gotten easier. The fact is, they haven't. Tanya has the people skills of plant life. It's like a special kind of tone-deafness, only instead of not hearing the music, she's deaf to nuances, to subtleties, to euphemisms, small talk, and white lies. Ask her how she's doing, and you'll get a full and lengthy explication of her latest work/health crisis, complete with an invitation to look at her latest surgical scar. Tell her that you liked whatever she cooked (and Lord knows you'll be lying), and she'll regale you with endless recipes, each with a story behind it ("My mother cooked this for me, I remember, the night after she came home from the hospital. . . .").

At the same time, she's also incredibly thin-skinned, prone to public crying fits, and temper tantrums that conclude with her either locking herself in my ex-bedroom, if we're home, or stomping away from wherever we are, if we're out. And she dotes on my mother in the most annoying way you could imagine, following her around like a lovestruck puppy, always reaching to hold her hand, touch her hair, rub her feet, tuck a blanket around her.

"Sick," pronounced Josh.

"Immature," said Lucy.

"I don't get it," is what I said. "Having somebody treat you that way for, like, a week would be nice . . . but where's the challenge? Where's the excitement? And what do they talk about?"

"Nothing," said Lucy. The three of us had come home for Chanukah, and we were sitting around the family room after the guests had gone home and my mother and Tanya had gone to bed, all of us holding the gifts Tanya had woven for us. I had a rainbow-colored scarf ("You can wear it to the Pride Parade," Tanya offered). Josh had mittens, also in the gay-pride rainbow, and Lucy had an odd-looking bundle of yarn that Tanya had explained was a muff. "It's to keep your hands warm," she'd rumbled, but Lucy and I had already dissolved into gales of laughter, and Josh was wondering in a whisper whether such a thing could be dropped to the bottom of the pool for a little summertime muff diving.

Nifkin, who'd been given a little rainbow sweater, was in my lap, sleeping with one eye open, ready to bolt for higher ground should the evil cats Gertrude and Alice appear. Josh was on the couch, picking out what sounded like the theme song from *Beverly Hills, 90210* on his guitar.

"In fact," said Lucy, "they don't talk at all."

"Well, what would they talk about?" I asked. "I mean, Mom's educated . . . she's traveled . . ."

"Tanya puts her hand over Mom's mouth when *Jeopardy* comes on," said Josh morosely, and switched to "Sex and Candy" on the guitar.

"Ew," I said.

"Yup," confirmed Lucy. "She says it's obnoxious how Mom shouts out the answers."

"It's probably just that she doesn't know any of them herself," said Josh.

"You know," said Lucy, "the lesbian thing is okay. It would've been all right . . ."

". . . if it had been a different kind of woman," I finished, and sat there, picturing a more appropriate same-sex love: say, a chic film professor from UPenn, with tenure and a pixie haircut and interesting amber jewelry, who'd introduce us to independent film directors and take my mother to Cannes. Instead, my mother had fallen for Tanya, who was neither well-read nor chic, whose cinematic tastes ran toward the later works of Jerry Bruckheimer, and who didn't own a single piece of amber.

"So what is it?" I asked. "What's the attraction? She isn't pretty . . ."

"That's for sure," said Lucy, shuddering dramatically.

"Or smart . . . or funny . . . or interesting . . ."

We all sat, silent, as it dawned on us what the attraction might be.

"I'll bet she's got a tongue like a whale," said Lucy. Josh made retching noises. I rolled my eyes, feeling queasy.

"Like an anteater!" cried Lucy.

"Lucy, cut it out!" I said. Nifkin woke up and started growling. "Besides, even if it is just sex, that'll only get you so far."

"How would you know?" said Lucy.

"Trust me," I said. "Mom'll get bored."

We all sat for a minute, thinking that over.

"It's like she doesn't care about us anymore," Josh blurted.

"She cares," I said. But I wasn't sure. Before Tanya, my mother had liked to do things with us . . . when we were all together. She'd visit me in Philadelphia, and Josh in New York. She'd cook when we came home, call us a few times a week, keep busy with her book clubs and lecture groups, her wide circle of friends.

"All she cares about is Tanya," said Lucy bitterly.

And I didn't have an argument for that. Sure, she'd still call us . . . but not as often. She hadn't visited me in months. Her days (not to mention her nights) seemed full of Tanya—the bike trips they went on, the tea dances they attended, the weekend long Ritual of Healing that Tanya had taken my mother to as a special three-month-anniversary surprise, where they'd burned sage and prayed to the Moon Goddess.

"It won't last," I said, with more conviction than I felt. "It's just an infatuation."

"What if it isn't?" Lucy demanded. "What if it's true love?"

"It's not," I said again. But inside, I thought that maybe it was. That this was it, and we'd all be stuck, saddled with this horrible, graceless emotional wreck of a creature for the rest of our lives. Or at least the rest of our mother's life. And after . . .

"Think of the funeral," I mused. "God. I can just hear her . . ." And I dropped my voice to a Tanya rasp. "Your mother would want me to have that," I growled. "But Tanya," I said in my own voice, ". . . that's my car!"

Josh's lips twitched upward. Lucy laughed. I did the Tanya-growl again.

"She knew how much it meant to me!"

Now Josh was out-and-out smiling. "Do the poem," he said.

I shook my head.

"C'mon, Cannie!" begged my sister.

I cleared my throat, and began to recite Philip Larkin. "They fuck you up, your mum and dad. They may not mean to, but they do."

"They fill you with the faults they had . . ." continued Lucy.

"And add some extra, just for you," said Josh.

"But they were fucked up in their turn, by fools in old-style hats and coats, Who half the time were soppy-stern, and half at one another's throats."

And we joined in together, the three of us, for the last stanza—the one I couldn't even bring myself to think of in my present predicament. "Man hands on misery to man, it deepens like the coastal shelf. Get out as early as you can, and don't have any kids yourself."

Then, at Lucy's suggestion, we all got to our feet—Nifkin included—and dropped our knitted items into the fireplace.

"Begone, Tanya!" Lucy intoned.

"Return, heterosexuality!" Josh implored.

"What they said," I echoed, and watched the pride muffler burn.

Back at home, I parked my bike in the garage, next to Tanya's little green car with its "A woman needs a man like a fish needs a bicycle" bumper sticker, hauled the gigantic frozen turkey out of the garage freezer, and set it in the sink to defrost. I took a quick shower and went into the Room Formerly Known as Mine, where I'd been camped out since my arrival. In between short bike rides and long baths and showers, I'd dragged enough blankets out of the linen closet to turn Tanya's futon into a triple-lined oasis. I had also dug a crate of books out of the basement and was working my way through all the hits of my childhood: *Little House on the Prairie, The Phantom Tollbooth,* the Narnia chronicles, and *The Five Little Peppers and How They Grew.* I was regressing, I thought bleakly. A few more days and I'd be practically embryonic myself.

I sat at Tanya's desk and checked my e-mail. Work, work. Old Person, Angry ("Your comments about CBS being the network for viewers who like their food prechewed were disgraceful!"). And a note from Maxi. "It's 98 degrees here every day," she wrote. "I'm hot. I'm bored. Tell me about Thanksgiving. What's the cast?"

I sat down to reply. "Thanksgiving is always a production in our house," I wrote. "Start off with me, and my mother, and Tanya, and Josh and Lucy. Then there's my mother's friends, and their husbands and kids, and whichever lost souls Tanya recruits. My mother makes dried turkey. Not intentionally dried, but because she insists on cooking it on the gas grill, and she hasn't quite figured out how to cook it long enough so that it's done, but not so long that it's not leathery.

Mashed sweet potatoes. Mashed potato potatoes. Some kind of green thing. Stuffing. Gravy. Cranberry sauce from a can." My stomach turned over even as I typed. I had pretty much stopped being nauseous during the last week, but just the thought of turkey jerky, Tanya's lumpy gravy, and canned cranberry cocktail was enough to make me grab for the saltines I'd packed.

"The food's not really the point," I continued. "It's nice to see people. I've known some of them since I was a little girl. And my mom builds a fire, and the house smells like wood smoke, and we all go around the table and name one thing we're thankful for."

"What will you say?" Maxi shot back.

I sighed, wriggling my feet in the thick wool socks I'd swiped from Tanya's L.L. Bean stash, and tugged the afghan I'd lifted from the family room tighter around me. "I'm not feeling especially thankful right now," I typed back, "but I'll think of something."

ELEVEN

Thanksgiving Day dawned crisp and cold and brilliantly sunny. I dragged myself out of bed, still yawning at ten in the morning, and spent a few hours outside raking leaves with Josh and Lucy while Nifkin kept watch on us, and on the stalking cats, from the porch.

At three that afternoon, I took a shower, blew my hair into some semblance of style, and put on lipstick and mascara, plus the wide-legged black velvet pants and black cashmere sweater I'd packed, hoping that the cumulative effect would be both stylish and slimming. Lucy and I set the table, Josh boiled and peeled shrimp, and Tanya bustled around the kitchen, making more noise than food, and breaking frequently for cigarettes.

At 4:30 the guests started to arrive. My mother's friend Beth came with her husband and three tall, blond sons, the youngest of whom was sporting a nose ring right through his septum, giving him the look of a baffled Jewish bull. Beth hugged me and started sliding trays of appetizers into the oven while Ben, the pierced one, started discreetly chucking salted nuts at Tanya's cats. "You look great!" Beth said, like she always says. It wasn't even close to being true, but I appreciated the sentiment. "I loved your story about Donny and Marie's new show. When you said how they were singing with LeAnn Rimes and it looked like they wanted to suck the lifeblood out of her . . . that was so funny!"

"Thanks," I said. I love Beth. Trust her to remember the "Mormon vampires" line, the one that I'd loved, too, even if it had occasioned half a dozen angry phone calls to my editor, a fistful of furious letters ("Dear Too-Bit reporter" my favorite one began), plus an earnest visit from two nineteen-year-old Brigham Young University students who were visiting Philadelphia and promised to pray for me.

Tanya contributed green beans with the crunchy canned onions on top and a can of undiluted Campbell's Cream of Mushroom soup mixed in, then galumphed into the family room and built a blazing fire. The house filled with the sweet smell of wood smoke and roasting turkey. Nifkin and Gertrude and Alice arranged a cease-fire and curled blissfully in front of the flames, all in a row. Josh passed around the shrimp he'd prepared. Lucy mixed Manhattans—she'd perfected them during a stint as a bartender that followed the topless dancing escapade but preceded her six weeks doing phone sex.

"You look lousy," she observed, handing me a drink. Lucy herself looked great, as always. My sister is just fifteen months younger than I am. People tell us we looked like twins when we were little. Nobody says that anymore. Lucy's thin—she always has been—and she wears her wavy hair short, so that the slightly pointed tips of her ears show when she shakes her head. She's got full, lush lips and big, brown Betty Boop eyes and she presents herself to the world like the star she thinks she ought to be. It's been years since I've seen her without a full face of makeup, her lips expertly outlined and colored, her eyebrows dramatically plucked, a tiny silver stud flashing and winking from the center of her tongue. She was dressed for the Thanksgiving feast in skintight black leather pants, high-heeled black boots, and a sequined pink sweater set. She looked like she'd just stepped out of a photo shoot, or stopped in for a quick drink before heading off to someone else's much more stylish holiday festivities.

"I'm a little stressed out," I said, yawning, handing the drink back, and wishing there was time for another nap.

My mother bustled around the table with the same placecards she'd used at Passover the year before. I knew there was one that said "Bruce" somewhere in the pile, and I hoped, for my sake, that she'd discarded it rather than crossing his name off and writing in someone else's as a way to economize.

The last time he'd been here it had been winter. Josh and Lucy and Bruce and I had stood on the porch, sipping the beers that Tanya refused to let us keep in the refrigerator. ("I'm in recovery!" she'd bleat, holding the offending bottles as if they were grenades.) Then we'd gone for a walk around the block. Halfway back, it had started to snow, unexpectedly. And Bruce and I stood, holding hands with our eyes shut and our mouths wide open, feeling the flakes like tiny wet kisses on our cheeks, long after everyone else went inside.

I closed my eyes against the memory.

Lucy stared at me. "Jeez, Cannie. Are you okay?"

I blinked back the tears. "Just tired."

"Hmmph," said Lucy. "Well, I'll just mash a little something special into your potatoes."

I shrugged, and made sure to avoid the potatoes at dinner. We followed my mother's Thanksgiving tradition, going around the table and talking about what we were thankful for that year. "I'm thankful for having found so much love," rasped Tanya, as Lucy and Josh and I winced and my mother took Tanya's hand.

"I'm thankful for having my wonderful family together," said my mother. Her eyes were glistening. Tanya kissed her cheek. Josh groaned. Tanya shot him a dirty look.

"I'm thankful . . ." I had to think for a while. "I'm thankful that Nifkin survived his bout with hemorrhagic gastroenteritis last summer," I finally said. At the sound of his name, Nifkin put his paw on my lap and whined beseechingly. I slipped him a piece of turkey skin.

"Cannie!" yelled my mother, "stop feeding that dog!"

"I'm thankful I still have an appetite after hearing about Nifkin's trouble," said Ben, who, in addition to the nose ring, was irritating his parents by sporting a "What Would Jesus Do?" T-shirt.

"I'm thankful that Cannie didn't dump Bruce until after my birthday, so that I got those Phish tickets," said Josh in his deep, deadpan baritone, which went nicely with his six-foot-tall, skin-and-bones frame, and the little goatee he'd grown since I'd seen him last. "Thanks," he stage-whispered.

"Think nothing of it," I whispered back.

"And I'm thankful," concluded Lucy, "that everyone's here to hear my big news!"

My mother and I exchanged anxious glances. Lucy's last big exciting news had been a plan—thankfully aborted—to move to Uzbekistan with a guy she'd met at a bar. "He's a lawyer over there," she'd said confidently, gliding smoothly over the fact that he was a Pizza Hut delivery guy over here. Before that, there'd been the plan for the bagel bakery in Montserrat, where she'd gone to visit a friend in medical school. "Not a bagel to be had down there!" she'd said triumphantly, and got as far as filling out the papers for a small business loan before Montserrat's long-dormant volcano erupted, the island was evacuated, and Lucy's bagel dreams died a hot molten death.

"What's the news?" asked my mother, looking into Lucy's shining eyes.

"I got an agent!" she trilled. "And he got me a photo shoot!"

"Topless?" asked Josh dryly. Lucy shook her head. "No, no, I'm done with all that. This is legitimate. I'm modeling rubber gloves."

"Fetish magazine?" I asked. I couldn't help myself.

Lucy's face fell. "Why doesn't anyone believe in me?" she demanded. Knowing my family, it was just a matter of time before somebody launched into Lucy's Catalogue of Failures—from school to relationships to the jobs she'd never kept.

I leaned across the table and took my sister's hand. She jerked her hand back. "No unnecessary touch!" she said. "What's with you, anyhow?"

"I'm sorry," I said. "We weren't giving you a chance." And that's when I heard the voice. Not God's voice, unfortunately, but Bruce's. *"Good,"* he said. *"That was nice."*

I looked around, startled.

"Cannie?" said my mother.

"Thought I heard something," I said. "Never mind."

And while Lucy prattled on about her agent, her photo shoot, and what she'd wear, all the while evading my mother's increasingly pointed questions about whether she was getting paid for this or what, I ate turkey and stuffing and glutinous green bean casserole, and thought about what I'd heard. I thought about how maybe even though I'd never see Bruce again, it might be possible to keep part of him, or of what we were together, if I could be more openhearted, and kind. For all of his lecturing, for every time he was didactic and condescending, I knew that he was basically a kind person, and I . . . well, I was too, in my private life, but it could be argued that I was making my living by being unkind. But maybe I could change. And maybe he'd like that, and someday like me better . . . and love me again. Assuming, of course, we ever even saw each other again.

Underneath the table, Nifkin twitched and growled at something chasing through his dream. My eyes were clear, and my head felt cool and ordered. It wasn't as if all of my problems were gone—as if any of them were gone, really—but for the first time since I'd seen the little plus sign on the EPT stick, it felt like I might be able to see myself safely through them. I had something to hold on to, now, no matter what choice I made—*I can be a better person,* I thought. *A better sister, a better daughter, a better friend.*

"Cannie?" said my mother. "Did you say something?"

I didn't. But at that moment I thought that I felt the faintest flutter in my belly. It might have been all the food, or all of my anxiety, and I knew it was much too early to really feel anything. But it felt like something. Like something waving at me. A tiny little hand, five fingers spread like a starfish, waving through the water. Hello and good-bye.

The last day of my Thanksgiving break, before I was going to make the trek back into town and pick up the pieces of my life where I'd left them, my mother and I went swimming. It was the first time I'd been back to the Jewish Community Center since I'd learned that it was the scene of my mother's seduction. After that, the steam room had never felt quite the same.

But I'd missed swimming, I realized, as I stood in the locker room and pulled on my suit. I had missed the tang of chlorine in my nose and the old Jewish ladies who'd parade through the locker room completely naked, completely unashamed, and swap recipes and beauty tips while they got dressed. The feel of the water, holding me up, and the way I could forget almost anything but the rhythm of my breath as I swam.

My mother swam a mile every morning, moving slowly through the water with a massive kind of grace. I kept up with her for maybe half of it, then slipped into one of the empty lap lanes and did a languid sidestroke for a while, thinking of nothing. Which I knew was a luxury I couldn't afford much longer. If I wanted to get things taken care of (and that was the phrase I was using in my mind), it would have to be soon.

I flipped on my back and thought about what I'd felt at Thanksgiving dinner. That tiny hand, waving. Ridiculous, really. The thing probably didn't have hands, and if it did, it certainly couldn't wave them.

I'd always been pro-choice. I had never romanticized pregnancies, intended or otherwise. I wasn't one of those women who sees her thirtieth birthday coming and starts cooing at anything in a stroller with drool on its chin. I had a few friends who'd gotten married and started their families, but I had many more friends in their late twenties and early thirties who hadn't. I didn't hear my clock ticking. I didn't have baby fever.

I rolled back over and commenced a lazy breaststroke. The thing was, I couldn't shake the feeling that it had been somehow decided for me. As if it was out of my control now, and all I was supposed to do was sit back and let it happen.

I blew a frustrated breath into the water, watching bubbles roil around me. I'd still feel better about all of this if I could have heard God's voice again, if I knew for sure that I was doing the right thing.

"Cannie?"

My mother swam into the lane beside me. "Two more laps," she said. We finished them together, matching each other breath for breath, stroke for stroke. Then I followed her into the locker room.

"Now," my mother began, "what is going on with you?"

I looked at her, surprised. "With me?"

"Oh, Cannie. I'm your mother. I've known you for twenty-seven years."

"Twenty-eight," I corrected.

She squinted at me. "Did I forget your birthday?"

I shrugged. "I think you sent a card."

"Is that what it is?" asked my mother. "Are you worried about getting older? Are you depressed?"

I shrugged again. My mother was sounding more worried.

"Are you getting any help? Are you talking to anyone?"

I snorted, imagining how useless the little doctor, drowning in her clothes, would be in a situation like this. "Now, Bruce is your boyfriend," she'd begin, flipping through her ever-present legal pad.

"Was," I'd correct.

"And you're thinking about . . . adoption?"

"Abortion," I'd say.

"You're pregnant," said my mother.

I sat up straight, my mouth falling open. "What?"

"Cannie. I'm your mother. A mother knows these things."

I drew my towel tight around me and wondered whether it would be too much to hope that this was one of the few things my mother and Tanya hadn't made a bet about.

"And you look just like I did," she continued. "Tired all the time. When I was pregnant with you I slept fourteen hours a day."

I didn't say anything. I didn't know what to say. I knew I would have to start talking about it to someone, at some point, but I didn't have words ready.

"Have you thought about names?" my mother asked me.

I gave a short, barking laugh. "I haven't thought about anything," I said. "I haven't thought about where I'll live, or what I'll do . . ."

"But you're going to . . ." Her voice trailed off delicately.

"Seems that way," I said. There. Out loud. It was real.

"Oh, Cannie!" She sounded—if it's possible—at once thrilled and brokenhearted. Thrilled, I guess, that she'd get to be a grandmother (unlike me, my mother was prone to cooing over anything in a stroller).

And brokenhearted because this wasn't a situation you'd wish for your daughter.

But it was my situation. I saw it then, that moment, in the locker room. This was what was going to happen—I was going to have this baby, Bruce or no Bruce, broken heart or no broken heart. It felt like the right choice. More than that, it felt almost like my destiny—the way my life was supposed to unfold. I just wished that whoever had planned it would drop me a clue or two about how I was going to provide for myself and a child. But if God wasn't going to speak up, I'd figure it out myself.

My mother stood up and hugged me, which was gross, considering that we were both wet from the pool, and her towel didn't quite make it around her front. But whatever. It felt good to have someone's arms around me.

"You're not mad?" I asked.

"No, no! How could I ever be mad?"

"Because . . . well. This isn't the way I wanted it . . ." I said, briefly letting my cheek rest against her shoulder.

"It never is," she told me. "It's never just the way you think that it'll be. Do you think I wanted to have you and Lucy down in Louisiana, a million miles away from my family, with those horrible army doctors and cockroaches big as my thumb. . . ."

"At least you had a husband," I said. "And a house . . . and a plan . . ."

My mother patted my shoulder briskly. "Husbands and houses are negotiable," she said. "And as for a plan . . . we'll figure it out."

She didn't ask the $64,000 question until we were dried off and dressed and in the car on our way home.

"I'm assuming that Bruce is the father," she said.

I leaned my cheek against the cool glass. "Correct."

"And you're not back together?"

"No. It was . . ." How could I possibly explain to my mother what had happened?

"Not to worry," she said, effectively ending my attempts to think of an appropriate euphemism for sympathy fuck. We drove past the industrial park and the fruit and vegetable stand, over the mountain, on our way home. Everything looked familiar, because I'd driven past it a million times, growing up. I would swim with my mother early Saturday mornings, and we'd drive home together, watching the sleeping towns wake up, on our way to get warm bagels and fresh-squeezed orange juice and have breakfast together, the five of us.

Now, everything looked different. The trees had gotten taller, the houses looked somehow shabbier. There were new traffic lights at a few of the more dangerous intersections, new houses with raw-looking wooden walls and torn-up lawns on streets that hadn't existed when I was in high school. Still, it felt good, and comfortable, to be riding beside my mother again. I could almost pretend that Tanya had stayed in her obsessive-compulsive codependent ex-girlfriend's apartment and out of my mother's life . . . and that my father hadn't abandoned us so completely . . . and that I wasn't in my current condition.

"Are you going to tell Bruce?" she finally asked.

"I don't know. We aren't exactly talking right now. And I think . . . well, I'm sure that if I told him, he'd try to talk me out of it, and I don't want to be talked out of it." I paused, thinking it over. "And it just seems . . . I mean, if I were him, if I were in his position . . . it's a lot to burden somebody with. That they've got a child out in the world. . . ."

"Do you want him in your life?" my mother asked me.

"That's not really the issue. He's made it pretty clear that he doesn't want to be in my life. Now, whether he wants to be in . . ." I stumbled, trying to say it for the first time, "in our child's life . . ."

"Well, it's not completely up to him. He'll have to pay child support."

"Ugh," I said, imagining having to take Bruce to court and justify my behavior in front of a judge and jury.

She kept talking: about mutual funds and compound interest and some television show she'd seen where working mothers set up hidden videocameras and found their nannies neglecting their babies while they (the nannies, not the babies, I presumed) watched soap operas and made long-distance phone calls to Honduras. It reminded me of Maxi, prattling on about my financial future.

"Okay," I told my mother. My muscles felt pleasantly heavy from the swimming, and my eyelids were starting to droop. "No Honduran nannies. I promise."

"Maybe Lucy could help out some," she said, and glanced at me when we were stopped at a red light. "You've been to your ob/gyn, right?"

"Not yet," I said, and yawned again.

"Cannie!" She proceeded to lecture me on nutrition, exercise during pregnancy, and how she'd heard that vitamin E in capsule form could prevent stretch marks. I let my eyes close, lulled by the sound of her voice and the turning wheels, and I was almost asleep when we pulled into the driveway. She had to shake me awake, saying my name gently, telling me that we were home.

It was a wonder she let me go back to Philadelphia that night. And as it was, I drove home with my trunk stuffed with about ten pounds of Tupperware'd turkey and stuffing and pie, and only after giving her my solemn promise that I'd make an appointment with a doctor first thing in the morning, and that she could come visit soon.

"Wear your seat belt," she said, as I loaded a protesting Nifkin into his carrier.

"I always wear my seat belt," I said.

"Call me as soon as you know the due date."

"I'll call! I promise!"

"Okay," she said. She reached over and brushed her fingertips against my cheek. "I'm proud of you," she said. I wanted to ask her why. What had I done that anyone could be proud of? Getting knocked up by a guy who wanted nothing else to do with you wasn't exactly the stuff she could brag to her book-club friends about, or that I could send in to the *Princeton Alumni Weekly*. Single motherhood might be getting more acceptable among the movie-star set, but from what I'd seen from my divorced colleagues, it was nothing but a hardship for real-life women, and it certainly wasn't a cause for celebration, or pride.

But I didn't ask. I just started the car and drove down the driveway, waving back at her until she disappeared.

Back in Philadelphia, everything looked different. Or maybe it was just that I was seeing it differently. I noticed the overflow of Budweiser cans in the recycling bin in front of the second-floor apartment as I made my way upstairs, and heard the shrill laugh track of a sitcom seeping beneath the door. Out on the street, somebody's car alarm went off, and I could hear glass breaking somewhere nearby. Just background noise, stuff I'd barely notice most of the time, but I'd have to start noticing now . . . now that I was responsible for somebody else.

Up on the third floor, my apartment had grown a thin layer of dust in the five days I'd been away, and it smelled stale. No place to raise a child, I thought, opening windows, lighting a vanilla-scented candle, and finding the broom.

I gave Nifkin fresh food and water. I swept the floors. I sorted my laundry to wash the next day, emptied the dishwasher, put the leftovers in the freezer, then rinsed and hung my bathing suit to dry. I was halfway through making a grocery list, full of skim milk and fresh apples and good things to eat, before I realized I hadn't even checked my voice mail to see if anyone . . . well, to see if Bruce . . . had called me. A long shot, I knew, but I figured I'd at least give him the benefit of the doubt.

And when I found that he hadn't called, I felt sad, but nothing like the sharp, jittery, anxious-sick sadness I'd had before, nothing like the overwhelming certainty that I would die if he didn't love me that I'd felt that night in New York with Maxi.

"He loved me," I whispered to the neatly swept room. "He loved me, but he doesn't love me anymore, and it's not the end of the world."

Nifkin raised his head from the couch, looked at me curiously, then fell back asleep. I picked up my list. "Eggs," I wrote. "Spinach. Plums."

TWELVE

"You're what?!?"

I bowed my head over my decaffeinated skim-milk latte and toasted bagel. "Pregnant. With child. Expecting. In a delicate condition. Bun in the oven. PG."

"Okay, okay, I've got it." Samantha stared at me, full lips parted, brown eyes shocked and wide-awake, even though it was only 7:30 in the morning. How?

"The usual way," I said lightly. We were in Xando, the neighborhood coffee shop that turned into a bar after six at night. Businessmen perused their *Examiner*s, harried moms with strollers gulped coffee. A good place, clean and bright. Not a place for making scenes.

"With Bruce?"

"Okay, maybe it wasn't the usual way. It was right after his father died. . . ."

Samantha gave a great exasperated sigh. "Oh, God, Cannie . . . what did I tell you about sex with the bereaved?"

"I know," I said. "It just happened."

She allowed herself another sigh, then reached for her DayTimer, all brisk efficiency, even though she was still wearing black leggings and a T-shirt from Wally's Wings advising "We Choke Our Own Chickens." "Okay," she said. "Did you call the clinic?"

"No, actually," I said. "I'm going to keep it."

Her eyes got very wide. "What? How? Why?"

"Why not? I'm twenty-eight years old, I've got enough money . . ."

Samantha was shaking her head. "You're going to ruin your life."

"I know my life's going to change. . . ."

"No. You didn't hear me. You're going to ruin your life."

I set down my coffee cup. "What do you mean?"

"Cannie . . ." She looked at me, her eyes beseeching. "A single mother . . . I mean, it's hard enough to meet decent men as it is . . . do you know what this is going to do to your social life?"

Truthfully, I hadn't given it much thought. Now that I'd gotten my mind around losing Bruce irrevocably, I hadn't even started thinking about who I might wind up with, or whether there'd ever be anybody else.

"Not just your social life," Samantha continued, "your whole life. Have you thought about how this is going to change everything?"

"Of course I have," I said.

"No more vacations," said Samantha.

"Oh, come on . . . people take babies on vacations!"

"Are you going to have money for that? I mean, I'm assuming you'll work . . ."

"Yeah. Part-time. That's what I'd figured. At least at first."

"So your income will go down, and you'll still be spending money on child care for when you are at work. That's going to have a major impact on your standard of living, Cannie. Major impact."

Well, it was true. No more three-day weekends in Miami just because USAir had a cheap flight and I felt like I needed some sun. No more weeks in Killington in a rented condo, where I'd ski all day and Bruce, a nonskiier, would smoke dope in the Jacuzzi and wait for my return. No more $200 pairs of leather boots that I absolutely had to have, no more $100 dinners, no more $80 afternoons at the spa where I'd pay some nineteen-year-old to scrub my feet and tweeze my eyebrows.

"Well, people's lives change," I said. "Things happen that you don't plan for. People get sick . . . or lose their jobs . . ."

"But those are things they don't have any control over," Samantha pointed out. "Whereas this is a situation you can control."

"I've made up my mind," I said quietly. Samantha was undeterred.

"Think about bringing a child into the world with no father," she said.

"I know," I told her, holding up my hand before she could say anything else. "I've thought about this. I know it's not ideal. It's not what I'd want, if I could choose. . . ."

"But you can choose," said Samantha. "Think about everything you're going to have to manage by yourself. How every single responsibility is going to be on your shoulders. Are you really ready for that? And is it fair to have a baby if you're not?"

"But think of all the other women who do it!"

"What, like welfare mothers? Teenage girls?"

"Sure! Them! There's lots of women who have babies, and the babies' fathers aren't around, and they're managing."

"Cannie," said Samantha, "that's no kind of life. Living hand-to-mouth . . ."

"I've got some money," I said, sounding sullen even to my own ears.

Samantha took a sip of coffee. "Is this about Bruce? About holding on to Bruce?"

I looked down at my clasped hands, at the wadded-up napkin between them. "No," I said. "I mean, I guess it involves that . . . somewhat by default . . . but it's not like I set out to get pregnant so I could get my hooks back in him."

Samantha raised her eyebrows. "Not even subconsciously?"

I shuddered. "God, I hope my subconscious isn't as unenlightened as that!"

"Enlightenment has nothing to do with it. Maybe, deep down, some part of you was hoping . . . or is hoping . . . that once Bruce finds out, he'll come back to you."

"I'm not going to tell him," I said.

"How can you not tell him?" she demanded.

"Why should I?" I shot back. "He's moved on, he's found some-body else, he doesn't want to be involved with me, or my life, so why should I tell him? I don't need his money, and I don't want whatever scraps of attention he'd feel obligated to throw me. . . ."

"But what about the baby? Doesn't the baby deserve to have a father in its life?"

"Come on, Samantha. This is Bruce we're talking about. Big, dopey Bruce? Bruce with the ponytail and the 'Legalize It' bumper sticker . . ."

"He's a good guy, Cannie. He'd probably be a really good father."

I bit my lip. This part hurt to admit or even to think about, but it was probably the truth. Bruce had been a camp counselor for years. Kids loved him, ponytail or not, dopiness or not, dope or not. Every time I'd seen him with his cousins or his former campers they were always vying with each other to sit next to him at dinner, or play bas-ketball with him, or have him help them with their homework. Even when our relationship was at its worst, I never doubted that he'd be a wonderful father.

Samantha was shaking her head. "I don't know, Cannie. I just don't know." She gave me a long, sober look. "He's going to find out, you know."

"How? We don't know any of the same people anymore . . . he lives so far away . . ."

"Oh, he'll find out. I've seen enough soap operas to guarantee you that. You'll run into him somewhere . . . he'll hear something about you . . . he'll find out. He will."

I shrugged, trying to look brave. "So he finds out I'm pregnant. It doesn't mean I have to tell him that it's his. Let him think I was sleep-ing around on him." Even though I felt struck through with grief at the thought that Bruce would ever have cause to think that. "Let him think I went to a sperm bank. The point is, he doesn't have to know." I looked at Samantha. "And you don't have to tell him."

"Cannie, don't you think he's got a right to know? He's going to be a father. . . ."

"No, he's not. . . ."

"Well, there's going to be a child born that's his. What if he wants to be a father? What if he sues you for custody?"

"Okay, I saw that Sally Jessy, too. . . ."

"I'm serious," said Samantha. "He could do that, you know."

"Oh, please." I shrugged, trying to look less worried than I was. "Bruce can barely keep track of his rolling papers. What would he want with a baby?"

Samantha shrugged. "I don't know. Maybe nothing. Or maybe he'd think that a child needs . . . you know . . . a male role model."

"So I'll let it hang around Tanya," I joked. Samantha wasn't laughing. She looked so upset I felt like offering her a hug, until I realized I'd sound just like Tanya at her most Anonymous. "It's going to be okay," I said, keeping my voice light, and convincing.

Samantha looked at me. "I hope so," she said quietly. "I really do."

"You're what?" asked Betsy, my editor. To her credit, she recovered a lot faster than Samantha did.

"Pregnant," I repeated. I was getting a little tired of playing this particular cut on the soundtrack of my life. "With child. Knocked up. Bun in the oven . . ."

"Oh. Okay. Oh, my. Um. . . ." Betsy peered at me from behind her thick glasses. "Congratulations?" she offered tentatively.

"Thanks," I said.

"Is there, um, going to be a wedding?" she asked.

"Not in the forseeable future, no," I said briskly. "Will that be a problem?"

"Oh, no, no! Of course not! I mean, of course, the paper would never discriminate, or anything. . . ."

I was suddenly very, very tired. "I know," I said. "And I know it's going to be weird for people . . ."

"The less explaining you do, the better," said Betsy. We were in the conference room with the door closed and the shades pulled, which meant I could only see my colleagues from the knees down. I recognized Frank the copy-editor's beat-up loafers slowing as they made their way to the mailroom, followed closely by Tanisha the photo clerk's stack-heeled Mary Janes, moving at a ridiculously snail-like pace. I was sure, if I had the full-body view, their heads would all be swiveling toward me, trying to figure out why Betsy and I were in here, whether I was in some kind of trouble, and what the trouble was. I was sure that once they'd made the obligatory stop at their mailboxes, they'd make a sharp right to the desk of Alice, longtime departmental secretary and depository of all things juicy and scandalous. Heck, if someone else were in here with Betsy right now, I'd be doing the exact same thing. It's the downside of working with people who poke and pry and investigate for a living. You don't wind up with much of a private life.

"If I were you I wouldn't say a word," Betsy said. She was in her forties, a short, quick-witted woman with a shock of white-blond hair who'd lived through sexism, corporate takeovers, budget cutbacks, and half a dozen different editors in chief, all men, and all with their own unique visions of what the *Examiner* should do. She was a survivor, and my mentor at the paper, and I trusted her to give me good advice.

"Well, eventually I'm going to have to say something. . . ."

"Eventually," she said. "But for now I would say nothing." She looked at me, not unkindly. "It's hard, you know," she said.

"I know," I said.

"Will you have any . . . help?"

"If you mean, is Bruce going to ride in on a white horse and marry me, probably not. But my mother and Tanya will help out . . . and maybe my sister, too."

Betsy had come prepared. She pulled a copy of the union contract out of her briefcase, then a notebook and a calculator. "Let's see what we can do for you."

What she came up with sounded more than fair—six weeks of paid leave after the birth, and if I wanted, six more weeks of unpaid leave after that. Then I'd have to work three days a week to keep my health benefits, but Betsy said she'd be amenable to having me work one of the days from home, as long as I was reachable. She tapped out my new salary-to-be on a calculator. Oof. Worse than I thought it would be . . . but still livable. At least, that's what I hoped. How much would day care cost? And baby clothes . . . and furniture . . . and food. I saw my carefully maintained nest egg—the one I'd built up, figuring I'd need it someday to pay for a wedding, or maybe a house—dwindling down to nothing before my eyes.

"We'll work it out," Betsy told me. "Don't worry." She gathered up her papers and sighed. "At least, try not to worry more than you absolutely have to. And let me know if I can help."

"Eight weeks," said my gynecologist, in her melodious clipped British voice. "Or perhaps nine."

"Eight," I said faintly. It's hard to be emphatic when you're flat on your back, with your feet up in stirrups and your legs spread.

Gita Patel—at least, that was the name on the tag clipped on to her lab coat—set her instruments down and slid around on her wheeled stool to face me, as I struggled into a sitting position. She was about my age, I guessed, with shiny black hair pulled into a low bun at the nape of her neck. She wasn't the one I usually saw in this HMO-run hidey-hole of a doctors' office, located one level below the street on Delancey, but she had the first available appointment, and, thanks to my mother's ceaseless chorus of "Have you seen a doctor yet," I decided not to wait. So far, I thought, it was working out. Dr. Patel had gentle hands, and a pleasant way about her.

"You are feeling well?" she asked.

"Fine. Just a little tired. Well, very tired, actually."

"No nausea?" Wow. I even loved the way she said "nausea."

"Not for the last few days."

"Very well, then. Let us discuss your plans." She tilted her head ever so slightly toward the waiting room. I admired the discretion of the gesture even as I shook my head.

"No. It's just me."

"Very well," she said again, and handed me some glossy brochures. My HMO's name was emblazoned at the top. "Little Sprouts" read the title. Ugh. "Helping our members as they begin one of life's most exciting journeys!" Double ugh.

"Now then. I will see you monthly for the next five months, then every two weeks for your eighth month, and then weekly until it is time to deliver." She flipped some pages on the calendar. "I am giving you a due date of June 15 . . . understanding, of course, that babies come when they please."

I left with my purse rattling with bottles of vitamins and folic acid, my head spinning with lists of things I couldn't eat and things I'd have to buy and calls I'd have to make. Forms to fill out, birthing classes to register for, a fact sheet on episiotomies that I didn't even want to look at in my current state of mind. It was December, and the weather had finally gotten cold. A brisk wind kicked dried-up leaves into the corners as I walked, my thin jacket wrapped tight around me. I could smell snow in the air. I was tired down to my bones, and my head was spinning, but I had one more stop left.

Fat Class was just getting out when I arrived. I found my classmates, and Dr. K., exiting the Weight and Eating Disorders offices, chatting happily, bundled up in sweaters and winter coats that looked as if they were being worn for the first time that year.

"Cannie!" Dr. K. waved and walked over. He was wearing khakis, a denim shirt, and a tie. No white lab coat, for once. "How have you been?"

"Oh, okay," I told him. "I'm sorry I missed class. I meant to stop by earlier. . . ."

"Why don't we step into my office," said Dr. K.

We did. He sat behind his desk, I took the chair opposite, not realizing until I'd sat down that I wasn't just tired, I was completely exhausted.

"It's good to see you," he said again, looking at me expectantly.

I took a deep breath. Get through this, I told myself. Get through this, and you'll be able to go home and go to sleep.

"I'm going to, um . . . stay pregnant. So I have to drop out of the program," I told him. He nodded, as if this was what he'd been waiting to hear.

"I'll make arrangements for the department to send you a check," he said. "And we'll be starting new studies next fall, if you're still interested."

"I don't think I'm going to have a lot of free time," I said.

He nodded. "Well, we'll miss you in class. You really bring a certain something."

"Oh, you're just saying that. . . ."

"No, I'm not. That imitation of the female fat cell you did two weeks ago . . . you really should think about stand-up."

I sighed. "Stand-up's hard. And I've got . . . a lot of things to think about right now."

Dr. K. reached for a notebook and a pen. "You know, I actually think we might have some kind of nutrition workshop for expectant mothers," he said, clearing books and papers away, locating his telephone directory. "I mean, since you've paid already, you might as well get something . . . Or, of course, if you just want a refund, we can definitely do that. . . ."

He was being so nice. Why was he being so nice to me? "No, that's okay. I just wanted to say that I had to drop out, and that I'm sorry. . . ."

I took a deep breath, looking at him looking at me from across the desk, his eyes so kind. And then I was crying again. What was it about this room, and this poor man, that every time I sat across from him I wound up in tears?

He handed me the Kleenex. "Are you all right?"

"I'm fine. I'm fine. I'll be okay. . . . I'm sorry. . . ."

And then I was crying so hard that I couldn't speak. "I'm sorry," I said again. "I think this is one of the first-trimester things, where everything makes you cry." I patted my purse. "I've got a list in here somewhere . . . things you're supposed to take, things you're supposed to feel . . ."

He was reaching over me, pulling a white lab coat off the coat rack.

"Stand up," he said. I stood up, and he draped the coat over my shoulders. "I want to show you something," he said. "Come with me."

He led me into an elevator, then down a hall, through a door marked "Staff Only" and "Keep Out," through another door marked "Emergency Only! Alarm Will Sound!" But the alarm didn't sound as he pushed open the door. And suddenly we were outside, on the roof, with the city spilled out beneath our feet.

I could see City Hall. I was practically at eye level with the statue of Billy Penn on top. There was the PECO building, studded with glistening lights . . . the twin towers of Liberty Place, shining silver . . . tiny cars, inching down infinitesimal streets. The rows of Christmas lights and neon wreaths marching down Market Street to the waterfront. The Blue Cross RiverRink, with tiny skaters moving in slow circles. And then the Delaware River, and Camden. New Jersey. Bruce. It all looked very far away.

"What do you think?" Dr. K. asked. I think I must have jumped when he finally started talking. For a moment, I'd forgotten him . . . forgotten everything. I was so wrapped up in the view.

"I've never seen the city like this," I told him. "It's amazing."

He leaned against the door and smiled. "I think you'd have to pay a pretty hefty rent in one of the Rittenhouse Square high-rises to get a view like this," he said.

I turned toward the river again, feeling the wind blow cool on my face. The air tasted delicious. All day long—or at least since Dr. Patel had given me the pamphlet listing Common Complaints of the First Trimester—I'd noticed that I could smell everything, and that most of what I could smell made me feel sick. Car exhaust . . . a whiff of dog crap from a trash can . . . gasoline . . . even things I normally enjoyed, like the scent of coffee wafting out of the Starbucks on South Street came to me at ten times their normal intensity. But up here the air smelled like nothing, as if it had been specially filtered for me. Well, me and whatever rich balcony-lined-penthouse-dwellers were lucky enough to have regular access.

"Feeling better?" he asked.

"Yeah."

Dr. K. sat down, cross-legged, and motioned for me to join him. Being careful not to sit on his lab coat, I did.

"Do you feel like talking about it?"

I shot him a quick sideways glance. "Do you want to listen?"

He looked embarrassed. "I don't mean to pry. . . . I know it's not any of my business. . . ."

"Oh, no, no, it's not that. I just don't want to bore you." I sighed. "It's the oldest story in the world, I guess. Girl meets boy, girl loves boy, girl dumps boy for reasons she still doesn't really understand, boy's father dies, girl goes to try to comfort him, girl winds up pregnant and alone."

"Ah," he said carefully.

I rolled my eyes at him. "What, you thought it was someone else?"

He didn't say anything, but in reflected light from the streets below, I thought he looked abashed. I hunkered around until I was sitting facing him.

"No, c'mon, really. You thought I found another guy that fast? Please," I snorted. "Give me a little less credit."

"I guess I thought . . . well, I guess I really hadn't thought about it."

"Well, believe me, it takes a lot longer than a few months before I meet someone who likes me, and who wants to see me naked, and before I get comfortable enough to actually let them." I looked at him sideways again. What if he thought I was flirting? "Just FYI," I added lamely.

"I'll file that away," he said somberly. He seemed so serious, I had to laugh.

"Tell me something . . . how do people know when you're kidding? Because you always sort of sound the same way."

"Which is what? Nerdy?" He spent a long time saying the word *nerdy*, which, of course, made him sound . . . a little nerdy.

"Not exactly. Just serious all the time."

"Well, I'm not." He actually appeared to be offended. "I actually have a very fine sense of humor."

"Which I'm just somehow managing to completely miss," I teased.

"Well, considering that the handful of times we've spoken, you've been having some extravagant life crisis, I haven't been at my funniest."

Now he was definitely sounding offended.

"Point taken," I said. "I'm sure you're very funny."

He looked at me suspiciously, thick brows furrowed. "How do you know?"

"Because you said you were. People who are funny know that they're funny. People who aren't funny will say, 'My friends say I've got a great sense of humor.' Or 'My mother says I've got a great sense of humor.' That's when you know you're in trouble."

"Oh," he said. "So if you were to describe yourself, you'd say you were funny?"

"No," I sighed, looking out at the night sky. "At this point, I'd say that I was fucked."

We sat in silence for a minute. I watched the skaters turn.

"Have you thought about what you're going to do?" he finally asked. "You don't have to talk about it if you don't want to. . . ."

"No, no. I don't mind. I've only figured a few things out, really. I know that I'm going to keep it, even though it's probably not the most practical thing, and I know I'm going to cut back my schedule when the baby comes. Oh, and I know I'm going to maybe start looking for a new place to live, and see if my sister will be my birth coach."

Laid out like that, like a losing hand of cards fanned out on a table, it didn't seem like much.

"What about Bruce?" he asked.

"See, that's the part I haven't figured out yet," I said. "We haven't talked in weeks, and he's seeing someone else."

"Seriously?"

"Seriously enough for him to tell me about it. And to write about it."

The doctor considered this. "Well, that might not mean anything. He might just be trying to get back at you . . . or make you jealous."

"Yeah, well, it's working."

"But a baby . . . well, that changes everything."

"Oh, you read that pamphlet, too?" I hugged my knees into my chest. "After we broke up . . . after his father died, when I felt so miserable, and I wanted him back, and all, my friends kept telling me,

'You broke up with him, and you must have done it for a reason.' And I know that it's true. I think I did know, deep down, that we probably weren't supposed to be, you know, together for the rest of our lives. And it was probably my fault. . . . I mean, I've got this whole theory about my father, and my parents, and why I don't trust love. So I think that maybe even if he was perfect . . . or, you know, not perfect, but a good fit for me . . . that maybe I wouldn't have been able to see it, or I'd have tried to talk myself out of it. Or whatever."

"Or maybe he wasn't the right guy for you. They always taught us in medical school, when you hear hoofbeats . . ."

". . . don't look for zebras."

He grinned at me. "They said that in your medical school, too?"

I shook my head. "No. My father was a doctor. He used to say that all the time. But I don't know. I think this might actually be a zebra. I mean, I know how much I miss him, and how awful I felt when I found out he had somebody else, and I think that I blew it . . . that he was actually supposed to have been the love of my life, my husband." I swallowed hard, my throat closing around that word. "But now . . ."

"Now what?"

"I miss him all the time." I shook my head, disgusted at my own mopiness. "It's like being haunted or something. And I don't have the luxury of being haunted right now. I need to think about myself, and the baby, and how I'm going to plan and get ready."

I looked at him. He'd taken off his glasses and was watching me intently.

"Can I ask you a question?" I said.

He nodded.

"I need a male perspective. Do you have any children?"

"None that I . . . I mean, no."

"See, you were going to say, 'None that I know of,' right?"

"I was, but I stopped myself," he said. "Well, almost."

"Okay. So no kids. How would you feel, if you'd been with someone, and then you weren't with her, and she came to you and said, 'Guess what? I'm having your baby!' Would you even want to know?"

"If it were me," he said, thoughtfully. "Well, yes. If it were me I'd want to know. I would want to be a part of the child's life."

"Even if you weren't with the mother anymore?"

"I think children deserve to have two parents involved with them, and who they become, even if the parents live apart. It's hard enough to grow up in this world. I think kids need all the help they can get."

That, of course, was not what I'd wanted to hear. What I'd wanted to hear was, *You can do this, Cannie! You can go it alone!* If I was going to be apart from Bruce—and there was ample evidence that I would—I wanted every assurance that a single parent was a fine and proper thing to be. "So you think I should tell him."

"If it were me," he said thoughtfully, "I would want to be told. And no matter what you do, or what he wants, you're still the one who ultimately gets to decide. What's the worst thing that can happen?"

"He and his mother sue me for custody and try to get the baby for themselves?"

"Wasn't that on Oprah?" he asked.

"Sally Jessy," I said. It was getting colder. I pulled the lab coat tight around me.

"Do you know who you remind me of?" he asked.

"If you say Janeane Garofalo, I'll jump," I warned him. I was forever getting Janeane Garofalo.

"No," he said.

"Your mother?" I asked.

"Not my mother."

"That guy on Jerry Springer who was so fat that the paramedics had to cut a hole in his house to get him out of it?"

He was smiling and trying not to. "Be serious!" he scolded me.

"Okay. Who?"

"My sister."

"Oh." I thought about it for a minute. "Is she . . ." And then I didn't know what to say. Is she fat? Is she funny? Did she get knocked up by her ex-boyfriend?

"She looked a little bit like you," he said. He reached out, his fingertip almost brushing my face. "She had cheeks like yours, and a smile like yours."

I asked the first thing I could think of. "Was she older or younger?"

"She was older," he said, keeping his eyes straight ahead. "She died when I was nine."

"Oh."

"A lot of my patients when they meet me want to know why I got into this line of medicine. I mean, there's no obvious connection. I'm not a woman, I've never had a weight problem . . ."

"Oh, sure. Rub it in," I said. "So your sister was . . . heavy?"

"No, not really. But it made her crazy." I could only see the side of his face as he smiled. "She was always on these diets . . . hard-boiled eggs one week, watermelon the next."

"Did she, um, have an eating disorder?"

"No. Just neuroses about food. She was in a car accident . . . that's how she died. I remember my parents were at the hospital, and nobody would tell me for the longest time what was going on. Finally my aunt, my mother's sister, came to my room and said that Katie was in Heaven, and that I shouldn't be sad, because Heaven was a wonderful place where you got to do all your favorite things. I used to think that heaven was a place full of Devil Dogs and ice cream and bacon and waffles . . . all the things that Katie wanted to eat, and would never let herself have." He turned to face me. "Sounds silly, doesn't it?"

"No. No, actually, that's kind of how I imagine Heaven myself." I felt terrible as soon as I'd said it. What if he thought that I was making fun of his poor dead sister?

"You're Jewish, right?"

"Yeah."

"I am, too. I mean, I'm half. My father was. But we weren't raised as anything." He looked at me curiously. "Do Jews believe in heaven?"

"No . . . not technically." I groped for my Hebrew school lessons. "The deal is, you die, and then it's just . . . like sleep, I think. There's no real idea of an afterlife. Just sleep. And then the Messiah comes, and everyone gets to live again."

"Live in the bodies they had when they were alive?"

"I don't know. I personally intend to lobby for Heidi Klum's."

He laughed a little bit. "Would you . . ." He turned to face me. "You're cold."

I had been shivering a little bit. "No, I'm okay."

"I'm sorry," he said.

"No, it's fine! I actually like hearing about other people's, um, lives." I had almost said "problems," but I'd caught myself just in time. "This was good."

But he was already on his feet and three long-legged strides ahead of me, almost to the door. "We should get you inside," he was muttering. He held the door open. I stepped into the stairwell, but didn't move, so that when he shut the door he was standing very close to me.

"You were going to ask me something," I said. "Tell me what it was."

Now it was his turn to look flustered. "I . . . um . . . the, uh, pregnancy nutrition classes, I think. I was going to ask you if you'd consider signing up for one of those."

I knew that wasn't it. And I even had a faint inkling that it might have been something completely different. But I didn't say anything. Maybe he'd just had a brief, fleeting thought of asking me . . . something . . . because he'd been talking about his sister and he felt vulnerable. Or maybe he felt sorry for me. Or maybe I was completely wrong. After the whole Steve debacle, and now with Bruce, I wasn't feeling very trusting of my instincts.

"What time do they meet?" I asked.

"I'll check," he said, and I followed him down the stairs.

THIRTEEN

After much deliberation and about ten rough drafts, I composed, and mailed, Bruce a letter.

> *Bruce,*
>
> *There is no way to sugar-coat this, so I'll just tell you straight out that I am pregnant. It happened the last time we were together, and I've decided to keep the baby. I am due on June 15.*
>
> *This is my decision, and I made it carefully. I wanted to let you know because I want it to be your choice to what extent you are involved in this child's life.*
>
> *I am not telling you what to do, or asking for anything. I have made my choices, and you will have to make yours. If you want to spend time with the baby, I will try my best to make that work out. If you don't, I understand.*
>
> *I'm sorry that this happened. I know it isn't what you need in your life right now. But I decided that this was something you deserved to know about, so you can make the choices you think are right. The only thing I ask is that you please not write about this. I don't care if you talk about me, but there's someone else at stake now.*
>
>

Take care,
Cannie
>

I wrote my telephone number, in case he'd forgotten, and mailed it off.

There was so much more that I wanted to write, like that I still pined for him. That I still had daydreams of him coming back to me, of us living together: me and Bruce, and the baby. That I was scared a lot of the time, and furious at him some of the time I wasn't scared, or so racked with love and longing and yearning that I was afraid to let myself even think his name, for fear of what I'd do, and that as much as I filled my days with things to do, with plans and lists, with painting the second bedroom a shade of yellow called Lemonade Stand and assembling the dresser I bought from Ikea, too often, I'd still find myself thinking about how much I wanted him back.

But I wrote none of those things.

I remembered when I was a senior in high school and how hard it was to wait for colleges to send out their letters and say whether they were taking you or leaving you. Trust me, waiting for the father of your unborn child to get back to you as to whether or not he's willing to be involved with you, or the baby, is a lot worse. For three days I checked my phone at home obsessively. For a week I drove home at lunchtime to check my mailbox, cursing myself for not having sent the letter via registered mail, so I'd at least know that he'd received it.

There was nothing. Day after day of nothing. I couldn't believe that he would be this cold. That he would turn his back on me—on us—so completely. But it was, it seemed, the truth of the matter. And so I gave up . . . or tried to make myself give up.

"It's like this," I addressed my belly. It was Sunday morning, two days before Christmas. I'd gone on a bike ride (I was cleared to ride until my sixth month, barring complications), put together a mobile made of brightly painted dog bones that I'd made, myself, from a book called *Simple Crafts for Kids,* and was rewarding myself with a long hot soak.

"I think that babies should have two parents. I believe that. Ideally, I'd have a father for you. But I don't. See, your, um, biological father is a really good guy, but he wasn't the right guy for me, and he's kind of having a rough time right now, and also he's seeing somebody else. . . ." This was probably more than my unborn child needed to know, but whatever. "So I'm sorry. But this is the way it is. And I'm going to try to raise you as best I can, and we'll make the best of it, and hopefully you won't wind up resenting me horribly and getting tattoos and piercings and stuff to externalize your pain, or whatever kids will be doing in about fifteen years, because I'm sorry, and I'm going to make this work."

I limped through the holidays. I made fudge and cookies for my friends instead of buying them stuff, and I tucked cash (less than I'd meted out the year before) into cards for my siblings. I drove home for my mother's annual holiday open house, where dozens of her friends, plus all of the members of the Switch Hitters and much of the roster of A League of Their Own fussed over me, offering good wishes, advice, the names of doctors and day-care centers, and a slightly used copy of *Heather Has Two Mommies* (the latter from a misguided short-stop named Dot, whom Tanya immediately took aside to inform that I wasn't a lesbian, just a dumped breeder). I stayed in the kitchen as much as I could, grating potatoes, frying latkes, listening to Lucy regale me with the story of how she and one of her girlfriends had convinced a guy they'd met at a bar to take them back to his place, then opened all the Christmas presents under his tree after he'd passed out.

"That wasn't very nice," I scolded.

"He wasn't very nice," said Lucy. "What was he doing, taking the two of us home while his wife was out of town?"

I agreed that she had a point.

"They're all dogs," Lucy continued loftily. "Of course, I don't have to tell you that." She gulped the clear liquid from her glass. Her eyes were sparkling. "I've got to get my holiday swerve on," she announced.

"Take your swerve outside," I urged her, and added another dollop of raw potato goo to the frying pan. I thought that Lucy was probably secretly delighted that it was me, not her, who'd wound up in this predicament. From Lucy, an unplanned pregnancy would have been almost expected. From me, it was shocking.

My mother poked her head into the kitchen. "Cannie? You're staying over, right?"

I nodded. Ever since Thanksgiving, I'd fallen into the pattern of spending at least one night every weekend at my mother's house. She cooked dinner, I ignored Tanya, and the next morning my mother and I would swim, slowly, side by side, before I'd stock up on groceries and whatever new-baby necessities her friends had donated, and head back to town.

My mother came to the stove and poked my latkes with a spatula. "I think the oil's too hot," she offered. I shooed her away, but she only retreated as far as the sink.

"Still nothing from Bruce?" she asked. I nodded once. "I can't believe it," she said. "It's not like him. . . ."

"Whatever," I said shortly. In truth, I thought my mother was right. This wasn't like the Bruce that I had known, and I was just as hurt and bewildered as anyone. "Evidently I've managed to bring out the worst in him."

My mother gave me a kind smile. Then she reached past me and turned the heat down. "Don't burn them," she said, and returned to the party, leaving me with a pan of half-cooked potato pancakes and all of my questions. *Doesn't he care?* I wondered. *Doesn't he care at all?*

All through the winter, I tried to keep busy. I made the rounds of my friends' parties, sipping spiced cider instead of eggnog or champagne. I went out to dinner with Andy, and went for walks with Samantha, and to birthing classes with Lucy, who'd agreed to be my birth coach "as long as I don't have to look at your coochie!" As it was, we'd almost got thrown out the first day. Lucy started hollering "Push! Push!" when all the teacher wanted to do was talk about how to pick a hospital. Ever since then, the mommy-and-daddy couples had given us a wide berth.

Dr. K. had become my new e-mail buddy. He'd write to me at the office once or twice a week, asking how I was doing, giving me updates on my friends from Fat Class. I learned that Esther had purchased a treadmill and lost forty pounds, and that Bonnie had found a boyfriend. "Let me know how you're doing," he would always write, but I never felt like telling him much, mostly because I couldn't figure out what box to put him in. Was he a doctor? A friend? I wasn't sure, so I kept things topical, telling him the latest pieces of newsroom gossip, and what I was working on, and how I was feeling.

Slowly, I started telling the people close to me what was going on, starting small, then moving in ever-widening circles—good friends, then not-so-good friends, a handful of coworkers, a half-dozen relatives. I did it in person, wherever possible, by e-mail, in Maxi's case.

"As it turns out," I began, "I am pregnant." I gave her the condensed, PG-13 version of the events. "Remember when I told you about the last time I saw Bruce, at the shiva call?" I wrote. "We had an encounter while I was at his house. That's how this happened."

Maxi's reply was instantaneous, two sentences long, and all in capital letters. "WHAT ARE YOU GOING TO DO?" she wrote. "DO YOU NEED HELP?"

I told her my plans, such as they were: have the baby, work part-time. "This isn't what I would have planned," I wrote, "but I'm trying to make the best of the situation."

"Are you happy?" Maxi e-mailed back. "Are you scared? What can I can do?"

"I'm sort of happy. I'm excited," I wrote. "I know my life will change, and I'm trying not to be too scared about how." I thought about her last question and told her that what I needed was for her to keep being my friend, to keep in touch. "Think good thoughts for me," I told her. "And hope that this all works out, somehow."

Some days, though, that didn't seem likely. Like the day I went to the drugstore to stock up on appealing pregnancy necessities including Metamucil and Preparation H and came across Bruce's latest "Good in Bed" column, a treatise on public displays of affection entitled "Oh, Oh, the Mistletoe."

"If it were up to me," he'd written, "I would hold E's hand forever. She has the most wonderful hands, tiny and slender and soft, so different from my own."

Or from mine, I'd thought sadly, staring at my own thick-fingered hands with their ragged nails and picked-over cuticles.

If it were up to me I'd kiss her on every street corner and hug her in front of live studio audiences. I don't need seasonal excuses, or random bits of greenery dangling from the ceiling as incentive. She's completely adorable, and I'm not shy about showing it.

It makes me unusual, I know. Lots of men would rather hold your shopping bags, your backpack, possibly even your purse, than hold your hand in public. They're okay kissing their mothers and sisters—years of conditioning have worn down their resistance—but they're not so great about kissing you when their friends can see. How to get your man over his hump? Don't stop trying. Brush his fingertips with yours while sharing popcorn at a movie, and hold his hand as you walk out the door. Kiss him playfully at first, and hope he'll reciprocate with more passion, eventually. Try tucking that mistletoe in your brassiere, or, better yet, that lacy garter belt you've never worn. . . .

Lacy garter belts. Oh, that hurt. I remembered how, for my birthday and for Valentine's Day, Bruce would show up with boxes full of plus-size lingerie. I refused to wear it. I told him I was shy. In truth, the stuff made me feel stupid. Regular-sized women are ashamed of their butts and bellies. How could I feel good about pouring myself into the teddies and thongs he'd somehow procured? It felt like a bad joke, like a mean trick, like a *Candid Camera* stunt, where as soon as I showed that I was dumb or gullible enough to think I'd look good in this stuff, Allen Funt and his crew would pop out of the closet, bright lights flashing and wide-angle lenses at the ready. No matter how Bruce tried to reassure me ("I wouldn't have bought it for you if I didn't want to see you wear it!") I just couldn't bring myself to even try.

I shut the magazine. I paid for my things, shoved them in my pocket, and trudged home. Even though I knew he'd written his December article months before he'd gotten my letter—if he'd gotten it at all—it still felt like a slap in my face.

Because I had no party plans (not to mention no one to kiss), I volunteered to work on New Year's Eve. I got out at 11:30, came home, bundled Nifkin in the little fleece sweatshirt he despised (in my heart, I was sure he thought it made him look silly . . . and in my heart, I had to admit he was right), and packed myself into my winter coat. I stuck a bottle of nonalcoholic grape juice into my pocket, and we walked down to Penns Landing and sat on the pier, watching the fireworks go off, as drunken teenagers and South Philly denizens screamed and groped and kissed each other all around us. It was 1999.

Then I went home and did something I probably should have done much earlier. I got a big cardboard box and started packing away all the things I had around that Bruce had given me, or the things that reminded me of him.

In went the half-melted globe candle that we'd lit together in Vermont, and in whose flickering sweetly scented light we'd made love. In went all of the letters he'd sent me, each folded neatly into its envelope. In went all the lingerie he'd bought me that I'd never worn, and the vibrator and the edible body oils and the pink fur-lined handcuffs, which were probably things I shouldn't have lying around anyhow, what with a baby on the way. In went a hand-painted glass bead necklace his mother had given me for my last birthday, and the leather bag from the birthday before that. After some deliberation I decided to hang on to the portable phone, which had managed to lose its association with Bruce . . . after all, he wasn't calling. And I kept the CDs from Ani DiFranco and Mary Chapin Carpenter, Liz Phair and Susan Werner. That was my music, not his.

I bundled it all up, taped the box, and walked it down to my storage area in the basement, thinking I could maybe sell some of the nicer stuff if it came to that, but for now, it would be out of sight, and maybe that would be enough. Or at least, a start. Then I came back upstairs and cracked open my new journal, a beautiful book with a marbled paper cover and thick lined pages. "1999," I wrote, as Nifkin hopped up and sat on the arm of the couch beside me, looking over my words with what I hoped was approval. "For my baby, whom I already love very much."

* * *

It rained through most of January and snowed almost constantly through February, turning everything white for about ten minutes, until the belching city busses and the guys hawking snot on the streets turned it gray again. I tried not to look at the red foil hearts in drugstore windows. I tried to avoid *Moxie*'s red-on-pink Valentine's Day issue to which Bruce, the cover informed me, had contributed a piece entitled "Make Him Wanna Holler: 10 Sizzling New Sex Tricks for the Erotic Adventuress." One ill-fated day I'd flipped to his column while waiting in line at the convenience store, and had been assaulted with a full-page picture of Bruce wearing lipstick-red silk boxer shorts and an expression of abject bliss as he lolled on bed with a woman I sincerely hoped was a *Moxie* model as opposed to the mysterious E. I'd thrust the magazine back into the rack as if I'd been burned, and decided, after in-person consultations with Samantha ("Just let it go, Cannie,") and e-mailed debate with Maxi ("I could have him killed, if you like,") that the best thing to do would be to just ignore it, and be grateful that February was a short month.

Time passed. I developed a new and interesting set of stretch marks, and started craving the imported Stilton cheese that they sold at Chef's Market on South Street for $16 a pound. A few times, I came close to slipping a wedge in my coat pocket and slinking out of the store, but I never did. Too embarrassing, I reasoned, having to explain my cheese habit to whoever would have to come and bail me out after my inevitable arrest.

I actually felt pretty good, which was how most of the relentlessly upbeat pregnancy books I'd read described the second trimester. "You'll feel radiant and alive, full of energy!" read one, beneath a picture of a radiant and alive-looking pregnant woman walking through a field of wildflowers, hand in hand with her devoted-looking spouse. It wasn't that great, what with the occasional overwhelming sleepiness, and my breasts aching so badly some days that I had fantasies of their falling off and rolling away, and the night I ate an entire jar of mango chutney while watching a rerun of *Total Request Live* on MTV. Occasionally—well, maybe more than occasionally—I'd feel so sorry for myself that I'd cry. All of my books had pictures of pregnant ladies with their husbands (or, in the more progressive ones, partners)—someone to rub cocoa butter on your belly and fetch you ice cream and pickles, to cheer you up and urge you on and help you pick out a name. I had nobody, I would mope, conveniently ignoring Samantha and Lucy and my mother's twice-a-night phone calls and weekly sleepovers. Nobody to dispatch to the convenience store in the middle of the night, nobody who'd stay up late debating the relative merits of Alice and Abigail, nobody to tell me not to be scared of the pain and not to be scared of the future and tell me that everything would be fine.

And it felt like things were getting more complicated instead of less. For one thing, people at work were starting to notice. Nobody'd come right out and asked me yet, but I was getting the occasional stare, or hearing the occasional hushed silence when I came into the ladies' room or the cafeteria.

One afternoon Gabby cornered me by my desk. She'd been gunning for me since the fall, when my forty-inch Sunday feature on Maxi ran on the front of the Entertainment section, much to the delight of my editors. They were thrilled that we were the only East Coast paper to have secured an interview with Maxi, and even more thrilled that we had the only story in which she spoke so candidly about her life, her goals, and her failed romances. I got a nice little bonus, plus a glowing note from the editor in chief, which I kept prominently posted on my cubicle wall.

All of this was good for me, but it meant that Gabby was in an increasingly foul mood—especially since I'd gotten the nod to write about the Grammys, while she'd been consigned to prewriting Andy Rooney's obituary, lest his health take a turn for the worse.

"Are you gaining weight?" she demanded.

I tried to turn the question around, the way *Redbook*'s latest "10 Tips for Handling Difficult People" advised, aware that people's ears had pricked up. "What an unusual question," I said through numb lips. "Why are you interested?"

Gabby just stared at me, refusing to bite. "You look different," she said.

"So what I'm hearing you say," I began, per *Redbook*'s instructions, "is that it's important to you that I always look the same?"

She gave me a long, angry stare, then huffed off. That suited me fine. I hadn't decided what to tell people, or when to tell them, and for the time being I was wearing oversized shirts and leggings and hoping they'd chalk my weight gain (six pounds in the first trimester, another four since Thanksgiving) up to holiday overindulgence.

And it was true that I was eating well. I had brunch every weekend with my mother, and dinner once or twice a week with my friends, who seemed to be operating on some kind of top-secret schedule. Every night, somebody would call, and offer to come over for coffee or meet for a bagel in the morning. Every day at work, Andy would ask if I wanted to share leftovers from whichever fabulous place he'd dined at the night before, or Betsy would take me to the tiny, excellent Vietnamese luncheonette two blocks over. It was as if they were afraid to leave me alone. And I didn't even care that I was their sympathy case or their project. I sucked it all up, trying to distract myself from missing Bruce and obsessing over the things I didn't have (security, stability, a father for my unborn child, maternity clothes that didn't make me look like a small ski slope). I went to work and to see Dr. Patel, and made arrangements for all of the classes and courses a new mother-to-be could want: Breast Feeding Basics, Infant CPR, Parenting 101.

My mother put the word out, and her friends all emptied their attics and their daughters' attics. By February, I had a changing table and a Diaper Genie, a crib and a car seat and a stroller that looked more luxurious (and more complicated) than my little car. I had boxes full of footie pajamas and little knitted caps, drooled-upon copies of *Pat the Bunny* and *Goodnight Moon,* and silver rattles with teeth marks. I had bottles and nipples and a nipple sterilizer. Josh gave me a $50 gift certificate to EBaby. Lucy gave me a packet of hand-drawn coupons agreeing to baby-sit once a week when the baby came ("as long as I don't have to change number two diapers!").

I gradually turned my second bedroom from a study into a nursery. I took the time I used to devote to the composition of screenplays and short stories and query letters to *GQ* and the *New Yorker*—to bettering myself, basically—and started a series of do-it-yourself home improvement projects. And, regretfully, I started spending money. I bought a sea-green rug that went nicely with the Lemonade Stand walls, and a Beatrix Potter calendar. I trash-picked a scarred rocking chair, had the seat recaned, and spray-painted it white. I started filling the bookshelf with every children's book I could scrounge from the book editor, plus books from home, and books I bought secondhand. Every night, I read to my belly . . . just to get into the habit, plus, because I'd read somewhere that babies are sensitive to the sound of their mother's voices.

And every night, I'd dance. I'd pull the forever-dusty metal blinds down, light a few candles, kick off my shoes, crank up the music, and move. It wasn't always a happy dance. Sometimes I'd blast early Ani DiFranco and think about Bruce in spite of myself as Ani roared out "You were never very kind, and you let me way down every time . . ." But I'd try to dance happily, for the baby's sake, if not my own.

Was I lonely? Like crazy. Living without Bruce, and without the possibility of his eventual return, of even ever seeing him again, and knowing that he'd totally rejected me and our baby, felt like trying to live without oxygen. Some days I'd get angry and be furious at him for letting me stay with him so long . . . or for not coming back when I wanted him to. But I'd try to put the anger in a box, the way I'd put away his gifts, and keep moving forward.

Sometimes I couldn't help but wonder whether it was only pride that was keeping us apart, and whether it wouldn't be smarter for me to call him, or better yet, go see him, and just beg until he took me back. I wondered if maybe, despite everything he'd said, he did still love me. I'd wonder if he ever had. I'd try to make myself stop thinking these things, but my mind would churn and churn, until I'd have to get up and do something. I polished my silverware, child-proofed the cabinets, cleaned my closets. My apartment, for the first time ever, was neat, even beautiful. Too bad my head was such a mess.

FOURTEEN

"The thing that every single woman has to remember," said Samantha, as we walked along Kelly Drive on a brisk, breezy early morning in April, "is that if he wants to talk to you, he'll call. You just have to keep repeating that. 'If he wants to talk to me, he'll call.'"

"I know," I said mournfully, resting my hands on the ledge of my belly, which I could do since I had officially started showing the week before. Being pregnant was strange, but it did have a few benefits. Instead of having people—okay, men—look at me with disinterest and/or scorn because I was a Larger Woman, people looked at me with kindness, now that I was visibly pregnant. It was a nice change. It even made me feel a little bit better about my own appearance—at least for a few minutes every now and then.

"I'm actually doing better," I said. "I'm trying to be proactive. Whenever I think of him, I force myself to think of something about the baby. Something that I have to do, or buy, or sign up for."

"Sounds good. How's work going?"

"Not bad," I said. Truthfully, work was a little weird. It was strange to be doing things that would have had me so excited . . . or nervous . . . or upset . . . or happy, just a year ago, and have them feel like they barely mattered. A personal audience with Craig Kilborn over lunch in New York, to discuss his show's new direction? Eh. A nasty spat with Gabby over which one of us was going to get to write the postmortem on *The Nanny*? Whatever. Even my coworkers' increasing and not-so-surreptitious glances, from my belly (burgeoning) to my third left finger (bare) didn't seem to matter. Nobody'd worked up the nerve to actually ask me anything yet, but I was ready for the questions when they came. Yes, I'd say, I'm pregnant. No, I'd tell them, not with the father any more. That, I thought, would maybe hold them . . . provided I could change the subject to their own pregnancy/birth/child-rearing stories.

"So what's on the agenda for today?" Samantha asked.

"More shopping."

Samantha groaned.

"I'm sorry, but I really just need a few more things from the maternity place. . . ."

I knew that Samantha was trying to be a good sport about shopping with me. But I could tell it wasn't easy. For one thing, unlike any other woman I'd ever known, she loathed shopping. For another, I was pretty sure she was getting sick of everybody assuming we were lesbian lovers.

While Samantha was extolling the virtues of mail-order catalogues and Internet shopping, a guy jogged by us. Tall, lean, shorts and a ratty-looking sweatshirt advertising some college or another. Typical jogger on Kelly Drive on a Saturday. Except that this one stopped.

"Hi, Cannie!"

I stopped and squinted, my hands resting protectively on my belly. Samantha stopped, too, gaping. The Mystery Jogger pulled off his baseball cap. It was Dr. K..

"Hey!" I said, smiling. Wow. Outside of that horrible fluorescent-lit building, outside of his white lab coat and glasses, he was kind of cute . . . for an older guy.

"Introduce me to your friend," Samantha practically purred.

"This is Dr. Krushelevansky." I pronounced it slowly and correctly, I think, because he smiled at me. "From the University of Philadelphia program I was doing."

"Peter. Please," he said.

Handshakes all around, as two rollerbladers almost crashed into us. "We'd better get moving," I said.

"I'll walk with you," he said, "if that's okay. I need to cool down. . . ."

"Oh, sure! Absolutely!" said Samantha. She gave me a short but significant look, which I took to mean, "Is he single, and is he Jewish, and if he is, what possible excuse could you have for not mentioning him to me?"

I gave her a brief shrug and raised eyebrows, which I was certain she would understand as, "I have no idea if he's single, and aren't you supposed to be taken?" Samantha seemed to have broken her bad-luck streak of third-date lunacy and was still with her yoga instructor. Many of our non-Bruce discussions revolved around whether he was too Zen to consider marrying.

Meanwhile, completely oblivious to our eyebrow-encrypted messages, Dr. K. was introducing himself to Nifkin, who'd been the object of several discussions during Fat Class.

"So you're the famous little guy," he said, as Nifkin demonstrated his vertical leap, bouncing higher and higher each time. "He should be in the circus," Dr. K. told me, rubbing Nifkin vigorously behind his ears as Nifkin preened.

"Yeah, well, a few more pounds and I'll go, too. They still hire fat ladies, right?"

Samantha glared at me.

"You look very healthy," Dr. K. pronounced. "How's work?"

"Good, actually."

"I read your piece on The View," he said. "I thought you were absolutely right . . . it does remind me of Thunderdome."

"Five girls enter, one girl leaves," I intoned. He laughed. Samantha looked at him, looked at me, did a few quick equations in her head, and grabbed Nifkin's leash.

"Well!" she said cheerfully. "Thanks for walking with me, Cannie, but I really need to get going." Nifkin whined as she started dragging him toward where she'd parked her car. "I'll see you later," she said. "Have fun shopping!"

"You're going shopping?" asked Dr. K.

"Yeah, I need some . . ." What I actually needed was new underwear, as my Jockey For Her briefs were no longer covering the waterfront, but I was damned if I was going to tell him that. "Groceries," I said weakly. "I was heading over to Fresh Fields. . . ."

"Would you mind if I came?" he asked. "I actually need to pick up a few things. I could drive you," he offered.

I squinted up at him in the sunshine. "Tell you what. If you can meet me in an hour, we can get breakfast, then shop," I said.

He told me that he'd lived in Philadelphia for seven years but had never been to the Morning Glory Diner, my absolute favorite breakfast spot. If there's one thing I love, it's introducing people to my food finds. I walked home, took a quick shower, pulled on a variation on my standard outfit (black velvet leggings, giant tunic top, lace-up Chuck Taylor low-tops in a subtle shade of periwinkle that I'd bought for $10), then met him at the diner, where, blessedly, there wasn't even a line—a total fluke on a weekend. I was feeling pretty good about things as we slid into a booth. He looked nice, too—he'd showered, I thought, and changed into khakis and a button-down plaid shirt.

"I'll bet it's weird for you, going out to eat with people," I said. "They probably feel very self-conscious about ordering what they really want."

"Yes," he said, "I have noticed some of that."

"Well, you're in for a treat," I told him, and flagged down a dreadlocked waitress in a halter top with a tattoo that snaked across her exposed belly. "I'll have the neighborhood fritatta with provolone cheese and roasted peppers, a side of turkey bacon, a biscuit, and would it be possible to get potatoes and grits instead of just one or the other?"

"Sure thing," she said, and wiggled her pen toward the doctor.

"I'll have what she's having," he said

"Good boy," she said, and twitched off toward the kitchen.

"It's brunch," I said, by way of explanation. He shrugged a little bit. "You're eating for two," he said. "How have . . . things . . . been?"

"If by 'things' you mean my situation, it's going fine. I'm actually feeling a lot better now. Still kind of tired, but that's about it. No more dizzy, no more barfing, no being so exhausted that I fall asleep on the toilet at work. . . ."

He was laughing. "Did that happen?"

"Just once," I said. "But it's better now. Even though I realize that my life has turned into one of the lesser songs in the Madonna catalogue, I limp along." I passed a hand dramatically across my brow. "Eh-lone."

He squinted at me. "Was that supposed to be Garbo?"

"Hey, don't hassle the pregnant lady."

"That was the worst Garbo imitation I have ever heard."

"Yeah, well, I do it better if I've been drinking." I sighed. "God, do I miss tequila."

"Tell me about it," said our waitress, as she deposited our heaping plates on the table. We tucked in.

"This is really good," he said between mouthfuls.

"Isn't it?" I said. "They make the best biscuits. The secret is lard."

He looked at me. "Homer Simpson."

"Very good."

"You do Homer much better than you do Garbo."

"Yeah. Wonder what that says about me?" I changed the topic before he could answer. "Do you ever think about cheese?"

"Constantly," he said. "I'm tormented, really. I lie awake at night, just thinking . . . about cheese."

"No, seriously," I said, and poked at my fritatta. "Like, who invented cheese? Who said, 'Hmm, I'll bet this milk would taste really delicious if I let it sit until a rind of mold grew around it?' Cheese had to be a mistake."

"I never thought about that," he said. "But I have wondered about Cheez Whiz."

"Philadelphia's official food!"

"Have you ever looked at the list of ingredients for Cheez Whiz?" he asked. "It's frightening."

"You want to talk about frightening, I'll show you the fact sheet on episiotomies my doctor gave me," I said. He swallowed hard. "Okay, not while you're eating," I amended. "But seriously, what is it with the medical profession? Are you guys trying to scare the human race into celibacy?"

"Are you nervous about labor?" he asked.

"Hell, yes. I'm trying to find a hospital that'll give me that Twilight Sleep thing." I looked at him hopefully "You can prescribe stuff, right? Maybe you could slip me a little something before the fun starts."

He was laughing at me. He really did have a very nice smile. His full lips were bracketed by deep laugh lines. I wondered idly how old he really was. Younger than I'd thought at first, but still probably fifteen years older than me. No wedding ring, but that didn't mean anything. Plenty of guys didn't wear them. "You'll do fine," he said.

He gave me the rest of his biscuit and didn't even flinch when I ordered hot chocolate, and insisted that brunch was his treat, and that, in fact, he really owed me for introducing him to the diner.

"Where to next?" he said.

"Oh, you can just drop me off at Fresh Fields. . . ."

"No, no. I'm at your disposal."

I looked at him sideways. "Cherry Hill Mall?" I proposed, barely hoping. The Cherry Hill Mall was over the river in New Jersey. It had a Macy's, two maternity shops, and a M.A.C. counter. And my own car was on a weekend loan to Lucy, who'd gotten a job as a singing flower delivery girl on her heartfelt assurances that yes, she could provide her own transportation, while waiting for her spokesmodel career to take off.

"Let's go."

His car was a sleek silver, some kind of heavy sedan-type thing. The doors closed with an authoritative chunk, and the motor sounded much more ostentatious than my modest little Honda ever had. The inside was immaculate, and the passenger seat looked . . . under-utilized. Like the upholstery was still untouched by human buttocks.

We got on 676 and drove over the Ben Franklin Bridge, over the Delaware River, which sparkled in the sun. The trees were covered with the faintest green fuzz, and the sun was shining off the water. My legs were pleasantly tired from the walk, and I was pleasantly full from the food, and, as I rested my hands on my belly, I felt something that it took me a minute to identify. Happy, I finally figured out. I felt happy.

I warned him in the parking lot. "When we go into the stores, they might think that you're the, uh . . ."

"Father?"

"Um, yeah."

He smiled at me. "How do you want me to handle it?"

"Hmm." I actually hadn't thought that part through, so enraptured was I with being in this big, steady, powerful-sounding car, looking at springtime through the window and feeling happy. "Let's just play it by ear."

And it wasn't bad, really. At the department store, where I purchased a Pregnancy Packables kit (long dress, short dress, skirt, pants, tunic top, all in some engineered, indestructable, stretchy and guaranteed stainproof black fabric), the aisles were crowded and we were pretty much ignored. Same deal at Toys "R" Us, where I bought blocks, and at Target, where I had coupons for buy-one-get-one baby wipes and Pampers. I could feel the girl at Baby Gap looking from him to me and back again as she rang up my stuff, but she didn't say anything. Not like the woman at Pea in the Pod, who'd told me and Samantha last week that she thought we were both very brave, or the woman the week before at Ma Jolie who'd assured me that "Daddy will just love!" the leggings I was trying on.

Dr. K. was very nice to shop with. Quiet, but willing to offer an opinion when asked, and to carry all my packages and even hold my backpack. He bought me lunch at the food court (sounds tacky, but the Cherry Hill food court is actually quite nice), and didn't seem perturbed at my four bathroom stops. During the last one he even ducked into a pet store and bought a rawhide bone at least as long as Nifkin was. "So he won't feel neglected," he explained.

"He's going to love you," I said. "That's going to be a first. Nifkin usually works as my first line of elimination with . . ." Dates, I was thinking. But this wasn't a date. "New friends," I finally said.

"Did he like Bruce?"

I smiled, remembering how the two of them had existed in a fragile détente that felt like it would rupture into full-scale war if I'd only turn my back long enough. Bruce had grudgingly agreed to let Nifkin sleep in my bed, like he was used to, and Nifkin had reluctantly conceded that Bruce had a right to exist at all, but there'd been any number of raised voices, insults, and chewed shoes, belts, and wallets in between. "I think Bruce was always about two minutes from dropkicking Nifkin somewhere far away. He wasn't exactly a dog person. And Nifkin isn't easy." I leaned back in the new-smelling car seat, feeling the late-afternoon sunshine streaming through the sunroof, warming my head.

He smiled at me. "Tired?"

"A little bit," I said, and yawned. "I'll take a nap when I'm home."

I gave him directions to my street, and he nodded approvingly as he turned onto it. "Pretty," he said. I looked at it, trying to see what he saw: the just-budding trees arcing over the sidewalks, the pots full of flowers in front of the brick townhouses.

"Yeah," I said. "I was lucky to find it."

When he offered to help me carry things upstairs, I wasn't about to turn him down, even though I was thinking, as I toted diapers up to the third floor, what my place would look like to him. He probably lived in the suburbs, in one of those grand old houses on the Main Line with, like, sixteen bedrooms and a stream running through the front yard, not to mention kitchens that did not boast Harvest Gold appliances, circa 1978. At least my place was relatively neat, I told myself. I opened the door, and Nifkin catapulted himself into the hall, hurtling into the air. Dr. K. laughed.

"Hey, Nif," he said, as Nifkin sniffed the rawhide bone through three plastic bags and went into a seizure of joy. I dumped my bags on the couch and hurried to the bathroom as Nifkin tried to burrow into the bag. "Make yourself comfortable!" I yelled.

When I emerged he was standing in the second bedroom where

I'd been trying to piece together a crib from one of my mother's friends. The crib had come to me unassembled, without directions, and possibly missing important pieces.

"This doesn't look right," he murmured. "Mind if I give it a go?"

"Sure," I said, startled and pleased. "If you actually get it together I'll owe you big-time."

He smiled at me. "You don't owe me anything," he said. "I had fun today."

Before I could think of what to make of that, the telephone rang. I excused myself, grabbed the portable, and flopped gracelessly onto the bed.

"Cannie!" bellowed a familiar British accent. "Where've you been?"

"Shopping," I said. Well, this was a surprise, too. Maxi and I had been corresponding through e-mail and the occasional telephone call at work. She talked about her travails on the set of *PlugIn,* the futuristic sci-fi thriller in which she was costarring with a hot young actor who required not one, not two, but three full-time "sobriety managers" to keep him in line, and e-mailed me investment tips and articles about how I should set up a fund for the baby. I'd write her back, talking about work, mostly, and my friends . . . and my plans, such as they were. She didn't ask many questions about the impending arrival—good manners, maybe, I thought.

"I have news," she said. "Big. Huge. The hugest. Your screenplay," she began breathlessly. I swallowed hard. Of all the things we'd talked about in the months since our meeting in New York, my screenplay hadn't come up once. I'd assumed that Maxi had forgotten about it, hadn't read it, or had read it and decided that it was so terrible it would be better for our friendship if she never spoke of it again.

"I loved it," she said. "The character of Josie is such a perfect heroine. She's smart, and stubborn, and funny, and sad and I would be honored to play her."

"Sure," I said, still not understanding what was happening. "Start eating."

"I fell in love with the part," Maxi continued, ignoring me, her words tumbling over each other, faster and faster. "And you know I've got this deal with this studio, Intermission . . . I showed the script to my agent. She showed it to them. They loved it, too . . . especially the idea of me as Josie. And so, with your permission . . . Intermission would like to buy your screenplay, for me to star in. Of course, you'd be involved the whole way through . . . I think that both of us should be able to sign off on any changes to the script, and, of course, on major casting decisions, not to mention who's going to be the director . . ."

But I wasn't listening. I lay back on the bed, my heart suddenly feeling fierce and strange and enormously excited. Making my movie, I thought to myself, a huge smile spreading over my face. Oh, my God, it's finally happening, somebody's going to make my movie! I'm a writer now, I've really made it, maybe I'll be rich!

And that's when I felt it. Like a wave cresting inside of me. Like I myself was in the ocean, being gently tumbled, over and over, by a wave. I dropped the phone and put both hands on my belly, and then came a gentle, almost inquisitive series of tap, tap, taps. Moving. My baby was moving.

"You're here," I whispered. "You're really here?"

"Cannie?" said Maxi. "Are you okay?"

"I'm fine!" I said, and started laughing. "I'm perfect."

Suzie Lightning

PART FOUR

Sugar Lightning

FIFTEEN

I'd never had any luck with Hollywood. To me, the movie industry was like a guy you lusted after from across the high school cafeteria—so good-looking, so perfect, that you just knew he'd never notice you, and that if you asked him to sign your yearbook at graduation he'd stare at you blankly and grope for your name.

It was an unrequited love affair, but I'd never stopped trying. Every few months I'd importune agents with query letters asking if they were interested in my screenplay. I'd wind up with nothing to show for my troubles but a fistful of preprinted rejection postcards ("Dear aspiring writer," they'd begin), or occasionally a semipersonal letter advising me that they were no longer handling unsolicited material, unknown writers, novice writers, unproduced writers, or whatever they were using as the derogatory term du jour.

Once, the year before I met Bruce, an agent did meet with me. The thing I remember most about our appointment was that during the entire ten minutes or so he granted me, he never once said my name, or removed his sunglasses.

"I read your screenplay," he said, pushing it across the table toward me with his fingertips, as if it was too distasteful to risk full palm contact. "It was sweet."

"Sweet's not good?" I asked—the obvious conclusion one would draw from the expression on his face.

"Sweet is fine, for children's books, or TGI Fridays on ABC. For movies, well . . . we'd prefer it if your heroine blew something up." He tapped his pen across the title page. *Star Struck,* it read. Except he'd doodled little fangs coming out of the S's, so they looked like snakes. "Also, I've got to tell you, there's only one fat actress in Hollywood. . . ."

"That's not true!" I exploded, abandoning my strategy of smiling politely and keeping quiet, not sure what I was more offended by—his use of the term "fat actress," or the notion that there was only one of them.

"One bankable fat actress," he amended. "And really, the reason is, nobody wants to see movies about fat people. Movies are about escape!"

Well. "So . . . what do I do now?" I asked.

He shook his head, already pushing himself back from the table, already reaching for his cell phone and his valet parking stub. "I just can't see getting involved with this project," he had told me. "I'm sorry." Another Los Angeles lie.

"We're anthropologists," I murmured to Nifkin, and to the baby, as we flew over what might have been Nebraska. I hadn't brought any of my baby books with me, but I figured, if I couldn't read, I could at least explain. "So just think of it as an adventure. And we'll be home before you know it. Back in Philadelphia, where we're appreciated."

We—me, and Nifkin, and my belly, which had gotten to the point where I pretty much regarded it as a separate thing—were in first class. Actually, as best I could tell, we were first class. Maxi'd sent a limo to my apartment, which had whisked me the nine miles to the airport, where a block of four seats had been reserved in my name and nobody so much as batted an eyelash at the presence of a small and terrified rat terrier in a green plastic carrying case. We were currently airborne, at our cruising altitude of 30,000 feet, and I had my feet up on a pillow, a blanket spread over my legs, a chilled glass of Evian with a twist of lime in my hand, and a glossy assortment of fresh magazines fanned out on the seat beside me, beneath which Nifkin reposed. *Cosmo, Glamour, Mademoiselle, Mirabella, Moxie.* The brand-new April issue of *Moxie.*

I picked it up, hearing my heart start thumping, feeling the sick feeling in the pit of my belly, and the familiar cold sweat at the back of my neck.

I put it down. Why should I upset myself? I was happy, I was successful, I was flying to Hollywood first class to collect a bigger paycheck than he'd ever see in his life, not to mention the mandatory hobnobbing with superstars.

I picked it up. Put it down. Picked it up again.

"Shit," I muttered, to no one in particular, and flipped to "Good in Bed."

"The Things She Left Behind," I read.

"I don't love her anymore," the article began.

When I wake up in the morning, she isn't the first thing that I think of—whether she's here, and when I'll see her, and when I can hold her again. I wake up and think about work, my new girlfriend, or, more likely, my family, and my mother, and how she'll manage in the wake of my father's recent death.

I can hear our song on the radio and not instantly punch up another station. I can see her byline and not feel like someone large and angry is stomping on top of my heart. I can go to the Tick Tock Diner, where we used to go for late-night omelets and fries, where we'd sit side by side in a booth and grin dopey grins at each other. I can sit in that same booth without remembering how she'd start off sitting across from me and then, halfway through, get up and plop herself down beside me. "I'm just being sociable," she'd say, every time. "I'm paying you a visit. Hello, neighbor!" she'd say, and kiss me, and kiss me until the waitress with the blond bouffant and the coffee pot in each hand would stop and shake her head.

I have reclaimed the Tick Tock. Once it was our place, now

it's my place again. It's right on my way home from work, and I like the spinach and feta omelet, and I can even order it sometimes without remembering how she'd bare her teeth at me in the parking lot, demanding to know whether she had spinach stuck between them.

It's the little things that get me, every time.

Last night I was sweeping—my new girlfriend was coming over, and I wanted things to look nice—and I found a single kibble of dog food, wedged in a crack between the tiles.

I returned the obvious stuff, of course, the clothes and the jewelry, and I tossed out the rest. Her letters are boxed up in my closet, her picture's banished to the basement. But how do you guard against a single kibble's worth of her dog's Purina Small Bites that's somehow survived, undetected, for months, only to surface in your dustpan and send you reeling? How do people survive this?

Everyone has history, my girlfriend says, trying to soothe me. Everyone has baggage, everyone carries parts of their past around. She's a kindergarten teacher, a student of sociology, a professional empath; she knows the right things to say. But it makes me furious to find C.'s cherry Chap Stick in my glove box, a single blue mitten in the pocket of my winter coat. Furious, too, over the things I can't find: my tie-dye tank top and the Cheesasaurus Rex T-shirt I got for sending in three box tops from Kraft Macaroni and Cheese, because I know she's got them and I'll never get them back.

I think that when relationships end there should be Thing Amnesty Day. Not right away, when you're both still raw and broken and aching and probably prone to ill-advised sex, but down the road, when you can still be civil, but before you've completed the process of turning your former beloved into just a memory.

Turning your former beloved into a memory, I thought sadly. So that's what he's doing. Except . . . well, turning a former lover into a memory is one thing, but turning a child into a minor distraction, into something you can't even be bothered with . . . well, that was something else. Something infuriating. Ill-advised sex, indeed! What about the consequences of his little slip-up!

> But for now, I hired a cleaning crew for my apartment. The floors, I told them, showing them the kibble I'd found, muttering dire predictions about bugs and mice and other assorted vermin. But really, I am haunted by memories.
>
> I don't love her anymore. But that doesn't mean it doesn't hurt.

Oof. I leaned back in the plush, double-wide leather-clad reclining seat and closed my eyes, feeling the most potent and horrible mixture of sadness and fury—and sudden, overwhelming hope—that for a minute I thought I'd throw up. He'd written this three months ago. That was how long magazines took to print things. Had he seen my letter? Did he know I was pregnant? And what was he feeling now?

"He still misses me," I murmured, with my hand on my belly. So did that mean there was hope? I thought for a minute that maybe I'd mail him his Cheesasaurus Rex T-shirt, as a sign . . . as a peace offering. Then I remembered that the last thing I'd mailed him was news that I was having his baby, and he hadn't even bothered to pick up the phone and ask me how I was.

"He doesn't love me anymore," I reminded myself. And I wondered how E. felt, reading this . . . E. the kindergarten teacher with her sweet talk of baggage and her small, soft hands. Did she wonder why he wrote about me, after all this time? Did she wonder why he still cared? *Did* he care, or was that just my wishful thinking? And if I called, what would he say?

I turned restlessly in my seat, flipping the pillow, then scrunching it against the window and leaning against it. I closed my eyes, and when I opened them, the captain was announcing our descent into beautiful Los Angeles, where the sun was shining and the winds were from the southwest and where it was a perfect 80 degrees.

* * *

I got off the plane with my pockets full of little gifts the flight girls had pressed upon me, packets of Mint Milanos and foil-wrapped chocolates and complimentary eye masks and washcloths and socks. I had Nifkin's carrier in one hand, my bag in the other. In the bag was a week's worth of underwear, my Pregnancy Packable kit, minus the long skirt and tunic, which I was wearing, and a few fistfuls of assorted hygiene products that I'd thrust in at the last minute. A nightgown, some sneakers, my telephone book, my journal, and a dog-eared copy of *Your Healthy Baby*.

"How long will you be?" my mother had asked the night before I'd left. The boxes and bags of what I'd bought at the mall were still strewn in the hallway and kitchen, like fallen bodies. But the crib, I'd noticed, was put together perfectly. Dr. K. must have done it while I was on the phone with Maxi.

"Just a weekend. Maybe a few days longer." I told her.

"You told this Maxi person about the baby, right?" she'd fretted.

"Yes, Mom, I told her."

"And you'll call, right?"

I rolled my eyes, told her yes, and walked Nifkin over to Samantha's, to give her the good news.

"Details!" she demanded, handing me a cup of tea and settling on her couch.

I told her what I knew: that I'd be selling my screenplay to the studio, that I'd need to find an agent, and that I'd be meeting some of the producers. I didn't mention that Maxi had urged me to find a place to stay for a while, in case I wanted to be in California for the inevitable revisions and rewrites.

"That is completely unbelievable!" Samantha said, and hugged me. "Cannie, it's just great!"

And it was great, I mused, as I trudged down the jetway with Nifkin's case banging against my leg. "Airport," I murmured to the baby. And there, at the gate, was April. I recognized her instantly from New York. Same knee-high black leather boots, only now her hair was drawn up into a ponytail at the top center of her head, and there was something strange happening between her nose and her chin. It took me a minute to figure out that she was smiling.

"Cannie!" she said, and waved and took my hand. "It's such a pleasure to finally meet you!" She raked her eyes over me in the way that I'd remembered, lingering just a beat or two too long on my stomach, but her smile was firmly in place by the time her eyes met mine. "A towering talent," she pronounced. "Loved the screenplay. Loved it, loved it. As soon as Maxi showed it to me, I told her two things. I said, Maxi, you are Josie Weiss, and I said, I cannot wait to meet the genius who created her."

I thought briefly about telling her that we had, in fact, already met, and it had been the single worst reporting experience of that month, possibly the entire year. I wondered if she'd hear me if I whispered "hypocrite" to the baby. But then I decided, why rock the boat? Maybe she genuinely didn't recognize me. I hadn't looked pregnant the last time she'd seen me, any more than she'd been smiling.

April bent to peer into the carrying case. "And you must be little Nifty!" she cooed. Nifkin started growling. April appeared not to notice. "What a beautiful dog," she said. I snorted back laughter, and Nifkin continued to growl so hard that his cage was vibrating. Nifkin has many fine qualities, but beauty is not among them.

"How was your flight?" April asked me, blinking rapidly and smiling still. I wondered if this was how she treated her famous clients. I wondered if I was a client already, if Maxi had gone ahead and signed a pact in blood, or whatever one did to acquire the services of someone like April.

"Fine. Very nice, really. I've never been in first class before."

April linked her arm through mine like we were grade-school chums. Her forearm fit neatly below my right breast. I tried to ignore it. "Get used to it," she advised me. "Your whole life's about to change. Just sit back and enjoy the ride!"

April deposited me in a suite in the Beverly Wilshire, explaining that the studio was putting me up there for the night. Even if it was for one night only, I felt like Julia Roberts in *Pretty Woman,* if they'd gone with the indie-alterna ending, where the prostitute winds up pregnant and alone, with only her little dog for comfort.

The suite might very well be the one where they filmed *Pretty Woman*. It was big, and bright, and deluxe in every way. The walls were covered in gold and cream striped wallpaper, the floors were lined with ultra-plush beige carpeting, and the bathroom was a study in marble shot through with veins of gold. The bathroom was also, I noted, the size of my living room back home, with a bathtub big enough to accommodate a vigorous game of water polo, if I'd been so inclined.

"Fancy schmancy," I noted for the baby, and opened a pair of French doors to find a bed that looked big as a tennis court, all done in crisp white sheets, topped with a fluffy pink and gold comforter. Everything was clean and new-smelling and so gorgeous I was almost afraid to touch it. There was also an elaborate bouquet waiting for me beside the bed. "Welcome!" read the card, from Maxi.

"Bouquet," I informed the baby. "Very expensive, probably." Nifkin had bounded out of his carrier and was busily making a sniffing tour of the suite. He glanced at me briefly, then rose up on his hind legs to dip his nose toward the toilet. Once that had passed muster, he scampered into the bedroom.

I got him settled on a pillow on the bed, and took a bath, and wrapped myself in the Wilshire robe. I called room service and ordered hot tea and strawberries and fresh pineapple, and liberated some Evian and a box of Choco Leibniz, king of all cookies, from the minibar, without even blanching at the $8 price tag, which was at least triple what the cookies would have cost in Philadelphia. Then I lay back on two of the six pillows that came with the bed and clapped my hands together, laughing. "I'm here!" I crowed, as Nifkin barked to keep me company. "I did it!"

Then I called every single person I could think of.

"If you eat at any of Wolfgang Puck's restaurants, get the duck pizza," counseled Andy, in full food-critic mode.

"Fax me anything before you sign it," urged Samantha, and proceeded to spout five minutes' worth of lawyer-ese before I calmed her down.

"Take notes!" said Betsy.

"Take pictures!" said my mother.

"You brought my head shots, right?" demanded Lucy.

I promised that I'd lobby for Lucy, take notes for future columns for Betsy and pictures for Mom, fax anything legal-looking to Samantha and eat duck pizza for Andy. Then I noticed the business card propped on one of the pillows, engraved with the words *Maxi Ryder.* Under her name was the single word *Garth,* a telephone number, and an address on Ventura Boulevard. "Be there at 7 o'clock. Drinks and amusements to follow," it said.

"Drinks and amusements," I murmured, and stretched out on the bed. I could smell the fresh flowers, and could hear the faint sound of cars buzzing from thirty-two floors below. Then I closed my eyes and didn't wake up until it was 6:30. I splashed water on my face, scrambled into my shoes, and hurried out the door.

Garth turned out to be *the* Garth, hairdresser to the stars, although at first I thought the cab had dropped me off at an art gallery. It was an easy mistake to make. Garth's salon lacked the typical trappings: the row of sinks, the stacks of thumbed-through magazines, the receptionist's desk. In fact, there didn't seem to be anyone at all inside the high-ceilinged room, decorated with a single chair, a single sink, and a single floor-to-ceiling antique mirror except . . . Garth.

I sat in the chair while the man who'd put the buttery chunks into Britney Spears's tresses, who'd given Hillary her highlights and Jennifer Lopez henna, lifted and replaced sections of my hair, touching and scrutinizing it with the cool detachment of a scientist, and tried to explain myself.

"See, you're not supposed to color your hair when you're pregnant," I began. "And I wasn't expecting to get pregnant, so I'd just had my highlights done, and they've been growing out for six months and I know it looks terrible . . ."

"Who did this to you?" Garth asked mildly.

"Um, the pregnancy or the highlights?"

He smiled at me in the mirror and picked up another piece of my hair. "These weren't done . . . here?" he asked delicately.

"Oh, no. In Philadelphia." Blank look from Garth. "In Pennsylvania."
Truth was, I'd gotten it done at the beauty school on Bainbridge Street,
and I thought they'd done a pretty good job, but from the look on his face
I could tell that Garth would not agree.

"Oh, dear," he breathed quietly. He took a comb, a little spritz-
bottle of water. "Do you have any strong feelings about, um . . ." I
could tell he was groping for the kindest word to describe what was
happening on top of my head.

"I have lots of strong feelings, but none about my hair," I told
him. "Do with me what you will."

It took him close to two hours: first cutting, then combing, then
snipping the ends, then rinsing my head in a garnet-red solution he
swore was completely natural, chemical free, derived from only the
purest organic vegetables and absolutely guaranteed not to harm my
unborn child.

"You're a screenwriter?" Garth said once I'd been rinsed. He was
holding my chin, tilting my head this way and that.

"Unproduced, so far."

"Things are going to happen for you. You've got that aura."

"Oh, that's probably just the soap from the hotel."

He leaned in close and started tweezing my eyebrows. "Don't tear
yourself down," he told me. He smelled of some wonderful cologne,
and, even inches from my face, his skin was flawless.

Once he'd shaped my brows to his satisfaction, he rinsed out my
hair, blew it dry, and spent about half an hour applying different creams
and powders to my face. "I don't wear much makeup," I protested.
"Chap Stick and mascara. That's pretty much it."

"Don't worry. This is going to be subtle."

I had my doubts. He'd already brushed three different shades of
shadow around my eyes, including one that looked practically violet.
But when he whipped the cape off me and twirled me to face the mirror, I felt sorry for even thinking about doubting him. My skin was
glowing. My cheeks were the color of a perfect, ripe apricot. My lips
were full, a warm wine color, curling with a faint hint of amusement
even though I wasn't aware that I was smiling. And I didn't notice the

eyeshadow, just my eyes, which seemed much bigger, much more compelling. I looked like myself, only more so . . . like the best, most happy version of myself.

And my hair . . .

"This is the best haircut I've ever had," I told him. I ran my fingers through it slowly. It had gone from a raggedy mouse-brown bob with a few haphazard highlights to a rich, shimmering tortoiseshell color, shot through with strands of gold and bronze and copper. He'd cut it short, the tendrils just brushing my cheeks, and let its natural wave remain in place, and he'd tucked it behind my ear on one side, giving me the look of a gamine. Sure, a pregnant gamine, but who was I to complain? "This may be the best haircut anyone's ever had."

The sound of applause came from the doorway. And there was Maxi, wearing a black slip dress with spaghetti straps and black sandals. She had diamond studs in her ears and a single diamond on a thin silver chain around her neck. The dress tied around her neck and left her back bare almost enough to display butt cleavage. I could see the tender buds of her shoulderblades, each marble-sized vertebra, the perfectly symmetrical sprinkling of freckles on her shoulders.

"Cannie! My God," she said, studying first my hair, and then my belly. "You're . . . wow."

"Did you think I was kidding?" I said, and laughed at her awed expression.

She knelt down in front of me. "Can I . . ."

"Sure," I said. She laid one hand flat on my belly, and, after a moment, the baby obligingly kicked.

"Ooh!" said Maxi, yanking her hand back as if she'd been burned.

"Don't worry. You won't hurt her. Or me."

"So it's a girl?" asked Garth.

"Nothing official. I just have a feeling," I said.

Maxi, meanwhile, was circling me as if I were a piece of property she was thinking about buying. "What does Bruce have to say about this?" she inquired.

I shook my head. "Nothing, as far as I know. I haven't heard from him."

Maxi stopped circling and stared at me, her eyes wide. "Nothing? Still?"

"Not kidding," I said.

"I could have him killed," Maxi offered. "Or even just beaten up. I could send, say, half a dozen angry rugby players with baseball bats to break his legs . . ."

"Or his bong," I suggested. "It'd probably hurt him worse."

Maxi grinned. "Do you feel okay? Are you hungry? Or sleepy? Do you feel like going out, because if you don't, that's no problem at all. . . ."

I grinned at her, and tossed my fabulous hair. "Of course I want to go out! I'm in Hollywood! I've got makeup on! Let's go!"

I offered Garth a credit card, but he shooed me away, telling me not to worry, it was all taken care of, and if I'd only promise to come back in six weeks to have my ends trimmed he'd consider that payment enough. I thanked him and thanked him until Maxi dragged me out the door. Her small silver car was pulled up to the curb. I got in carefully, aware of my shifting center of gravity . . . and aware that, next to Maxi, even with my fabulous new hair and gorgeous Garth-enhanced complexion, even in my semichic black matte tunic and skirt and not unhip black slides, I still felt like a dowdy dirigible. A gamine dirigible, at least, I thought, as Maxi zoomed across three lanes of honking cars and accelerated through a yellow light.

"I arranged for the doormen at the hotel to look in on Nifkin, in case we're out late," she shouted, as the warm night wind blew in our faces. "Also, I rented him a cabana."

"Wow. Lucky Nifkin."

It wasn't until two traffic lights later that I thought to ask where we were going. Maxi perked up instantly. "The Star Bar! It's one of my favorite places."

"Is it a party?"

"Oh, it's always a party there. Great sushi, too."

I sighed. I couldn't eat raw fish or drink alcohol. And even though I was excited to celebrate and see the stars, I knew it wouldn't be long before the thing I wanted most was the bed in that big gorgeous hotel suite. I never liked late nights or loud parties much before I was pregnant, and I found myself liking them even less since. I'd stay for a little while, I told myself, and then plead pregnant lady exhaustion and make a break for home.

Maxi gave me the rundown on who might be there, as well as any pertinent back-story of which a newcomer such as myself should be aware. The famous actor and actress, married for seven years, I learned, were faking it. "He's gay," Maxi murmured, "and she's been getting it on with her personal trainer for years."

"How cliché!" I whispered back. Maxi laughed and leaned in closer. The ingenue, star of last summer's second-biggest action picture, might offer me Ecstasy in the ladies' room ("at least, she offered it to me," said Maxi). The hip-hop princess who reportedly didn't make a move without her Baptist, Bible-carrying mother was "a real wild one," said Maxi. "Sleeps with boys, and girls, and both at the same time, while Maman's off leading revivals in Virginia." The fiftyish director just got out of the Betty Ford Clinic; the fortysomething leading man had been diagnosed as a sex addict during his last stint at Hazelden; and the much-gossiped-about art-house director wasn't actually a lesbian, although she was perfectly happy to feed the rumor mill. "Straight as an arrow," said Maxi, sounding disgusted. "I think she's even got a husband stashed in Michigan."

"The horror!" I said. Maxi giggled, grabbing my arm. The elevator doors slid open, and two gorgeous guys wearing white shorts and white dress shirts swung open ten-foot-high glass doors, revealing a bar that looked like it was suspended in the night sky. Windows wrapped around the length of the room. There were dozens of small white-cloth-covered tables for two and for four, covered with dozens of flickering votive candles. The walls were hung with gossamer ivory curtains that billowed gently in the night breeze. The bar was backlit with blue neon, and the bartender was a six-foot-tall woman in a midnight-blue cat-suit, dispensing martinis with her face as gorgeous and still as a carved African mask. Maxi gave my arm a final squeeze, whispered, "I'll be back in a jiff," and darted off to air-kiss people I'd only seen in movies. I leaned against one of the pillars and tried not to stare.

There was the hip-hop princess, with tiny braids cascading from the crown of her head almost to her waist. There were the long-married superstars, looking for all the world like a devoted couple, and the non-lesbian art-house director, in a starched tuxedo shirt and a red bow tie. Dozens of waiters and waitresses zipped around. They all wore white—white pants, white shorts, white tank tops, and absolutely pristine white sneakers. It made the place look like the world's most chic hospital, except the staff carried oversized martinis instead of bedpans, and everyone was beautiful. My hands itched for a pen and a notebook. I had no business being at a place like this, surrounded by people like these, unless I was taking notes for a future newspaper article in which I'd quite possibly be sarcastic. I didn't belong here just as myself.

I walked to the windows, which overlooked a lit swimming pool in which nobody was swimming. There was a tiki bar with the requisite thatched roof and torches, thronged with people—all young, all gorgeous, most of them pierced and tattooed and looking like they were on their way to shoot a music video. Beyond that, smog, and Calvin Klein billboards, and the glittering lights of the city.

And there, with his back to the room, with a glass in his hand, staring off into the night, was . . . oh, God, was it? Yes. Adrian Stadt. I could recognize him from the shape of his shoulders, the set of his hips. Lord knows I'd spent enough time mooning over his pictures. His hair was cut short, and the back of his neck glimmered in the dim room.

Adrian wasn't handsome in the classic rugged-leading-man mode, and he wasn't one of the latest crop of androgynous pretty boys, either. He was more boy-next-door—medium height, regular features, unremarkable brown hair, and standard-issue brown eyes. What made him special, appearance-wise, was his smile—the sweet, crooked grin that exposed an ever-so-slightly chipped front tooth (he always told interviewers that he'd done it falling out of his treehouse at age nine). And those regular brown eyes could convey a thousand variations on bafflement, bewilderment, befuddlement—in short, all of the *b* words necessary to playing the lead in a romantic comedy. Taken by themselves, the pieces were nothing special, but put them together and you had a bona fide Hollywood hottie. At least, that's what *Moxie* called him in the "Men We Crave!" issue.

I'd been thankfully immune to teenage crushes, had never papered my locker with pictures of New Edition or anything, but I had feelings for Adrian Stadt. Watching him on *Saturday Night!* as he cringed and whined his way through impressions of Kid Picked Last for Kickball Team or sang the faux-operatic "PTA Mother's Lament," I'd felt that if we'd known each other, we could have been friends . . . or more. Of course, judging from his popularity, millions of other women felt exactly the same way. But how many of them were standing in the Star Bar on a warm spring night in Los Angeles, with the object of their affection in front of them?

I shuffled back until I was leaning against a pillar, trying to hide so I could stare, uninterrupted, at Adrian Stadt's back and trying to decide whether I'd call Lucy or Samantha first with the news. Things were going fine until a gaggle of skinny girls on stilettos surged into the room and planted themselves in front of, behind, and all around me. I felt like an elephant who'd blundered into a herd of sleek, fast, gorgeous antelope, and I couldn't see an easy way to blunder my way back out.

"Hold this a sec?" the tallest, blondest, thinnest of the girls asked me, indicating her silvery pashmina shawl. I took the shawl, then stared at her, feeling my mouth gape open. It was Bettina Vance, lead singer of the chart-topping power punk band Screaming Ophelia— one of my late-night dancing favorites when I was in a bitter mood.

"I love your music," I blurted, as Bettina snatched a martini.

She looked at me, bleary-eyed, and sighed. "If I had a nickel for every fat girl who said that to me . . ."

I felt as shocked as if she'd thrown ice water in my face. All this makeup, my great haircut, new clothes, all of my success, and all the Bettina Vances of the world would see was another fat girl, sitting alone in her room, listening to rock stars sing about lives they couldn't even dream about, lives they would never know.

I felt the baby kick then, like a little fist rapping sternly at me from the inside, like a reminder. Suddenly, I thought, the hell with her. I thought, I'm someone, too.

"Why would you need donations? Aren't you rich already?" I inquired. A few of the gazelles tittered. Bettina rolled her eyes at me. I reached into my purse and, thankfully, felt my fingers close around what I needed. "Here's your nickel," I said sweetly. "Maybe you can start saving for your next nose job."

The titters turned to outright laughter. Bettina Vance was staring at me.

"Who are you?" she hissed.

A few answers occurred: A former fan? An angry fat girl? Your worst nightmare?

Instead, I went for the simple, understated, and, not coincidentally, true answer. "I'm a writer," I said softly, forcing myself not to retreat or look away.

Bettina glared at me for what felt like an unbelievably long time. Then she snatched her shawl out of my hands and stalked off, taking her gaggle of size zeros with her. I leaned back against the pillar, shaking, and ran one hand over my belly. "Bitch," I whispered to the baby. One of the men who'd been hanging at the edge of the crowd smiled at me, then walked away before his face could really register. In the instant it took me to figure out who he was, Maxi was back at my side.

"What was that all about?" she asked.

"Adrian Stadt," I managed.

"Didn't I tell you he was here?" asked Maxi impatiently. "Jesus, what's with Bettina?"

"Never mind Bettina," I burbled. "Adrian Stadt just smiled at me! Do you know him?"

"A little bit," she said. "Do you?"

I rolled my eyes. "Oh, yeah," I said. "He's in my bowling league back in Philadelphia."

Maxi looked puzzled. "Isn't he from New York?"

"Kidding," I told her. "Of course I don't know him! But I'm a major fan." I paused, debating whether to tell Maxi that Adrian Stadt had basically inspired my screenplay. Just as Josie Weiss was me, Avery Trace was Adrian, only with a different name, and without the annoying penchant for dating supermodels. Before I'd decided what to say, she connected the dots. "You know, he'd be a perfect Avery," she murmured. "We should talk to him."

She headed toward the window. I froze. She turned around.

"What's wrong?"

"I can't just walk up to him and start talking."

"Why not?"

"Because I'm . . ." I tried to think of a nice way to say, "in a completely different league than handsome, famous movie stars." I arrived at ". . . pregnant."

"I think," said Maxi, "that pregnant people are still allowed to converse with nonpregnant people."

I hung my head. "I'm shy."

"Oh, you are not shy. You're a reporter, for heaven's sake!"

She had a point. It was true that, in my working life, I could, and have, routinely just walked up to people far more powerful or influential or better-looking than me. But not Adrian Stadt. Not the guy I'd allowed myself a one-hundred-page daydream about. What if he didn't like me? Or what if, in person, I didn't like him? Wouldn't it be better to just preserve the fantasy?

Maxi shifted from foot to foot. "Cannie . . ."

"I'm better on the phone," I finally muttered. Maxi sighed, charmingly, the way she did everything. "Wait here," she said, and hurried to the bar. When she came back there was a cell phone in her hand.

"Oh, no," I said when I saw it. "I had bad luck with that phone."

"It's a different phone," said Maxi, squinting at the numbers she'd drawn on her hand with what looked like lipliner. "Smaller. Lighter. More expensive." The phone started ringing. She handed it to me. Across the room, in front of the room-length windows, Adrian Stadt flipped his own phone open. I could see his lips moving, reflected in the glass.

"Hello?"

"Don't jump," I said. It was the first thing I could think of. As I spoke, I moved so I was standing behind a pillar draped in white silk, hidden from his view, but in a spot where I could still see his reflection in the window. "Don't jump," I said again. "Nothing could be that bad."

He gave a short, rueful laugh. "You don't know," he said.

"Sure I do," I said, with the phone in a death grip in my suddenly sweaty hand. I couldn't believe this was happening. I was talking— flirting, even!—with Adrian Stadt. "You're young, you're handsome, you're talented . . ."

"Flatterer," he said. He had a wonderful voice, low and warm. I wondered why he always spoke in that weird whiny singsong in his movies, if he really sounded like this.

"But it's true! You are. And you're in this wonderful place, and it's a beautiful night. You can see the stars."

Another bitter burst of laughter. "Stars," he sneered. "Like I'd want to."

"Not those stars," I said. "Look out the window," I told him. I watched his eyes as he did what I said. "Look up." He tilted his head. "See that bright star, just off to your right?"

Adrian squinted. "I can't see anything. Pollution," he explained. He turned from the window, scanning the crowd. "Where are you?"

I ducked even farther behind my pillar. When I swallowed, I could hear my throat click.

"Or at least tell me who you are."

"A friend."

"Are you in this room?"

"Maybe."

His voice took on a faint, teasing edge. "Can I see you?"

"No. Not yet."

"Why not?"

"Because I'm shy," I said. "And wouldn't you like to get to know me better this way?"

He smiled. I could see his lips curving in the window. "How do I know you're real?" he asked.

"You don't," I said. "I could be a figment of your imagination."

He turned around swiftly, and for a second I felt his eyes on me. I dropped the phone, picked it up, clicked it off, and handed it back to Maxi, all in one motion that I would like to think was smooth, but probably wasn't.

Instantly, the phone started ringing. Maxi flipped it open. "Hello?"

I could hear Adrian's voice. "Figment? Figment, is that you?"

"Hold, please," Maxi said crisply, and handed the phone back to me. I slipped back behind my pillar.

"Star 69 is the bane of human existence in the nineties," I began. "Whatever happened to anonymity?"

"Anonymity," he repeated slowly, as if it was the first time he'd said the word.

"Just think," I continued, "of the generations of pubescent boys who are never going to be able to make hang-up calls to the girls they've got crushes on. Think of how they'll be stunted."

"You're funny," he said.

"It's a defense mechanism," I replied.

"So can I see you?"

I held the phone as tightly as I could and didn't answer.

"I'm going to keep calling until you let me see you."

"Why?" I asked.

"Because you sound very nice. Can't I buy you a drink?"

"I don't drink," I said.

"Don't you ever get thirsty?" he asked, and I laughed in spite of myself.

"Let me see you," he said.

I sighed, straightened my tunic, cast a quick glance around to make sure Bettina Vance was elsewhere, then walked up behind him and tapped him on his shoulder. "Hey," I said, hoping that he'd get the full impact of my hair and makeup before getting to my belly. "Hi."

He turned, slowly. In person, he was adorable. Taller than I'd imagined, and so cute, so sweet looking. And drunk. Very, very drunk.

He smiled at me. I picked up my phone. He grabbed my wrist. "No," he said, "face-to-face."

I turned the telephone off.

He was so handsome up close. On the screen he looked cute, not gorgeous, but in the flesh he was amazing, with beautiful brown eyes, and . . .

"You're pregnant," he blurted.

Okay, not precisely a news flash, but it was something.

"Yeah," I said. "I'm pregnant. I'm Cannie."

"Cannie," he repeated. "Where's your, um . . ." And he waved one arm in the air in a vague way that I took to mean "baby's father."

"I'm here by myself," I said, deciding to let it go at that. "Actually, I'm here with Maxi Ryder. "

"I'm here alone," he said, as if he hadn't heard me. "I'm always alone."

"Now, I know that isn't true," I said. "I happen to be aware that you are dating a German medical student named Inga."

"Greta," he murmured. "We broke up. You've got some memory."

I shrugged and tried to look modest. "I'm a fan," I said. I was trying to figure out whether it would be completely tacky to ask for his autograph, when Adrian grabbed my hand.

"I have an idea," he said. "Do you want to go outside?"

"Outside?" Did I want to go outside with Adrian Stadt? Did the Pope wear a big hat? I nodded so hard I was worried I'd give myself whiplash, and darted off into the halter-topped, miniskirted masses in search of Maxi. I located her at last in the crush by the bar. "Listen," I said, "I'm going outside with Adrian Stadt for a minute."

"Oh, you are, are you?" she said archly.

"It's not like that."

"Oh, no?"

"He seems kind of . . . lonely."

"Hmph. Well, remember, he is an actor." She thought about it. "Well, actually, a comedian who makes movies."

"We're just going for a walk," I said, feeling desperate not to upset or offend her, but even more desperate to get back to Adrian.

"Whatever," she said airily. She scribbled her number on a napkin and held out her hand for the cell phone. "Give me a call from wherever you are."

I handed her the phone, tucked the number into my purse, and rolled my eyes. "Oh, right. I'll be off seducing him. It'll be very romantic. We'll be snuggling on the couch, and I'll kiss him, and he'll tell me he adores me, and then my unborn child will kick him in the ribs."

Maxi stopped looking sulky.

"And then I'll film the whole thing, and sell the rights to Fox, and they'll turn it into a special. *World's Kinkiest Threesomes*."

Maxi laughed. "Okay. Just be careful."

I kissed her on the cheek and, unbelievably, found that Adrian Stadt was still waiting. I smiled at him, and he led me to the elevator, down and out the door, where we found ourselves standing in front of what looked like a highway. No benches, no grass, not even a lowly bus shelter, or a sidewalk to stroll on.

"Huh," I said.

Adrian, meanwhile, was looking even more tipsy than he had in the Star Bar. The fresh air didn't seem to be having the sobering effect I was hoping for. He grabbed at my hand, managing to get my wrist instead, and pulled me close to him . . . well, as close as my belly would allow.

"Kiss me," he said, and I laughed out loud at the absurdity of it. *Kiss me!* Like a line from a movie! I was looking over his shoulder for the inevitable bright lights and milling extras and director ready to yell "Cut!" when Adrian took his thumb and traced it along my cheek, then down over my lips. It was a move that I was pretty sure I'd seen him perform on screen, but I found that I didn't much care. "Cannie," he whispered. Just hearing him say my name was making me throb in places I hadn't expected to feel anything until the baby came. "Kiss me." He brought his lips down to mine, and I tilted my face up, and my body away, as his hand curved behind my neck and held my head like it was something precious. Oh, so sweet a kiss, I thought, and then his lips were back on mine, harder, his hand more insistent, as the traffic rushed by us and I felt myself melting, forgetting my resolve, my history, my name.

"Come with me," he offered, raining kisses on my cheeks, my lips, my eyelids.

"I'm staying at a hotel . . . ," I murmured weakly, realizing as soon as the words were out of my mouth that it sounded like the cheapest come-on ever. And what was going on here, anyhow? Could he really be that lonely? Did he have a thing for pregnant women? Was this perhaps his idea of a joke? "Do you want to maybe . . ." I tried to think quickly. If I were in Philadelphia, if I were standing on a street being groped by the ultimate object of my desire who was very very drunk, what would I suggest? But, of course, I couldn't think of a thing. Nothing in my life had even come close. "Go to a bar?" I finally offered. "A diner, maybe?"

Adrian reached into his pocket and produced what I figured must be a valet ticket. "How about a ride?" he said.

"Can we . . ." I thought quickly. "Can we go to see the beach? It's such a beautiful night. . . ." Which was not exactly true. It was an extremely smoggy night, but at least it was warm, and there was a breeze.

Adrian rocked back and forth on his feet and gave me a sweet, slightly dopey grin. "Sounds like a plan," he said.

First, though, there was the not inconsequential matter of getting him to surrender the keys.

"Ooh, a convertible," I cooed when a small red car arrived at the curb. "I've never driven one." I shot him my most coy and charming glance. "Could I drive it?" He handed over the keys without a word, then sat beside me quietly, not saying much except to tell me where I should turn.

When I glanced over he had his hand pressed to his forehead.

"Headache?" I asked. He nodded with his eyes shut. "Beer before liquor?"

He winced. "Ecstasy before vodka, actually," he said.

Oof. I guessed if I was going to stay in Hollywood, I'd have to get used to people casually confessing to recreational drug use. "You don't look ecstatic," I ventured.

He yawned. "Maybe I'll ask for a refund," he said, and glanced at me sideways. "So, you're, um . . . when are you . . ."

"I'm due on June fifteenth," I said.

"So your, um, husband's back in . . ."

I decided to end the game of fill-in-the-blank. "I'm from Philadelphia, and I don't have a husband. Or a boyfriend."

"Oh!" said Adrian, sounding like he felt himself to be on firmer ground. "So, your partner's back there?"

I laughed. I couldn't help it. "No partner, either. Just your classic single unwed mother." I gave him the briefest bare-bones outline of the story: me and Bruce, our breakup and twenty-minute-long reconciliation, the pregnancy, the screenplay, and my flight to California a scant twelve hours ago.

Adrian nodded, but didn't ask any questions, and I couldn't look at him to read his face. I just kept driving. Finally, after a series of twists and turns I knew I couldn't hope to remember, let alone repeat on my own, we found ourselves parked on a bluff overlooking the ocean. And in spite of the smog, it was magnificent: the smell of salt water, the rhythmic sound of the waves on the shore, the feel of all that water, all that power and motion, so close to us . . .

I turned toward Adrian. "Isn't this great?" I asked. He didn't answer. "Adrian?"

No movement. I leaned toward him slowly, like a big-game hunter approaching a lion. He didn't stir. I edged closer still. "Adrian?" I whispered. No murmured endearments, no inquiries as to the subject of my screenplay, or the nature of my life in Philadelphia. Instead, I heard snoring. Adrian Stadt had fallen asleep.

I couldn't help but laugh at myself. It was a classic Cannie Shapiro moment: out on the beach with a gorgeous movie star, with the wind whipping the waves and the moonlight gleaming on the water and a million stars in the sky, and he's passed out.

Meanwhile, I was stranded. And getting cold, too, with the wind blowing off the water. I looked in the car in vain for a blanket or a stray sweatshirt. Nothing doing. It was four in the morning, according to the glowing green hands of my watch. I decided I'd give him half an hour, and if he didn't wake up and start moving I'd . . . well, I'd figure something out.

I turned the engine on so I'd have heat, and music from the Chris Isaak CD he had in the CD player. Then I sat back, wishing I'd worn a jacket, keeping one eye on Adrian, who was snoring to beat the band, the other on my watch. It was . . . well, pathetic, really, but also a little bit funny. My big trip to Hollywood, I thought ruefully. My romance. Maybe I was the kind of girl who deserved to be mocked in magazines, I thought . . . then I shook my head. I knew how to take care of myself. I knew how to write. And I had one of the things that I wanted most in the world—I'd sold my screenplay. I'd have money, comfort, some measure of fame. And I was in Hollywood! With a movie star!

I glanced to my right. Said movie star was still not moving. I leaned closer. He was breathing harshly, and his forehead was covered in sweat.

"Adrian?" I whispered. Nothing. "Adrian?" I said in a normal voice. I didn't see as much as an eyelid twitch. I bent over and shook his shoulders lightly. Nothing happened. When I let him go he flopped bonelessly back into the bucket seat. Now I was getting worried.

I slipped one hand into his pocket, trying not to think of the potential tabloid headlines ("*Saturday Night!* Star Molested by Wannabe Screenwriter!") and found his cell phone. After a little fumbling, I produced a dial tone. Great. So now what?

Then it hit me. I reached into my purse and pulled Dr. K's business card out of my wallet. He'd told us in one Fat Class session that he didn't sleep much, and was usually in the office by 7 A.M., and it was later than that on the East Coast by now.

I held my breath and punched his numbers. "Hello?" said his deep voice.

"Hey, Dr. K. It's Cannie Shapiro."

"Cannie!" he said, sounding happy to hear from me, and not at all alarmed by the fact that I was calling long-distance in what was, for me, the wee hours of the morning. "How was your trip?"

"Just fine," I said. "Well, so far so good. Except now I seem to have a problem."

"Tell me," he said.

"Well, I, um . . ." I paused, thinking. "I made a new friend," I said.

"That's good," he said encouragingly.

"And we're at the beach, in his car, and he's kind of passed out, and I can't get him to wake up."

"That's bad," he said.

"Yeah," I agreed, "and it's not even the worst date I've been on. So normally I'd just let him sleep, except he told me before he'd been drinking and also taking Ecstasy . . ."

I paused, and heard nothing. "It's not what you think," I said weakly, even though I had no real idea what he was thinking, except that it was probably some combination of my name and words like "flaky."

"So he's passed out?" asked Dr. K.

"Well, yeah. Basically." I sighed. "And I thought I was being fairly amusing."

"But he's breathing?"

"Breathing, but sweating," I elaborated. "And not waking up."

"Touch his face, and tell me how his skin feels."

I did. "Hot," I reported. "Sweaty."

"Better than cool and clammy. We don't want that," he told me. "Try this. I want you to make a fist . . ."

"Done," I reported.

"Now rub your knuckles along his sternum. His breastbone. Do it pretty hard . . . we're trying to see if he reacts."

I leaned over and did as he instructed, pressing hard. Adrian flinched and said a word that might have been "mother." I re-settled myself in my seat and told Dr. K. what had happened.

"Very good," he said. "I think your gentleman caller is going to be just fine. But I think you should do two things."

"Go ahead," I said, tucking the phone under my chin and turning back to Adrian.

"First, turn him on his side, so in case he does vomit, he won't be in danger of aspirating any."

I nudged Adrian until he was semi-sideways. "Done," I said.

"The other thing is just to stay with him," he said. "Check on him every half hour or so. If he turns cool or starts shaking, or if his pulse becomes irregular, I'd dial 911. Otherwise, he should be fine in the morning. He might feel nauseous, or achy," he cautioned, "but there won't be any permanent damage done."

"Great," I said, cringing inwardly as I imagined what the morning would be like, when Adrian woke up with the mother of all hangovers and found himself beside me.

"You might want to take a washcloth, dip it in cool water, wring it out, and put it on his forehead," said the doctor. "That is, if you're feeling merciful."

I started laughing. I couldn't help it. "Thank you," I said. "Really. Thanks a lot."

"I hope things improve," he said cheerfully. "But it sounds like you've got this situation in hand. Will you call me and let me know how it turns out?"

"Absolutely. Thank you again," I said.

"Take care of yourself, Cannie," he said. "Call if you need anything else."

We hung up, and I considered. Washcloth? I looked in the glove compartment and found only a car lease agreement, a few CD jewel boxes, and two pens. I looked in my own purse: lipstick that Garth had given me, wallet, keys, address book, a panty liner that *What to Expect When You're Expecting* told me to carry.

I looked at Adrian. I looked at the panty liner. I figured that what he didn't know wouldn't hurt him, so I got out of the car, made my way carefully to the water, dipped the panty liner, walked back up, and laid it tenderly upon his forehead, trying not to giggle while I did it.

Adrian opened his eyes. "You're so sweet," he slurred.

"Hey, Sleeping Beauty!" I said. "You're awake! I was getting worried . . ."

Adrian appeared not to hear me. "I bet you'll be a terrific mother," he said, and closed his eyes again.

I smiled, settling myself back in my seat. A terrific mother. It was the first time I'd really thought about it—the actual act of mothering. I'd thought about giving birth, sure, about the logistics of caring for a newborn, too. But I'd never given much consideration to what kind of mother I, Cannie Shapiro, age almost twenty-nine, would be.

I cupped my hands around my belly as Adrian snored softly beside me. A good mother, I thought, bemused. But what kind? Would I be one of those cool mothers that all the kids in the neighborhood liked, the ones who served sweetened fruit punch and cookies instead of skim milk and fruit, who wore jeans and funky shoes and could actually talk to her kids, instead of just lecture them? Would I be funny? Would I be the kind of mom they'd want to be the room mother, or show up on Career Day? Or would I be one of those worried mothers, always hovering by the door, waiting for my child to come home, always running after it, clutching a sweater, a raincoat, a handful of tissues?

You'll be you, said a voice in my head. My own mother's voice. I recognized it instantly. I would be me. I had no other choice. And that wouldn't be so bad. I'd done all right by Nifkin, I reasoned. That was something.

I leaned my head against Adrian's shoulder, figuring that he wouldn't mind. And that was when I thought of something else.

I plucked his phone out of my purse, then dug out the napkin with Maxi's number, and held my breath until I heard her bright, British, "Hello."

"Hey, Maxi," I whispered.

"Cannie!" she cried. "Where are you?"

"On the beach," I said. "I'm not sure exactly where, but . . ."

"You're with Adrian?" she asked.

"Yes," I whispered. "And he's kind of passed out."

Maxi started laughing . . . and in spite of myself, I started laughing, too. "So help me out. What's the etiquette here? Do I stay? Do I go? Do I, like, leave him a note?"

"Where are you, exactly?" asked Maxi.

I looked around for a sign, for a light, for something. "I remember the last street we were on was Del Rio Way," I said. "And we're right on a bluff, maybe twenty-five yards over the water. . . ."

"I know where that is," Maxi said. "At least, I think I do. It's where he shot the love scene for *Estella's Eyes.*"

"Great," I said, trying to remember whether anyone had passed out during that particular scene. "So what should I do?"

"I'm going to give you directions to my house," she told me. "I'll be waiting."

Maxi's directions were perfect, and in twenty minutes' time we were pulling into the driveway of a small, gray-shingled house on the beach. It was the kind of place I might have picked out, given my druthers, and probably several million dollars.

Maxi herself was waiting in the kitchen. She'd swapped her dress and updo for a pair of black leggings, a T-shirt, and pigtails, which would have looked ridiculous on 99.9 percent of the female population, but looked adorable on her. "Is he still passed out?"

"Come see," I whispered. We walked back to the car where Adrian still lay in the passenger's seat, his mouth gaping open, his eyes sealed shut, and my panty liner still perched on his forehead.

Maxi burst out laughing. "What is that?"

"It was the best I could do," I said defensively.

Still giggling, Maxi grabbed a copy of *Variety* from what I took to be her recycling bin, rolled it up, and poked Adrian in the arm. Nothing. She moved the magazine lower and poked him in the belly. No response.

"Huh," said Maxi. "Well, I don't think he's dying, but maybe we should bring him inside."

Slowly and carefully, with much grunting and giggling, we maneuvered Adrian out of the car and onto Maxi's living room couch—a gorgeous white leather construction that I very much hoped Adrian would not defile.

"We should turn him on his side, in case he throws up . . ." I suggested, and stared at Adrian. "Do you really think he's okay?" I asked. "He was taking Ecstasy . . ."

"He'll probably be fine," she said dismissively. "But maybe we should stay with him." She peered at me. "You must be exhausted."

"You, too," I said. "I'm sorry about this . . ."

"Cannie, don't worry! You're doing a good deed!"

She looked at Adrian, then at me. "Slumber party?" she asked.

"Sounds like a plan," I said.

While Maxi went off, presumably to gather bedding material, I took off Adrian's shoes, then socks. I slid his belt out of its loops, unbuttoned his shirt, pulled off the panty liner and replaced it with a dishtowel I'd found in the kitchen.

Then while Maxi piled blankets and pillows on the floor, I washed the makeup off my face, struggled into a Maxi-provided T-shirt, and thought of what I could do to make myself useful.

There was a fireplace in the center of the living room—a perfect-looking, pristine fireplace with a stack of birch logs in the grate in its center. And I knew how to make fires. This was good.

I couldn't find newspaper, so I tore pages of *Variety*, twisted them into pretzels, put them underneath the wood, checked to make sure the flue was open, checked to make sure that the wood was actual wood, and not some decorator's ceramic critique of wood, then lit a match from the matchbook I'd grabbed at the Star Bar, in hopes of proving to Samantha and Andy and Lucy that I'd actually been there. The paper flared, then the logs started burning, and I rocked back on my heels, satisfied.

"Wow," said Maxi, snuggling into her pile of blankets, turning her face toward the fire's glow. "How'd you learn to do that?"

"My mother taught me," I said. She looked at me expectantly, so I told the story . . . to Maxi, and, I thought, to my baby, too, of how we'd all go fishing on Cape Cod, and how my mother would build a fire to keep us warm . . . how we'd sit in a circle—my father, my sister, my brother, and me—roasting marshmallows and watching my mother standing in the water, tossing the silvery filament of line out into the gray-black water, with her shorts rolled up and her legs strong and tanned and solid.

"Good times," Maxi repeated, rolling over and falling asleep. I lay there for a while, my eyes wide open in the darkness, listening to her deep, quiet breaths and Adrian's snoring.

Well, here you are, I told myself. The fire was dying down to embers. I could smell the smoke on my hands and in my hair, and I could hear the waves moving on the shore, and see the sky lightening from black to gray. Here you are, I thought. You Are Here. I cupped my hands around my belly. The baby turned, swimming in her sleep, executing what felt like a backflip. Her, I thought. A girl, for sure.

I sent out a good-night prayer to Nifkin, who I figured would be fine for one night on his own in a luxury hotel. Then I closed my eyes and conjured my mother's face over those Cape Cod fires, so happy and at peace. And, feeling happy and at peace myself, I finally fell asleep.

SIXTEEN

When I woke up it was 10:30 in the morning. The fire was out. So were Adrian and Maxi.

As quietly as I could I made my way to the second floor. Polished hardwood floors, modern maple shelves and dressers, mostly empty. I wondered how Maxi felt, inhabiting and abandoning a series of houses, like a caterpillar casting aside its cocoon. I wondered if it bothered her at all. I knew it would bother me.

The bathroom brimmed with all manner of plush towels and fancy soaps and shampoos in sample-sized bottles. I took a long, hot shower, brushed my teeth with one of the brand-new, still-wrapped toothbrushes I found in the medicine cabinet, then got dressed in the T-shirt and clean pajama bottoms I'd found in one of the dresser drawers. I was sure I'd need a blow dryer and possibly an assistant to even attempt to replicate what Garth had done to my hair the night before, but I didn't see either one nearby. So I pulled back sections of my hair, pinning them with the bobby pins, cementing the whole thing with a dime-sized dollop of some rich and delicious-smelling French styling potion. At least that's what I hoped it was. At my father's insistence, I'd taken Latin in high school. Useful for acing the SATs, not any good for those mornings after when you found yourself unexpectedly having to translate the names of movie star's toiletries.

When I came back downstairs Maxi was still asleep, curled like an adorable kitten on top of a pile of blankets. But where Adrian had slumbered, there was only a single sheet of notepaper.

I picked it up. "Dear Cassie," it began, and I snorted laughter. Well, I thought, at least he was close. And I'd certainly been called worse. "Thank you very much for taking care of me last night. I know that we don't know each other well . . ."

And here I snorted again. Don't know each other well! We'd barely exchanged five sentences before he'd passed out!

". . . but I know that you're a kind person. I know you'll be a wonderful mother. I'm sorry I had to leave in such a hurry, and that I won't get to see you again any time soon. I'm off to location, in Toronto, this morning. So I hope you'll enjoy this while you're in California."

This? What was this? I unfolded the note completely, and a silver key fell into what remained of my lap. A car key. "The lease is up next month," Adrian had written on the back of the piece of paper, along with the name and address of a Santa Monica car dealership. "Drop it off when you're ready to go home. And enjoy!"

I got slowly to my feet, walked to the window, and held my breath as I raised the blinds. Sure enough, there was the little red car. I looked from the key in my hand to the car in the driveway, and pinched myself, waiting to wake up and find that this was all a dream . . . that I was still asleep in my bed in Philadelphia, with a pile of pregnancy planning books on my beside table and Nifkin curled on the pillow next to my head.

Maxi yawned, rose gracefully off the floor, and came to stand at the window beside me. "What's going on?" she asked.

I showed her the car, and the key, and the note. "I feel like I'm dreaming," I said.

"Least he could do," said Maxi. "He's just lucky you didn't go through his pockets and take pictures of him naked."

I gave her a wide-eyed innocent look. "Was I not supposed to do that?"

Maxi grinned at me. "Sit tight," she said. "I'm going to fetch your dog, and then we'll plan your conquest of Hollywood."

* * *

I'd expected Maxi's cupboards to be bare, except maybe for the foods I thought that starlets subsisted on—Altoids, fizzy water, perhaps some spelt or brewer's yeast or whatever the diet gurus had decreed they should be eating.

But Maxi's shelves were stocked with all the basics, from chicken broth to flour and sugar and spices, and the refrigerator had fresh-looking apples and oranges, milk and juice, butter and cream cheese.

Quiche, I decided, and fruit salad. I was slicing kiwis and straw-berries when Maxi returned. She'd changed into a pair of black pedal-pushers and a cherry-red cap-sleeved T-shirt, with big black sun-glasses and what I took to be fake ruby barrettes in her hair, and Nifkin was sporting a patent-leather red collar studded with the same jewels, and a matching red leash. They both looked very grand. I served Maxi and then, in the absence of kibble, gave Nifkin a small portion of quiche.

"This is so beautiful," I said, admiring the sun glinting on the water, the fresh breeze stirring the air.

"You should stay for a while," Maxi suggested.

I shook my head. "I need to wrap things up and head back . . . ," I began, and then stopped. Really, why did I have to hurry back? Work could wait—I still had vacation time stored up. Missing a few prebaby classes wouldn't be the end of the world. A room with a view of the ocean was enticing, especially given Philadelphia's fitful, slushy spring. And Maxi was reading my mind.

"It'll be great! You can write, I'll go to work, we can have dinner parties, and fires. Nifkin can hang out . . . I'll set up a stock portfolio for you . . ."

I wanted to jump up and down with the joy of it, but I wasn't sure the baby would approve. It would be incredible out here. I could wade in the surf. Nifkin could chase seagulls. Maxi and I could cook. There had to be strings attached. I just couldn't figure out which ones, or where. And on that morning, with the sun shining and the waves rolling in, it seemed easier to let this wonderful adventure unfold than to spend much more time trying.

* * *

Things happened very quickly after that.

Maxi drove me to a skyscraper with bluish-silver glass walls and a trendy eatery on the bottom level. "I'm taking you to meet my agent," she explained, punching the button for the seventh floor.

I racked my brain for appropriate questions. "Is she . . . does she handle writers?" I asked. "Is she good?"

"Yes, and very," said Maxi, marching me down the hall. She rapped sharply on an open door and stuck her head inside.

"That's bullshit!" said a woman's voice, floating out into the hallway. "Terence, that's absolute crap. This is the project you're looking for, and he's absolutely going to have it done by next week . . ."

I peered over Maxi's shoulder, expecting the voice to belong to a chain-smoking dame with platinum hair and possibly shoulder pads, with an unfiltered cigarette in one hand and a cup of black coffee in the other . . . a female version of the reptilian sunglassed guy who'd told me there were no fat actresses in Hollywood. Instead, perched behind the giant slab of a desk was a strawberry-blond pixie with creamy skin and freckles. She wore a pale-green jumper and a lace-scalloped lilac-colored T-shirt and a pair of Keds on her child-sized feet. Her hair was gathered into a haphazard bun with a pale blue scrunchy. She looked as if she were maybe twelve years old.

"That's Violet," Maxi said proudly.

"Bull-SHIT!" said Violet again. I fought down the urge to put my hands on my belly where I imagined the baby's ears would be.

"What do you think?" Maxi whispered.

"She's . . . um," I said. "She looks like Pippi Longstocking! Is she old enough to be using language like that?"

Maxi cracked up. "Don't worry," she said. "She might look like a Girl Scout, but she's plenty tough."

With a valedictory "Bullshit," Violet hung up the phone, got to her feet, and extended her hand. "Cannie. A pleasure," she said, sounding like a regular person, not like a fire-breathing dragon who'd been channeling Andrew Dice Clay just moments before. "I really enjoyed your screenplay. Do you know what I liked best about it?"

"The curse words?" I ventured.

Violet laughed. "No, no," she said. "I loved that your lead character had such faith in herself. So many romantic comedies, it seems, the female lead has to be rescued somehow . . . by love, or by money, or a fairy godmother. I loved that Josie just rescued herself, and believed in herself the whole time."

Wow. I'd never thought about it quite that way. To me, Josie's story was wish fulfillment, pure and simple—the story of what could happen if one of the stars I interviewed in New York ever looked at me and saw more than a potential puff piece in plus-size female form.

"Women are going to fucking love this movie," Violet predicted.

"I'm so glad you think so," I said.

Violet nodded, yanked the scrunchy out of her hair, ran her fingers through it, and gathered her curls into a marginally neater version of the same bun. "We'll talk more later," she said, gathering a legal pad, a fistful of pens, a copy of my screenplay, and what looked like a copy of a contract. "For now, let's make you some money."

In the end it turned out that little Violet was an ace negotiator. Maybe it was just that the sound of that brassy voice and nonstop stream of obscenities coming out of her adorable little person was so jarring that the trio of young guys in sharp suits wound up staring more than they did contesting her assertion that my script was worth it. In the end the amount of money they gave me—one chunk to be delivered within five days of signing, the other to be handed over the day filming began, a third chunk for "first look" at whatever I wrote next—was pretty unbelievable. Maxi hugged me, and Violet hugged both of us. "Now go out there and make me proud," she said, before traipsing back to her office, looking for all the world like a fourth-grader coming in from afternoon recess.

By five o'clock that afternoon I was sitting back on Maxi's deck with a bowl of chilled grapes in my lap and a flute of nonalcoholic sparkling grape juice in my hand, feeling the most incredibly sweet relief. Now I could buy whatever house I wanted, or hire a nanny, even take a whole year off of work when the baby came. And whatever rewriting I had to do, it wouldn't be as bad as facing Gabby, and her nonstop stream criticism, both of the to-the-face and behind-the-back variety. It couldn't be as bad as straining over the seventh draft of my letter to Bruce. Those things were work. This would just be play.

I talked for hours that afternoon, screaming out the joyous news to my mother, to Lucy and Josh, to Andy and Samantha, to assorted relatives and colleagues, to anyone I could think of who'd share in my happiness. Then I called Dr. K. at his office.

"It's Cannie," I said. "I just want you to know that everything's fine."

"Your friend's feeling better?"

"Much better," I said, and explained it—how Adrian had recovered, how I'd decided to stay at Maxi's, how tiny little Violet had gotten me all of this money.

"It's going to be a great movie," Dr. K. said.

"I can't even believe it," I said, for perhaps the thirtieth time that afternoon. "It doesn't even feel real."

"Well, just enjoy it," he said. "It sounds like you're off to a wonderful start."

Maxi watched the whole thing bemusedly, and threw a tennis ball for Nifkin until he collapsed, panting, next to a pile of seaweed.

"Who's that one?" she asked, and I explained.

"He's . . . well, he was my doctor, when I was trying to lose weight, before I got pregnant. Now he's a friend, I guess. I called him last night to ask him about Adrian."

"It sounds like you like him," she said, waggling her eyebrows, Groucho Marx style. "Does he make house calls?"

"I have no idea," I said. "He's very nice. Very tall."

"Tall's good," said Maxi. "So what now?"

"Dinner?" I suggested.

"Oh, that's right," said Maxi. "I forgot that you're multitalented. You can write, and cook, too!"

"Don't get your hopes up," I said. "Let me see what else is in the fridge."

Maxi smiled. "I've got a better idea of something we should do first," she said.

* * *

The guard at the front of the jewelry store nodded at me and Maxi, and swung the heavy glass door open wide.

"What are we doing here?" I whispered.

"Buying you a treat," said Maxi. "And you don't have to whisper."

"What are you, my sugar daddy?" I scoffed.

"Oh, no," Maxi said very seriously. "You're going to buy something for yourself."

I gaped at her. "What? Why? Shouldn't you be encouraging me to save? I've got a baby on the way. . . ."

"Of course you're going to save," said Maxi, sounding eminently sensible. "But my mother always told me that every woman should have one beautiful, perfect thing that she bought for herself . . . and you, my dear, are now in a position to do just that."

I took a deep breath, like I was about to dive into deep water, rather than just walk through a jewelry store. The room was full of glass cases, at the level of what used to be my waist, and each case was full of a treasure trove of ornaments, all arranged artfully on pads of black and dove-gray velvet. There were emerald rings, sapphire rings, slender bands of platinum set with diamonds. There were dangling amber earrings and topaz brooches, bracelets of silver mesh so fine I could barely make out the links, and cuffs of hammered gold. There were glittering charm bracelets bearing tiny ballet slippers and miniature car keys . . . sterling silver earrings in the shape of plump Valentine hearts . . . interlocked bands of pink and yellow gold . . . glittering pins shaped like ladybugs and sea horses . . . diamond tennis bracelets of the kind that Bruce's mother had worn. . . . I stopped walking and leaned against a counter, feeling more than a little bit overwhelmed.

A saleswoman in a neat navy suit appeared behind it as quickly as if she'd been teleported over. "What can I show you?" she asked warmly. I pointed tentatively at smallest pair of diamond earrings that I saw. "Those, please," I asked.

Maxi peered over my shoulder. "Not those," she scoffed. "Cannie, they're tiny!"

"Shouldn't something on my body be tiny?" I asked.

Maxi looked at me, puzzled. "Why?"

"Because . . ." I said. My voice trailed off.

Maxi grabbed my hand. "You know what?" she said. "I think you look fine. I think you look wonderful. You look happy . . . and healthy . . . and, and pregnant . . ."

"Don't forget that," I said, laughing.

The saleswoman, meanwhile, was unfolding a piece of black velvet and laying earrings out on top of the case—the itsy-bitsy pair I'd requested first, then another pair about twice as large. The diamonds were each about the size of a SunMaid raisin, I thought, and cupped them in my hand, watching them sparkle, flashing blue and violet.

"They're gorgeous," I said softly, and lifted them up to my ears.

"They suit you," said the saleswoman.

"We'll take them," Maxi said, sounding very certain. "And don't bother wrapping them. She'll wear them home."

Later, in the car, with my new earrings sending spangled rainbows against the roof whenever the sunlight flashed through them, I tried to thank her—for taking me in, for buying my screenplay, for making me believe in a future where I deserved such things. But Maxi just brushed it off. "You deserve nice things," she said kindly. "It shouldn't come as a surprise, Cannie."

I took a deep breath. *Friend,* I whispered to the baby. To Maxi, I said, "I'm going to make you the best dinner you've ever had."

"I don't understand this," said my mother, who was checking in with her daily afternoon phone call/interrogation session. "And I've got five minutes to figure it out."

"Five minutes?" I tucked the phone closer to my chest and squinted at my toes, trying to decide whether it was possible to survive in Hollywood with badly chipped toenail polish, or if I'd be fined by the pedicure police. "Why are you in such a hurry?"

"Preseason softball," my mother said briskly. "We're scrimmaging the Lavender Menace."

"Are they any good?"

"They were last year. But you're changing the subject. Now, you're living with Maxi . . . ," my mother began, her voice trailing off hopefully. Or at least I thought that's what I detected.

"We're just friends, Ma," I said. "The platonic kind."

She sighed. "It's not too late, you know."

I rolled my eyes. "Sorry to disappoint."

"So what are you doing?"

"I'm having fun," I said. "I'm having a great time." I barely knew where to start. I'd been in California for almost three weeks, and every day, it seemed, Maxi and I went on some adventure, some little trip in Adrian's red convertible, which felt more and more like an enchanted chariot, or a magic carpet, every day. Last night after dinner we'd walked all the way to Santa Monica Pier, and bought greasy, salty-sweet french fries and frozen pink lemonade, which we'd eaten while dangling our feet in the water. The day before we'd gone to a farmer's market downtown, where we'd filled a backpack with raspberries and baby carrots and white peaches, which Maxi distributed to her fellow cast members (except for her costar because, she reasoned, he'd see the peaches as an invitation to make Bellinis— "and I don't want to be the one responsible for his falling off the wagon this time").

There were things in California that I still hadn't gotten used to— the uniform beauty of the women, for one, the way every other person I saw in the coffee bars or gourmet grocery stores looked vaguely familiar, like they'd played the girlfriend or the second banana's buddy on some quickly cancelled sitcom from 1996. And the car culture of the place astonished me—everyone drove everywhere, so there weren't any sidewalks or bicycle lanes, just endless traffic jams, smog as thick as marmalade, valet parking everywhere—even, unbelievably, at one of the beaches we'd visited. "I have now, officially, seen everything," I told Maxi. "No, you haven't," she'd replied. "On the Third Street Promenade there's a dachshund dressed up in a sequined leotard that's part of a juggling act. Once you've seen that, you've seen everything."

"Are you working at all?" asked my mother, who didn't sound impressed with tales of juggling dachshunds and white peaches.

"Every day," I told her, which was true. In between adventures, and outings, I was spending at least three hours a day on the deck with my laptop. Violet had sent me a script so larded with notes it was practically unreadable. "DO NOT PANIC," she'd written in lavender-colored ink on the title page. "Purple notes are mine, red notes are from a reader the studio hired, black from the guy who may or may not wind up directing this—and most of what he says is bullshit, I think. Take everything with a grain of salt, they are SUGGESTIONS ONLY!" I was gradually working through the thicket of scribbled marginalia, cross-outs, arrows, and Post-it addenda.

"So when are you coming home?" my mother asked. I bit my lip. I still didn't know, and I'd have to make up my mind—and soon. My thirtieth week was quickly approaching. After that, I'd either have to find a doctor in Los Angeles and have the baby here, or find a way to get home that didn't involve an airplane.

"Well, please let me know your plans," my mother said. "I'd be delighted to give you a ride home from the airport, and maybe even look at my grandchild before his or her first birthday . . ."

"Ma . . ."

"Just a motherly reminder!" she said, and hung up.

I got to my feet and walked down to the sand, Nifkin bouncing at my heels, hoping he'd get to chase his tennis ball into the waves.

I knew that I'd have to figure it out eventually, but things were going so well that it was hard to think of anything but the next perfect, sunny day, the next delicious meal, the next shopping trip or picnic or walk on the beach under the starry sky. Aside from the occasional memory of Bruce and our happier times together, and absent the uncertainty of not knowing what would happen next in my life, my time at the beach house was basic unmitigated bliss.

"You should stay here," Maxi would say. I never said yes, but I never said no, either. I tried to figure it out the way I'd once investigated my brides, turning the question over and over in my mind: Could this life fit me? Could I really live this way?

I thought about it at night, when my work was done and the food was cooking, and Nifkin and I would stroll along the water's edge.

"Stay or go?" I'd ask, waiting for an answer—from the dog, from the baby, from the God who had failed to instruct me back in November. But no answer came—just the waves and, eventually, the starlit night.

On my third Saturday morning in California Maxi walked into the guest bedroom, flinging open the curtains and snapping her fingers at Nifkin, who darted to her side, ears pricked up alertly, like the world's smallest guard dog. "Up and at 'em!" she said, bouncing on the balls of her feet. "We're going to the gym!"

I struggled to sit up. "Gym?" I asked. She was dressed for it, I saw. Her auburn curls were drawn up into a high ponytail, and she was wearing a form-fitting black unitard, bright white socks, and pristine white sneakers.

"Don't worry," Maxi told me. "Nothing too exerting." She sat on the side of my bed and pointed at a schedule from someplace called the Inner Light Education Center. "See . . . here?"

"Self-actualization, meditation, and visualization," read the course description.

"To be followed by masturbation?" I asked.

Maxi gave me an evil look. "Don't knock it," she said. "This stuff really works."

I went to the dresser and started searching for appropriate self-actualization wear. I figured I'd tag along, and use the meditation session to see if I couldn't come up with a plausible bit of dialogue between Josie, the heroine of my screenplay, and her soon-to-be-ex boyfriend. Or I'd contemplate my future, and what I'd do with it. Self-actualization and visualization sounded like New Age foolishness to me, but at least it wouldn't be a waste of my time.

The Inner Light Education Center was a low-slung white wood building perched on top of a hill. There were wide glass windows, and a deck lined with sea grass and pots of impatiens. There was, thankfully, no valet parking.

"You're really going to like this," said Maxi, as we made our way to the door. I'd wriggled into Maxi's oversized T-shirt, which was becoming less oversized by the day, plus a pair of leggings and sneakers, and the obligatory baseball cap and shades—the one part of her look I'd been able to adapt for myself.

"You know, in Philadelphia this place would be a cheesesteak stand," I grumbled.

We entered a large, airy room with mirrors on the walls, a piano in one corner, and the smell of sweat and, faintly, sandalwood incense. Maxi and I found spots near the back, and when Maxi went to fetch us folding foam mats, I checked out the crowd. There was a pack of supermodel-looking stunners in the front, but also a few older women —one with actual undyed gray hair—and a guy with a long, flowing white beard and a T-shirt reading "I Got the Crabs at Jimmy's Crab Shack." Definitely a long way from the Star Bar, I thought happily, as the instructor walked through the door.

"Let's all get to our feet," she said, bending to put a compact disc into the player.

I stared, and blinked, for there, in front of me, was a bona fide Larger Woman . . . in a shiny electric-blue leotard and black tights, no less. She was maybe ten years older than me, with a deep tan, and brown hair that fell halfway down her back, held off her wide, unlined face with a band that matched her leotard. Her body reminded me of those little fertility dolls that archeologists dug out of ruins—sloping breasts, wide hips, unapologetic curves. She had pink lipstick and a tiny diamond stud in her nose, and she looked . . . comfortable. Confident. Happy with herself. I stared at her, unable to help myself, wondering if I'd ever looked that happy, and whether I could ever learn how, and how I'd look with a nose-piercing.

"I'm Abigail," she announced. Abigail! I thought. My top female-baby name contender! This had to be a sign. Of what, I wasn't sure, but definitely something good. "And this is self-actualization, meditation, and visualization. If you're in the wrong place, please leave now." Nobody did. Abigail smiled at us and hit a button on the stereo. The sound of flutes and soft drumming filled the room. "We're going to start off with some stretching and deep breathing, and then we're going to do what's called a guided meditation. You'll all sit in what-ever position you find comfortable, and you'll close your eyes, and I'm going to guide you through imagining different situations, different possibilities. Shall we begin?"

Maxi smiled at me. I smiled back. "Okay?" she whispered, and I nodded, and before I knew it I was sitting cross-legged on a cushioned mat on the floor, with my eyes closed and the flutes and drums ringing faintly in my ears.

"Imagine a safe place," Abigail began. Her voice was low and soothing. "Don't try to choose it. Just close your eyes and see what comes."

I thought for sure I'd see Maxi's deck, or maybe her kitchen. But what I saw as Abigail repeated "safe place," was my bed . . . my bed at home. The blue comforter, the brightly colored pillows, Nifkin perched on top like a small furry hood ornament, blinking at me. I could tell by the slant of the light through the blinds that it was evening, when I'd come home from work. Time to walk the dog, time to call Samantha to see when she wanted to head to the gym, time to flip through my mail and hang up my clothes and settle in for the night. . . . And suddenly I was swept up in a wave of such wretched homesickness, such longing for my city, my apartment, my bed, that I felt faint.

I struggled to my feet. My head was full of pictures of the city—the coffee shop on the corner, where Samantha and I shared iced cappucinos and confidences and horror stories about men . . . the Reading Terminal in the morning, full of the smell of fresh flowers and cinnamon buns . . . Independence Mall on my way home from work, the wide green lawns crammed with tourists craning for a glimpse of the Liberty Bell, the dogwood trees full of pink blossoms . . . Penn's Landing on a Saturday, with Nifkin straining at his leash, trying to catch the seagulls who skimmed and dipped low over the water. My street, my apartment, my friends, my job . . . "Home," I whispered, to the baby—to myself. And I whispered "bathroom," to Maxi, and made my way outside.

I stood in the sunshine, breathing deeply. A minute later I felt a tap on my shoulder. Abigail was standing there with a glass of water in her hand.

"Are you okay?"

I nodded. "I just started feeling a little . . . well, homesick, I guess," I explained.

Abigail nodded thoughtfully. "Home," she said, and I nodded. "Well, that's good. If home's your safe place, that's a wonderful thing."

"How do you . . ." I couldn't find the words for what I wanted to ask her. How do you find happiness in a body like yours . . . like mine? How do you find the courage to follow anything anywhere if you don't feel like you fit in the world?

Abigail smiled at me. "I grew up," she said, in response to the question I hadn't asked. "I learned things. You will, too."

"Cannie?"

Maxi was squinting at me in the sunlight, looking concerned. I waved at her. Abigail nodded at both of us. "Good luck," she said, and walked back inside, hips churning, breasts wobbling, proud and unashamed. I stared after her, wishing I could whisper *role model* to the baby.

"What was that about?" asked Maxi. "Are you okay? You didn't come back, I thought you were giving birth in the stall or something . . ."

"No," I said. "No baby yet. I'm fine."

We drove back home, Maxi chattering excitedly about how she'd visualized herself winning an Oscar and tastefully, graciously, and very emphatically denouncing every single one of her rotten ex-boyfriends from the podium. "I almost started laughing when I visualized the look on Kevin's face!" she crowed, and shot me a glance at the next red light. "What'd you see, Cannie?"

I didn't want to answer her . . . didn't want to hurt her feelings by telling her that I thought my happiness lay approximately three thousand miles from the beach house and the California coastline, and from Maxi herself. "Home," I said softly.

"Well, we'll be there soon enough," Maxi said.

"Can-nie," Samantha wailed on the phone the next morning, sounded decidedly unlawyerly. "This is ridiculous! I insist that you come back.

Things are happening. I broke up with the yoga instructor and you weren't even here to hear about it . . . ."

"So tell me," I urged her, staving off a pang of guilt.

"Never mind," Sam said airily. "I'm sure whatever I'm enduring isn't as interesting as your movie-star friends and their breakups . . ."

"Now, Sam," I said, "you know that isn't true. You're my absolute best friend, and I want to hear all about the evil yoga guy . . ."

"Never mind that," said Sam. "I'd rather talk about you. What's the deal? Are you, like, on permanent vacation? Are you going to stay there forever?"

"Not forever," I said. "I just . . . I'm not sure what I'm doing, really." And I was desperate, at that moment, not to have to talk about it anymore.

"I miss you," Sam said plaintively. "I even miss your weird little dog."

"I won't be gone forever," I said. It was the only thing I knew for sure was true.

"Okay, subject change," said Samantha. "Guess who called me? That hunky doctor we ran into on Kelly Drive."

"Dr. K!" I said, feeling a sudden rush of happiness at his name, along with a twinge of guilt that I hadn't called him since the day I'd signed with Violet. "How'd he get your number?"

Samantha's voice turned chilly. "Evidently," she said, "and despite my explicit request, you once again listed me as your emergency contact when you filled out some kind of form for him."

This was a point of some contention. I always listed Samantha as my emergency contact when I went on bike trips. Samantha had been less than delighted to learn this.

"Honestly, Cannie, why don't you just list your mother?" she asked now, reiterating the complaint she'd made many times before.

"Because I'm worried that Tanya would answer the phone and have my body buried at sea," I said.

"Anyhow, he called because he wanted to know how things were going, and if I had your address; I guess he wants to send you something."

"Great!" I said, wondering what it was.

"So when are you coming home?" Sam asked again.

"Soon," I told her, relenting.

"Promise?" she demanded.

I laid my hands on my belly. "I promise," I said, to both of them.

The next afternoon, the mailbox yielded a box from Mailboxes & More on Walnut Street, Philadelphia.

I carried it out onto the deck and opened it. The first thing I saw was a postcard with a picture of a small, wide-eyed, anxious-looking Nifkin-esque dog on the front. I turned it over. "Dear Cannie," it read. "Samantha tells me you'll be in Los Angeles for a while, and I thought you might like something to read. (They do read out there, right?) I've enclosed your books, and a few things to remind you of home. Feel free to call me if you want to say hello." It was signed "Peter Krushelevansky (from the University of Philadelphia)." Under the signature was a postscript: "Samantha also tells me that Nifkin's gone West Coast, so I've sent a little something for him, too."

Inside the box I found a postcard of the Liberty Bell, and one of Independence Hall. There was a small tin of dark chocolate-covered pretzels from the Reading Terminal, and a single, slightly squashed Tastykake. At the bottom of the box my fingers encountered something round and heavy, wrapped in layers and layers of the *Philadelphia Examiner* ("Gabbing with Gabby," I noted, was devoted to Angela Lansbury's latest made-for-TV movie). Inside I found a shallow ceramic pet food bowl. The letter *N* was emblazoned on the inside, painted bright red and outlined in yellow. And around the outside of the bowl were a series of portraits of Nifkin, each accurate right down to his sneer and his spots. There was Nifkin running, Nifkin sitting, Nifkin on the floor devouring a rawhide bone. I laughed delightedly. "Nifkin!" I said, and Nifkin barked and came running.

I set the bowl down for Nifkin to sniff. Then I called Dr. K..

"Suzie Lightning!" he said, by way of greeting.

"Who?" I said. "Huh?"

"It's from a Warren Zevon song," he said.

"Huh," I said. The only Warren Zevon song I knew was the one about lawyers, guns, and money.

"It's about a girl who . . . travels a lot," he said.

"Sounds interesting," I said, making a mental note to look up the lyrics. "I'm calling to thank you for my presents. They're wonderful."

"You're welcome," he told me. "I'm glad you like them."

"Did you paint Nifkin from memory? It's amazing. You should have been an artist."

"I dabble," he acknowledged, sounding so much like Dr. Evil, of Austin Powers fame, that I burst out laughing. "Actually, your friend Samantha lent me some pictures," he explained. "But I didn't use them much. Your dog has a very distinctive look."

"You're too kind," I said truthfully.

"They opened up a paint-your-own-pottery studio around the corner from campus," he explained. "I did it there. It was some kid's fifth birthday party, so there were eight five-year-olds painting coffee mugs, and me."

I grinned, picturing it—tall, deep-voiced Dr. K. folded into a chair, painting Nifkin as the little kids gawked.

"So how are things going out there?"

I gave him the condensed version, telling him about shopping with Maxi—the cooking I'd been doing, the farmer's market I'd found. I described the little house on the beach. I told him that California felt both wonderful and unreal. I told him that I was walking every morning and working every day and how Nifkin had learned to retrieve his tennis ball from the surf.

Dr. K. made interested noises, asked pertinent follow-up questions, and proceeded directly to the big one. "So when are you coming home?"

"I'm not sure," I said. "I'm on leave right now, and I'm still fine-tuning a few things with the screenplay."

"So . . . will you give birth out there?"

"I don't know," I said slowly. "I don't think so."

"Good," was all he said. "We should have breakfast again when you come back."

"Sure," I said, feeling a pang for Sam's Morning Glory. There was no place like it out here. "That would be great." I heard Maxi's car in the garage. "Hey, I've kind of got to run . . . ."

"No problem," he said. "Call me any time."

I hung up the phone smiling. I wondered how old he was, really. I wondered if he liked me as more than a patient, as more than just another one of the big girls shuttling in and out of his office, each with her own tale of heartache. And I decided that I'd like to see him again.

The next morning Maxi proposed another trip.

"I still can't believe that you have a plastic surgeon," I grumbled, heaving myself into the low-slung little car, thinking that only in this city, at this moment in time, would a twenty-seven-year-old actress with perfect features keep a plastic surgeon on retainer.

"Necessary evil," Maxi said crisply, powering past several lesser vehicles and zooming into the fast lane.

The surgeon's office was a study in gray and mauve, all cool marble floors and glossy walls and even glossier receptionists. Maxi pulled off her oversized sunglasses and had a quiet talk with the woman behind the desk while I strolled, examining the poster-sized photographs of the doctors that lined the wall, wondering which one would have the pleasure of plumping up Maxi's lips and erasing the invisible lines around her eyes. Dr. Fisher was a Ken doll-looking blond. Dr. Rhodes was a brunette with arched eyebrows who looked about my age, but probably wasn't. Dr. Tasker was the jovial Santa Claus of the bunch—minus, of course, the roly-poly cheeks and double chin. And Dr. Shapiro . . .

I stood there, frozen, staring up at the larger-than-life picture of my father. He was thinner, and he'd shaved off his beard, but it was unquestionably him.

Maxi strolled over, her heels clicking on the floor. When she saw the look on my face, she grabbed my elbow and led me to a chair. "Cannie, what is it? Is it the baby?"

I tottered back to the wall on legs that felt like lengths of ossified wood, and pointed. "That's my dad."

Maxi stared at the picture, then at me. "You didn't know he was out here?" she asked. I shook my head.

"What should we do?"

I nodded toward the door and started walking as fast as I could. "Leave."

"So that's what's become of him," I said. Maxi and Nifkin and I were out on the deck, drinking raspberry iced tea. "Liposuction in L.A." I worked my tongue around it, trying the concept on for size. "Sounds like the beginning of a bad joke, doesn't it?"

Maxi looked away. I felt sorry for her. She'd never seen me this upset, and she didn't have any idea of how to help me. And I didn't know what to tell her.

"Sit tight," I said, getting to my feet. "I'm going to go for a walk."

I walked down by the water, passed the rollerbladers in bikinis, the volleyball games, the screaming, Popsicle-sticky kids. I passed the vendors on stilts, the piercing parlors, and the four-pairs-for-ten-dollars sock vendors, and the dreadlocked teenagers sitting on park benches, playing their guitars, and homeless people in layers and layers of clothes, splayed like corpses underneath the palm trees.

As I walked I tried to lay things out in front of me, to organize them, like they were pictures at an exhibition, framed and hung on a gallery wall.

I pictured my family as it had once been—the five of us on the lawn at Rosh Hashanah, posing in our best clothes: my father with his beard neatly trimmed and his hands on my shoulder; me with my hair twisted back in barrettes, the barest buds of breasts pushing at the front of my sweater, both of us smiling.

I pictured us all five years later: my father gone; me, fat and sullen and scared; my mother, frantic; my brother, miserable; and Lucy with her Mohawk and her piercings and late-night telephone callers.

More pictures: my college graduation. My mother and Tanya, their arms around each other's shoulders, at their softball league championship game. Josh, six feet tall and thin and solemn, carving a turkey at Thanksgiving. Years of holidays, the four of us arrayed around the dining room table, my mother at the head and my brother opposite her, various boyfriends and girlfriends showing up, fading out, all of us trying hard to look like there was nothing missing there.

I moved on. There I was, standing proudly in front of my first apartment, holding a copy of my first newspaper story, pointing at the headline "Budget Debate Postponed." Me and my first boyfriend. Me and my college sweetheart. Me and Bruce in the ocean, laughing at the camera, squinting in the sun. Bruce at a Grateful Dead concert, in a hackey-sack circle, one foot extending in mid-kick, a beer in his hand and his hair flowing loose over his shoulders. Then I made myself step back and move on.

I stood and let the ocean cool my feet and felt . . . nothing. Or maybe it was the end of love that I was feeling, the cool empty place that's left inside you where all that heat and pain and passion used to be, the slick of wet sand after the tide finally rolls back out.

Okay, I thought. Here you are. You Are Here. And you move forward because that's the way it works; that's the only place you can go. You keep going until it stops hurting, or until you find new things to hurt you worse, I guess. And that is the human condition, all of us lurching along in our own private miseries, because that's the way it is. Because, I guess, God didn't give us any choice. You grow up, I remembered Abigail telling me. You learn.

Maxi was sitting on the deck where I'd left her, waiting.

"We need to go shopping," I said.

She rose quickly to her feet. "Where?" she asked. "For what?"

I laughed, and heard the tears inside of it, and wondered if she could hear them, too. "I need to buy myself a wedding ring."

SEVENTEEN

The receptionist at my father's office didn't seem at all perturbed at the long pause before I told her why I was calling.

I had a scar, I finally explained, and I wanted Dr. Shapiro to have a look at it. I gave Maxi's cell phone number as my own and gave Lois Lane as my name, and the receptionist didn't sound the least bit curious. She just gave me a ten A.M. appointment for Friday and warned me that the traffic could be brutal.

So on Friday morning I started out early. My hair was freshly trimmed (Garth had obliged, even though it had only been four weeks, not six). And on my left hand I wore not only the plain gold band I'd imagined but a diamond of such breathtaking enormity, such improbable size, that I could barely keep my eyes on the road.

Maxi had brought it home from the set, promising that no one would miss it, and that it would be just the thing to announce to my father in general and the world at large that I'd arrived.

"But let me ask you," she began that morning, over buttermilk waffles and peach and ginger tea. "Why do you want your father to think you're married?"

I stood up and opened the curtains, looking out at the water. "I don't know, really. I don't even know if I'll wear the rings when I go see him."

"You must have thought about it," said Maxi. "You think about everything."

I looked at the rings on my fingers. "I guess it's that he said nobody would ever love me, that nobody would ever want me. And I feel like if I see him, and I'm pregnant and I'm not married . . . it'll be like he was right."

Maxi looked at me as if this were the saddest thing she'd ever heard. "But you know that's not true, right?" she asked. "You know how many people love you."

I drew a shaky breath. "Oh, sure," I said. "It's just . . . with this . . . it's hard to be reasonable." I looked at her. "It's family, you know? Who was ever reasonable about family? I just . . . I want to know why he did what he did. I want to at least be able to ask the question."

"He might not have answers," Maxi told me. "Or, if he does, they might not be the ones you want to hear."

"I just want to hear something," I said raggedly. "I just feel like . . . I mean, you only get two parents, and my mom's . . ." I gave a vague, general wave of my hand to indicate lesbianism and an inappropriate life partner. My finger flashed in the sunlight. "I just feel like I have to try."

The nurse who led me into the cubicle had breasts as symmetrical and rounded as twin halved cantaloupes. She handed me a plush terrycloth robe and a clipboard full of forms to fill out. "Doctor will be with you shortly," she said, clicking on a high-powered light and shining it on my face, where I'd invented a scar. "Huh," she said, scrutinizing the scar. "That hardly looks like anything."

"It's deep, though," I said. "I can see it in pictures. It shows up there."

She nodded as if this made perfect sense to her and backed out of the room.

I sat on a beige armchair, making up lies to put on the forms and wishing that I had a scar—some physical sign to show the world—to show him—what I'd been through, and what I'd survived. Twenty minutes later, there was a brisk knock at the door, and my father walked in.

"So what brings you here today, Ms. Lane?" he asked, his eyes on my chart. I sat quietly, saying nothing. After a moment, he looked up. There was an irritated expression on his face, a stop-wasting-my-time look that I recognized from my childhood. He stared at me for a minute with nothing registering on his face but more annoyance. Then he saw.

"Cannie?"

I nodded. "Hello."

"My God, what . . ." My father, a man with an insult for every occasion, was for once gratifyingly speechless. "What are you doing here?"

"I made an appointment," I said.

He winced, took off his glasses, and pinched the bridge of his nose—another pose I'd remembered well. It usually presaged a temper tantrum, anger of some sort.

"You just disappeared," I said. He started shaking his head and opened his mouth, but I wasn't about to let him start without saying my piece. "None of us knew where you were. How could you do that? How could you just walk out on all of us like that?" He said nothing . . . just stared at me—through me—as if I were any hysterical patient, shrieking that her thighs still felt lumpy or her left nipple was higher than her right one. "Don't you care about us? Don't you have a heart? Or is that a stupid question to ask someone who sucks cellulite out of thighs for a living?"

My father glared at me. "You don't need to be condescending."

"No, what I needed was a father," I said. I hadn't realized how angry, how furious at him I was until I'd seen him, standing there in his crisp white doctor's coat, his manicured fingernails, his tan, and his heavy gold watch.

He sighed, as if the conversation bored him; as if I bored him, too. "Why are you here?"

"I didn't come here looking for you, if that's what you're asking. A friend of mine had an appointment, and I came with her. I saw your picture," I continued. "Not very smart, you know? For someone trying to stay undercover. . . ."

"I'm not trying to stay undercover," he said irascibly. "That's nonsense. Did your mother tell you that?"

"Then how come none of us know where you are?"

"You wouldn't have cared if you did," he muttered, picking up the clipboard he'd come in with.

I was so flabbergasted, he actually had his hand on the doorknob before I could think of what to say. "Are you crazy? Of course we would have cared. You're our father. . . ."

He put his glasses back on. I could see his eyes behind them, a weak, watery brown. "And you're all grown up now. All of you are."

"You think just because we're older it doesn't matter what you did to us? You think needing your parents in your life is something you outgrow, like training wheels or a high chair?"

He raised himself up to his full five feet, eight and a half inches, and gathered the cloak of authority, of Doctor-ness, around him as palpably as if he'd been pulling on a heavy winter coat. "I think," he said, speaking slowly and precisely, "that lots of people are disappointed by the lives that they wind up with."

"And that's what you want to be to us? A disappointment?"

He sighed. "I can't help you, Cannie. I don't know what you want, but I can tell you this—I've got nothing to give you. Any of you."

"We don't want your money. . . ."

He looked at me almost kindly. "I'm not talking about money."

"Why?" I asked him. My voice was cracking. "Why have kids and leave them? That's the part I don't understand. What did we do . . ." I gulped. "What did any of us do that was so awful that you never wanted to see us again?" I knew, even as I was saying the words, even as I was thinking them, that it was ridiculous. I knew that no child could be that bad, that wrong, that ugly, could be anything to cause a parent to leave. I knew that it was no fault of ours. We weren't to blame, I thought to myself. I could let it go; I could set the burden down, I could be free.

Except, of course, that knowing something in your head is different than feeling it in your heart. And I knew at that moment that Maxi had been right. Whatever my father could say, whatever answer he could provide, whatever excuse he could muster, it wouldn't be right. And it wouldn't ever be enough.

I stared at him. I waited for him to ask me something, to ask what had become of me: Where did I live, and what did I do, and whom had I decided to spend my life with? Instead he looked at me again, shook his head once, and turned toward the door.

"Hey!" I said.

He turned to look at me, and my throat closed up. What did I want to tell him? Nothing. I wanted him to ask *me* things: how are you, who are you, what's happened to you, who have you become. I stared at him, and he said nothing—just walked away.

I couldn't help myself. I reached for him, for some sign, for something, as he was walking out the door. I felt my fingertips graze the back of that crisp white coat. He never stopped walking. He never even slowed down.

When I came back, I put the rings in their little velvet box. I washed the makeup off my face and the gel out of my hair. Then I called Samantha.

"You won't believe it," I began.

"Probably not," she said. "So tell me."

And I did. "He didn't ask me a single question," I told her at the end. "He didn't want to know what I was doing out here, or what I was doing with my life. I don't even think he noticed I was pregnant. He just didn't care."

Samantha sighed. "That's awful. I can't even imagine how you must feel."

"I feel . . ." I said. I looked out at the water, then up at the sky. "I feel like I'm ready to come home."

Maxi nodded when I told her, sadly, but didn't ask me to stay.

"You're done with the screenplay?" she asked.

"I've been done for a few days," I told her. She surveyed the bed, where I'd laid my things out—my clothes and books, the teddy bear I'd bought for the baby one afternoon in Santa Monica.

"I wish we could have done more," she said with a sigh.

"We did plenty," I said, and hugged her. "And we'll talk . . . and e-mail . . . and you'll visit when the baby comes. . . ."

Maxi's eyes lit up. "Aunt Maxi," she proclaimed. "You'll have to have it call me Aunt Maxi. And I'm going to spoil it rotten!"

I smiled to myself, imagining Maxi treating little Max or Abby like a two-legged Nifkin, dressing the baby in outfits she'd picked out to match her own. "You're going to be a fabulous aunt," I said.

She insisted on driving me to the airport, helping me check my luggage, waiting with me at the gate even though everyone from the flight attendants on down were staring at her like she was the rarest exhibit in the zoo.

"This is going to wind up on *Inside Edition,*" I warned her, giggling and crying a little bit as we hugged each other for the eighteenth time. Maxi kissed my cheek, then bent down and gave my belly a little wave.

"You've got your ticket?" she asked me.

I nodded.

"Got milk money?"

"Oh, yes," I said, smiling, knowing how true it was.

"Then you're good to go," she said.

I nodded, and sniffled, and hugged her tight. "You're a wonderful friend," I told her. "You're the greatest."

"Be careful," she replied. "Travel safe. Call me as soon as you get there."

I nodded, saying nothing, because I didn't trust myself to speak, and turned away from her, toward the walkway, the plane, and home.

First class was more crowded this time than it had been on my way out. A guy about my age and exactly my height, with curly blond hair and bright blue eyes, took the seat next to me as I was struggling to get the seat belt (much tighter this time) around myself. We nodded politely at each other. Then he pulled out a sheaf of important-looking legal documents with "Confidential" stamped all over them, and I pulled out my *Entertainment Weekly.* He shot a sidelong glance at my reading matter and sighed.

"Jealous?" I asked. He smiled, nodded, and pulled a roll of candy from his pocket.

"Would you like a Mento?" he asked.

"Is that really the singular?" I replied, taking one. He gazed at the roll of Mentos, then looked at me and shrugged. "You know," he said, "that's a good question."

I reclined the seat. He was kind of cute, I mused, and clearly had a good job, or at least the paperwork to make it look like he had a good job. That was what I needed—just a regular guy with a good job, a guy who lived in Philadelphia and read books and adored me. I snuck another look at Mr. Mento and contemplated giving him my card . . . and then I pulled myself up short, hearing my mother's voice and Samantha's voice converging in my head in one loud, desperate shriek: *Are you crazy?*

Maybe in another lifetime, I decided, pulling the blanket up under my chin. But this one would work out okay. Maybe my father was never going to be my father again, maybe my mother would stay yoked to the Dread Lesbian Tanya forever. Maybe my sister would always be unstable, and maybe my brother would never learn how to smile. But I could still find good in the world. I could still find beauty. And someday, I told myself, before I fell asleep, maybe I'd even find someone else to love. "Love," I whispered to the baby. And then I closed my eyes.

If you wish for something hard enough, the fairy tales teach us, you can get it in the end. But it's hardly ever the way you thought it would be, and the endings aren't always happy ones. For months, I had been wishing for Bruce, dreaming of Bruce, conjuring a memory of his face and holding it in front of me as I fell asleep, even when I tried not to. In the end, it was almost like I'd wished him into being, that I'd dreamed so hard and so often that he couldn't help but appear before me.

It happened just the way Samantha had said it would. "You'll see him again," she'd told me that morning months ago when I told her that I was expecting. "I've seen enough soap operas to guarantee it."

I got off the plane, yawning to clear my clogged-up ears, and there, in the waiting area directly across from me, beneath a sign that read "Tampa/St. Pete's" was Bruce. I felt my heart lift, thinking that he'd come for me, that, somehow, he'd come for me, until I saw that he was with some girl I'd never seen before. Short, pale, her hair in a pageboy. Light blue jeans, a pale yellow Oxford shirt tucked in. Nondescript, fade-into-the-woodwork clothes, medium features and a medium frame. Nothing remarkable about her at all except for her thick unruly eyebrows. My replacement, I presumed.

I froze in place, paralyzed by the horrible coincidence, the outrageous misfortune of this. But if it was going to happen, this would be the place—the giant, soulless Newark International Airport, where travelers from New York, New Jersey, and Philadelphia converged in search of transatlantic flights and/or cheap domestic airfare.

For about five seconds I stood stock-still and prayed that they wouldn't see me. I tried to edge off to the side of the lounge, to skirt the entire area, thinking that there had to be some way to duck onto the escalator, grab my bags, and escape. But then Bruce's eyes locked on mine, and I knew it was too late.

He bent down, whispering something to the girl, who turned her head away before I could get a good look. Then he crossed the concourse, walking right toward me, wearing a red T-shirt that I'd snuggled up against a hundred times and blue shorts that I remembered seeing him put on, and pull off, just as often. I sent up a quick prayer of thanks for Garth's haircut, for my tan, for my diamond earrings, and endured a sudden spasm of misery that I wasn't still wearing that grand and gaudy diamond ring. It was completely superficial, I knew, but I hoped I looked good. As good as somebody seven and a half months pregnant could look after a six-hour plane trip, at least.

And then Bruce was right in front of me, looking pale and solemn. "Hey, Cannie," he said. His eyes fell to my midsection as if it were magnetized. "So you . . ."

"That's right," I said coolly. "I'm pregnant." I stood up straight and tightened my grip on Nifkin's case. Nifkin, of course, had smelled Bruce and was in the midst of trying to leap out and greet him. I could hear his tail thumping as he whined.

Bruce raised his eyes to the computerized board over the doorway I'd just passed through. "You're coming from L.A.?" he asked, showing that his reading abilities had not diminished during our time apart.

I gave another curt nod, hoping he couldn't tell how badly my knees were shaking. "What are you doing here?" I asked.

"Vacation," he said. "We're going to Florida for the weekend."

We, I thought bitterly, staring at him. He looked just the same. A little thinner, maybe, with a few more strands of gray in his ponytail, but still, same old Bruce, right down to his smell, to his smile, and the half-laced doodled-on basketball sneakers. "How nice for you," I said.

Bruce didn't take the bait. "So were you in L.A. for work?"

"I had some meetings on the coast," I said. I have always wanted to say that to someone.

"The *Examiner* sent you to California?" he asked.

"No, I had meetings about my screenplay," I said.

"You sold your screenplay?" He seemed genuinely happy for me. "Cannie, that's great!"

I said nothing, glaring at him. Of all the things I needed from him—love, support, money, the bare acknowledgment that I existed, that our baby existed, and that any of it mattered to him, his congratulations felt exceedingly paltry.

"I . . . I'm sorry," he finally managed. And with that I was furious. How rotten of him, I thought, showing up at an airport to take Little Miss Pageboy on vacation, mouthing his pathetic apology, as if it could undo the months of silence, the worry I'd gone through, the anguish of missing him and figuring out how to provide for a baby on my own. And I was furious, too, for his complacency. He didn't care—not about me, not about the baby. He'd never called, never asked, never *cared*. Just left me—left us—all alone. Who did this remind me of?

I knew, at that moment, that my anger wasn't really for him. It was for my father, of course, the Original Abandoner, the author of all of my insecurities and fears. But my father was three thousand miles away from me, with his back eternally turned. If I could only step back and look at it clearly, I'd see that Bruce was just some guy, like a thousand other guys, right down to the pot and the ponytail and the half-intended slipshod lazy life, right down to the dissertation he'd never finish, the bookshelves he'd never build, and the bathtub he'd never clean. Guys like Bruce were as common as white cotton socks sold in six-packs at the Wal-Mart, if not as clean, and all I'd have to do to acquire another one would be to show up at a Phish concert and smile.

But Bruce, as opposed to my father, was right here . . . and he was far from innocent. After all, hadn't he left me, too?

I set Nifkin down and turned to face Bruce, feeling all of my fury—years of it—curl in my chest and rise to my throat. "You're *sorry?*" I spat.

He took a step backward. "I am sorry," he said, and his voice was so sad it sounded like he was being ripped open from the inside. "I know I should have called you, but . . . I just . . ."

I narrowed my eyes. He dropped his hands. "It was just too much," he whispered. "With my father and all."

I rolled my eyes to show what I thought of that excuse, and to make it clear that he and I would not be exchanging tender reminiscences of Bernard Guberman, or anything else, anytime soon.

"I know how strong you are," he told me. "I knew you'd be okay."

"Well, I have to be, don't I, Bruce? You didn't leave me much of a choice."

"I'm sorry," Bruce said again, looking even more wretched. "I . . . I hope you'll be happy."

"I can feel those good wishes radiating right off you," I retorted. "Oh, wait. My mistake. That's just pot smoke." It felt as if a part of me had detached from my body, floated up to the ceiling, and was watching this scene unfold in terror . . . and in great sadness. *Cannie, oh, Cannie,* a little voice mourned, *this isn't who you're angry at.*

"And you know what?" I asked him. "I'm sorry about your father. He was a man. You, you're nothing but a boy with big feet and facial hair. And you're never going to be anything else. You'll never be more than a third-rate writer at a second-rate magazine, and God help you when you can't peddle any more memories of what we had together."

The girlfriend sidled up to his side and laced her fingers through his. I just kept talking. "You'll never be as good as me, and you're always going to know that I was the best you ever had."

The girlfriend attempted to say something, but I wasn't going to stop.

"You're always going to be some big goofy guy with a bunch of tapes in cardboard shoeboxes. The guy with the rolling papers. The guy with the Grateful Dead bootleg. Good old Bruce. Except that shtick gets tired after sophomore year. It gets old, the same way that you're getting old. It's unimproved, just like your writing. And you know what else?" I stepped right up to him, so we were practically toe to toe. "You're *never* going to finish that dissertation. And you're *always* going to live in New Jersey."

Bruce stood there, stunned. His mouth was literally gaping open. It wasn't a good look, emphasizing as it did his weak chin, and the network of wrinkles around his eyes.

The girlfriend looked up at me.

"Leave us alone," she said in a little squeaky voice. My new Manolo Blahnik slides gave me an extra three inches and I felt Amazonian, powerful, untroubled by this little wisp of a thing who barely cleared my shoulders. I gave her my very best shut-up-and-let-the-smart-people-talk look, the one I'd perfected over the years on my siblings. I wondered if she'd ever heard of tweezers. Sure, she could probably be looking at me and wondering whether I'd ever heard of Slim-Fast . . . or of birth control, for that matter. I found that I didn't much care.

"I don't think I was actually saying anything to you," I said, and dredged up a line from the Take Back the Night March, circa 1989. "I don't believe in blaming the victim."

That snapped Bruce back to reality. He tightened his grip on her hand. "Leave her alone," he said.

"Oh, Jesus." I sighed. "Like I'm the one doing anything to either one of you. For your information," I told the girlfriend, "I wrote him exactly one letter when I found out I was pregnant. One letter. And I won't do it again. I've got plenty of money, and a better job than he does, in case he neglected to mention that when he gave you our history, and I'm going to do just fine. I hope the two of you are very happy together." I picked up Nifkin, tossed my great hair, and breezed past a security guard. "I'd search his luggage," I said, loud enough for Bruce to hear, "he's probably holding."

And then, still being pregnant, I went to the bathroom to pee.

My knees felt like water, my cheeks were hot. Hah, I thought. Hah!

I stood, flushed, and opened the cubicle door. And there was the new girlfriend, her arms crossed against her meager chest.

"Yes?" I inquired politely. "You have a comment?"

Her mouth twisted. She had, I noticed, a bit of an overbite.

"You think you're so smart," she said. "He never really loved you. He told me he didn't." Her voice was getting higher. Squeak, squeak, squeak. She sounded like a little stuffed animal, the kind that bleated when you squeezed it.

"Whereas you," I said, "are obviously the real love of his life." I knew, deep in my heart, in my good heart, that whatever quarrel I had, it wasn't with her. But it was as if I couldn't help myself.

Her lip curled, literally curled, like Nifkin's when we played with his fluffy toys.

"Why don't you leave us alone?" she hissed.

"Leave you alone?" I repeated. "Leave you alone? See, this is the theme you keep coming back to, and I don't understand it. I'm not doing anything to either one of you. I live in Philadelphia, for heaven's sake. . . ."

And then I saw it. Something in her face, and I knew what it was.

"He's still talking about me, right?" I asked.

She opened her mouth to say something. I decided I didn't want to stay around and hear it. I was suddenly enormously tired. I ached for sleep, for home, for my bed.

"He doesn't," she began.

"I don't have time for this," I told her, cutting her off. "I've got a life." I tried to walk past her, but she was standing right by the sink, not giving me the room to pass.

"Move," I said shortly.

"No," she said. "No, you listen to me!" She put her hands on my shoulders, trying to get me to hold still, shoving me slightly. One minute I was up, trying to get past her, and the next minute my foot slipped on a puddle of water. My ankle buckled, turning underneath me. And I fell sideways, slamming my belly into the hard edge of the sink.

Bright pain flared, and I was lying on my back, lying on the floor, my ankle twisted at an angle I knew couldn't mean anything good, and she was standing above me, panting like an animal, her cheeks flushed hectic red.

I sat up, putting both palms flat on the floor, and grabbed for the sink, when I felt a sudden tearing cramp. When I looked down and saw that I was bleeding. Not a lot, but . . . well, blood is not something you want to see anywhere below the belt when you're only halfway through month seven.

Somehow I yanked myself to my feet. My ankle hurt so badly I felt sick, and I could feel blood trickling down my leg.

I stared at her. She stared back, following my gaze down to where the blood was falling in thick drips. Then she clapped one hand over her mouth, turned, and ran.

Things were starting to go fuzzy around the edges, and waves of pain were making their way through my belly. I'd read about this. I knew what it meant, and I knew that it was too early, that I was in trouble. "Help," I tried to say, but there was no one there to hear. "Help . . . ," I said again, and then the world went gray, then black.

PART FIVE

Joy

EIGHTEEN

When I opened my eyes, I was underwater. In a swimming pool? The lake at summer camp? The ocean? I wasn't sure. I could see the light above me, filtered through the water, and I could feel the pull of what was underneath me, the dark depths I couldn't make out.

I'd spent most of my life in the water swimming with my mother, but it was my father who'd taught me how, when I was little. He'd flip a silver dollar into the water, and I'd follow it down, learning how to hold my breath, how to go deeper than I thought I could, how to propel myself back to the top. "Sink or swim," my father would tell me when I'd come up empty-handed and sputtering and complaining that I couldn't, that the water was too cold or too deep. *Sink or swim.* And I'd go back into the water. I wanted the silver dollar, but, more than that, I wanted to please him.

My father. Was he here? I turned around frantically, paddling, trying to flip myself up toward where I thought the light was coming from. But I was getting dizzy. I was getting all turned around. And it was hard to keep paddling, hard to stay afloat, and I could feel the bottom of the ocean tugging at me, and I thought how nice it would be just to stop, not to move, to let myself float to the bottom, to sink into the soft silt of a thousand seashells ground down fine, to let myself sleep . . .

Sink or swim. Live or die.

I heard a voice, coming from the surface.

What is your name?

Leave me alone, I thought. *I'm tired. I'm so tired.* I could feel the darkness pulling me, and I craved it.

What is your name?

I opened my eyes, squinting in the bright white light.

Cannie, I muttered. *I'm Cannie, now leave me alone.*

Stay with us, Cannie, said the voice. I shook my head. I didn't want to be here, wherever here was. I wanted to be back in the water, where I was invisible, where I was free. I wanted to go swimming again. I shut my eyes. The silver dollar flashed and glittered in the sunlight, arcing through the air, plunging into the water, and I followed it back down.

I closed my eyes again and saw my bed. Not my bed in Philadelphia, with its soothing blue comforter and bright, pretty pillows, but my bed from when I was a little girl—narrow, neatly made, with its red and brown paisley spread tucked tight around it and a spill of hardcover books shoved underneath. I blinked and saw the girl on the bed, a sturdy, sober-faced girl with green eyes and brown hair in a ponytail that spilled over her shoulders. She was lying on her side, a book spread open before her. Me? I wondered. My daughter? I couldn't be sure.

I remembered that bed—how it had been my refuge as a little girl, how it had been the one place I felt safe as a teenager, the place my father would never come. I remember spending hours there on weekends, sitting cross-legged with a friend on the other side of the bed, with the telephone and a melting pint of ice cream between us, talking about boys, about school, about the future, and how our lives would be, and I wanted to go back there, wanted to go back so badly, before things went wrong, before my father's departure and Bruce's betrayal, before I knew how it all turned out.

I looked down, and the girl on the bed looked up from her book, up at me, and her eyes were wide and clear.

I looked at the girl, and she smiled at me. *Mom,* she said.

* * *

Cannie?

I groaned as if waking from the most delicious dream and slitted my eyes open again.

Squeeze my hand if you can hear this, Cannie.

I squeezed weakly. I could hear voices burbling above me, heard something about blood type, something else about fetal monitor. Maybe this was the dream, and the girl on the bed was real? Or the water? Maybe I really had gone swimming, maybe I'd swum out too far, gotten tired, maybe I was drowning right now, and the picture of my bed was just a little something my brain had whipped up by way of last-minute entertainment.

Cannie? said the voice again, sounding almost frantic. *Stay with us!*

But I didn't want to be there. I wanted to be back in the bed.

The third time I closed my eyes I saw my father. I was back in his office in California, sitting up straight on his white examining table. I could feel the weight of diamonds on my finger, in my ears. I could feel the weight of his gaze upon me—warm and full of love, like I remembered it from twenty years ago. He was sitting across from me, in his white doctor's coat, smiling at me. *Tell me how you've been,* he says. *Tell me how you turned out.*

I'm going to have a baby, I told him, and he nodded. *Cannie, that's wonderful!*

I'm a newspaper reporter. I wrote a movie, I told him. *I have friends. A dog. I live in the city.*

My father smiled. *I'm so proud of you.*

I reached for him and he took my hand and held it. *Why didn't you say so before?* I asked. *It would have changed everything, if I'd just known you cared. . . .*

He smiled at me, looking puzzled, like I'd stopped speaking English, or like he'd stopped understanding it. And when he took his hands away I opened mine and found a silver dollar in my palm. *It's yours,* he said. *You found it. You always did. You always could.*

But even as he spoke he was turning away.

I want to ask you something, I said. He was at the door, like I remembered, his hand on the knob, but this time he turned and looked at me.

I stared at him, feeling my throat go dry, saying nothing.

How could you? is what I thought. *How could you leave your own children?* Lucy was just fifteen, and Josh was only nine. How could you do that; how could you walk away?

Tears slid down my face. My father walked back to me. He pulled a carefully folded handkerchief from his breast pocket, where he always kept them. It smelled like the cologne he always wore, like lemons, and the starch the Chinese laundry place put in, like they always did. Very carefully, my father bent down and wiped away my tears.

Then there was the darkness below me again, and the light above.

Sink or swim, I thought ruefully. And what if I wanted to sink? What was there to keep me afloat?

I thought of my father's hand on my cheek, and I thought of the steady green-eyed gaze of the girl on the bed. I thought about what it felt to take a warm shower after a long bike ride, to slip into the ocean on a hot summer day. I thought about the taste of the tiny strawberries Maxi and I had found at the farmer's market. I thought about my friends, and Nifkin. I thought about my own bed, lined with flannel sheets softened from many trips through the dryer, with a book on the pillow and Nifkin perched beside me. And I thought for a minute about Bruce . . . not about Bruce specifically, but the feeling of falling in love, of being loved, of being worthy. *Treasured,* I heard Maxi say.

So okay, I thought. Fine. I'll swim. For myself, and for my daughter. For all the things I love, and everyone who loves me.

When I woke up again I heard voices.

"That doesn't look right," said one. "Are you sure it's hanging the right way?"

My mother, I thought. Who else?

"What's this yellow stuff?" demanded another voice—young, female, crabby. Lucy. "Probably pudding."

"It's not pudding," I heard in a raspy growl. Tanya.

Then: "Lucy! Get your finger out of your sister's lunch!"

"She's not going to eat it," Lucy said sulkily.

"I don't know why they even brought food," Tanya rumbled.

"Find some ginger ale," said my mother. "And some ice cubes. They said she can have ice cubes when she wakes up."

My mother leaned close. I could smell her—a combination of Chloe and sunscreen and Pert shampoo. "Cannie?" she murmured. I opened my eyes—for real this time—and saw that I wasn't underwater, or in my old bedroom, or in my father's office. I was in a hospital, in a bed. There was an IV taped to the back of my hand, a plastic bracelet with my name on it around my wrist, a semicircle of machines beeping and chirping around me. I lifted my head and saw down to my toes—no belly looming up between my face and my feet.

"Baby," I said. My voice sounded strange and squeaky. Someone stepped out of the shadows. Bruce.

"Hey, Cannie," he said, sounding sheepish, looking wretched, and horribly ashamed.

I waved him away with the hand that didn't have a needle stuck in it. "Not you," I said. "My baby."

"I'll get the doctor," said my mother.

"No, let me," said Tanya. The two of them looked at each other, then hustled out of the room as if by mutual agreement. Lucy shot me a quick unreadable look and dashed out behind them. Which left just me and Bruce.

"What happened?" I asked.

Bruce swallowed hard. "I think maybe the doctor better tell you that."

Now I was starting to remember—the airport, the bathroom, his new girlfriend. Falling. And then blood.

I tried to sit up. Hands eased me back onto the bed.

"What happened?" I demanded, my voice spiraling toward hysteria. "Where am I? Where's my baby? What happened?"

A face leaned into my line of sight—a doctor, no doubt, in a white coat with the obligatory stethoscope and plastic name tag.

"I see you're awake!" he said heartily. I scowled at him. "Tell me your name," he said.

I took a deep breath, suddenly aware that I was hurting. From my belly button on down it felt like I'd been torn open and sewn back together sloppily. My ankle throbbed in time with my heartbeat. "I'm Candace Shapiro," I began, "and I was pregnant . . ." My voice caught in my throat. "What happened?" I begged. "Is my baby okay?"

The doctor cleared his throat. "You had what's known as placenta abruptio," he began. "Which means that your placenta separated from your uterus all at once. That's what caused the bleeding . . . and the premature labor."

"So my baby . . . ," I whispered.

The doctor looked somber.

"Your baby was in distress when they brought you in here. We did a cesarean section, but because we didn't have the fetal monitor in place, we aren't sure whether she was deprived of oxygen, and if so, for how long."

He kept talking. Low birth weight. Premature. Underdeveloped lungs. Ventilator. NICU. He told me that my uterus was torn during the delivery, that I was bleeding so badly, they had to take "radical steps." Radical as in my uterus was now gone. "We hate to have to do this to young women," he said gravely, "but the circumstances left us no choice."

He droned on and on about counseling, therapy, adoption, egg harvesting, and surrogates until I wanted to scream, to claw at his throat, to force him to give me the answer to the only question I cared about anymore. I looked at my mother, who bit her lip and looked away as I struggled to sit up. The doctor looked alarmed, and tried to ease me back down onto my back, but I wasn't going. "My baby," I said. "Is it a boy or girl?"

"A girl," he said—reluctantly, I thought.

"Girl," I repeated, and started to cry. My daughter, I thought, my poor daughter whom I couldn't keep safe, not even on her way into the world. I looked at my mother, who'd come back and was leaning against the wall, blowing her nose. Bruce put his hand awkwardly on my arm.

"Cannie," he said, "I'm sorry."

"Get away from me," I wept. "Just go." I wiped my eyes, shoved my matted hair behind my ears, and looked at the doctor. "I want to see my baby."

They eased me into a wheelchair, sore and stitched up, hurting all over, and wheeled me to the Neonatal Intensive Care Unit. I couldn't go in, they explained, but I could see her through the window. A nurse pointed her out. "There," she said, gesturing.

I leaned so close my forehead pressed on the glass. She was so small. A wrinkled pink grapefruit. Limbs no bigger than my pinky, hands the size of my thumbnail, a head the size of a smallish nectarine. Tiny eyes squinched shut, a look of outrage on her face. A dusting of black fuzz on top of her head, a nondescript beige-ish hat on top of that. "She weighs almost three pounds," the nurse who was pushing me said.

Baby, I whispered, and tapped my fingers against the windows, drumming a soft rhythm. She hadn't been moving, but when I tapped she pinwheeled her arms. Waving at me, I imagined. *Hi, baby,* I said.

The nurse watched me closely. "You okay?"

"She needs a better hat," I said. My throat felt thick, clotted with grief, and there were tears running down my face, but I wasn't crying. It was more like leaking. As if I was so full of sadness and a strange, doomed kind of hope that there was nowhere for it to go but out. "At home, in her room, the yellow room with the crib, in the dresser, the top drawer, I've got lots of baby hats. My Mom has keys. . . ."

The nurse leaned down. "I have to bring you back," she said.

"Please make them give her a nicer hat," I repeated. Stupid, stubborn. She didn't need fashionable headgear, she needed a miracle, and even I could see that.

The nurse bent closer. "Tell me her name," she said. And sure enough, there was a piece of paper taped to one end of the box. "BABY GIRL SHAPIRO," it read.

I opened my mouth, not sure what would happen, but when the word came I knew instantly, in my heart, that it was right.

"Joy," I said. "Her name is Joy."

When I came back to my room Maxi was there. A quartet of candy-stripers clustered at the door of my room, their faces like blossoms, or balloons packed tight together. Maxi pulled a white curtain close around my bed, shutting them out. She was dressed more soberly than I'd ever seen her—black jeans, black sneakers, a hooded sweatshirt—and she was carrying roses, a ridiculous armload of roses, the kind of garland you'd drape around a prizewinning horse's neck. Or lay across a casket, I thought grimly.

"I came as soon as I heard," she said, her face drawn. "Your mother and sister are outside. They'll only let one of us in at a time."

She sat beside me and held my hand, the one with the tube in it, and didn't seem alarmed when I didn't look at her, or even squeeze back. "Poor Cannie," she said. "Have you seen the baby?"

I nodded, brushing tears from my cheeks. "She's very small," I managed, and started to sob.

Maxi winced, looking helpless, and dismayed at being helpless.

"Bruce came," I said, weeping.

"I hope you told him to go to hell," said Maxi.

"Something like that," I said. I wiped my non-needled hand across my face and wished for Kleenex. "This is disgusting," I said, and hic-coughed a sob. "This is really pathetic and disgusting."

Maxi leaned close, cradling my head in her arm. "Oh, Cannie," she said sadly. I closed my eyes. There was nothing left for me to ask, nothing else to say.

After Maxi left I slept for a while, curled up on my side. If I had any dreams, I didn't remember them. And when I woke up Bruce was standing in the doorway.

I blinked and stared at him.

"Can I do anything?" he asked. I just stared, saying nothing. "Cannie?" he asked uneasily.

"Come closer," I beckoned. "I don't bite. Or push," I added meanly.

Bruce walked toward my bed. He looked pale, edgy, twitchy in his own skin, or maybe just unhappy to be near me again. I could see a sprinkling of blackheads on his nose, standing out in sharp relief, and I could tell from his posture, from the way his hands were crammed in his pockets and how his eyes never left the linoleum, that this was killing him, that he wanted to be anywhere but here. *Good,* I thought, feeling rage bubble up in my chest. Good. Let him hurt.

He settled himself on the chair next to my bed, looking at me in quick little peeks—the drainage tubes snaking out from beneath my sheet, the I.V. bag hanging beside me. I hoped that he was sickened by it. I hoped that he was scared.

"I can tell you exactly how many days it's been since we talked," I said.

Bruce closed his eyes.

"I can tell you exactly what your bedroom looks like, exactly what you said the last time we were together."

He grabbed for me, clutching blindly. "Cannie, please," he said. "Please. I'm sorry." Words I once thought I would have given anything to hear. He started crying. "I never wanted . . . I never meant for this to happen. . . ."

I looked at him. I didn't feel love, or hate. I didn't feel anything but a bone-deep weariness. Like I was suddenly a hundred years old, and I knew at that moment I would have to live a hundred more years, carrying my grief around like a backpack full of stones.

I closed my eyes, knowing that it was too late for us. Too much had happened, and none of it was good. A body in motion stays in motion. I'd started the whole thing by telling him I'd wanted to take a break. Or maybe he'd started it by asking me out in the first place. What did it matter anymore?

I turned my face to the wall. After a while, Bruce stopped crying. And a while after that, I heard him leave.

I woke up the next morning with sunlight spilling across my face. Instantly my mother hurried through the door and pulled a chair up beside my bed. She looked uncomfortable—she was good about crack-ing jokes, laughing things off, keeping a stiff upper lip and soldiering on, but she wasn't any good with tears.

"How are you doing?" she asked.

"I'm shitty!" I shrieked, and my mother pulled back so fast that her wheeled chair scooted halfway across the room. I didn't even wait for her to pull herself back toward me before continuing my tirade. "How do you think I am? I gave birth to something that looks like a junior-high science experiment, and I'm all cut open and I h-h-hurt . . ."

I put my face in my hands and sobbed for a minute. "There's something wrong with me," I wept. "I'm defective. You should have let me die. . . ."

"Oh, Cannie," my mother said, "Cannie, don't talk that way."

"Nobody loves me," I cried. "Dad didn't, Bruce didn't . . ."

My mother patted my hair. "Don't talk that way," she repeated. "You have a beautiful baby. A little on the petite side, for the time being, but very beautiful." She cleared her throat, got to her feet, and started pacing—typical Mom behavior when there was something painful coming.

"Sit down," I told her wearily, and she did, but I could see one of her feet jiggling anxiously.

"I had a talk with Bruce," she said.

I exhaled sharply. I didn't even want to hear his name. My mother could tell this from my face, but she kept talking.

"With Bruce," she continued, "and his new girlfriend."

"The Pusher?" I asked, my voice high and sharp and hysterical. "You saw her?"

"Cannie, she feels just awful. They both do."

"They should," I said angrily. "Bruce never even called me, the whole time I was pregnant, then the Pusher does her thing . . ."

My mother looked shaken by my tone. "The doctors aren't sure that's what caused you to . . ."

"It doesn't matter," I said querulously. "I believe that's what did it, and I hope that dumb bitch does, too."

My mother was shocked. "Cannie . . ."

"Cannie what? You think I'm going to forgive them? I'll never forgive them. My baby almost died, I almost died, I'll never have another baby, and now just because they're sorry, it's all supposed to be okay? I'll never forgive them. Never."

My mother sighed. "Cannie," she said gently.

"I can't believe you're taking their side!" I yelled.

"I'm not taking their side, Cannie, of course I'm not," she said. "I'm taking your side. I just don't think it's healthy for you to be so angry."

"Joy almost died," I said.

"But she didn't," said my mother. "She didn't die. She's going to be fine. . . ."

"You don't know that," I said furiously.

"Cannie," said my mother. "She's a little underweight, and her lungs are a little underdeveloped . . ."

"She was deprived of oxygen! Didn't you hear them! Deprived of oxygen! There could be all kinds of things wrong!"

"She looks just the way you did when you were a baby," my mother said impatiently. "She's going to be fine. I just know it."

"You didn't even know you were gay until you were fifty-six!" I shouted. "How am I supposed to believe you about anything!"

I pointed toward the door. "Go away," I said, and started to cry.

My mother shook her head. "I'm not going," she said. "Talk to me."

"What do you want to hear about?" I said, trying to wipe my face off, trying to sound normal. "My my asshole ex-boyfriend's idiot new girlfriend pushed me, and my baby almost died. . . ."

But what was really wrong—the part that I didn't think I'd be able to bring myself to say—was that I had failed Joy. I'd failed to be good enough, pretty enough, thin enough, lovable enough, to keep my father in my life. Or to keep Bruce. And now, I'd failed at keeping my baby safe.

My mother wheeled in close again and wrapped her arms around me.

"I didn't deserve her," I wept. "I couldn't keep her safe, I let her get hurt . . ."

"What gave you that idea?" she whispered into my hair. "Cannie, it was an accident. It wasn't your fault. You're going to be a wonderful mother."

"If I'm so great, why didn't he love me?" I wept, and I wasn't even sure who I was talking about—Bruce? My father? "What's wrong with me?"

My mother stood up. I followed her eyes to the clock on the wall. She watched me watching, and bit her lip. "I'm sorry," she said softly, "but I have to run out for a few minutes."

I wiped my eyes, buying time, trying to process what she'd told me. "You have to . . ."

"I have to pick up Tanya at her continuing education class."

"What, Tanya forgot how to drive?"

"Her car's in the shop."

"And what is she studying today? Which facet of herself is she addressing?" I inquired. "Codependent granddaughters of emotionally distant grandparents?"

"Give it a rest, Cannie," my mother snapped, and I was so stunned that I couldn't even think to start crying again. "I know you don't like her, and I'm sick of hearing about it."

"Oh, and now is the time you decided to bring it up? You couldn't wait until maybe your granddaughter makes it out of intensive care?"

My mother pursed her lips. "I'll talk to you later," she said, and walked out the door. With her hand on the doorknob, she turned to face me one more time. "I know you don't believe it, but you're going to be fine. You have everything you need. You just have to know it in your own heart."

I scowled. *Know it in my own heart*. It sounded like New Age crap, like something she'd pirated from one of Tanya's stupid *Healing Your Hurt* workbooks.

"Sure," I called after her. "Go! I'm good at being left. I'm used to it."

She didn't turn around. I sighed, staring at my blanket and hoping none of the nurses had heard me spouting third-rate soap opera dialogue. I felt absolutely wretched. I felt hollow, like my insides had been scooped out and all that was left was echoing emptiness, vacant black holes. How was I going to figure out how to be a decent parent, given the choices my own parents had made?

You have everything you need, she'd told me. But I couldn't see what she meant. I considered my life and saw only what was missing—no father, no boyfriend, no promise of health or comfort for my daughter. Everything I need, I thought ruefully, and closed my eyes, hoping that I'd dream again of my bed, or of the water.

When the door opened again an hour later I didn't even look up.

"Tell it to Tanya," I said, with my eyes still shut. "'Cause I don't want to hear it."

"Well, I would," said a familiar deep voice, "but I don't think she has much use for my kind . . . and also, we haven't really been introduced."

I looked up. Dr. K. was standing there, with a white bakery box in one hand and a black duffel bag in the other. And the duffel bag appeared to be wriggling.

"I came as soon as I heard," he began, folding himself into the seat my mother had recently occupied, setting the box on my nightstand and the duffel bag on his lap. "How are you feeling?"

"Okay," I said. He looked at me carefully. "Well, actually lousy."

"I can believe it, after what you've been through. How is . . ."

"Joy," I said. Using her name felt strange . . . presumptuous somehow, as if I was testing fate by saying it out loud. "She's small, and her lungs are a little underdeveloped, and she's breathing with a ventilator . . ." I paused and swiped a hand across my eyes. "Also, I had a hysterectomy, and I seem to be crying all the time."

He cleared his throat.

"Was that too much information?" I asked through my tears.

He shook his head. "Not at all," he told me. "You can talk to me about anything you want to."

The black duffel bag practically lurched off his lap. It looked so funny I almost smiled, but it felt as if my face had forgotten how. "Is that a perpetual motion machine in your bag, or are you just glad to see me?"

Dr. K. glanced over his shoulder at the closed door. Then he leaned close to me. "This was kind of a risk," he whispered, "but I thought . . ."

He lifted the bag onto the bed and eased the zipper open. Nifkin's nose popped out, followed by the tips of his oversized ears, and then, in short order, his entire body.

"Nifkin!" I said, as Nifkin scrambled onto my chest and proceeded to give my entire face a tongue-bath. Dr. K held him, lifting him clear of my various tubes and attachments, as Nifkin licked away. "How did you . . . where was he?"

"With your friend Samantha," he explained. "She's outside."

"Thank you," I said, knowing that the words couldn't begin to express how happy he'd made me. "Thank you so much."

"No problem," said the doctor. "Here . . . look. We've been practicing." He lifted Nifkin and set him on the floor. "Can you see?"

I propped myself up on my elbows and nodded.

"Nifkin . . . SIT!" said Dr. K., in a voice every bit as deep and authoritative as James Earl Jones's telling the world that this . . . is CNN. Nifkin's butt hit the linoleum at lightning speed, his tail wagging triple-time. "Nifkin . . . DOWN!" And down went Nifkin, flat on his belly, looking up at Dr. K. with his eyes sparkling and his pink tongue curled as he panted. "And now, for our final act . . . PLAY DEAD!" And Nifkin collapsed onto his side as if he'd been shot.

"Unbelievable," I said. It really was.

"He's a fast learner," said Dr. K., loading the now-squirming terrier back into the duffel bag. He bent back to me. "Feel better, Cannie," he said, and rested one of his hands on top of mine.

He walked out and Samantha walked in, hurrying over to my bed. She was in full lawyer garb—a sleek black suit, high-heeled boots, a caramel-colored leather attaché case in one hand and her sunglasses and car keys in the other. "Cannie," she said, "I came . . ."

". . . as soon as you heard," I supplied.

"How do you feel?" asked Sam. "How's the baby?"

"I feel okay, and the baby . . . well, she's in the baby intensive-care place. They have to wait and see."

Samantha sighed. I closed my eyes. I suddenly felt completely exhausted. And hungry.

I sat up, tucking another pillow behind my back. "Hey, what time is it? When's dinner? You don't have, like, a banana in your purse or something?"

Samantha rose to her feet, grateful, I thought, to have something to do. "I'll go check . . . hey, what's this?"

She pointed at the bakery box that Dr. K. had left behind.

"Don't know," I said. "Dr. K. brought it. Take a look."

Sam ripped through the string and opened the box, and there, inside, was an éclair from the Pink Rose Pastry Shop, a wedge of chocolate bread pudding from Silk City, a brownie still in its Le Bus wrapping paper, and a pint of fresh raspberries.

"Unbelievable," I murmured.

"Yum!" said Samantha. "How does he know what you like?"

"I told him," I said, touched that he'd remember. "For Fat Class, we had to write down what our favorite foods were." Sam cut me a sliver of éclair, but it tasted like dust and stones in my mouth. I swallowed to be polite, sipped some water, then told her that I was tired, that I wanted to sleep.

I stayed in the hospital another week, healing, while Joy got bigger and stronger.

Maxi showed up every morning for a week and sat beside me and read from *People, In Style,* and *Entertainment Weekly* magazines, embroidering each story from her own personal stash of anecdotes. My mother and sister stayed with me in the daytime, making conversation, trying not to linger too long at the pauses that came where I would normally be saying something smart-ass. Samantha came every night after work and regaled me with Philadelphia gossip, about the antiquated former stars Gabby had interviewed and the how Nifkin had taken to stopping, mid-walk, and planting himself in front of my apartment building and refusing to budge. Andy came with his wife and a box of Famous Fourth Street chocolate chip cookies and a card that everyone in the newsroom had signed. "Get Well Soon," it read.

I didn't think that would be happening, but I didn't tell him that.

"They're worried about you," Lucy whispered when my mother was in the hall, talking about something with the nurses.

I looked at her and shrugged.

"They want you to talk to a psychiatrist."

I said nothing. Lucy looked very serious. "It's Dr. Melburne," she said. "I had her for a while. She's horrible. You better cheer up and start talking more, or else she's going to ask you about your childhood."

"Cannie doesn't have to talk if she doesn't want to," said my mother, pouring a cup of ginger ale that nobody would drink. She straightened my flowers, plumped my pillows for the fourteenth time, sat down, then got up again, looking for something else to do. "Cannie can just rest."

Three days later, Joy took her first breaths without the ventilator.

Not out of the woods yet, the doctors warned me. Have to wait and see. She could be fine, or things could go wrong, but probably she'll be okay.

And they let me hold her, finally, lifting up her four-pound-six-ounce body and cradling her close, running my fingertips over each of her hands, each fingernail impossibly small and perfect. She clutched at my finger fiercely with her own tiny ones. I could feel the bones, the push of her blood beneath her skin. *Hang on,* I thought to her. *Hang in there, little one. The world is hard a lot of the time, but there're good things here, too. And I love you. Your mother loves you, baby Joy.*

I sat with her for hours until they made me go back to bed, and before I left I filled out her birth certificate, and my handwriting was clear and firm. Joy Leah Shapiro. The Leah was for Leonard, Bruce's father's middle name. Leah, the second sister, the one Jacob didn't want to marry. Leah, the trick bride, the one her father sent down the aisle in disguise.

I bet Leah had a more interesting life anyhow, I whispered to my baby, holding her hand, with me in my wheelchair and her in her glass box that I forced myself not to see as a coffin. I bet Leah went on hiking trips with her girlfriends and had popcorn and Margaritas for dinner, if that's what she wanted. I'll bet she went swimming naked and slept under the stars. Rachel probably bought Celine Dion CDs and those Franklin Mint collectible plates. She was probably boring, even to herself. She never went on an adventure, never took a chance. But you and me, baby, we're going to go on adventures. I will teach you how to swim, and how to sail, and how to build a fire . . . everything my mother taught me, and everything else I've learned. Just make it out of here, I thought, as hard as I could. Come home, Joy, and we'll both be fine.

Two days later, I got part of my wish. They sent me home, but decided to keep Joy. "Just for another few weeks," said the doctor, in what I'm sure he imagined was a comforting tone. "We want to make sure that her lungs are mature . . . and that she's gained enough weight."

I burst into bitter laughter at that one. "If she takes after her mother," I announced, "that shouldn't be a problem. She'll gain weight like a champ."

The doctor gave me what he no doubt believed was a comforting pat on the shoulder. "Don't worry," he said. "Things should be fine."

I limped out of the hospital, blinking, in the warm May sunshine, and eased myself into my mother's car, sitting quietly as we drove back home. I saw the leaves, the fresh green grass, the St. Peter's schoolgirls in crisp plaid jumpers. I saw, but didn't see. To me, the whole world looked gray. It was as if there was no room inside of me for anything except fury and fear.

My mother and Lucy unloaded my bags from the trunk and walked me to my building. Lucy carried my bags. My mother walked slowly beside me, and Tanya huffed behind us. My leg muscles felt wobbly and underused. My stitches ached, my ankle itched in its walking cast. It turned out that I'd only sprained my ankle when I'd fallen, but nobody had thought to look at my legs until days later, so the foot had stayed bent, and the tendons stayed torn, which meant a walking cast for six weeks: small potatoes, in relation to everything else I was dealing with.

I fumbled through my purse. My wallet, the half-empty pack of chewing gum, a Chap Stick and a book of matches from the Star Bar looked like relics from another life. I was groping for my keys when Lucy put her key into the first-floor door.

"I don't live here," I said.

"You do now," said Lucy. She was beaming at me. My mother and Tanya were, too.

I limped across the threshold, my cast thumping on the hardwood floors, and stepped inside, blinking.

The apartment—a twin of mine up on the third floor, all dark wood and circa 1970s fixtures—had been transformed.

Sunlight streamed in from windows that hadn't been there before, sparkling on the pristine, polished maple floors that had been neither pristine nor polished nor maple when I'd last seen the place.

I walked slowly into the kitchen, moving as if I were underwater. New cabinets stained the color of clover honey. In the living room were a new couch and love seat, overstuffed and comfortable, upholstered in buttery yellow denim—pretty, but sturdy, I remember telling Maxi, as I pointed out things I coveted in the latest issue of *Martha Stewart Living* one lazy afternoon. A beautiful woven rug in garnet and dark blue and gold covered the floor. There was a flat-screen TV and a brand new stereo in the corner, stacks of brand-new baby books on the shelves.

Lucy was practically dancing, beside herself with joy. "Can you believe it, Cannie? Isn't it amazing?"

"I don't know what to say," I told her, moving down the hall. The bathroom was unrecognizable. The Carter administration-era pastel wallpaper, the ugly dark wood vanity, the cheap stainless steel fixtures, and the cracked toilet bowl—all gone. Everything was white tile, with gold and navy accents. The tub was a whirlpool bath, with two showerheads, in case, I guessed, I wanted to bathe with a partner. There were new glass-fronted cabinets, fresh lilies in a vase, a profusion of the thickest towels I ever felt stacked on a brand-new shelf. A tiny white tub for giving the baby a bath sat on one counter, along with an assortment of bath toys, little sponges cut into the shapes of animals, and a family of rubber duckies.

"Wait until you see the baby's room!" Lucy crowed.

The walls were painted Lemonade Stand yellow, just the way I'd done them upstairs, and I recognized the crib that Dr. K. had put together. But the rest of the furniture was new. I saw an ornate changing table, a dresser, a white wood rocking chair. "Antiques," Tanya breathed, running one thick fingertip along the curved whitewashed wood that was tinged very faintly pink. There were framed pictures on the walls—a mermaid swimming in the ocean, a sailboat, elephants marching two by two. And in the corner was what looked like the world's smallest branch of Toys "R" Us. There was every toy I'd ever seen, plus a few I hadn't. A set of building blocks. Rattles. Balls. Toys that talked, or barked, or cried, when you squeezed them, or pulled their strings. The exact same rocking horse I'd admired in a shop in Santa Monica two months ago. Everything.

I sank slowly down into the yellow denim love seat, underneath the hanging mobile of delicate stars and clouds and crescent moons, next to a three-foot-high Paddington Bear.

"There's more," said Lucy.

"You won't even believe it," said my mother.

I wandered back to the bedroom. My plain metal bedframe had been replaced with a magnificent wrought-iron canopy bed. My pink sheets had been swapped for something gorgeous—rich stripes of white and gold, tiny pink flowers.

"That's two-hundred-thread-count cotton," Lucy boasted, ticking off the merits of my new linens, pointing out the pillow shams and dust ruffle, the hand-knotted carpet (yellow, with a border of pink roses) on the floor, opening the closet to show off yet more of the pinkish-whitewashed antique furniture—a nine-drawer dresser, a bedside table topped with a gorgeous spray of daffodils in a blue ginger jar.

"Open the blinds," said Lucy.

I did. There was a new deck outside the bedroom window. There was a big clay pot of geraniums and petunias, benches and a picnic table, a gas grill the size of a Volkswagen Bug in the corner.

I sat down—collapsed, really—onto the bed. There was a tiny

card on the pillow, the kind you'd get with a bouquet of flowers. I slid it open with my thumbnail.

"Welcome home," it read on one side. "From your friends," said the other.

My mother and Lucy and Tanya stood in a line, regarding me, waiting to hear my approval.

"Who . . . ," I started. "How . . ."

"Your friends," said Lucy impatiently.

"Maxi?"

The three of them exchanged a sneaky look.

"Come on, you guys. It's not like I've got other friends who could afford all this."

"We couldn't stop her!" Lucy said.

"Really, Cannie, that's true," said my mother. "She wasn't taking no for an answer. She knows all of these contractors . . . she hired a decorator to find you all these things . . . there were people working in here, like, around the clock . . ."

"My neighbors must have loved that," I said.

"Do you like it?" asked Lucy.

"It's . . ." I lifted my hands, and let them sink into my lap. My heart was beating too fast, pushing pain into every part of my body that hurt. I thought of the word that I needed. "It's amazing," I finally said.

"So what do you want to do?" asked Lucy. "We could go to Dmitri's for dinner . . ."

"There's a documentary about lesbians of size at the Ritz," rasped Tanya.

"Shopping?" asked my mother. "Maybe you want to stock up on groceries while we're here to help you carry things."

I got to my feet. "I think I'd like to go for a walk," I said.

My mother and Lucy and Tanya looked at me curiously.

"A walk?" my mother repeated.

"Cannie," my sister pointed out, "your foot's still in a cast."

"It's a walking cast, isn't it?" I snapped. "And I feel like walking." I got to my feet. I wanted to exult in this. I wanted to feel happy. I was surrounded by the people I loved; I had a beautiful place to live. But I felt like I was looking at my new apartment through a dirty mirror, like I was feeling the crisp cottons and plush carpets through thick rubber gloves. It was Joy—not having Joy. None of this would feel right until my baby came home, I thought, and I was suddenly so angry that my arms and legs felt weak with the force of it, and my fists and feet tingled with the desire to hit and kick. Bruce, I thought, Bruce and the goddamn fucking Pusher. This should be my triumph, goddammit, except how can I be happy with my baby still in the hospital, when Bruce and his new girlfriend were the ones who put her there?

"Fine," said my mother uneasily. "So we'll walk."

"No," I said. "By myself. I want to be by myself right now."

They all looked puzzled, even worried, as they filed out the door.

"Call me," said my mother. "Let me know when you're ready for Nifkin to come back."

"I will," I lied. I wanted them out already, out of my house, my hair, my life. I felt like I was burning up, like I had to move or explode. I stared out the window until they'd all piled in the car and driven off. Then I pulled on a jogging bra, a ratty T-shirt, a pair of shorts, a single sneaker, and thumped out of the house and onto the hot sidewalks, determined not to think about my father, about Bruce, about my baby, about anything. I would just walk. And then, maybe, I'd be able to sleep again.

May drifted into June, and all of my days were built around Joy. I'd go to the hospital first thing in the morning, walking the thirty blocks to the Children's Hospital of Philadelphia as the sun came up. Robed and masked and gloved, I'd sit beside her on a sterile rocking chair in the NICU, holding her tiny hand, brushing her lips with my fingertips, singing her the songs we'd danced to months before. Those were the only moments I didn't feel the rage consuming me; the only times I could breathe.

And when I felt the anger coming back, when I'd feel my chest tightening and my hands wanting to hit something, I'd leave her. I'd go home to pace the floors and pump my breasts, to clean and scrub floors and counters that I'd cleaned and scrubbed the day before. And I'd take long, furious walks through the city, with my ankle in the increasingly filthy walking cast, charging through yellow lights and shooting evil glances at any car that dared inch toward the intersection.

I got used to the little voice in my head, the one from the airport, the one that had floated up to the ceiling and watched me rage at Bruce while mourning quietly that he wasn't the one. I got used to the voice asking *Why?* every morning, when I laced up my sneakers and yanked a succession of nondescript shirts over my head . . . and asking *Why?* again at night, when I'd play my messages back—ten, fifteen messages from my mother, my sister, from Maxi, and Peter Krushelevansky, from all of my friends—and then erase each one without ever calling back, until the day I started erasing them without even listening. *You're too sad,* the voice would murmur, as I stomped up Walnut Street. *Take it easy,* said the voice, as I gulped scalding black coffee, cup after cup, for breakfast. *Talk to someone,* said the voice. *Let them help.* I ignored it. Who could help me now? What was there left for me but the streets and the hospital, my silent apartment, and my empty bed?

I let the voice mail keep taking my calls. I instructed the post office that I would be out of town for an indefinite period and to please hold my mail. I let my computer gather dust. I stopped checking my e-mail. And on one of my walks I dropped my pager into the Delaware River without missing a single step. The cast came off, and I started going on even longer walks—four hours, six hours, meandering loops through the city's worst neighborhoods, past crack dealers, hookers of the male and female variety, dead pigeons in gutters, the burned-out skeletons of cars, without seeing any of it, and without being afraid. How could any of this hurt me, after what I'd already lost? When I ran into Samantha on the street, I told her I was too busy to hang out, shifting from foot to foot with my eyes on the horizon so I wouldn't have to see her worried face. Getting things ready, I explained, waiting to be off again. The baby's coming home soon.

"Can I see her?" Sam asked.

Instantly, I shook my head. "I'm not ready . . . I mean, she's not ready."

"What do you mean, Cannie?" asked Sam.

"She's medically fragile," I said, trying out the term I'd heard over and over in the baby intensive care ward.

"So I'll stand outside and look at her through the window," said Sam, looking perplexed. "And then we'll go have breakfast. Remember breakfast? It used to be one of your favorite meals."

"I've got to go," I said brusquely, trying to edge my way around her. Samantha didn't budge.

"Cannie, what is going on with you, really?"

"Nothing," I said, shoving past her, my feet already moving, my eyes fixed far ahead. "Nothing, nothing, everything is fine."

NINETEEN

I walked and walked, and it was as if God had fitted me with special glasses, where I could only see the bad things, the sad things, the pain and misery of life in the city, the trash kicked into corners instead of the flowers planted in window boxes. I could see husbands and wives fighting, but not kissing or holding hands. I could see little kids careering through the streets on stolen bicycles, screaming insults and curses, and grown men who sounded like they were breakfasting on their own mucus, leering at women with unashamed, lecherous eyes. I could smell the stink of the city in summer: horse piss and hot tar and the grayish, sick exhaust the buses spewed. The manhole covers leaked steam, the sidewalks belched heat from the subways churning below.

Everywhere I looked, I just saw emptiness, loneliness, buildings with broken windows, shambling addicts with outstretched hands and dead eyes, sorrow and filth and rot.

I thought that time would heal me and that the miles would soothe my pain. I waited for a morning where I woke up and didn't instantly imagine Bruce and the Pusher dying horrible gruesome deaths . . . or, worse yet, losing my baby, losing Joy.

I would walk to the hospital at the break of dawn and sometimes before, and walk laps around the parking lot until I felt calm enough to walk inside. I would sit in the cafeteria gulping cup after cup of

water, trying to smile and look normal, but inside, my head was spinning furiously, thinking knives? guns? car accident? I would smile
and say hello, but really, in my head I was plotting revenge.

I imagined calling the university where Bruce had taught freshman English and telling them how he'd only passed his drug test by
ingesting quarts and quarts of warm water spiked with goldenseal
that he bought from a 1-800 line in the back pages of *High Times*.
Urine Luck, the stuff was called. I could tell them he was showing up
stoned at work—he used to do it, probably he still was doing it, and if
they watched him long enough they'd see. I could call his mother, call
the police in his town, have him arrested, taken away.

I imagined writing to *Moxie,* including a picture of Joy in the
NICU, growing bigger, growing stronger, but still a pathetic sight,
run through with tubes, breathing on a ventilator more often than
not, with who knew what horrors strewn in her future—cerebral
palsy, learning disabilities, blind, deaf, retarded, a menu of disasters
that the doctors hadn't mentioned. I'd gone online, to sites with
names like preemie.com, reading first-person stories from parents
whose children had survived, horribly damaged; who'd come home on
oxygen or sleep apnea monitors or with holes cut in their throats so
they could breathe. I read about kids who grew up with seizure disorders, learning disabilities, who never quite caught up, never quite got
right. And I read stories about the babies who died: at birth, in the
NICU, at home. "Our Precious Angel," they'd be headlined. "Our
Darling Daughter."

I wanted to copy these stories and e-mail them to the Pusher,
along with a photograph of Joy. I wanted to send her a picture of my
daughter—no letter, no words, just Joy's picture, sent to her house,
sent to her school, sent to her boss, to her parents if I could find them,
to show them all what she'd done, what she'd been responsible for. I
found myself planning walking routes that would bring me by gun
shops. I found myself looking in their windows. I didn't go inside yet,
but I knew that was next. And then what?

I didn't let myself answer the question. I didn't let myself think
beyond the image, the picture that I treasured: Bruce's face when he

opened his door and saw me standing there with a gun in my hand; Bruce's face when I said, "I'll show you sorry."

Then one morning I was burning past a newsstand and I saw the new issue of *Moxie,* the August issue, even though it was only just July, and so hot that the air shimmered and the streets turned sticky in the sun. I yanked a copy off the rack.

"Miss, you gonna pay for that?"

"No," I snarled, "I'm going to rob you." I tossed two bucks and change on the counter and started flipping furiously through the pages, wondering what the headline would be. "My Daughter the Vegetable?" "How to Really, Really Screw Up Your Ex's Life?"

Instead I saw a single word, big black letters, a somber incongruity in *Moxie*'s light-hearted, pastel-heavy lineup. "Complications," it said.

"Pregnant," says the letter, and I can't read any more. It's as if the very word has poleaxed me and left me paralyzed, save for the icy crawling along the back of my neck, the beginning of dread.

"I don't know an easy way to say this," she has written, "so I'll just say it. I am pregnant."

I remember sixteen years ago standing on the bimah in my synagogue in Short Hills, looking over the crowd of friends and relatives and mouthing those time-honored words, "Today I am a man." Now, feeling this rush of ice to my stomach, feeling my palms start to sweat, I know the truth: Today, I am a man. For real, this time.

"Not quite," I said, so loudly that the homeless people loping along the sidewalks stopped and stared. Not hardly. A man. A man would have called me. At least sent a postcard! I turned my attention back to the page.

But I'm not a man. As it turns out, what I am is a coward. I tuck the letter in a notebook, stuff the notebook in a desk drawer, lock the drawer, and accidentally on purpose, lose the key.

They say—they being the great philosophers, or possibly the cast of *Seinfeld*—that breaking up is like pushing over a Coke machine. You can't just do it, you have to set the thing in motion, rock it back and forth a few times. For C. and me it wasn't like that. It was a clean, swift break—a thunderclap. Intense and awful and over in seconds.

Liar, I thought. Oh, you liar. It wasn't a thunderclap, it wasn't even a breakup, I just told you I wanted some time!

Then, less than three months later, my father died.

I went back and forth with the telephone in my hand, her number still first on my speed-dial. Call her? Don't call her? Was she my ex or my friend?

In the end I opted for her friendship. And later, when a houseful of mourners picked over deli trays in my mother's kitchen, I opted for more

And now, three months later, I am still mourning my father, but I'm feeling as if I'm over C., truly and completely. I know what real sadness is now. I can explore it every night like a kid who's lost a tooth and can't stop tonguing the pulpy, wounded, empty space where the tooth once was.

Except now she's pregnant.

And I don't know whether she's set out to trick me or trap me, whether I'm even the father, whether she's pregnant at all.

"Oh, this is unbelievable," I announced to Broad Street at large. "This is fucking unbelievable!"

And, the thing is, I'm too chicken to ask.

It's your choice, I imagine I say with my silence. Your call, your game, your move. I manage to silence the part of me that wonders, that wants to know how she chose: whether she went to the clinic on Locust Street and marched past the protestors with their pictures of bloody dead babies; whether she did it in a doctors' office, whether she went with a friend, or a new lover, or alone. Or whether she's marching around her hometown right now with a belly as big as a beachball and books full of baby names.

I don't ask, or call. I don't send a check, or a letter, or even a card. I'm done, empty, dried out and cried out. There's nothing left for her or for a baby if there is one.

When I let myself think about it I get furious at myself (how could I have been so dumb?) and furious at her (how could she have let me?). But I try not to let myself think of it too much. I wake up, work out, go to the office, and go through the motions, try to keep the tip of my tongue away from that hole in my smile. But deep down I know that I can only postpone this so long, that even my cowardice can't stave off the inevitable. Somewhere in my desk, tucked in a notebook and locked in a drawer, there's a letter with my name on it.

"You're late!" the head nurse scolded, and smiled at me to show she didn't mean it. I had the copy of *Moxie* curled up like I meant to smack a dog with it. "Here," I said, handing it off. She barely spared it a glance. "I don't read this stuff," she said. "It's worthless."

"I agree," I said, heading toward the nursery.

"There's someone here to see you," she said.

I walked to the nursery and sure enough, there was a woman standing at my window, the window in front of Joy's Isolette. I could see short, impeccably coiffed gray hair, an elegant black pantsuit, a platinum diamond tennis bracelet around one wrist. A light whiff of Allure was in the air, her freshly polished fingernails glittered under the fluorescent lights. The Ever-Tasteful Audrey had put together just the right ensemble for going to visit her son's illegitimate premature firstborn.

"What are you doing here?" I demanded.

Audrey gasped and took two giant steps backward. Her face went two shades paler than her Estée Lauder foundation.

"Cannie!" she said, and pressed one hand against her chest. "I . . . you scared me."

I stared at her, saying nothing, as her eyes moved over me, unbelieving.

"You're so thin," she finally said.

I looked down and observed with not much interest that this was true. All that walking, all that plotting, my only food a snatched bite of bagel or banana and cup after cup of bitter black coffee, because the taste matched the way I felt inside. My refrigerator held bottles of breast milk and nothing else. I couldn't remember the last time I sat down and ate a meal. I could see the bones in my face, the jut of my hipbones. In profile, I was Jessica Rabbit: nonexistent butt, flat belly, improbable bosom, thanks to the milk. If you didn't get close enough to notice that my hair was dirty and matted, that I had giant black circles under my eyes and that, most likely, I smelled bad, I was an actual babe.

The irony had not been lost on me: After a lifetime of obsession, of calorie counting, Weight Watching, and StairMastering, I'd found a way to shed those unwanted pounds forever! To free myself of flab and cellulite! To get the body I'd always wanted! I should market this, I thought hysterically. The Placenta Abruptio Emergency Hysterectomy Premature and Possibly Brain-Damaged Baby Diet. I'd make a fortune.

Audrey fingered her bracelet nervously. "I guess you're wondering . . . ," she began. I said nothing, knowing exactly how hard this was for her. Knowing, and not giving a damn. A part of me wanted to see her twist in the wind like this, to struggle for the words. A part of me wanted her to suffer.

"Bruce says you won't speak to him."

"Bruce had a chance to speak to me," I told her. "I wrote and told him I was pregnant. He never called."

Her lips trembled. "He never told me," she whispered, half to herself. "Cannie, he is so sorry about what happened."

I snorted, so loud I was afraid I'd bother the babies. "Bruce is a day late and a dollar short."

She bit her lip, twirling the bracelet. "He wants to do the right thing."

"Which would be what?" I asked. "Having his girlfriend refrain from any more attempts on my baby's life?"

"He said that was an accident," she whispered.

I rolled my eyes.

"He wants to do the right thing," she repeated. "He wants to help out. . . ."

"I don't need money," I said, deliberately crude, spelling it out. "Not his or yours, either. I sold my screenplay."

Her face lit up, so glad that we were on a happy subject. "Honey, that's wonderful!"

I said nothing, hoping she'd fall apart in the face of my silence. But Audrey was braver than I'd given her credit for.

"Could I see the baby?" she asked.

I shrugged and stabbed one finger at the window. Joy was in the center of the nursery. She looked less like an angry grapefruit; more like a cantaloupe, perhaps, but still tiny, still frail, still with the science-fiction-looking ventilator attached to her face more often than not. The chart at the end of her glass crib read "Joy Leah Shapiro." She was wearing just a diaper, plus pink and white striped socks and a little pink hat with a pompom on top. I'd brought the nurses my stash, and every morning they made sure that Joy got a different hat. She was far and away the best chapeau'd baby in all of the NICU.

"Joy Leah," whispered Audrey. "Is she . . . did you name her after my husband?"

I nodded once, swallowing hard around the lump in my throat. I can give her this much, I thought. After all, she wasn't the one who ignored me, who didn't call me, who had caused me to fall into a sink and almost lose my baby.

"Will she be all right?"

"I don't know," I said. "Probably. They say probably. She's still small, and she has to get bigger, her lungs have to grow until she can breathe on her own. Then she'll come home."

Audrey wiped her eyes with the Kleenex she extracted from her purse. "And you'll stay here? You'll raise her in Philadelphia?"

"I don't know," I told her. Honest to a fault. "I don't know if I want to go back to the paper, or maybe back out to California. I have friends there." But even as I said it, I wondered if it was true. After dashing off a perfunctory thank-you note that couldn't begin to express the gratitude I should have felt for everything she'd done for me, I'd been giving Maxi the same silent treatment as all of my friends. Who knew what she was thinking, or whether she even thought she was my friend still?

Audrey straightened her shoulders. "I would like to be a grand-mother to her," she said carefully. "No matter what happened between you and Bruce. . . ."

"What happened," I repeated. "Did Bruce tell you I had a hys-terectomy? That I'll never have another baby? Did he happen to men-tion that?"

"I'm sorry, Cannie," she said again, sounding shrill and helpless and even a little scared. I shut my eyes, slumping against the glass wall.

"Just go," I told her. "Please. We can talk about this some other time, but not right now. I'm too tired."

She put her hand on my shoulder. "Let me help you," she said. "Can I get you something? Some water?"

I shook my head, shook her hand off, turned my face away. "Please," I said. "Just go." And I stood there, turned away from her, with my eyes shut tight, until I heard her soles slap-slapping back down the hallway. That was where the nurse found me, leaning against the wall and crying, with my hands curled into fists.

"Are you okay?" she asked, and touched my shoulder. I nodded, and turned toward the door.

"I'll be back later," I told her. "I'm going for a walk."

That afternoon, I walked for hours, until the streets, the sidewalks, the buildings turned into a grayish blur. I remember that I bought a

Snapple lemonade somewhere, and a few hours later I stopped at a bus station to pee, and I remember that at one point the ankle I'd had the cast on started throbbing. I ignored it. I kept walking. I walked south, then east, through strange neighborhoods, over trolley tracks, past burned-out drug houses, abandoned factories, the slow, brackish twist of the Schuylkill. I thought maybe, somehow, I would walk all the way to New Jersey. *Look,* I would say, standing in the lobby of Bruce's high-rise apartment building like a ghost, like a guilty thought, like a wound you'd thought had scabbed over that had suddenly started to bleed. *Look at what's become of me.*

I walked and walked until I felt something strange, an unfamiliar sensation. A pain in my foot. I looked down, lifting my left foot, and watched in dumb confusion as the sole slowly peeled off the bottom of my filthy sneaker and flopped onto the street.

A guy sitting on a stoop across the street whooped laughter. "Hey!" he shouted, as I stared stupidly from shoe to sole and back again, trying to make sense of it. "Baby needs a new pair of shoes!"

My baby needs a new pair of lungs, I thought, limping and looking around. Where am I? The neighborhood wasn't familiar. None of the street names rang any bells. And it was dark. I looked at my watch. 8:30, it said, and for a minute I didn't know whether it was morning or night. I was sweaty and grimy and exhausted . . . and lost.

I dug in my pockets, looking for answers, or at least cab fare. I found a five-dollar bill, a fistful of change, and some assorted lint.

I looked for landmarks, for a pay phone, for something.

"Hey," I called to the guy on the stoop. "Hey, where am I?"

He cackled laughter, rocking back on his heels. "Powelton Village! You in Powelton Village, baby!"

Okay, then. That was a start.

"Which way's University City?" I called.

He shook his head. "Girl, you lost! You all turned around!" His voice was deep and resonant, and sounded Southern. He lifted himself off his stoop and walked over to me—a middle-aged black man in a white undershirt and khakis. He peered closely at my face. "You sick?" he finally asked.

I shook my head. "Just lost," I said.

"You go to the college?" he continued, and I shook my head again, and he moved even closer, his expression growing more concerned.

"Are you drunk?" he asked, and I had to smile.

"No, really," I said. "I just went for a walk and got lost."

"Well, you better get found," he said. For one sick, terrifying moment I was absolutely certain he was going to start talking to me about Jesus. But he didn't. Instead, he took a long, careful inventory of me, from my falling-apart sneakers, up my scabby, bruised shins, to the shorts that I'd folded over twice at the waistband so they wouldn't slide down off my hips, and the T-shirt I'd been wearing for five days running, and my hair that had grown past my shoulders for the first time in more than a decade, and was doing a sort of impromptu dreadlock thing in the absence of being washed and brushed.

"You need help," he finally said.

I bowed my head and nodded. Help. This was true. I needed help.

"You got people?"

"I do," I told him. "I have a baby," I began, and then my throat closed up.

He raised his arm and pointed. "University City that way," he said. "You go to the corner of 45th Street, the bus take you straight there." He dug in his pocket, found a slightly tattered bus transfer pass, and pressed it into my hand. Then he bent and looked at my shoe. "Stay here," he said. I stood, stock-still, afraid to move so much as a muscle. Afraid of what, exactly, I wasn't sure.

The man came out of his house with a silver roll of duct tape in his hand. I lifted my foot, and he wrapped tape around and around it, holding the sole in place.

"Be careful," he said. *Keffel,* the word sounded like. "You a mother now, you need to be careful."

"I will," I said. I started limping off toward the corner he'd pointed at.

As filthy as I was, with duct-taped shoes and tears cutting slow tracks through the grime on my cheeks, nobody spared me so much as a glance on the bus. Everyone was too wrapped up in their own private coming-home-from-work thoughts—dinner, children, what was on TV, the minutiae of normal lives. The bus heaved and groaned its way across town. Things started looking familiar again. I saw the stadium, the skyscrapers, the far-off glimmering white tower of the *Examiner* building. And then I saw the University of Philadelphia's Weight and Eating Disorders office, where I'd gone a million years ago. When the only thing I thought I had to worry about was not being thin.

Get found, I thought, and pulled the "Stop Requested" cord so hard I thought for a moment I'd yanked it off. I took an elevator up to the seventh floor, thinking that I'd find all the lights out and the doors locked, wondering why I was even bothering.

But his light was on, and his door was open.

"Cannie!" said Dr. K., beaming. Beaming until he stood up, came around the desk, and got a good whiff of me. And a good look.

"I'm a success story," I said, and tried to smile. "Look at me! Forty pounds of ugly flab gone in just months!" I swiped one hand across my eyes. "I'm thin," I said, and started crying. "Yay, me."

"Sit down," he said, and closed the door. He put his arm around my shoulders and eased me toward his couch, where I sat, sniffling and pathetic.

"Cannie, my God, what happened to you?"

"I went for a walk," I began. My tongue felt thick and furry, and my lips felt cracked. "I got lost," I said. My voice had gone strange and croaky. "I went for a walk, and I got all turned around. I got lost, but now I'm trying to be found."

He put his hand on my head, stroking gently. "Let me take you home."

I let him lead me to the elevator, out the door, into his car. On the way out, he stopped at a soda machine and bought a cold can of Coke. I grabbed it without asking and guzzled the whole thing down. He didn't say a word, not even when I burped hugely. He pulled into a convenience store and came out with a quart of water and an orange Popsicle.

"Thanks," I rasped, "that's very nice of you." I drank the water, sucked on the Popsicle.

"I've been trying to call you," he said. "At work and at home."

"I'm very busy," I recited.

"Is Joy home yet?"

I shook my head.

He looked at me. "Are you okay?"

"Busy," I croaked again. My breasts were aching. I looked down and was unsurprised to see two circular stains beneath the V of sweat from my collarbone down.

"Busy with what?" he asked.

I shut my mouth. I hadn't really planned any dialogue beyond "busy."

At a stoplight, he looked over at me, staring at my face. "Are you okay?"

I shrugged. The car behind us honked, but he didn't move. "Cannie," he said kindly. A single tear trickled down my cheek. He reached out to brush it away. I jerked back as if I'd been burned.

"No!" I shrieked. "Don't touch me!"

"Cannie, my God, what's the matter?"

I shook my head, stared at my lap, where the ruins of the Popsicle were melting. We drove in silence for a while, the car purring beneath us, cool air whispering from the air conditioner over my knees and my shoulders.

At another traffic light, he started to talk again. "How's Nifkin? Did he remember anything I taught him?" He glanced at me quickly. "You remember when we visited you, right?"

I nodded. "I'm not crazy," I said. But even as I said it, I wasn't sure whether it was true. Did crazy people know they were crazy? Or did they think they were perfectly normal, all the while doing crazy things, wandering around filthy and with their shoes falling apart and their heads so full of rage it felt as if they'd explode?

We drove for a few more blocks in silence. I couldn't think of what to say, what to do next. I knew that there were questions I should ask him, points that I should make, but it felt as if my head was full of buzzing static.

"Where are we going?" I finally managed. "I should go home. Or to the hospital. I should go back there."

We pulled up at a red light. "Are you working?" he asked me. "I haven't seen your byline. . . ."

It had been so long since I'd had this kind of normal cocktail-party conversation with anyone, it took me a while to get the words sorted out right. "I'm on leave."

"Are you eating right?" He squinted sideways at me in the dark. "Or maybe I should ask, are you eating anything?"

I shrugged. "It's hard. With the baby. With Joy. I go to the hospital to see her twice a day, and I'm getting things ready at home. . . . I walk a lot," I finished up.

"I can see that," he said.

Another few blocks of silence, another red light. "I've been thinking about you," he said. "I was hoping you'd stop by, or call. . . ."

"Well, I did, didn't I?"

"I thought maybe we could see a movie. Or go to that diner again."

It sounded so bizarre I almost laughed. Was there a time I'd gone to dinner, to movies, when my every thought hadn't been about my baby and my rage?

"Where were you going, when you got lost?"

"For a walk," I said in a small voice. "Just for a walk."

He shook his head but didn't question me. "Why don't you let me take you to my place? I'll make you dinner."

I considered this. "Do you live near the hospital?"

"Even closer than you. I'll take you as soon as you like."

I nodded once, giving in.

I was quiet on the elevator ride to the sixteenth floor, quiet as he unlocked his door, apologizing for the mess, asking if I still liked chicken and did I want to use the phone? I nodded for chicken, shook my head for phone, and walked through his living room slowly, running my hands along the spines of his books, considering the framed family pictures, seeing but not really seeing. He disappeared into the kitchen, then emerged with a stack of folded things: a fluffy white towel, a pair of sweatpants and a T-shirt, miniature bars of soap and bottles of shampoo from a hotel in New York City.

"Would you like to freshen up?" he offered.

The bathroom was big and clean. I stripped off my shirt, then my shorts, halfheartedly trying to remember when they'd been clean. From the look and smell, I surmised that it had been a while. I folded them, then folded them again, then decided the hell with it and tossed them in the trash. I stood under the water for a long time, with my eyes closed, and thought of nothing but the feeling of the water on my face. *Found,* I told myself. *Try to get found.*

When I come out of the shower, dressed, with my hair toweled dry, he was putting food on the table.

"Welcome back," he said, smiling at me. "Is this okay?"

There was a tossed salad, a small roast chicken, a platter of potato pancakes, which I hadn't seen anyone serve outside of Chanukah in years. I sat down. The food actually smelled good—the first time anything had smelled good to me in a while.

"Thank you," I said.

He piled my plate high, and didn't talk while I ate, although he watched me carefully. Every once in a while I'd look up and see him . . . not staring, exactly. Just watching me.

Finally, I pushed my plate away. "Thank you," I said again. "That was really good."

He led me over to the couch and handed me a ceramic bowl full of chocolate ice cream and mango sorbet.

"Ben and Jerry's," he said. I stared at him, my head still staticky, remembering that he'd brought me dessert once before, when I was in the hospital. "Remember when we talked about ice cream in class?"

I looked at him blankly.

"When we were talking about trigger foods?" he prompted. And I remembered then, sitting around the table a million years ago, talking about things I liked to eat. It felt unbelievable that I had ever liked anything . . . that I'd enjoyed regular stuff. Food, and friends, and going for walks and to movies. Could I ever have a life like that again? I wondered. I wasn't sure . . . but I thought that maybe I could try.

"Do you remember all of your patients' favorite foods?" I asked.

"Only my favorite patients," he said. He sat in the armchair across from me while I ate it, slowly, savoring each mouthful. I sighed when I was finished. It had been so long since I'd eaten this well; so long since anything had tasted good.

He cleared his throat. I figured that was my cue to go. He probably had plans for the night. He possibly even had a date. I racked my brain and tried to remember. What day was it? Was it the weekend?

I yawned, and Dr. K. smiled at me. "You look so tired," he said. "Why don't you rest for a while?"

His voice was so warm, so soothing. "You like tea, not coffee, right?" I nodded. "I'll be right back," he said.

He went to the kitchen and I stretched out my legs on the couch, and by the time he came back I was half asleep. My eyelids felt so heavy. I yawned, and tried to sit up, as he handed me a mug.

"Where were you going today?" he asked.

I turned my head away, reaching for the blanket that was draped over the back of the couch. "I just went for a walk. I guess I got kind of lost or something. I'm fine, though. You shouldn't worry. I'm fine."

"You're not," he said, sounding almost angry. "You're very obviously not fine. You're half-starved, you're stomping around the city, you quit your job . . ."

"Leave of absence," I corrected. "I'm on a compassionate leave of absence."

"You don't have to be ashamed to ask for help."

"I don't need help," I told him, reflexively. Because that was my reflex, ingrained as a teenager, honed over the years. *I'm okay. I can handle it. I'm fine.* "I've got everything under control. I'm fine. We're fine. Me and the baby. We're fine."

He shook his head. "How are you fine? You're not happy. . . ."

"Why should I be happy?" I shot back. "What's to be happy about?"

"You have a beautiful baby. . . ."

"Yeah, no thanks to anyone else."

He stared at me. I stared back, furious. Then I put down my tea and got to my feet.

"I should go."

"Cannie . . ."

I looked for my socks and my duct-taped shoes. "Could you take me home?"

He looked distressed. "I'm sorry . . . I didn't mean to upset you."

"You haven't upset me. I'm not upset. But I want to go home."

He sighed, and looked down at his feet. "I thought . . ." he mumbled.

"Thought what?"

"Nothing."

"Thought what?" I repeated, more insistently.

"It was a bad idea."

"Thought what," I said again, in a tone that wasn't taking no for an answer.

"I thought that if you came here, you'd relax." He shook his head, seeming stunned by his own hopes, his own presumptions. "I thought maybe you'd want to talk about things. . . ."

"There's really nothing to talk about," I said. But I said it more gently. He had given me dinner, clean clothes, an orange Popsicle, a ride. "I'm okay. Really. I am."

We stood for a minute, and something passed between us, some small easing of the tension. I could feel the blisters on both feet, and how my cheeks felt tight and painful with sunburn. I could feel the cool thin cotton of his T-shirt on my back, and how nice it was, and my belly full of good food, and how nice that was. And I could feel my breasts, which ached dully.

"Hey, you wouldn't happen to have a breast pump in here?" I asked. My first attempt at a joke since I'd woken up in the hospital.

He shook his head. "Would ice help?" he asked. I nodded, and sat back down on the couch, where he brought me ice wrapped in a towel. I turned my back to him and tucked the ice under my shirt.

"How's Nifkin?" he asked again.

I shut my eyes. "With my mom," I muttered. "I sent him to stay with her for a while."

"Well, don't let him stay away too long. He'll forget his tricks." He took a sip of his tea. "I was going to teach him how to speak, if we'd had a little more time together."

I nodded. My eyelids were feeling heavy again.

"Maybe some other time," he said. He kept his eyes politely averted as I shifted the ice around. "I'd like to see Nifkin again," he said. He paused and cleared his throat. "I'd like to see you, too, Cannie."

I looked at him. "Why?" A rude question, I knew, but I felt like I was past the point of good manners . . . of any manners, really. "Why me?"

"Because I care about you."

"Why?" I asked again.

"Because you're . . ." He let the last word hang there. When I looked at him he was waving his hands in the air, like he was trying to sculpt phrases out of the air. "You're special."

I shook my head.

"You are."

Special, I thought. I didn't feel special. I felt ridiculous, really. I felt like a spectacle of a woman, a sob story, a freak. How must I look, really? I imagined myself on the street that night, my shoe falling apart, sweaty and filthy, my breasts leaking. They should take a picture, put my poster up in every junior high school, staple it in bookstores next to the Harlequin novels and the self-help books about finding your soulmate, your life partner, your one true love. I could be a warning; I could turn girls away from my fate.

I must have dozed off then, because when I came awake with a start, with my cheek against the blanket and the towel full of ice melting in my lap, he was sitting right across from me.

He'd taken his glasses off, and his eyes were gentle.

"Here," he said. He had something in his arms, cradled like a baby. Pillows. Blankets. "I made up the guest bedroom for you."

I walked there in a daze, aching from exhaustion. The sheets were cool and crisp, the pillows like an embrace. I let him draw back the covers, help me onto the bed, tuck them up over me, smooth the blanket over my shoulders. His face seemed so much softer without his glasses, in the dark.

He sat on the edge of the bed. "Will you tell me why you're so angry?" he asked.

I was so tired, and my tongue felt heavy and slow in my mouth. It was like being drugged, or hypnotized; like dreaming underwater. Or maybe I would have told anyone, if I'd let anyone get close enough to ask. "I'm mad at Bruce. I'm mad that his girlfriend pushed me, and I'm mad that he doesn't love me. I'm mad at my father, I guess."

He raised an eyebrow.

"I saw him . . . in California. . . ." I paused to yawn, to fight the words out. "He didn't want to know me." I passed my hands over my belly, or where my belly had been. "The baby . . . ," I said. My eyelids felt freighted, so heavy I could barely keep them open. "He didn't want to know."

He brushed the back of his hand against my cheek, and I leaned into his touch like a cat, unthinking. "I'm so sorry," he said. "You've had a lot of sadness in your life."

I breathed in, then out, pondering the truth of this. "That's not exactly a news flash," I said.

He smiled. "I just wanted you to know," he said, "I wanted to see you, so I could tell you . . ."

I stared at him, wide-eyed in the dark.

"You don't have to do everything alone," he said. "There are people who care about you. You just have to let them help."

I sat up then. The sheets and blankets fell around my waist. "No," I told him, "that's wrong."

"What do you mean?" he asked.

I shook my head, once, impatiently. "Do you know what love is?"

He considered the question. "I think I heard a song about it once."

"Love," I said, "is the rug they pull out from under you. Love is Lucy always lifting the football at the last second so that Charlie Brown falls on his ass. Love is something that every time you believe in it, it goes away. Love is for suckers, and I'm not going to be a sucker ever again." When I closed my eyes I could see myself as I was, months ago, lying on the bathroom floor, highlights in my hair and makeup on my face, the expensive shoes and fancy clothes and diamond earrings that couldn't keep me safe, couldn't keep the wolf from my door.

"I want a house with hardwood floors," I said, "and I don't want anyone else to come inside."

He was touching my hair, saying something. "Cannie," he repeated. I opened my eyes.

"It doesn't have to be that way."

I stared at him in the dark. "How else could it be?" I asked, quite reasonably.

He leaned forward and kissed me.

He kissed me, and at first I was too shocked to do anything, too shocked to move, too shocked to do anything but sit there, perfectly still, as his lips touched mine.

He pulled his head back. "I'm sorry," he said.

I leaned toward him. "Hardwood floors," I whispered, and I realized I was teasing him, and that I was smiling, and it had been so long since I had smiled.

"I will give you whatever I can," he said, looking at me in a way that made it clear that he was, somehow, oh miracle of miracles, taking this all seriously. And then he kissed me again, pulled the sheets up to my chin, pressed his warm hand on top of my head, and walked out of the room.

I listened as the door closed and as he settled his long body onto the couch. I listened until he'd clicked the lights off and his breathing became deep and regular. I listened, holding the blankets tight around me, holding that feeling of being safe, of being tucked in and taken care of, around me. And I thought clearly then, for the first time since Joy had been born. I decided, right there in that strange bed in the dark, that I could go on being scared forever, that I could keep walking, that I could carry my rage around, hot and heavy in my chest forever. But maybe there was another way. *You have everything you need,* my mother had told me. And maybe all I needed was the courage to admit that what I needed was someone to lean on. And then I could do it— could be a good daughter, and a good mother. Maybe I could even be happy. Maybe I could.

I slipped out of bed. The floor was cool on my bare feet. I moved stealthily through the darkness, out of the room, easing the door shut behind me. I went to him there on the couch, where he'd fallen asleep with a book falling from his fingers. I sat on the floor beside him and leaned so close that my lips practically touched his forehead. Then I closed my eyes and took a deep breath and jumped into the water. "Help," I whispered.

His eyes opened instantly, as if he hadn't been sleeping, but waiting, and he reached out one hand and cupped my cheek.

"Help," I said again, as if I were a baby, as if this was a word I'd just learned and could not stop repeating. "Help me. Help."

Two weeks later Joy came home. She was eight weeks old, and she'd topped seven pounds and was finally breathing on her own. "You'll be fine," the nurses told me. Except I decided that I wasn't ready to be by myself yet. I was still too hurt inside, still too sad.

Samantha offered to let us stay with her. She'd take leave from work, she said, she had weeks built up, she'd do whatever it took to get her house ready. Maxi volunteered to fly in or, alternately, to fly us both up to Utah, where she was shooting a cowgirl epic with the unwieldy title *Buffalo Girls 2000*. Peter, of course, was first in line to tell us that we could stay with him or that, if I wanted, he could stay at my place with us.

"Forget it," I told him. "I've learned my lesson about giving men the milk for free and then expecting them to buy the cow."

He turned a gratifying shade of crimson. "Cannie," he began, "I didn't mean . . ."

And I laughed, then. It was still feeling good to laugh. I'd gone too long without it. "Kidding," I said, and looked at myself ruefully. "Believe me, I'm in no shape to think about that for a while."

In the end, I decided to go home—home to my mother and horrible Tanya, who'd agreed to put her loom in storage for the duration and give me and Joy back the Room Formerly Known as Mine. Actually, they were both glad to have us. "It's so nice to hold a baby again!" said my mother, considerately ignoring the fact that tiny, bristly, sickly Joy, with her sleep apnea monitor and myriad health concerns, was not exactly the sort of baby a grandmother would dream about.

I thought it would be for a week or two—just a chance for me to regroup, to rest, to get used to taking care of a baby. In the end, we stayed for three months, me in the bed that had been mine when I was a girl, and Joy in a crib beside me.

My mother and Tanya let me be. They brought trays of food to my door and cups of tea to my bedside. They retrieved my CDs and a half-dozen books from my apartment, and Tanya presented me with an afghan in purple and green. "For you," she said shyly. "I'm sorry about what happened." And she was, I realized. She was sorry, and she was trying—she'd even managed to quit smoking. For the baby, my mother had told me. That was nice.

"Thanks," I said, and wrapped it around me. She smiled like the sun coming out.

"You're welcome," she said.

Samantha came a few times a week, bringing me treats from the city—grilled grape leaves from the Vietnamese food stall in the Reading Terminal, fresh plums from a farm in New Jersey. Peter visited, too, bringing books, newspapers, magazines (never *Moxie,* I was pleased to note), and little gifts for Joy, including a tiny T-shirt that read "Girl Power."

"That is so great," I said.

Peter smiled, and reached into his briefcase. "I got you one, too," he said.

"Thanks," I said.

Joy stirred in her sleep. Peter looked at her, then at me. "So how are you really?"

I stretched my arms over my head. I was very very tan, from all that time walking in the sun, but things had started to change. I was taking showers, for one thing. I was eating, for another. My hips and breasts were coming back, and I felt okay with it . . . like I recognized myself again. Like I was reclaiming not only my body, but the life I'd left behind. And all things considered, it hadn't been such a bad life. There were things that I had lost, true, and people who wouldn't ever love me again, but there was also . . . potential, I thought, and I smiled at Peter. "Better," I told him. "I guess I'm doing better now."

* * *

Then one morning in September, I woke up and felt like walking again.

"Do you want some company?" Tanya rasped.

I shook my head. My mother watched me lace up my sneakers, her brow furrowed. "Do you want to take the baby?" she asked.

I stared at Joy. I hadn't even considered it.

"She might like some fresh air," said my mother.

"I don't think so," I said slowly.

"She won't break," said my mother.

"She might," I replied, feeling my eyes fill. "She almost did before."

"Babies are stronger than you give them credit for," she said. "Joy's going to be okay . . . and you can't keep her inside forever."

"Not even if I home-school?" I asked. My mother grinned and handed me the Snugli baby carrier. Awkwardly, I strapped it over my chest, and lifted Joy inside.

She was so small, still, so small, she felt like an autumn leaf against me. Nifkin looked at me and pawed my leg, whining softly. So I hitched him to his leash and took him, too. We walked slowly, down to the edge of the driveway, then out onto the street, moving at a pace that would have made an arthritic snail look speedy. It was the first time I'd been out on the street since I'd arrived, and I felt terrified—of the cars, of the people, of everything, I thought ruefully. Joy nestled against me with her eyes closed. Nifkin marched beside me, growling at cars that went by. "Look, baby," I whispered against Joy's downy head. "Look at the world."

When we got back from our morning walk Peter's car was parked in the driveway. Inside, my mother and Tanya and Peter were sitting around the kitchen table.

"Cannie!" said my mother.

"Hello," said Peter.

"We were just talking about you," Tanya said. Even after close to a month smoke-free, she still sounded like Marge Simpson's sisters.

"Hey," I said to Peter, pleased to see him. I gave a genial wave, then unstrapped Joy, wrapped her in a blanket, and sat down with her in my lap. My mother poured me tea as Joy stared at Peter, wide-eyed. He'd been over before, of course, but she'd always been asleep. So this was their first real meeting.

"Hello, baby," Peter said solemnly. Joy screwed up her face and started to cry. Peter looked distressed.

"Oh, I'm sorry," he began.

"Don't worry about it," I told him, turning Joy so that she faced me, and rocking her until her sobs subsided into whimpers, then hiccoughs, then quiet.

"She isn't used to men," said Tanya. I thought of at least six snappy comebacks to that, but prudently kept my mouth shut.

"I think babies are scared of me," Peter said, sounding mournful. "I think it's my voice."

"Joy's heard all kinds of voices," I said tartly. My mother shot me an evil look. Tanya didn't seem to notice.

"She's not scared," I said. She was, in fact, asleep, her lips slightly parted and her eyelashes long and dark against her rosy cheeks where there were still tears drying. "Here," I said, "see?"

I wiped her face and tilted Joy toward him so he could see. He leaned down, looking at her. "Wow," he said reverently. He reached out one long, slender finger and gently touched her cheek. I beamed down at Joy, who promptly woke up, took one look at Peter, and started bawling again.

"She'll get over it," I said. "Rude baby!" I whispered in her ear.

"Maybe she's hungry," said Tanya.

"Wet diaper," suggested my Mom.

"Disappointed with ABC's prime-time lineup," I said.

Peter cracked up.

"Well, she's a very discerning viewer," I said, bouncing Joy against my shoulder. "She really liked *Sports Night.*" Once she'd settled down, I helped myself to tea, and to a fistful of the chocolate-chip cookies in the center of the table. I added an apple from the fruit bowl and went to work.

Peter looked at me approvingly. "You look much better," he pronounced.

"You say that every time you see me," I told him.

"You do," he insisted. "Much healthier."

And it was true. With three meals a day, plus snacks, I was quickly regaining my old prediet Anna Nicole Smith proportions. And I continued to welcome the changes. I could see it all differently now. My legs were sturdy and strong, not fat or ungainly. My breasts now had a purpose besides stretching out my sweaters and making it hard to find a non-beige bra. Even my waist and hips, riddled with silvery stretch marks, suggested strength, and told a story. I might be a big girl, I reasoned, but it wasn't the worst thing in the world. I was a safe harbor and a soft place to rest. Built for comfort, not for speed, I thought, and giggled at myself. Peter smiled at me. "Much healthier," he said again.

"They'll kick you out of the weight-loss center if it gets out about your telling me that," I said.

He shrugged as if it didn't matter. "I think you look fine. I always did," he said. My mother was beaming. I shot her a mind-your-own-business look and settled Joy in my lap.

"So," I said, "what brings you to these parts?"

"Actually," he said, "I was wondering if you and Joy would like to go for a ride."

I felt my chest tighten again. Joy and I hadn't gone anywhere in the car since her arrival, except for checkups at the hospital. "Where to?" I asked, trying to sound casual.

"Down the shore," he said, using the typical Philadelphia construction. "Just for a little drive."

It sounded nice. It also sounded absolutely terrifying. "I'm not sure," I said regretfully. "I'm not sure she's ready."

"She's not ready, or you're not ready?" asked my helpful mother. I sent her an even more intense mind-your-own-business look.

"I'll be there," Peter said. "So you'll have medical assistance, if you need it."

"Go on, Cannie," said my mother.

"It'll be good for you," urged Tanya.

I stared at him. He smiled at me. I sighed, knowing I was defeated. "Just a short ride," I said, and he nodded, eager as a schoolboy, and stood up to help me.

* * *

Of course, it took a while—forty-five minutes, to be precise, and three bags full of diapers, hats, socks, sweaters, stroller, bottles, blankets, and assorted baby paraphernalia, all shoved in the trunk—before we were ready to leave. Then Joy got stowed in the infant seat, I sat on the passenger's side, Peter took the wheel, and we headed down to the Jersey shore.

Peter and I talked a little at first—about his job, about Lucy and Maxi and how Andy'd actually gotten a death threat after savaging one of Philadelphia's famous old fish-houses that had been coasting on its reputation and so-so snapper soup for decades. Then, when we turned on to the Atlantic City Expressway, he smiled at me and touched a button on the dashboard, and the roof over our heads slid away.

"A moon roof!" I said, impressed.

"Thought you'd like it!" he shouted back.

I looked back at Joy, tucked snug in her infant seat, wondering if the wind would be too much. But she actually looked like she was enjoying it. The little pink ribbon I'd tied in her hair, so that everyone would know she was a girl, was bobbing in the breeze, and her eyes were wide open.

We drove to Ventnor and parked in a lot two blocks from the beach. Peter unfolded Joy's complicated carriage while I got her out of the car, wrapped her in more blankets than the warm September day merited, and set her into the carriage. We walked slowly down to the water, me pushing, Peter walking beside me. The sunshine felt wonderful, thick as honey on my shoulders, making my hair glow.

"Thank you," I said. He shrugged and looked embarrassed.

"I'm glad you like it," he said.

We walked on the boardwalk—up for twenty minutes, back for another twenty, because I'd decided I didn't want Joy outside for more than an hour. Except the salt air didn't seem to be bothering her. She'd fallen fast asleep, her little rosebud mouth slack, her pink ribbon coming unfurled, and her fine brown hair curling around her cheeks. I leaned close to hear her breathing, and to check her diaper. She was fine.

Peter returned to my side with a blanket in his arms. "Want to sit on the beach?" he asked.

I nodded. He unfolded the blanket, I unstrapped Joy, and we walked down close to the water and sat there, watching the waves break. I worked my toes into the warm sand, and stared at the white foam, the blue-green depths, the black edge of the ocean against the horizon, and thought of all the things I couldn't see: sharks and bluefish and starfish, whales singing to each other, secret lives that I would never know.

Peter draped another blanket over my shoulders, and let his hands linger there for a few seconds.

"Cannie," he began. "I want to tell you something."

I gave him what I hoped was an encouraging smile.

"That day on Kelly Drive, when you and Samantha were walking," he said, and cleared his throat.

"Right," I said. "Go on."

"Well," he said. "I, um . . . I'm not actually a jogger."

I looked at him, confused.

"I just . . . well, I remember how in class you used to say you went on bike rides there, and you'd go for walks, and I didn't feel that I could call you . . ."

"So you started jogging?"

"Every day," he confessed. "Morning and night, and sometimes on my lunch hour. Until I saw you."

I sat back, surprised by the extent of his dedication, knowing that if it were me, no matter how much I felt that I wanted to see the other person, it probably wouldn't be enough to get me to jog. "I, um, have shinsplints now," he mumbled, and I burst out laughing.

"It serves you right!" I said. "You could've just called me . . ."

"But I couldn't," he said. "First of all, you were a patient . . ."

"Was a patient," I said.

"And you were, um . . ."

"Pregnant with another man's child," I supplied.

"You were oblivious!" he exclaimed. "Completely oblivious! That was the worst part! There I was, mooning after you, giving myself shinsplints . . ."

I giggled some more.

"And first you were sad about Bruce, who even I could tell wasn't right for you . . ."

"You were hardly objective," I told him, but he wasn't through.

"And then you were in California, and that wasn't right for you, either. . . ."

"California's very nice," I said, in California's defense.

He sat down next to me and wrapped his arms around my shoulders, pulling me and Joy tightly against him. "I thought you were never coming home," he said. "I couldn't stand it. I thought I'd never see you again, and I didn't know what to do with myself."

I smiled at him, turning so I could look him in the eye. The sun was setting over us, and seagulls swooped and squawked above the waves.

"But I did come home," I said. "See? No shinsplints necessary."

"I'm glad," he said, and I leaned against him, letting him support me, with the setting sun glowing in his hair and the warm sand cradling my feet, and my baby, my Joy, safe in my arms.

"So I guess the question is," I began, in his car on the way home, "what do I do with my life now?"

He smiled at me quickly before turning his eyes back to the road. "I was actually thinking more along the lines of whether you wanted to stop for dinner."

"Sure," I said. Joy was asleep in her infant seat. We'd lost her pink ribbon somewhere, but I could see sand glittering on her bare feet. "So now that we've got that settled . . ."

"Do you want to go back to work?" he asked me.

I thought about it. "I think so," I said. "Eventually. I miss it," I said. Knowing, as soon as I said it, that it was the truth. "I don't think I've ever gone this long without writing something. God help me, I even miss my brides."

"So what do you want to write?" he asked. "What do you want to write about?"

I considered the question.

"Newspaper articles?" he prompted. "Another screenplay? A book?"

"A book," I scoffed. "As if!"

"It could happen," he said.

"I don't think I've got a book in me," I said.

"If you did," he said seriously, "I'd devote all of my medical training to getting it out."

I laughed. Joy woke up and made a questioning noise. I looked back and waved at her. She stared at me, then yawned and went back to sleep.

"Maybe not a book," I said, "but I would like to write something about this."

"Magazine article?" he suggested.

"Maybe," I said.

"Good," he said, sounding like it had been settled once and for all. "I can't wait to see it."

The next morning, after I'd walked with Joy, had breakfast with Tanya, talked to Samantha on the phone, and made plans to see Peter the next night, I went down to the basement and fetched the dusty little Apple that had gotten me through four years of Princeton. I wasn't expecting much, but when I plugged it in it chugged and bleeped and lit up obligingly. And even though the keyboard felt strange under my hands, I took a deep breath, wiped the dust from the screen, and started writing.

Loving a Larger Woman

by Candace Shapiro

When I was five I learned to read. Books were a miracle to me—white pages, black ink, and new worlds and different friends in each one. To this day, I relish the feeling of cracking a binding for the first time, the anticipation of where I'll go and whom I'll meet inside.

When I was eight I learned to ride a bike. And this, too, opened my eyes to a new world that I could explore on my own—the brook that burbled through a vacant lot two streets over, the ice-cream store that sold homemade cones for a dollar, the orchard that bordered a golf course and that smelled tangy, like cider, from the apples that rolled to the ground in the fall.

When I was twelve I learned that I was fat. My father told me, pointing at the insides of my thighs and the undersides of my arms with the handle of his tennis racquet. We'd been playing, I remember, and I was flushed and sweaty, glowing with the joy of movement. You'll need to watch that, he told me, poking me with the handle so that the extra flesh jiggled. Men don't like fat women.

And even though this would turn out not to be absolutely true—there would be men who would love me, and there would be people who'd respect me—I carried his words into my adulthood like a prophecy, viewing the world through the prism of my body, and my father's prediction.

I learned how to diet—and, of course, how to cheat on diets. I learned how to feel miserable and ashamed, how to cringe away from mirrors and men's glances, how to tense myself for the insults that I always thought were coming: the Girl Scout troop leader who'd offer me carrot sticks while the other girls got milk and cookies; the well-meaning teacher who'd ask if I'd thought about aerobics. I learned a dozen tricks for making myself invisible—how to keep a towel wrapped around my midsection at the beach (but never swim), how to fade to the back row of any group photograph (and never smile), how to dress in shades of gray, black, and brown, how to avoid seeing my own reflection in windows or in mirrors, how to think of myself exclusively as a body—more than that, as a body that had fallen short of the mark, that had become something horrifying, unlovely, unlovable.

There were a thousand words that could have described me—smart, funny, kind, generous. But the word I picked—

the word that I believed the world had picked for me—was
fat.

When I was twenty-two I went out into the world in a suit
of invisible armor, fully expecting to be shot at, but determined that I wouldn't get shot down. I got a wonderful job,
and eventually fell in love with a man I thought would love
me for the rest of my life. He didn't. And then—by accident—I got pregnant. And when my daughter was born
almost two months too soon I learned that there are worse
things than not liking your thighs or your butt. There are
more terryifing things than trying on bathing suits in front of
three-way department-store mirrors. There is the fear of
watching your child struggling for breath, in the center of a
glass crib where you can't touch her. There is the terror of
imagining a future where she won't be healthy or strong.

And, ultimately, I learned, there is comfort. Comfort in
reaching out to the people who love you, comfort in asking for
help, and in realizing, finally, that I am valued, treasured,
loved, even if I am never going to be smaller than a size sixteen, even if my story doesn't have the Hollywood-perfect
happy ending where I lose sixty pounds and Prince Charming
decides that he loves me after all.

The truth is this—I'm all right the way I am. I was all
right, all along. I will never be thin, but I will be happy. I will
love myself, and my body, for what it can do—because it is
strong enough to lift, to walk, to ride a bicycle up a hill, to
embrace the people I love and hold them fully, and to nurture
a new life. I will love myself because I am sturdy. Because I did
not—will not—break.

I will savor the taste of my food and I will savor my life, and
if Prince Charming never shows up—or, worse yet, if he drives
by, casts a cool and appraising glance at me, and tells me I've
got a beautiful face and have I ever considered Optifast?—I
will make my peace with that.

And most importantly, I will love my daughter whether she's

big or little. I will tell her that she's beautiful. I will teach her to swim and read and ride a bike. And I will tell her that whether she's a size eight or a size eighteen, that she can be happy, and strong, and secure that she will find friends, and success, and even love. I will whisper it in her ear when she's sleeping. I will say, Our lives—your life—will be extraordinary.

I read through it twice, cleaning up the punctuation, fixing the numerous typos. Then I stood up and stretched, placing my palms flat against the small of my back. I looked at my baby, who was beginning to resemble an actual infant of the human species, rather than some miniaturized, prickly fruit-human hybrid. And I looked at myself: hips, breasts, butt, belly, all of the problem areas I'd once despaired of, the body that had caused me such shame, and smiled. In spite of everything, I was going to be fine.

"We both are," I said to Joy, who did not stir.

I called information, then dialed the number in New York. "Hello; *Moxie*," said a chirpy subteen-sounding secretary. My voice didn't tremble even slightly when I asked for the managing editor.

"May I ask what this is in reference to?" the secretary singsonged.

"My name is Candace Shapiro," I began. "I'm the ex-girlfriend of your 'Good in Bed' columnist."

I heard a sharp intake of breath on the other end of the line. "You're C.?" she gasped.

"Cannie," I corrected.

"Ohmygod! You're, like, real!"

"Very much so," I said. This was turning out to be very amusing.

"Did you have the baby?" asked the girl.

"I did," I said. "She's right here, sleeping."

"Oh. Oh, wow," she said. "You know, we were wondering how that turned out."

"Well, that's why I'm calling," I said.

TWENTY

The good thing about naming ceremonies for Jewish baby girls is that they're not tied to a specific time. With a boy, you've got to do the bris within seven days. A girl, you can do it in six weeks, three months, whenever. It's a newer service, a little bit free-form, and the rabbis who do namings tend to be accommodating, New Age-ish types.

Joy's naming was on December 31, on a crisp, perfect winter morning in Philadelphia. Eleven o'clock in the morning, with brunch to follow.

My mother was among the first wave of arrivals. "Who's my big girl?" she cooed, lifting Joy from her crib. "Who's my bundle of joy?" Joy chuckled and waved her arms. My beautiful daughter, I thought, feeling my throat catch at the sight of her. She was almost eight months old, and still it felt like every time I saw her she was a miracle.

And even strangers said she was a miraculously beautiful baby, with peachy skin, wide eyes, sturdy limbs pillowed with cushiony rolls of fat, and a wonderfully happy way about her. I'd named her perfectly. Unless she was hungry, or her diaper was wet, Joy was always smiling, always laughing, observing the world closely through her wide, watchful eyes. She was the happiest baby I knew.

My mother handed her over, then impulsively reached and hugged us both. "I am so proud of you," she said.

I hugged her hard. "Thank you," I whispered, wishing that I could tell her what I really wanted to, that I could thank her for loving me when I was a girl, and for letting me go now that I was a woman. "Thank you," I said again. My mother gave me a final squeeze, and kissed Joy on top of her head.

I filled Joy's white tub with warm water and gave her a bath. She cooed and clucked as I poured the water over her, washing her legs, her feet, her fingers, her sweet little baby behind. I rubbed on lotion, dusted her with powder, snapped her into a white knitted dress and put a white hat with roses embroidered around the edges on her head. "Baby," I whispered in her ear, "baby Joy." Joy waved her fists in the air like the world's tiniest triumphant athlete and gurgled a liquid string of syllables, like she was having a conversation in a language none of us had learned.

"Can you say mama?" I asked.

"Ahh!" Joy announced.

"Not even close," I said.

"Oo," she said, looking at me with her big, clear eyes, as if she understood every word.

Then I handed her off to Lucy and went to take my own shower, to do my hair and face, to practice the speech I'd been writing for days.

I could hear the doorbell chiming, the door opening and closing, people coming inside. The caterers had come first, and Peter had come second, with two boxes wrapped in silver paper and a bouquet of roses. "For you," he'd said, and put the flowers in a vase. Then he took Nifkin for a walk and emptied the dishwasher while I finished getting things in order.

"What a sweetheart," said one of the caterer's assistants. "I don't think my husband even knows where the dishwasher is."

I smiled my thanks without bothering to correct her. It was all too confusing to explain to strangers . . . like telling them I'd gone through the day with all my clothes on backward. First comes love, then comes marriage, then comes baby in a baby carriage. Even little kids knew how it was supposed to go. But what could I do? I reasoned. What happened happened. I couldn't undo my history. And if it had given me Joy, there was no way I would want to.

I walked into the living room with Joy in my arms. Maxi was there, and she smiled at me, giving me the tiniest of waves. Samantha was next to her, and next to Sam were my mother and Tanya, Lucy and Josh, Betsy and Andy and Andy's wife, Ellen, and two of the nurses from the hospital who'd taken care of Joy. And, in one corner, was Audrey, impeccably turned out in crisp cream-colored linen. Peter was standing beside her. All my friends. I bit my lip and looked down to keep from crying. The rabbi asked for silence, then asked for four people to come forward to hold the posts of the huppah. It was my grandmother's, I saw, recognizing the fine old lace from my cousins' weddings. It was the huppah I would have been married under, had I gotten things in the right order. At naming ceremonies the huppah is meant to shelter the baby and the husband and wife. But I'd made prior arrangements, and at the rabbi's request everyone crowded under the huppah with me. My baby would get her name surrounded by all of the people who'd loved and sustained us, I decided, and the rabbi had said that it sounded fine to her.

Joy was awake and alert, taking it all in, beaming as if she knew she was the center of attention, as if there was no doubt that it was exactly where she was meant to be. Nifkin sat politely by my feet.

"Shall we begin?" asked the rabbi. She gave a short speech about Israel and Jewish tradition, and how Joy was being welcomed into the religion handed down from Abraham, Isaac, and Jacob, and also Sarah, Rebecca, and Leah. She chanted a blessing, said prayers over bread and wine, daubed a cloth in Manischevitz and pressed it against Joy's lips. "Ooh!" Joy chortled, and everybody laughed. "And now," said the rabbi, "Joy's mother, Candace, will tell how she chose the name."

I took a deep breath. Joy looked at me with her wide eyes. Nifkin was very still against my leg. I pulled a notecard out of my pocket.

"I've learned a lot this year," I began. I took a deep quavering breath. *Don't cry,* I told myself. "I learned that things don't always turn out the way you planned, or the way you think they should. And I've learned that there are things that go wrong that don't always get fixed or get put back together the way they were before. I've learned that some broken things stay broken, and I've learned that you can get through bad times and keep looking for better ones, as long as you have people who love you." I stopped and swiped my hand across my eyes. "I named my baby Joy because she is my joy," I said, "and she's named Leah after her father's father. His middle name was Leonard, and he was a wonderful man. He loved his wife, and his son, and I know that he would have loved Joy, too."

And that was all. I was crying, Audrey was crying, my mother and Tanya were holding each other, and even Lucy, who tended to go non-reactive at sad occasions ("It's the Prozac," she'd explain), was wiping away tears. The rabbi observed this all, a bemused look on her face. "Well," she finally said, "shall we eat?"

After the bagels and whitefish salad, after butter cookies and apple cake and mimosas, after Nifkin had devoured a quarter pound of Nova lox and been sick behind the toilet, after we'd opened the gifts and I'd spent fifteen minutes telling Maxi that Joy, wonderful baby that she was, was really not going to be needing a strand of cultured pearls until at least her eighteenth birthday, after we'd cleared away the wrapping paper and put away the leftovers and the baby and I had taken a nap, Peter and Joy and I walked down to the river to wait for the century's end.

I was feeling good about things, I thought, as I bundled Joy into her stroller. Preproduction on my movie was beginning. My version of "Loving a Larger Woman" had come out at the end of November, replacing Bruce's column. The response, the managing editor told me, had been overwhelming, with every woman who'd ever felt too big, too little, too ugly or strange to fit in or be worthy of love writing in to praise my courage, to decry B's selfishness, to share their own stories about being big and female in America, and to offer best wishes to baby Joy.

"I've never seen anything like this," the managing editor had said, describing the piles of mail, baby blankets, baby books, teddy bears, and assorted religious and secular good-luck icons that had filled the

Moxie mailroom. "Would you consider writing for us regularly?" She had it all figured out—I'd do monthly dispatches from the single-mom front, ongoing updates on my life and Joy's. "I want you to tell us what it's like to live your life, in your body—to work, to date, to balance your single friends with your obligations as a mother," she said.

"What about Bruce?" I asked. I was thrilled with the chance to write for *Moxie* (and even more thrilled once they'd told me what it paid), but I was less than enamoured with the thought of seeing my articles appear next to Bruce's every month, watching him tell readers about his sex life while I filled them in on spit-up and poopy diapers and how I could never find a bathing suit that fit.

"Bruce's contract hasn't been renewed," she said crisply. Which was just fine with me, I said, and happily agreed to her terms.

I spent December settling back into my new apartment, and my life. I kept things easy. I'd wake up in the mornings and get dressed and dress the baby, put Nifkin on his leash, push Joy in the stroller, walk to the park, sit in the sun. Nifkin would fetch his ball, the neighbors would fuss over Joy. After, I'd meet Samantha for coffee, and practice being out in public, around cars and buses and strangers and the hundred thousand other things I'd learned to be afraid of after Joy came into the world so abruptly.

Along those lines, I found a therapist, too: a warm woman about my mother's age with a comforting way about her, plus an endless supply of Kleenex, who did not seem at all alarmed when I spent the first two sessions crying nonstop, and the third one telling the once-upon-a-time story of how much my father had loved me and how it had hurt me when he'd left, rather than addressing what surely seemed like the more pertinent issues at hand.

I called Betsy, my editor, and made arrangements to come back part-time, to pitch in on some big projects, to work from home if I was needed. I called my mother and made a standing date: Every Friday night, dinner at her house, and Joy and I would sleep over so we could go to Wee Ones swimming class at the Jewish Center the next morning. Joy took to the water like a little duck. "I've never seen anything like it," Tanya would growl, as Joy paddled her arms, looking adorable in a small pink bathing suit with ruffles all over the bottom. "She's going to swim like a fish!"

I called Audrey and apologized . . . well, I did whatever apologizing I could, in between her nonstop apologies for Bruce. She was sorry for how he'd behaved, sorry he hadn't been there for me, sorriest of all that she hadn't known so she could have made him do the right thing. Which, of course, wasn't possible. You can't make grownups do what they don't want to do. But I didn't say any of that.

I told her I'd be honored if she would have a role in Joy's life. She asked, very nervously, if I had any intention of letting Bruce have a role in Joy's life. I told her that I didn't . . . but I told her that things change. A year ago I couldn't have imagined myself with a baby. So who knows? Next year maybe Bruce will come over for brunch or a bike ride, and Joy will call him Daddy. Anything's possible, right?

I didn't call Bruce. I thought about it and thought about it, turned it over and over in my mind, and looked at it from every angle I could think of, and in the end I decided that I couldn't. I'd been able to let go of a lot of the anger . . . but not all of it. Maybe that too would come in time.

"So you haven't talked to him at all?" Peter asked, as he walked alongside me, balancing one hand beside mine on Joy's stroller.

"Not once."

"You don't hear from him?"

"I hear . . . things about him. It's this very Byzantine system. Audrey tells my mother, who tells Tanya, who tells everyone she knows, including Lucy, who usually tells me."

"How do you feel about that?"

I smiled at him, beneath the sky, which had finally gone completely black. "You sound like my shrink." I took a deep breath and huffed it out, watching it turn into a silver cloud and blow away. "It was awful at first, and it still is sometimes."

His voice was very gentle. "But only sometimes?"

I smiled at him. "Hardly ever," I said. "Hardly every anymore." I reached for his hand and he squeezed my fingers. "Things happen, you know? That's my one big lesson from therapy. Things happen, and you can't make them un-happen. You don't get do-overs, you can't roll back the clock, and the only thing you can change, and the only thing it does any good to worry about, is how you let them affect you."

"So how are you letting this affect you?"

I smiled sideways at him. "You're very persistent."

He looked at me seriously. "I have ulterior motives."

"Oh?"

Peter cleared his throat. "I wonder if you'd . . . consider me."

I tilted my head. "For the position of in-house diet counselor?"

"In-house something," he muttered.

"How old are you, anyway?" I teased. It was the one topic we'd never quite gotten around to during our trips to bookstores and the beach and to the park with Joy.

"How old do you think I am?"

I took my honest guess and revised it five years downward. "Forty?"

He sighed. "I'm thirty-seven."

I was so startled at that there was no way to even try to hide it. "Really?"

His voice, usually slow and deep and self-assured, sounded higher, hesitant, as he explained. "It's just that I'm so tall, I think . . . and my hair started going gray when I was eighteen . . . and, you know, being a professor, I think everyone just makes certain assumptions. . . ."

"You're thirty-seven?"

"Do you want to see my driver's license?"

"No," I said, "no, I believe you."

"I know," he began, "I know I'm still probably too old for you, and I'm probably not exactly what you had in mind."

"Don't be silly . . ."

"I'm not glamorous or quick on my feet." He looked down at his feet and sighed. "I'm kind of a plodder, I guess."

"Plotter? Like, *Murder, She Wrote?*"

A faint twitch of a smile lifted his lips. "Plodder. Like, one foot in front of the other."

"Especially now with the shinsplints," I murmured.

"And I . . . I mean, I really . . ."

"Have we come to the emotional part of the presentation?" I asked, still teasing. "You don't mind that I'm a larger woman?"

He wrapped his long fingers around my wrist. "I think you look like a queen," he said with such intensity that I was startled . . . and tremendously pleased. "I think you're the most amazing, exciting woman I've ever met. I think you're smart, and funny, and you have the most wonderful heart . . ." He paused, swallowing hard. "Cannie." And then he stopped.

I smiled—a private, contented smile—as he sat there, holding my wrist, waiting for my answer. And I knew what it was, I thought, looking at him looking at me. The answer was that I loved him . . . that he was as kind and considerate and loving a man as I could ever hope for. That he was warm-hearted, and decent, and sweet, and that we could have adventures together . . . me, and Peter, and Joy.

"Would you like to be the first man I kiss this millennium?" I inquired.

Peter leaned close. I could feel his warm breath on my cheek. "I would like to be the only man you kiss this millennium," he said emphatically. And he brushed my neck with his lips . . . then my ear . . . then my cheek. I giggled until he kissed my lips to quiet me. Snuggled against my chest, squeezed between us, Joy gave a little shout and waved one fist in the air.

"Cannie?" Peter whispered, his voice pitched low, for my ears only, and one hand in his jacket pocket. "I want to ask you something."

"Shh," I said, knowing in my heart what his question was, and what my answer would be. *I do,* I thought. *I will.* "Shh," I said, "they're starting."

Above our heads, fireworks burst, in great blooms of color and light. Silver sparks showered down, racing toward the river, and the night was full of explosions and the whistling shrieks as the spent firecrackers hurtled through the night and into the water. I looked down. Joy's face was rapt, her eyes wide, both her arms extended, as if she wanted to embrace what she was seeing. I smiled at Peter, holding up one finger, asking him with my eyes to wait. Then I unstrapped Joy from her carryall, putting my hands under her armpits, holding her in front of me as I scrambled to my feet. Ignoring the good-natured shouts of "Down in front!" and, "Hey, lady, be careful!" I stood on the ledge, letting the cold and the light pour down over my hair, my face, and my daughter. I raised my arms over my head and lifted Joy up toward the light.

ACKNOWLEDGMENTS

Good in Bed would not have been possible without my brilliant, patient, and devoted agent, Joanna Pulcini, who plucked Cannie from obscurity, cleaned her up, and found her a home. I'm grateful to Liza Nelligan's careful reading and good advice. I also thank my editor, Greer Kessel Hendricks, whose keen eye and invaluable suggestions made this a much better book.

Thanks to Greer's assistant, Suzanne O'Neill, and Joanna's assistant, Kelly Smith, who answered a thousand questions and held my hand.

Thanks to Linda Michaels and Teresa Cavanaugh, who helped Cannie see the world, and Manuela Thurner, the German translator of *Good in Bed*, who caught a dozen discrepancies and learned the meaning of Tater Tot.

From elementary school through college, I was gifted with teachers who believed in me, and in the power of words: Patricia Ciabotti, Marie Miller, and most especially John McPhee.

I work with, and have learned from, the best people in the business at *The Philadelphia Inquirer*. Thanks to Beth Gillin, editor extraordinaire, and Gail Shister, Jonathan Storm, Carrie Rickey, Lorraine Branham, Max King, and Robert Rosenthal.

Thanks to my friends, who inspired me and amused me, especially Susan Abrams, Lisa Maslankowski (for the medical advice), Bill Syken, Craig and Elizabeth LaBan, and Scott Andron. Thanks to my sister Molly, my brothers Jake and Joe, and my grandmother Faye Frumin, who always believed in me, and to my mother, Frances Frumin Weiner, who still can't believe it. Thanks to Caren Morofsky, for being a very good sport.

Thanks to my muse, Wendell, King of All Dogs.

And finally, thanks to Adam Bonin, first reader and traveling companion, who made the journey worthwhile.

CERTAIN GIRLS

BY JENNIFER WEINER

ONE

When I was a kid, our small-town paper published wedding announcements, with descriptions of the ceremonies and dresses and pictures of the brides. Two of the disc jockeys on one of the local radio stations would spend Monday morning picking through the photographs and nominating the Bow-Wow Bride, the woman they deemed the ugliest of all the ladies who'd taken their vows in the Philadelphia region over the weekend. The grand prize was a case of Alpo.

I heard the disc jockeys doing this on my way to school one morning—"Uh-oh, bottom of page J-6, and yes . . . *yes,* I think we have a contender!" Jockey One said, and his companion snickered and replied, "There's not a veil big enough to hide *that* mess." "Wide bride! Wide bride!" Jockey One chanted before my mother changed the station back to NPR with an angry flick of her wrist. After that, I became more than a little obsessed with the contest. I would pore over the black-and-white head shots each Sunday morning as if I'd be quizzed on them later. Was the one in the middle ugly? Worse than the one in the upper-right-hand corner? Were the blondes always prettier than the brunettes? Did being fat automatically mean you were ugly? I'd rate the pictures and fume about how unfair it was, how just being born with a certain face or body could turn you into a punch line. Then I'd worry for the winner. Was the dog food actually delivered to the couple's door? Would they return from the honeymoon and find it there, or would a well-meaning parent or friend try to hide it? How would the bride feel when she saw that she'd won? How would her husband feel, knowing that he'd chosen the ugliest girl in Philadelphia on any given weekend, to love and to cherish, until death did them part?

I wasn't sure of much back then, but I knew that when—if— I got married, there was no way I'd put a picture in the paper. I was pretty certain, at thirteen, that I had more in common with the bow-wows than the beautiful brides, and I was positive that the worst thing that could happen to any woman would be winning that contest.

Now, of course, I know better. The worst thing would not be a couple of superannuated pranksters on a ratings-challenged radio station oinking at your picture and depositing dog food at your door. The worst thing would be if they did it to your daughter.

I'm exaggerating, of course. And I'm not really worried. I looked across the room at the dance floor, just beginning to get crowded as the b'nai mitzvah guests dropped off their coats, feeling my heart lift at the sight of my daughter, my beautiful girl, dancing the hora in a circle of her friends. Joy will turn thirteen in May and is, in my own modest and completely unbiased opinion, the loveliest girl ever born. She inherited the best things I had to offer—my olive skin, which stays tan from early spring straight through December, and my green eyes. Then she got my ex-boyfriend's good looks: his straight nose and full lips, his dirty-blond hair, which, on Joy, came out as ringlets the deep gold of clover honey. My chest plus Bruce's skinny hips and lean legs combined to create the kind of body I always figured was available only thanks to divine or surgical intervention.

I walked to one of the three bars set along the edges of the room and ordered a vodka and cranberry juice from the bartender, a handsome young man looking miserable in a ruffled pale blue polyester tuxedo shirt and bell-bottoms. At least he didn't look as tormented as the waitress beside him, in a mermaid costume, with seashells and fake kelp in her hair. Todd had wanted a retro seventies theme for the party celebrating his entry into Jewish adulthood. His twin sister, Tamsin, an aspiring marine biologist, hadn't wanted a theme at all and had grudgingly muttered the word "ocean" the eleventh time her mother had asked her. In between pre-party visits to Dr. Hammermesh to have her breasts enlarged, her thighs reduced, and the millimeters of excess flesh beneath her eyes eliminated, Shari Marmer, the twins' mom, had come up with a compromise. On this icy night in January, Shari and her husband, Scott, were hosting three hundred of their nearest and dearest at the National Constitution Center to celebrate at Studio 54 Under the Sea.

I passed beneath a doorway draped with fake seaweed and strands of dark blue beads and wandered toward the table at the room's entrance. My place card had my name stenciled in elaborate script on the back of a scallop shell. Said shell contained a T&T medallion, for Tamsin and Todd. I squinted at the shell and learned that my husband, Peter, and I would be sitting at Donna Summer. Joy hadn't picked up her shell yet. I peered at the whirling mass of coltish girls until I saw Joy in her knee-length dark blue dress, performing some kind of complicated line dance, hands clapping, hips rocking. As I watched, a boy detached himself from a cluster of his friends, crossed the room with his hands shoved in his pockets, and said something to my daughter. Joy nodded and let him take her hand as he led her underneath the strobe that cast cool bubbles of bluish light.

My Joy, I thought as the boy shifted his weight from foot to foot, looking like he was in desperate need of the bathroom. It isn't politically correct to say so, but in the real world, good looks function as a get-out-of-everything-free card. Beauty clears your path, it smooths the way, it holds the doors open, it makes people forgive you when your homework's late or you bring the car home with the gas gauge on E. Joy's adolescence would be so much easier than mine. Except . . . except. On her last report card, she'd gotten one A, two B's, and two C's instead of her usual A's and B's (and worlds away from the straight A's I'd gotten when I was her age and had more brains than friends). "She just doesn't seem as engaged, as present," her teacher had said when Peter and I had gone in for our parent-teacher conference. "Is there anything unusual going on at home?"

Peter and I had shaken our heads, unable to think of a thing—no divorce, certainly, no moves, no deaths, no disruptions. When the teacher had folded her eyeglasses on her desk and asked about boyfriends, I'd said, "She's *twelve*." The teacher's smile had been more than a little pitying. "You'd be surprised," she said.

Except I wouldn't. Other mothers, maybe, but not me. I kept a close watch on my daughter (too close, she'd probably say). I knew her teachers, the names of her friends, the horrible, whiny boy singer she likes, the brand of twenty-bucks-a-bottle shampoo on which she blows the bulk of her allowance. I know the way she struggles with reading, and is a whiz at math, and that her favorite thing in the world to do is swim in the ocean. I know that apricots are her favorite fruit, that Tamsin and Todd are her best friends, that she worships my little sister and is terrified of needles and bees. I'd know if anything had changed, and Joy's life, I explained, was the same as it had ever been. Her teacher had smiled and patted my knee. "We see it a lot with girls her age," she'd said, putting her glasses back on and glancing at the clock. "Their worlds just get bigger. I'm sure she'll be fine. She's got involved parents and a good head on her shoulders. We'll just keep an eye on things."

As if I don't do that already, I'd thought. But I'd smiled and thanked Mrs. McMillan and promised to call with any concerns. Of course, thirty minutes later, when I'd gone straight to the source and asked Joy whether anything was wrong, my interrogation had been met with the shrug/eye-roll combination that is the hallmark of adolescent girls everywhere. When I'd said, "That's not an answer," she'd replied, "Seventh grade's harder than sixth," and opened her math book to let me know definitively that the conversation was over.

I'd wanted to call her pediatrician, a psychologist, her old speech therapist, at the very least the school's principal and guidance counselor. I'd made a list of possibilities: tutoring centers and homework-help websites, support groups for parents of premature children or kids with hearing loss. Peter had talked me out of it. "It's one quarter of seventh grade," he'd argued. "All she needs is time."

Time, I thought now. I sipped my drink and shoved the worries away. I've gotten good at that. At the age of forty-two, I've decided, ruefully, that I'm slightly inclined toward melancholy. I don't trust happiness. I turn it over as if it were a glass at a flea market or a rug at a souk, looking for chipped rims or loose threads.

But not Joy, I thought as I watched my daughter shuffle back and forth with the boy's hands on her hips, laughing at something he'd said. Joy is fine. Joy is lovely and lucky. And in the manner of almost-thirteen-year-olds everywhere, my daughter has no idea how lovely, or how lucky, she is.

"Cannie!" Shari Marmer's voice cut across the crowded atrium of the Constitution Center, where guests were clustered, waiting to take their seats for dinner. I clutched my shell and my drink and gave a halfhearted wave as she hustled over, all bright red lips and blepharo-plasty, a new diamond solitaire trapped in the Grand Canyon of her cleavage. "Yoo-hoo! Can-nie!" Shari singsonged. I groaned inwardly as she grabbed my arm with her French manicure. When I tried to pull away, her hand came with me and ended up lodged beneath my right breast. My embarrassment was instant and excruciating. Shari didn't appear to notice.

"You and Peter are sitting with us," she said. She swept me into the dining room, where I saw thirty tables for ten draped in aquama-rine tablecloths with seashell centerpieces, topped with glittering disco balls.

"Great!" I said. *Why?* I wondered. Shari and Scott had relatives, grandparents, actual friends who should have been sitting with them. And it wasn't as if Shari and I needed to catch up. Our kids were best friends, and even though we'd never become friends ourselves, we had years of shared history and saw each other plenty. Just last month we'd spent an entire day together, rehashing our latest reality-TV fixation and grating thirty pounds of potatoes for our synagogue's annual preschool Latkefest. Peter and I could've been over at Gloria Gaynor with the Callahans, or at Barry Gibb with Marisol Chang, whom I'd loved since I'd met her ten years ago in Music Together class.

"What do you think?" Shari asked me, waving her toned, sculpted, and possibly lipo'd arm at the room as we made our way toward the head table.

"It's fantastic," I said loyally. "And Tamsin and Todd did a wonderful job."

She tightened her grip on my arm. "Do you really think so?"

"They were great. The party's fantastic. You look amazing." That, at least, was the undisputable truth. Eight years older than me, Shari had been in advertising in New York before marriage and motherhood. Her job now was self-maintenance, and she worked at it harder than I'd worked at any paid employment I'd ever had. Frying potato pancakes in the synagogue's kitchen, I'd listened, awestruck and exhausted, as Shari had described her rounds: the personal trainer, the yoga and pilates, the facials, the waxing, the laser treatments and the eyelash tinting, the low-cal, low-carb meals delivered each morning to her door. It was, perhaps, the one good thing about never having been beautiful—you didn't have to kill yourself trying to hold on to something you'd never had in the first place.

"And the party?" Shari fretted. "It's not too much?"

"Not at all!" I lied.

Shari sighed as a gold-medallioned, Jheri-curled DJ, who was a dead ringer for a pre-incarceration Rick James, led her parents to the front of the room for the blessing over the bread. "Tamsin's furious. She says that marine biology is a serious science, and that I'm . . ." Her bejeweled fingers hooked into air quotes. " 'Trivializing her ambitions' with seashell centerpieces and mermaid costumes." She blinked at me with her newly widened eyes. "I think the waitresses look cute!"

"Adorable," I said.

"They should," Shari muttered. "I had to pay them extra to wear bikinis. Something about the health code." She towed me through the crowd, past the tables draped in ocean-blue tablecloths, and over to Donna Summer. Of the ten people at the table, six were family, two were me and Peter, and numbers nine and ten were the programming director of the city's public radio station and his wife. I waved at my husband, who was standing in the corner, deep in conversation with a gastroenterologist of our acquaintance. *Better Peter than me,* I thought, and sank into my seat.

The elderly woman to my left peered at my place card, then at my face. My heart sank. I knew what was coming. "Candace Shapiro? Not Candace Shapiro the writer?"

"Former," I said, trying to smile as I spread my napkin over my lap. Suddenly the gastroenterologist wasn't looking so bad. Ah well. I supposed I should be flattered that Shari still thought my name was worth dropping. I'd written one novel under my own name almost ten years ago and, since then, had produced a steady stream of science fiction under a pseudonym. The pay for sci fi was a lot worse than the royalties for fiction, but anonymity turned out to suit me much better than my fifteen minutes of fame had.

My seatmate placed one spotted, shaking hand on my forearm. "You know, dear, I've had a book inside me for the longest time."

"My husband's a doctor," I told her gravely. "I'm sure he could help you get it out."

A puzzled look crossed the aged party's face.

"Sorry," I said. "What's your idea?"

"Well, it's about a woman who gets divorced after many years of marriage . . ."

I smiled, sipped my drink, and tried to turn her synopsis into a pleasant blur of sound. A minute later, Peter appeared at my side. I shot him a grateful smile as he took my hand.

"Excuse me," he said to the woman. "They're playing our song. Cannie?"

I got to my feet and followed him to the dance floor, where a few grown-up couples had worked their way in among the kids. I waved at Joy, stretched up to plant a quick kiss on the dimple in Peter's chin, and leaned in to his tuxedoed chest. It took me a minute to recognize the music. " 'Do It Till You're Raw' is our song?"

"I had to get you out of there, so it is now," he said.

"And here I was, hoping for something romantic." I sighed. "You know. 'I Had His Baby, But You Have My Heart.' " I rested my cheek on his shoulder, then waved at Shari and Scott Marmer as they fox-trotted past us. Scott looked euphoric, puffed up and proud of his children. His round brown eyes and his bald spot gleamed under the disco lights, along with his cummerbund, made of the same red satin as Shari's gown. "Can you believe that's going to be us this fall? I looked at Shari more closely. "Except I probably won't be getting my implants refreshed beforehand."

"No need," Peter said, and dipped me. When the song was over, I raised my hands to my hair, which felt fine, then dropped them to my hips, encased in black velvet. I thought I looked all right. No less an authority than my daughter had signed off on my ensemble. True, she'd done so with a less than enthusiastic *I guess it's okay,* and told me on our way into the building that if I took my shoes off at any point in the evening and wandered around like a homeless person, she would legally emancipate herself, which children were allowed to do these days.

I wondered, the way I always did on occasions like this, what people thought when they saw me and Peter together, and whether it was some incredulous version of *He's married to her?* Unlike poor, paunchy, balding Scott, Peter was tall and lean, and had only gotten better-looking as the years had progressed. Sadly, unlike the surgically improved Shari Marmer, the some could not be said of me. *Ah, well,* I thought. *I should look on the bright side.* Maybe they all assumed that I had the flexibility of a nineteen-year-old Romanian gymnast and the imagination of a porn star and could do all manner of crazy stuff in bed.

I squared my shoulders and lifted my head as the DJ played "Lady in Red" and Peter took me in his arms again. I was determined to be a good role model, to set a good example for my daughter, to be judged on the content of my character as opposed to the size of my thighs. And if I was going to be judged by the size of my thighs, let the word go out that I was actually an impressive seven pounds thinner than I was when I'd gotten married, thanks to an indescribably hellish six weeks on the Atkins Diet. Plus, except for a touch of arthritis and the occasional back spasm, I was disgustingly healthy, while Peter was the one who'd inherited a cholesterol problem that he had to treat with three separate medications.

I looked up to find him staring at me, his forehead slightly furrowed, eyes intent.

"What is it?" I asked hopefully. "Do you wanna go make out in a stairwell?"

"Let's take a walk." He snagged a few beef satay sticks and a plate from a passing waiter, added some raw vegetables and crackers, and led me up the staircase to the Signers' Hall, with life-size statues of the men who'd signed the Constitution.

I leaned against Ben Franklin and took a look around. "You know what? Our country was founded by a bunch of short, short men."

"Better nutrition these days," said Peter, setting his plate on a cocktail table by the railing and giving John Witherspoon a friendly slap on the back. "It's the secret to everything. And you're wearing heels."

I pointed at George Washington. "Well, so is he. Hey, did Ben Franklin have VD, or was that someone else?"

"Cannie," Peter said soberly. "We are in the presence of great men. Molded bronze replicas of great men. And you have to bring up venereal disease?"

I squinted at Ben's biography, on a small rectangular plaque on the back of his chair. It made no mention of any nasty souvenirs he might have picked up during his years in Paris. History was a whitewash, I thought, crossing the floor and leaning over the railing to look down at the hired dancers, gyrating wildly as a specially constructed Studio 54 emblem descended from the ceiling (instead of sniffing cocaine, the man on the moon appeared to be reading from the Torah). "This party is insane," I said.

"I've been thinking about something," Peter said, looking at me steadily over George Washington's wig.

I hoisted myself up onto the stool in front of our cocktail table. "Joy's party?" Our daughter's bat mitzvah, and the party that would follow, were many months away but had already emerged as a hot topic around our house.

"Not that." He took the seat across from me and looked at me sweetly, almost shyly, from underneath his long eyelashes.

"Are you dying?" I inquired. Then I asked, "Can I have your beef stick?"

Peter exhaled. His brown eyes crinkled in the corners and his teeth flashed briefly as he struggled not to smile.

"Those weren't related questions. I'm very sympathetic," I assured him. "I'm just also very hungry. But don't worry. I'll do the whole devoted-wife-of-many-years thing. Hold your hand, sleep by your bedside, have your body stuffed and mounted, whatever you like."

"Viking funeral," Peter said. "You know I want a Viking funeral. With flaming arrows and Wyclef Jean singing 'Many Rivers to Cross.'"

"Right right right," I said. I had an entire file on my laptop labeled "Peter's Demise." "If Wyclef's busy, should I try for Pras?"

Peter shrugged. "He could use the work, I guess."

"Well, you think it over. I really don't want you haunting me from beyond the grave because I hired the wrong Fugee. And do you want the music before or after they set your corpse on fire?"

"Before," he said, reclaiming his plate. "Once you light a corpse on fire, it's all downhill from there." He munched ruminatively on a carrot stick. "Maybe I could lie in state at the Apollo. Like James Brown."

"You might have to release an album first, but I'll see what I can do. I know people. So what's up?" I raised my eyebrow in a knowing manner. "Do you want a threesome?"

"No, I don't want a threesome!" he boomed. Peter has a very deep voice. It tends to carry. The three women in strapless gowns who'd wandered into the hall, presumably for some fresh air, stared at us. I gave them a sympathetic shrug and mouthed, *Sorry.*

"I want . . ." He lowered his voice and stared at me, his dark brown eyes intent. Even with all the little businesses of ten years of marriage between us, the conversations about when to get the roof fixed and where to send Joy for summer camp, his gaze could still melt me and make me wish we were somewhere all alone . . . and that I really was as limber as a Romanian gymnast.

"I want to have a baby," Peter said.

"You want . . ." I felt my heart start pounding, and my velvet dress suddenly felt too tight. "Huh. Didn't see that coming. Really?"

He nodded. "I want us to have a baby together."

"Okay," I said slowly. This was not the first time the possibility of a baby had come up over the course of our marriage. There'd be a story about some talk-show host or country singer on the news, the proud mother of twins or triplets "born with the help of a surrogate," an expression that always made me roll my eyes. It would be like me saying that the oil in my car had been "changed with the help of a mechanic," as if I had something to do with it other than paying the bill. But if we were going to have a baby who was biologically our own, there'd need to be a third party involved. Joy had been born two months early, via emergency C-section, which had been followed by an emergency hysterectomy. There'd be no more babies for me. Peter knew this, of course, and even though he'd pointed out the pieces about surrogates, he'd never pushed it.

Now, though, it looked like he was ready to push. "I'm fifty-four," he said.

I turned away and read out loud from James McHenry's plaque: " 'Physician, military aide, and politician.' And a very sharp dresser."

Peter ignored me. "I'm getting older. Joy's growing up. And there might be possibilities. You might have viable eggs."

I batted my eyelashes. "That is, hands down, the most romantic thing you've ever said to me."

Peter took my hand, and his face was so open, so hopeful, so familiar and dear that I was sick with regret that my one shot at natural motherhood had come via my stoned jerk of an ex-boyfriend instead of with my husband. "Don't you ever think about it?" he asked.

My eyelids started to prickle. "Well . . ." I shook my head and swallowed hard. "You know. Sometimes." Obviously I'd wondered. I'd daydreamed about a baby we'd make together, a sober little boy who'd look like Peter, with flashes of his dry humor, like heat lightning in the summer sky; one perfect little boy to go along with my perfect girl. But it was like dreaming about being in the Supremes, or winning a marathon, or, in my case, running a marathon: a fantasy for a lazy afternoon in the hammock, something to mull over while stuck on a runway or driving on the turnpike, nothing that would ever really happen.

"We're so happy now," I said. "We have each other. We have Joy. And Joy needs us."

"She's growing up," he said gently. "Our job now is to let her go."

I freed my hand and turned away. Technically, it was true. With any other going-on-thirteen-year-old, I'd agree unconditionally. But Joy was a different story. She needed special attention because of who she was, the things she struggled with—her hearing, her reading— and because of who I'd been.

"Our lives are wonderful, but everything's the same," he continued. "We live in the same house, we see the same people, we go to the Jersey shore every summer—"

"You like it there!"

"Things are good," he said. "But maybe they could be even better. It wouldn't kill us to try something new."

"Back to threesomes," I said, half to myself.

"I think we should at least take a look. See what's what." He pulled a business card out of his wallet and handed it to me. Dr.

Stanley Neville, reproductive endocrinologist, offices on Spruce Street—in the same building, I noted ruefully, as the doctor who treated my recently diagnosed arthritis. "He can do an ultrasound of your ovaries."

"Good times," I said, and gave him back the card. I thought of our lives, perfectly arranged, the three of us safe, cocooned from the world. My garden, after ten years of attention, was in full flower, with espaliered roses climbing the brick walls, hydrangeas with blue and violet blossoms as big as babies' heads. My house was just the way I'd always wanted it. Last month, seven years of searching had finally yielded the perfect green and gold antique grandfather clock that sat on top of the staircase and melodically bing-bonged the hours. Everything except for the tiny and no doubt fixable matter of Joy's grades was perfect.

Peter touched my shoulder. "Whatever happens, whether this works out or not, our life is good just the way it is. I'm happy. You know that, don't you?"

Beneath us, a parade of waiters and waitresses, in their bodysuits and bikinis, exited the kitchen bearing salad plates. I nodded. My eyelids were still burning, and there was a lump in my throat, but I wasn't about to start bawling in the middle of the Constitution Center. I could only imagine the gossip that would start if Shari got wind of it. "Okay," I said.

"Candace," he said fondly. "Please don't look so worried."

"I'm not worried," I lied. He handed me his plate, but for one of the rare times in recent memory, I wasn't hungry at all. So I set it back on the table and followed him down the stairs, past the windows and the moon hanging high in the sky, flooding the lawn with its silvery light.

SIMON &
SCHUSTER

Jennifer Weiner
In Her Shoes

Rose and Maggie think they have nothing in common but a
childhood tragedy, shared DNA and the same size feet, but they are
about to find out that they're more alike than they'd ever believe.

Rose Feller is thirty; a successful lawyer with high hopes of a
relationship with Jim, Mr Not-Quite-Right, a senior partner in her
firm. The last thing she needs is her messed-up, only occasionally
employed sister Maggie moving in: drinking, smoking, stealing her
money – and her shoes – and spoiling her chance of romance. If
only Maggie would grow up and settle down with a nice guy and a
steady job.

Maggie is drop dead gorgeous and irresistible to men. She's going
to make it big as a TV presenter, or a singer . . . or an actress. All
she needs is a lucky break. What she doesn't need is her uptight
sister Rose interfering in her life. If only Rose would lighten-up,
have some fun – and learn how to use a pair of tweezers.

'Like Helen Fielding, Weiner balances romantic formula with fresh
humor, deft characterizations and literary sensibility' Elaine
Showalter, *Guardian*

ISBN 978-1-84983-401-8

SIMON &
SCHUSTER

Jennifer Weiner

Best Friends Forever

A grand, hilarious, edge-of-your-seat story of love, betrayal and friendship renewed.

Addie Downs and Valerie Adler will be best friends forever. At least that's what nine-year-old Addie believes when Val moves into the house across the street. But in the wake of betrayal during their teenage years, Val is swept into the popular crowd, while mousy, sullen Addie becomes her school's scapegoat.

Fifteen years on, Val has found a measure of fame and fortune as the local weathergirl. Addie, meanwhile, lives alone in her parents' house, looking after her troubled brother and trying to meet Prince Charming on the internet. She's just returned from Bad Date No. 6, when she hears a knock at her door. There, on the step, is her long-gone best friend, with blood on the sleeve of her coat. 'Something terrible has happened,' Val tells Addie. 'Can you help me?'

ISBN 978-1-84739-023-3

SIMON &
SCHUSTER

Coming soon from Simon & Schuster ...

Jennifer Weiner

Fly Away Home

One mother, two daughters, three life-changing decisions

When Sylvie Serfer met Richard Woodruff in law school, she had wild curls, wide hips and lots of opinions. Decades later, Sylvie has remade herself as the ideal politician's wife – her hair dyed and straightened, her hippie-chick wardrobe replaced by tailored suits. At fifty-seven, she ruefully acknowledges that her job is staying twenty pounds thinner than she was in her twenties and tending to her senator husband.

Lizzie, the Woodruffs' youngest daughter, is a recovering addict, whose mantra HALT (Hungry? Angry? Lonely? Tired?) helps her keep her life under control. Still, at twenty-four, trouble always seems to find her.

Diana, an emergency room physician, has everything Lizzie failed to achieve – a husband, a young son, the perfect home – and yet she's trapped in a loveless marriage. With temptation waiting in one of the ER's exam rooms, she finds herself craving more.

When Richard's extra-marital affair makes headlines, the three women are drawn into the painful glare of the national spotlight. Once the press conference is over, each is forced to reconsider their lives, who they are and who they are meant to be.

ISBN 978-1-84739-025-7